PRAISE FOR

NEMESIS

A *NEW YORK TIMES* BESTSELLER

★ "There are many overworked adjectives for action books: page-turner, fast-paced, intense. For this book, multiply all of them. Reichs truly keeps readers guessing throughout, with twists on nearly every page."
—*BOOKLIST*, starred review

★ "Hooked readers will be tapping their fingers waiting for the sequel."
—*KIRKUS REVIEWS*, starred review

"Min is a self-assured female protagonist, and Noah is a refreshingly complex young man . . . This fast-paced exploration of the teen condition is recommended for lovers of science fiction, video games, and New Age dystopia."
—*SCHOOL LIBRARY JOURNAL*

"[I]t's [Min's] story that will . . . draw readers back to see where the cliffhanger ending leads."
—*THE BULLETIN OF THE CENTER FOR CHILDREN'S BOOKS*

"*Nemesis* will appeal to teens who enjoy a fast-paced, action-filled plot."
—*VOYA*

"Reichs pulls everything together at the book's end, and a plot twist few will see coming should leave readers eagerly awaiting the second book."
—*PUBLISHERS WEEKLY*

"Hard to put down . . . It's mysterious and dark, with plot twists galore. So strap yourself in and be prepared for a bumpy ride."
—*ROMANTIC TIMES*

"Brendan Reichs takes you on a twisty thrill-ride that will keep you guessing with characters you'll want to stay with."
—*BUSTLE*

"Part *Orphan Black* part *Lord of the Flies*."
—*TOR.COM*

"This tautly written YA suspense is unstoppable, luring you in with its every turn down a dark path you don't foresee."
—USA TODAY's *HAPPY EVER AFTER*

ALSO BY BRENDAN REICHS

GENESIS

BRENDAN
REICHS

PENGUIN BOOKS

PENGUIN BOOKS

An imprint of Penguin Random House LLC, New York

First published in the United States of America by G. P. Putnam's Sons, 2018
Published by Penguin Books, an imprint of Penguin Random House LLC, 2019

G. P. Putnam's Sons is a registered trademark of Penguin Random House LLC.

Visit us online at penguinrandomhouse.com

THE LIBRARY OF CONGRESS HAS CATALOGED THE G. P. PUTNAM'S SONS BOOKS EDITION AS FOLLOWS:
Names: Reichs, Brendan, author.
Title: Genesis / Brendan Reichs.
Description: New York, NY : G. P. Putnam's Sons, [2018]
Summary: "Min, Noah, and the sophomores of Fire Lake must fight to survive in
the second phase of Project Nemesis"—Provided by publisher.
Identifiers: LCCN 2017028972 (print) | LCCN 2017040531 (ebook)
| ISBN 9780399544989 (ebook) | ISBN 9780399544965 (hardcover)
Subjects: | CYAC: Survival—Fiction. | Conspiracies—Fiction. | Science fiction.
Classification: LCC PZ7.R264467 (ebook) | LCC PZ7.R264467 Gen 2018 (print)
| DDC [Fic]—dc23
LC record available at https://lccn.loc.gov/2017028972

Penguin Books ISBN 9780399544972

Printed in the United States of America.

Design by Marikka Tamura. Text set in Adobe Caslon Pro.

1 3 5 7 9 10 8 6 4 2

For Henry and Alice, my true north

<MEGACOM SYSTEM OVERRIDE INPUT—ACCEPTED>
<START SEQUENCE—INITIATED>
<USER—GUARDIAN . . . ACCEPTED> <CODE—ACCEPTED>
<BEGIN PROJECT NEMESIS PROGRAM PHASE TWO>
ENGAGED

PART ONE

CHAOS

1

NOAH

We went there to kill them all.

Fire and blood.

Blood and fire.

I stalked through the midnight-dark woods, making as little noise as possible.

Kyle was beside me. Akio a step behind. We stole through the bare trunks like smoke, stepping lightly in our snowshoes, a pack of hungry wolves scenting prey. The target was still a football field away and a hundred feet downslope, but experience had taught me to be wary.

I'd been killed twice that week already, ambushed both times. Had no interest in another death. Resetting in new places had been disorienting. Unnerving. The rules had changed, and I didn't know all the new ones yet. But I'd learn.

Reaching the tree line, I dropped to a knee and freed my boots from the snowshoes. An icy wind smacked me in the face, tingling my cheeks and scraping my nose like sandpaper. I peered down the plunging mountainside before me, a barren stretch of slope barely dusted with white despite deep drifts piled up on both sides.

A full moon hung low and huge in the sky, glowing like a candle. Squinting, I could see our objective: a log cabin at the bottom of the run—simple, rough-hewn, topped by a cedar-chip roof and a stone chimney. Soft yellow lamplight spilled from two blocky windows. Inhaling, I caught faint traces of burning pine.

I shook my head, nearly snorted in disbelief.

These classmates were cocky. They'd planted a double line of tiki torches that stabbed up the center of the slope. Angry orange flames danced in the heavy gusts, reflecting off the frozen landscape, creating pools of shadow and light among the encroaching trees.

The kids inside probably thought the torches made them safer. They didn't.

Echoes of their laughter had risen all the way to our base at the mountaintop chalet. I was living in the same suite the black-suited man had once occupied, back in the real world, before it died. Stepping out onto the ice-covered patio, I'd heard voices. Tasted wood smoke. Spotted the flickering pinpricks a mile away.

I clicked my tongue at the memory. This cabin was firmly outside of downtown limits. An expansion into my territory. They were testing me. Mistake.

I glanced right, across twenty yards of open ground to a thicket on the opposite side of the slope, searching for the second prong of my strike force. This empty stretch would've made an excellent moguls trail. My father had earmarked it for development—a project that would never happen, in a future that would never be.

Did time mean anything now? Did it exist inside the Program?

It'd been three weeks since the Guardian revealed the true nature of our existence. How the planet had been destroyed by a series of cataclysms, our physical bodies burned to crisps. That the sixty-four members of Fire Lake's sophomore class were all that remained of humanity, existing as digital lines of code inside a supercomputer buried deep underground.

Some couldn't accept it. Couldn't wrap their heads around the idea of being nothing more than ones and zeros. They walked around like zombies, or hid. A few even defied the Program, questioning its purpose. Refusing the Guardian's instructions, as if things were somehow up for debate.

Idiots. The Program *was* purpose. The last hope of our species. It was the greatest gift anyone had ever received. To rebel against it was madness. *Heresy.* The smartest minds on Earth had crafted a single way forward for a few lucky souls. Who were we to question its dictates?

I'd been murdered over and over back in the real world, never knowing why, wracked by the pain and humiliation of thinking I was crazy. But I'd had it all wrong.

I was being trained. Prepared. I'd been chosen to lead the human race. I was *special*, to a nearly paralyzing degree. The *hell* I'd give the middle finger to the defining achievement of all human existence. The stakes were way too high.

During the chaos at Town Hall, I'd been momentarily conflicted. The Guardian had disappeared back inside without further instructions. But I'd rallied quickly, focusing on what we'd been told. We had to sort ourselves. There'd be winners and losers. I needed to dominate the situation. And the first step was to carve out my own space.

So I did. Shooting Ethan had changed everything, for everyone.

Shooting Ethan? You mean shooting Min.

I flinched. Felt a heaviness in the pit of my stomach, even as I gritted my teeth.

She'd made her choice. Had given me *no* choice.

Min had rejected the Guardian, ignoring what we'd been prepared for. Everything we'd suffered through, *our whole lives,* as beta patients for Project Nemesis. She'd refused to see the truth—that the Program was our salvation. We *had* to follow its plan.

I'd been so angry. So frustrated and disappointed. I'd shot Min to make a point. To her and everyone else. *This* was our world now. Min would reset and be perfectly fine. The old rules didn't apply. The Guardian's rules were all that mattered.

It's not like I'd enjoyed it.

After the massacre, everyone had scattered. I'd retreated to my father's ski resort atop the northeastern slopes, the most defensible spot in the valley. To my surprise, several classmates had followed. People who understood the truth as I did.

The Program was everything. It required conflict. We would provide it.

But you don't even know why. You're flying blind.

I shook my head sharply to clear it. Try as I might, I hadn't been able to stamp out a nagging voice that was determined to weaken me. My failures in life—the sad puddles of self-recrimination and doubt that had hounded me for years—were trying to sabotage me here, but I rejected them. I was strong now. I'd stay strong. Spineless Noah Livingston was dead.

Movement across the gap. I spotted Zach, skinny and moon-faced, standing upright and exposed, and waving like a human archery target. Behind him Morgan and Leah were motioning for him to get down, but he ignored them, even shaking off Morgan's outstretched hand.

Smart girls. I should've put one of them in charge instead of Zach. Too late now.

Not all of my followers were brilliant. Zach had even killed himself once, just to see what it was like. Moron. Suicide *had* to be against the Program, and was therefore unthinkable. I was fully committed to winning this phase, whatever that meant. And right then, it meant giving the people down in that cabin a really bad night.

I lifted a single fist overhead, then made a chopping motion and pointed at our target. Zach straightened, scratching his cheek, but Leah flashed the okay sign. Her father was a National Guardsman, and her family owned the quarry at the western edge of the valley, which was why I'd chosen her for this mission. She had experience with flammables. Lifting two plastic canisters, Leah shoved one into Zach's stomach and began picking her way downslope. Zach stomped after her, with Morgan bringing up the rear.

"Let's go," I said to Akio and Kyle, keeping my voice firm.

5

I didn't relish what was coming, but I wasn't agonizing over it. And I could never show weakness in front of the others. They had to believe *I* was the scariest thing on the mountain. Or else why would they follow me? Who'd follow the Noah Livingston from life, a guy who never stood up for anything?

Min would.

Heat rose to my cheeks. Min shamed me, brought out all of my failings. All of the things I couldn't afford to be in this world. Would my flaws always haunt me, even here?

This was a mission.

Feelings didn't matter.

Not here, not in this virtual proving ground we inhabited.

I was doing what I was supposed to do.

Akio's soft features tightened as he handed a fuel canister to Kyle. He didn't want to do this, but could be counted on to follow orders. Fine by me. His conscience was irrelevant so long as he did his part. Akio had been the first to join me. If I trusted anyone, it was him.

Kyle smiled darkly. He was looking forward to the carnage, and I didn't care about that, either.

Snowshoes hidden, we crept down the mountain, sticking to the trees as we mirrored our teammates on the opposite side. Zach quickly became a disaster—stumbling through the frozen underbrush, snapping branches and grunting in annoyance. Morgan hissed at him, but he ignored her warning, stepping out onto the slope to avoid a patch of pricker bushes.

I shook my head. I shouldn't have included him, but I'd asked for volunteers and he'd spoken up first.

The wind sighed down to nothing. The night was as still as

death, and nearly as cold. No birds. No chirping insects. Every sloppy footfall echoed down the icy hillside between the bordering woods, setting my teeth on edge. Zach drew level with the first pair of torches, casting a long black shadow that arrowed sharply back up the mountain.

A clicking sound.

Leah and Morgan froze.

Zach stomped a few more steps, then stopped abruptly, glancing back over his shoulder.

Shots rang out. One. Two. A half dozen.

Zach dropped like a puppet with its strings cut, a dark stain spreading on the icy ground beneath him.

Leah dove behind a round-bellied oak and rolled, her thick braid whipping like a bicycle spoke. Morgan's body jerked as more cracks boomed up the mountainside. Then she slumped onto her butt, blubbering, glossy liquid spilling from her mouth.

Out on the slope, Zach's body shimmered and disappeared.

Leah was up and running, ignoring her fuel canister and Morgan's grasping hand as she bolted deeper into the forest. Three figures in dark ski jackets lurched from the shadows. After a cursory glance at Morgan, they tore after Leah, fanning out in an attempt to encircle her. Behind them, Morgan toppled over and stopped moving. Seconds later she vanished.

Two dead, another outnumbered and on the run. I didn't care.

These people weren't friends. The idea was nonsensical. As far as I was concerned, every kid in Fire Lake was my rival. I'd work with those I needed to, but I'd never lose sight of the goal. I had to win. I had to follow the rules and complete the phase.

Killing without knowing why? How is that strength?

"Enough," I hissed, startling my companions. Cheeks burning, I schooled my face to stillness. Doubt was poison, and I was letting it infect me at the worst time possible.

Dr. Lowell. Principal Myers. Sheriff Watson and all the others. Even Black Suit. They'd dedicated their lives to Project Nemesis, planning every detail. All so we had a chance to go on. I had to fulfill their vision. I had to live up to the faith they'd placed in me. I had to make the Program proud. Plus, Morgan and Zach would be back in the valley in a matter of minutes.

Kyle and Akio were backing away from the slope, preparing to bolt. I snapped my fingers, freezing them in their tracks. "Our scouts counted ten people," I whispered. "Three just went after Leah. Our job got easier."

Akio shifted, a hand shooting up to rub the back of his neck. Kyle swallowed, gave me a shaky thumbs-up. I turned and set off downhill, not watching to see if they followed. I knew they would.

We ghosted the remaining distance, sticking to the woods on our side, avoiding the flickering torchlight. I stopped in a copse of pine trees directly across from the cabin. The single window facing us was dark, perhaps a bedroom. It made for a clean approach.

A freezing gust swept down from the snowcapped heights, rattling branches and leaching the heat from my skin. I rubbed my flaking nose. Scanned for any sign we'd been seen. God, it was cold. But not for long.

I turned. Met the eyes of my companions in turn.

"Ready?"

Two nods.

I led them across open ground, past the line of torches to an ancient, billowing cedar standing beside the cabin like a sentinel. Just then the front door opened. We dove to the ground, crawling under the cedar's low-slung branches. Flattening onto my stomach, I held my breath, one hand creeping toward the pistol in the back of my waistband.

Derrick Morris stood blinking in the doorway, his silhouette unmistakable, skyscraper-tall and haloed in yellow light. He was woefully underdressed in jeans and a short-sleeve T-shirt. I don't think he was even wearing shoes.

"Lars? Charlie?" he called. "What the hell are y'all shooting at?" Derrick listened for a moment, rubbing his dark skin to ward off the chill. Then he shook his head, muttering to himself. "Trigger-happy derps, always popping off." The door closed. Voices rose within, but no one else came outside.

I eased up into a crouch. One of Ethan's top lieutenants was here, and he wasn't paying close enough attention. No guards. No lookouts. I guessed those people were all chasing Leah up the mountain. The rest weren't taking any extra precautions, even after hearing shots fired. We'd teach them quite a lesson.

I swiveled on one knee, tapped the canisters in my companions' hands, then pointed at the cabin. Spun an index finger. They nodded—one excited, the other scared to death. But they both moved forward, slinking toward the dark side of the house.

No shouts of alarm rang out. The door stayed firmly shut.

Akio and Kyle split apart, hugging the outside walls as they circled the building, dousing its wooden foundation with liquid. Then they scurried back to my position under the cedar, tossing the now-empty canisters aside.

On his knees, Kyle dug into his pocket and withdrew a book of matches. Leering darkly, he started to rise, but I stopped him with a hand to his chest. Kyle frowned, then nodded and sank back down.

I was in charge. I'd light the fire.

Crawling from beneath the branches, I gave the cabin a final inspection, every sense on high alert. It was time to finish the job.

I strode directly for the front door, making no effort to disguise my approach. Passing a woodpile, I snagged a long, thick branch, twirling it in my hands as I mounted the porch.

The door had a wide, refrigerator-style handle. I ran the branch through the opening until it extended all the way across the door frame. I paused, then stepped down and grabbed another tree limb, doubling the barricade.

No one came to the door. I almost laughed. A dark part of me was tempted to call out and give them a far-too-late warning, but I resisted the urge. The Program wanted results, not grandstanding.

I walked down to the yard. Grabbed a torch and carried it back to the house.

The wind dropped like an accomplice. The forest held its breath. Time stood still.

Because it *was* still. Time was as dead as me.

I tossed the torch at the base of the doorway. Felt the bone-deep concussion of fire being born as it raced along the fuel-drenched logs. Orange tendrils sprang up around the foundation, encircling the cabin, eating hungrily into wood.

Shouts. Screams.

The door began jerking inward as flames engulfed it, but the branches held. Then fists began to pound, rising in intensity as shrieks erupted to match. I stepped back into the yard, removed my father's Beretta 9 mm, and racked the slide. The wind returned, and a furnace blast of dry heat struck my face, forcing me to retreat a few more paces.

Smoke billowed. Enveloped the house in a whirly black fist.

The screaming reached a crescendo. The branches finally splintered and the door flew open. I fired into the inferno, emptying the Beretta's magazine. I quickly reloaded, but no one emerged. No one even got close. I put the gun away and watched the fire rage. Heard Akio throwing up behind me.

Six at least. Maybe seven.

Then I felt something . . . twist in my head. An electric charge that snapped and sizzled, matching the conflagration reflected in my eyes before vanishing as quickly as it came.

Kyle was yelling something, but couldn't get close. The cabin burned like a Roman candle, entrancing me. Then Akio raced forward and grabbed my arm, covering his face with a sleeve as he pointed toward the trees. I nodded as if coming awake. We should leave. Everyone inside was surely gone, transported to one of the four reset zones, waiting to rejoin the Program's version of reality.

This was a minor victory. A slap on the wrist. A warning.

My head felt thick and gummy. The front of my parka was a melted ruin. But the screech of breaking glass snapped me back into focus. Shrugging free of my companions, I trotted around to the rear of the cabin, dazed and confused but determined to finish anything left undone.

A girl had launched herself through the back window in a desperate attempt to avoid the flames, but it was clearly too late. The fire had left her unrecognizable. Breathing raggedly, she lay on the ground, her hands making red lines as she pawed at the snow.

The girl's eyes opened. She stared up at the sky with a silent plea. Then her head lolled, and a lock of gleaming black hair spilled onto her ruined cheek.

My heart stopped. The air left my lungs. I lurched forward, one hand shooting out as bile climbed my windpipe. Then I noticed the girl's melted leather boot with a smiley-face sticker on its heel. I gagged, coughed hard.

Not Min. But I knew who it was.

Something shifted inside me. A hairline crack. Water seeping into stone.

I swallowed, fingers trembling as I dropped my hand and squeezed it into a fist. I stood there, frozen, breathless, waiting for the body to disappear. Guilt—sharp and stinging—exploded within me. Burning like that must've been excruciating.

Inhuman.

I tried to brush the thought aside. This girl would wake up unharmed in minutes, alone in the woods without a scratch on her. She'd have done the same to me.

Piper. Her name is Piper Lockwood.

Piper's eyes found mine. We'd never been close, but she'd sat two rows in front of me in English Comp. She'd tap her toes

12

under her chair when bored, stickered boot heels smiling back at me.

The rift inside me deepened. Cracks spread like spiderwebs.

No. I wouldn't go back. I'd worked too hard to bury my demons.

But her body was still there, still quivering, still slumped atop a pile of dirty leaves. Her hand spasmed. A silver ring had melted around her pinky finger. The smell of roasted meat filled my nostrils, and I nearly emptied my stomach.

My teeth dug into my bottom lip. A cloud slipped in front of the moon, swamping the yard in darkness, leaving only the flames to whisper what we'd done.

My hand rose. Two shots rang out.

Akio gasped beside me, staring at Piper's now-still body as tears cut tracks down his ash-covered cheeks. "She didn't . . . This wasn't . . ." he stammered, his chin dropping to his chest.

I put a hand on his shoulder, somehow freed by his show of weakness. It clarified things like a magnifying glass. This was a different world, with different rules. Only the strong would survive, and that meant doing hard things. I had to be vigilant against my own inadequacy. "It's okay, man. It's best to send people along quickly."

So why'd it take you so long?

Akio nodded, staring at his boots. He wasn't cut out for this. Then a new wave of energy struck me, dwarfing the one from before.

My scalp tingled. Electricity ran up and down my limbs. It filled me. Remade me.

Suddenly I was back in the park beside town square, playing

basketball with my friends. Ethan and I were on the same team for once, and we were passing circles around the Nolan twins. The air was crisp, the sky so blue it felt unfair. A slight breeze swept up off the lake, ruffling my hair and tingling my sweat-slicked skin. I knew I was on fire, couldn't be guarded. That no one could stop me that day. Ethan knew it, too. He threw me the ball, backing up to give me room. I dribbled through my legs, wobbling Mike, then stepped back and shot over his out-stretched hand, the ball sliding through the net like prophecy. Ethan lifted me up and we whooped like idiots. I glanced over and saw Min sitting on the grass with Sarah and the other girls, her eyes rolling as she shook her head at us. My smile grew ten times wider.

The scene—memory?—winked out, but the elation remained.

I drank in the sensation. Felt galvanized, head to toe. I stared at my hands, flexing and unflexing my fingers. I was so close to the Program I could weep.

Fire and blood.

Blood and fire.

Program wants? Program gets.

This was my world. Or it would be soon.

"Guys?"

I glanced over at Kyle, who was chewing on his thumb, his face lit up by the bonfire raging behind us. He pointed. "Why's she still here?"

I turned. Stiffened. Piper had stopped moving, but hadn't vanished.

My blood ran cold, a dark corner of my mind jabbering for

attention. Piper was still lying on the frozen ground. She wasn't miles away, restored and repaired, waking up with only a bad memory for her trouble.

She wasn't moving. Or breathing. She refused to fade away.

Inside me, something snapped. Surety dissolved like a sand castle at high tide.

Piper's scorched body defied me like an accusation. The truth was inescapable.

Someone inside the Program hadn't reset.

You're a murderer.

2

MIN

In a minute, I was going to die.

Trapped inside an elevator of all places. I'd been stupid, and let myself get caught. It wasn't a screaming terror so much as incredibly frustrating. Tack and I badly needed the supplies I'd gathered, but now our enemies would get them. Either that or they'd plummet to the bottom with me, and no one would benefit.

What a waste. Food was becoming a problem.

I could hear the Nolan twins clunking around on the roof. A loud clang echoed through the shaft, followed by a horrible wrenching sound as they tried to release the support cables. The brothers, wonderful guys that they were, had every intention of dropping this elevator into the basement.

Why had I deviated from the plan?

The Marina Hotel was hard against the water at the western edge of town, eight stories of picture-perfect lakefront views. I'd gambled that the Skyline Café might not have been pillaged yet, like the downtown restaurants, but I'd been wrong. Soon-to-be-*dead* wrong. The top-floor eatery was being guarded by two of Ethan's goons. A snare for the unwary.

And I'd walked right into it, like a dumbass.

Of course they'd been watching the café—it was the highest vantage point in the village. Lower than the surrounding peaks, for sure, but still a great lookout position. At dawn I'd snuck up the stairs and into the kitchen, ready to bolt at the first sign of trouble. But I'd seen and heard no one. So, after raiding the pantry—cramming canned goods and boxes of noodles into two giant duffel bags—I'd decided to use the elevator to lug it all back down to street level.

Stupid. Stupid stupid stupid.

The elevator car had jerked to a stop between the fifth and sixth floors, and now the Doofus Brothers were trying to figure out how to make it fall the rest of the way down. Based on their muffled bickering, they weren't having an easy go of it. If I'd brought a gun like Tack had urged, I could've blasted them through the ceiling while they stood scratching their heads. Sent them back to the Program, hand in hand. But I'd left the gun in my ski jacket, which I'd stashed outside so I wouldn't rustle like a potato-chip bag as I snuck around the building.

Also stupid.

Not that I was confident with it. A simple Smith & Wesson revolver, I'd only learned to load and fire the thing two weeks ago, under Tack's critical tutelage. He'd gathered all his dad's weapons—a small arsenal—but I'd chosen the most basic one I could find. To begin with I could hit a barn door 50 percent of

17

the time in good conditions. I'd improved with practice, but was still no markswoman. Not that it mattered at the moment, since I was unarmed.

Something heavy clattered on the roof. A voice howled in pain, then both twins began shouting at once. I smirked despite myself. Maybe I could simply wait them out. Then I shivered, wondering if they'd think of blasting *me* through the ceiling.

I knew Sarah would prefer I be captured rather than killed—that was the smart move—but the twins didn't know who they had trapped. I'd refused to respond to their questions and threats. Chris and Mike weren't deep thinkers, but they did like breaking things. Since they couldn't pry the hatch open—I'd latched it from within; plus, *they* didn't know I wasn't armed—the brothers seemed content to drop the whole damn car down the shaft.

By sawing through a set of steel cables. Meant to hold up thousands of pounds.

And didn't these things have automatic brakes? It was a dumb idea altogether, but that wouldn't help me much. They'd give up soon and try a more direct method. I had zero doubt *they* had guns, and I was trapped inside a metal box with no place to hide.

Something hissed, punctuated by three sharp clacks and a low whoosh. I stared up through the ventilation slats. Spotted a nimbus of blue light.

The hairs on my neck stood. These boys had a blowtorch.

A screech, then the crackle of burning metal. Acrid smoke sank into the car.

The temperature rose and I began to sweat, my slick fingers hammering the buttons even though I knew it was useless. My breathing quickened as my pulse throttled up. Resetting aside, I *really* didn't want to free-fall six stories down an elevator shaft.

The first cable snapped with a metallic warble, and the car lurched. Frightened yelps echoed above as Chris and Mike scrambled off the roof. Then something popped with a high-pitched thrum and the elevator dropped another foot before jerking to a stop.

The car vibrated, tremors shivering up my legs as it battled with gravity. The twins began murmuring excitedly. Made shuffling noises. I tried to claw open the doors—hoping I'd fallen even with the next floor—but they refused to budge.

I punched the door, then sank down with my back to it. Rested my head against the warm metal. My hand throbbed. I'd broken a knuckle or two, but it didn't matter. I was going to die, and that was that. My hand would reset with the rest of me.

The thought wasn't scary—I was well past that by now—but the fact that death was no longer frightening made me unaccountably sad. It felt alien. Like a vital piece of my humanity had been stripped away.

If death couldn't scare me anymore, what was left? What was the point of anything? I shook my head at the *wrongness* of it all. Everything about the Program felt so . . . futile. How could there be justice in a world with no consequences? And without justice, what connected us as human beings? What was the point of existing at all?

Something clattered down one side of the car, stopping directly level with me.

A faint hiss echoed in the shaft.

Sweat exploded from my pores. Scrambling away from the noise, I pressed back into a corner. Buried my head between my knees and made myself small.

Damn it, this is going to hurt.

A roaring thunderclap. The wall exploded, shards of metal lacerating my arms and legs. Flames licked my skin and I screamed. Then my stomach did a somersault as the floor dropped from beneath my feet.

The elevator fell. I fell with it.

Contact. A horrible crunch.

My legs smashed up into my body.

The roof slammed down on top of me.

I gasped in pain, unable to scream as my chest caved inward. Flashes of light exploded behind my retinas. The world became soft and indistinct. The scent of copper filled my nose as I began to choke on my own blood.

My head swam. Images cycled through my mind at breakneck speed.

Me and Tack, way up high in a giant oak tree.

My body intertwined with Noah's on a crappy trailer-park couch.

My mother, sitting in her chair, rocking as she knit while a storm raged outside.

I don't want to live in a video game.

Everything faded to black.

I awoke in darkness.

For a terrifying moment, I imagined I was still trapped inside the mangled elevator car, broken but not quite dead. My arms lashed out wildly, encountered nothing but loose pebbles and a rough stone floor.

I sat up quickly. Realized I could move.

Pitching upright, I took stock of my body. Limbs felt fine. No breaks, bruises, gashes, or amputations. A light breeze ruffled my hair, tinged with the scents of wet rock and loamy earth. My eyes adjusted to the gloom. I was inside an enclosed space, yet still outdoors somehow. I could taste the chill night air. I was freezing.

Releasing a pent-up breath, I sat back and squeezed the bridge of my nose. Sighed. Then I blew into my fists for warmth, thanking my lucky stars that the fall had, in fact, killed me.

Dying sucked. It was painful and terrifying and the memories never left you alone. But to be badly wounded inside a demolished steel coffin—with no way to escape, and no one to save you—was a fate too awful to contemplate.

Much better to die and come back.

Reset. Again. But where?

I rose and slowly edged forward, until I spotted a brighter patch to my left. Sunlight was leaking between two walls of solid rock. The answer hit me: I was inside a cave.

Which meant I was at Noah's reset point, up near the western canyon rim, close to the downed bridge. Stumbling awkwardly for the exit, I stepped out to a clear, cold morning in the Bitterroot Mountains.

Are these peaks still called that? Is this technically Idaho at all?

I blew out a long breath, misting the air around my face. *Stop it.* That kind of thinking would drive me insane.

My classmates and I might be dead, but we also weren't.

21

We lived in *this* valley now, virtual or not. Philosophical hand-wringing was pointless. What I knew for sure was that I needed to get home, get warm, and find something to eat.

There was a small ice-rimmed pond outside the cave, surrounded by a circle of pine trees. I'd been here once before, with Noah, in what seemed like another lifetime.

It was one, actually. How depressing is that?

Noah's face invaded my thoughts, burning like a hot coal. My teeth clenched. For a moment I imagined him crashing through the pond's thin ice, then struggling to keep his head above water, begging me for the help I'd never give him again.

Stop it.

I jerked my head away, ashamed. My anger with Noah always simmered just below the surface. Sometimes its intensity frightened me. Other times it spilled out in tears.

I'd never reset in *his* spot before. Never anywhere but my clearing in the northern woods. But the reset points were randomized now. I hadn't died since the carnage at Town Hall, so this was my first taste of Phase Two. I didn't want there to be another, but our fates rode a roulette wheel, and only the Program knew what would happen next. My classmates and I were prisoners in every sense of the word.

Another face floated to the surface. The Guardian. My murderer's digital shadow, haunting me even here. *It* knew what was coming, but hadn't shared any details. The black-suited man's avatar was holed up in Town Hall like a spider pulling strings, unreachable until this new phase ended. Or so it claimed. But who could trust anything the Program said?

The rest of us? Left to fend for ourselves. Worse, left to savage each other.

I circled the pond to a deer trail leading down toward Fire Lake. How many murdered classmates had walked this path recently? The slaughter had reached a fever pitch last week, before vague battle lines had been drawn. Places where you'd catch a bullet for crossing into someone else's turf. Tack was scouting them all, but they were borders of smoke, with no real meaning. The fighting continued every day. It's hard to protect territory if your attackers don't worry about getting killed. They just try again.

As I rounded a bend, a tingling sensation swept over me. I whirled and pressed my hands against the invisible barrier I'd passed through, a boundary field isolating the reset zone. It was the same at the other three compass points. Once you exited, there was no going back. Outside the protective bubble I was fair game, and human predators prowled the valley.

Leaves rustled to my left. I tensed, fingers itching for a gun I didn't possess.

Tack emerged from the woods, a crooked smile on his face. "Ha! I'm two-for-two. I can track you like a bloodhound."

I wanted to gasp in relief, but my heart wouldn't stop thudding. I felt a twitch in my cheek, then my knees buckled and I nearly collapsed. Tack raced over and caught my arm, his smile evaporating. "Jesus, Min, are you okay?"

"Yes. Sure. Fine." I straightened and stepped back. Rubbed my cheeks with my palms. What the hell was that? Nerves? One death too many?

"You don't look fine." Tack was watching me like a hawk, concern plain on his face. "Sorry I scared you. God, I'm such a jackass. You just fell down an elevator shaft, and here I am jumping out of the bushes at you."

I cleared my throat, steadying myself. Forced a smile. "Really, I'm okay. Just a blood rush. How'd you know where I'd reset, anyway?"

He ran a hand through his unruly black hair, then shrugged. "I didn't. This was the closest zone. Twenty more minutes and I was heading back to the trailer park. With an empty stomach," he added significantly, his sharp blue eyes glinting with disapproval.

My mood soured. "I tried. They beat me."

"I'm starving. Try harder."

"What was I supposed to do?" I shot back, crossing my arms and bristling. "I can't haul two gym bags full of SpaghettiOs down eight flights of stairs, and the twins hijacked the elevator after I got inside."

"The *plan* was for you to toss the bags off the balcony," Tack reminded me unnecessarily. "That's why *I* was there. Standing outside. In the wind and snow." He stomped his feet, then burrowed his hands inside the front pouch of his hoodie. A show for my benefit, since I knew he rarely felt the cold. "Like I've been doing out *here* for the last hour."

"The balcony doors were locked," I snapped. "Breaking the glass would've been like sounding . . ." I trailed off as the last thing Tack said finally penetrated. "Wait, only an hour?"

Interesting. Resets were coming faster than before.

"Well, it took me a while to figure out what happened and

24

verify you were roadkill, then I had to slip out of town without anyone mounting my head over their fireplace. You were in the data stream for about ninety minutes, I'd guess."

"Stop calling it that." A shiver ran through me, and not just from the cold. I balled up my hands and tucked them into the sleeves of my sweater. It was still below freezing out despite the rising sun. "You don't know where we go between resets. No one does."

Tack noticed my discomfort, held up a finger. He stepped back into the woods and returned with my ski jacket, which I dove into gratefully. The revolver jabbed me in the ribs as I zipped up. Armed again. Yippee.

Tack shrugged, conceding the last word if not the point. He never stopped trying to figure out the Program, but everything he did was guesswork. We were adrift inside a circuit board, and no one had the answers. I felt like a hamster on a wheel.

"So what now?" Tack scuffed the dirt with his shoe, worry lines creasing his forehead. I sensed he was still annoyed I hadn't followed the plan. Or maybe just hungry, which in this case was essentially the same thing.

I sighed. "Back to the trailer park. What else?"

"We can't keep on like this, you know."

"I do know." Setting off along the trail. "You remind me every day."

I didn't want to talk about it, but Tack wouldn't let it go.

"We need food, Min." I heard his lazy footfalls follow me downhill. "We've ransacked ninety percent of our neighborhood. There's *maybe* enough to eat for another week. And I'm talking about trash food. *Beets*, Melinda. The devil's most garbage vegetable. Unless you want to get drunk a lot. How many calories are in a Bud Light? We're close to finding out."

Our former neighbors had proven to be thrifty shoppers and heavy drinkers. Some of our classmates might've found the situation ideal, but I'd kill for some bacon and eggs. Last night—in a drafty, dingy double-wide that used to belong to Francine the Cat Lady—Tack and I had split a box of Hamburger Helper, without the hamburger. Suboptimal.

But what were we supposed to do? Find some happy campers and persuade them to host a dinner party? Stroll downtown and talk Ethan into giving up his kingdom? It was laughable.

No one would listen to me. No one would take us in.

Why should they? What did I have to offer? I'd barely existed back in high school, and meant next to nothing to my classmates now. And I was fine with that. I didn't want anything to do with *them*, either. Not anymore, not after taking a bullet in the back. I didn't trust anyone except Tack.

"Come on." I tried to keep my voice light. "There's still that French-bread pizza over at the Jenkins place. Let's eat it tonight."

"Our victory pizza?" Tack snorted, drawing level with me as we reached the valley floor. "Sure, why not? It's not every day you fail completely and get compacted in a falling elevator. I bet nobody else has died that way."

I winced, sure Tack was right. That murder had been uniquely my own.

Lucky me.

3

MIN

We stepped cautiously through the gates.

Rocky Ridge Trailer Park had been home our entire lives, but these days you couldn't be too careful. We'd been gone for hours. Adrenaline coursed through my veins as I scanned for signs of unwelcome company.

Is it adrenaline? With our bodies dead, do biological terms even apply anymore?

Why can't I leave this stuff alone?

Questioning the basis of our reality gave me vertigo. Made me nauseous. More than that, it depressed me. Was this existence really being alive? At times I felt like a tortured soul tethered to Earth by things left undone, like in a bad romance movie, or maybe one about Christmas. But was I anything more than a vengeful ghost? Was this stupid Program denying me the eternal rest that everyone else on the planet was now enjoying?

Enough. I had to focus. Real or not, I was in no mood to get killed again.

Tack and I cut left, hugging the perimeter fence as we circled the neighborhood. We never walked straight down the main thoroughfare. Never went directly to our trailer du jour. We hadn't visited either of *our* old trailers since right after the massacre at Town Hall, and even then it was only to grab Wendell Russo's weapons and bolt. I tried not to think about the people who used to live here, or what happened to them. I had enough on my plate without mourning the entire community. Hell, the entire world.

We slept in a different unit every night. Tack's idea. Something about Fidel Castro. I'd thought he was being paranoid until Toby and six others came looking for us a week ago. We'd watched through slitted blinds as they kicked in the door to my mother's trailer, then Tack's father's, then searched half the units on the east side before giving up and heading back into town. Lazy, but they could return at any time.

I knew Ethan and Sarah were still looking for us. Ethan was obsessed with controlling the valley, and everyone in it, a directive from Project Nemesis. Those two had been told more from the start, and none of it good, back when the black-suited man had been slaughtering us as beta patients. Testing the secret military program we now found ourselves locked inside. But on that terrible day at Town Hall, the Guardian had spoken to everyone.

Phase Two has begun.

Uploaded sequences must be sorted.

You must find your place within the system.

What the hell did that even mean?

We didn't know. Nobody did. The purpose of the Program remained a complete mystery, fueling a bloody nightmare of fighting, carnage, and macho swagger in the valley that I wanted absolutely nothing to do with. Problem was, there was nowhere else to go.

So Tack and I ducked, weaved, and hid. My angry promise to fight back seemed almost laughable now. We had zero contact with the rest of our class. No one wanted anything to do with us, except maybe to crush us like bugs. Which was no surprise—who'd team up with the trailer-trash head case whose boyfriend shot her in the back? Her slacker friend who couldn't stop his mouth from running?

But weirdly enough, I was almost thankful we were running out of food. At least then *something* would happen. I realized I couldn't take this rabbit-hole life much longer. Each reset made my existence feel less real.

Then solve the problem. Find out what the Program wants.

The thought startled me so much, I stopped short. Was that what I wanted? Answers?

"Yo, Melinda?" Tack snapped his fingers, drawing me back to the present. "We're home. Unless you want to stare at that fire pit a few more minutes."

I gave him my most level glance, then shouldered him aside and reached for the ratty screen door. "Wait!" Tack squawked.

I paused, barely kept my eyes from rolling. "Tack, I'm cold. I think the coast is clear."

Tossing me a scolding look, Tack circled the trailer, scanning the snow for footprints. Then he checked the fishing wire strung across the door handle.

"Better safe than sorry," he said primly. We slipped inside, shrugging off our winter coats as I hurried to fire up the space heater.

Our current residence was a drab beige double-wide on the western edge of the community, overlooking the drop into Gullet Chasm. At first it had felt stupid holing up in our own neighborhood, but honestly, we couldn't think of a better location. No one else would choose it. Plus it had the advantage of hiding places—dozens of run-down mobile homes arranged in haphazard rows. No one could sneak up on us, or guess our shell game.

Two days ago a blizzard had swept down from the north, riming the lake and coating the valley in a thick white blanket. The temperature dropped into the teens. Winter Was Coming, as the Starks would say. There'd be snowpack from now until April, if seasons and months still applied.

I dropped onto a tired three-seater couch in the main room, ejecting a cloud of dust that stank of old footwear. This trailer had narrow bedrooms at both ends, so we each got our own. When there was only one Tack slept on a couch or recliner, depending on the decor. Although in a few particularly gross trailers we both did, then crossed them off our list.

Tack filled two mugs from the tap in the kitchenette, dropped in tea bags, and stuck them in the microwave. So far power and water were still running, but who knew how long that would last. A perk of the Program? Or were those facilities on autopilot and doomed to break down eventually? We'd filled rain barrels and hoarded batteries just in case.

Isolated like lepers in our little corner, we didn't know much about happenings in the rest of the valley. But we knew Ethan and Sarah still controlled downtown—and all the kids living there—cutting us off from the bulk of our classmates. Enough reason to keep our heads down.

Tack handed me a steaming mug and plopped into a moth-eaten easy chair. "So the Nolan dorks dropped you down a fucking elevator shaft, huh? Unreal."

The memory jangled my nerves, but I didn't have another dizzy spell.

"I hate that everyone is acting like animals," I grumbled, blowing into my mug. My numb fingers drank in the warmth, but I didn't want to burn my tongue. Pain was still very real in virtual Fire Lake. "Chris and Mike didn't even know it was me. When I wouldn't respond and they couldn't pop the hatch, they just said 'Screw it' and wrecked the whole damn thing, like a toy they didn't care about anymore. With a *person* inside."

Tack blew out a deep breath. "To be fair, they knew you wouldn't really die."

"That's not an excuse!" I slapped the couch's armrest, launching another dust plume skyward. "It *hurt* getting crushed to death. And what if I hadn't died? I'd still be trapped inside a crumpled tin can, writhing in agony. But I swear I heard them laughing."

Tack shifted uncomfortably, circling the rim of his mug with a finger. "It's human nature. People need rules, or they go crazy. Didn't you read *Lord of the Flies*? The CliffsNotes I scanned explained a lot. This anarchy? The violence? It's probably our new normal."

"Because no one knows what we're supposed to *do*." I kicked the coffee table with both feet, nearly spilling my tea and earning a disapproving look from my best friend. "The Program told us to 'vie for control.' But why? For what?"

Tack deepened his voice, quoting the Guardian's only other clue. "*You must create the proper population size and alignment. No more information will be given. Those who remain will move on.*' Simple and straightforward, right?"

I scraped a hand across my face, then let out a sigh that nearly didn't end. "Vague, useless gibberish. What are we trying to *accomplish*? It can't just be killing each other and coming back, over and over, like some twisted, never-ending video game. What would be the point of that?"

Tack lifted both palms. We debated this every day.

"Do you need to look at the map?" he asked suddenly.

"No. No I do not."

"I think you need to look at the map."

He rose and pulled the chair aside. Slid his masterpiece into view on the carpet.

"Tack, honestly, we don't ha—"

"As you know, Melinda," he interrupted smoothly, "I've spent a portion of each day cobbling together the strategic situation in Fire Lake valley." Tack stood, clasping his hands behind his back like a general addressing paratroopers. "Careful scouting has provided the following intelligence." He looked me squarely in the eye, lowering his voice with solemn dignity. "Many Bothans died to bring us this information."

I covered my face with both hands. "Tack, please, do you really—"

"Observe!" Removing a laser pointer from his pocket, he emblazoned the top left corner of a cardboard diagram executed in magic marker. A G.I. Joe had been taped there, representing the last known position of certain classmates. Updated religiously, Tack dragged this artistic catastrophe everywhere we went. And made me look at it all the freaking time.

"We now know a group led by Carl and Sam took over the miners' compound inside the quarry," Tack continued, gathering steam. "We know this because a crack surveillance team—"

"Meaning you."

"—was able to spot Sam conducting sensitive camp business just two days ago."

"You saw him pooping in a mineshaft."

Tack nodded seriously. "Initial reports suggest that perhaps a dozen people are with the cousins, and that they oppose Ethan's group in town."

I held on to my patience. Carl and Sam had bolted before anyone even knew about resets, right after Ethan killed Tack in the church. Rough-and-tumble guys who were tighter than brothers, they weren't the type to take orders from a wannabe dictator. A knot of kids had disappeared with them, infuriating Ethan, but he hadn't tracked them down before the Guardian appeared and all hell broke loose. We'd only noticed them because the quarry is directly above the trailer park, making us neighbors.

"So the cousins and some others are in the quarry," I said testily. "I already knew that."

Tack frowned, aimed his laser pointer at my forehead. "My sources indicate—"

"Tack—"

33

"—there are four, perhaps *five* major groups operating in the valley, with some scattered coyotes hiding out solo, or in pairs or threes." He flicked the red dot to the northeast corner of his map, where he'd drawn a crude hotel and ski lift. "Noah's team of murder-loving wackos are in his father's luxury ski lodge at the top of the slopes, attacking anyone who comes close. He's lost his damn mind. Seriously. Insanity sauce. He's a psychopath."

I turned away, hoping Tack wouldn't see the color drain from my face. Outside, clouds rolled in and the trailer darkened, leaden shadows pooling in the corners and creeping up the bare walls. The microwave leered at me from across the room, a ghastly black face sitting in broken-toothed judgment.

I didn't want to think about Noah again. This day had been trying enough.

Tack continued quickly, pointing the laser over Main Street. "Ethan, Sarah, and the superjerks hold all of downtown. That's the largest group by far—at least twenty to twenty-five people, maybe more. I can't get good intel on *exactly* how many others ran like we did, but the ones who stayed are probably all in. They control the grocery store, the shops, and most of the restaurants."

"The food supply," I said sourly.

"The food supply," Tack agreed. "Which means they have the upper hand on everyone. When the pantries inside empty houses dry up, loners are going to be in trouble. I bet some are already trickling back into town as they run out of Pop-Tarts. Ethan might be able to win this thing just by sitting tight."

I rubbed my face. *Win what?* "Have you learned anything about the summer camp?"

Tack's frown deepened. "No. There's definitely a group there,

34

but it's been impossible to figure out who's in it. Our best man was shot trying to sneak close enough to make an ID."

I arched an eyebrow.

"Our very best man."

"Okay, so people are mostly spread out in four main parties."

"Five, I think. Some folks are poking around in the swanky southwestern neighborhoods, but I can't tell if it's an offshoot of Ethan's group or a whole different set of classmates. I was planning on checking that out after you'd secured our supply of mac and cheese. But instead you fell down an elevator shaft."

"Right. My bad."

"We're in a tough spot," Tack admitted, spinning the chair back around and flopping into its cushy depths. "Without a re-supply we can't last here much longer, but Ethan has a monopoly on grocery shopping. We'll have to either start raiding other neighborhoods or find a hidden cache no one's gotten to first. But how many of those do you think are left?"

"None. Sarah's too smart. She'll have thought through logistics like we have, and she's got manpower for days."

Tack tapped his lip, then leaned forward. "We have to unite the groups opposing Ethan and Sarah. We'll need numbers to break their stranglehold. Without a unified front to challenge them, they can stamp out resistance one small pocket at a time."

I recoiled, crossing my arms as creases crinkled my forehead. "Who? *Us?* How are *we* going to do that? We don't have anything to offer, Tack. We're only having this conversation because we're about to starve."

"You're a beta patient for Project Nemesis. Everyone knows it."

"But that doesn't *mean* anything," I spat, suddenly, explosively angry. "Ethan and Noah might think it makes them gods, but the others won't listen to me just because I tell them how many times I've been killed."

Undeterred, Tack began ticking fingers. "There are only *four* betas. Ethan. Noah. Sarah. You. The other three are all running gangs, so why not you? The Guardian mentioned you specifically at Town Hall, so everyone knows you're important to the Program. I mean, *Jesus*, Min. You guys were tested for this your whole lives."

My voice hardened. "I wasn't *tested*, Tack. I was murdered. *Repeatedly*. And brought back time after time."

"So the conspiracy could create this virtual lifeboat," Tack countered, ignoring my not-so-subtle hint to let this topic go. "That means you're special. If you lead, people will follow. I know they will."

I just stared at him. "Me. Lead. Tack, have you been drinking?"

He spread his arms, cobalt eyes narrowing to pinpricks. "Do you agree that people need to work together to force some sense into Ethan?"

"Yes, but—"

"Then who's going to do it? It *has* to be you."

"I don't want to be in charge of anything." I'd scooted back on the couch as if to force a path through the trailer wall. "And you're talking crazy. No one will listen to me." I fought to keep my voice firm. "I'm the girl who got shot in the back, remember?"

His shoulders fell. "Min, that was—"

"Our classmates are all idiots, anyway," I said. I was in a

funk, and knew it, but Tack had blindsided me with this save-the-world crap. "If they had the sense to realize we have to unite against Ethan, they'd have done it already."

"We have to at least try." He was trying to sound confident. Suddenly, I felt ashamed.

Tack captured my gaze and held it. "You're a beta. But more than that, you're the type who *should* be running things. You care about fairness, and justice, all that noble crap. People know that." He sighed. "Without a new rallying point, Ethan and Sarah are the only game in town. People flock to strength when they're scared, even when it's wrong. If we want an alliance against them, someone is going to have to step up."

I took a deep breath. "For the sake of argument . . . what do you suggest?"

He brightened immediately, flourishing his laser pointer and aiming it at the G.I. Joe. "We visit the cousins. They're close by, clearly opposed to Ethan, and know how to take care of themselves. Plus, it must be awful up in that dirty miners' compound. Maybe we can persuade them to come down here and join us."

I suppressed a sigh. "Don't get your hopes up. Sam and Carl are survivalists. They wouldn't have chosen that spot if they didn't think they could last a long time. And I still don't see what we're bringing to the table."

Tack rose and slipped his hoodie on. "That's not 'victory pizza' talk, but I'll let it slide." He took two steps toward the door, then stopped and looked back at me. "We good?"

I stuck my tongue out at him, but nodded. Honestly, I did feel a little better having made a decision. "Go get that pizza, soldier. We'll need our strength for the hike."

Tack scratched his cheek. "When do you want to head out?"

"After lunch. A few hours should give us plenty of time to perfect the art of diplomacy."

Tack snorted, stepped outside. My spirits sank as soon as the door eased shut.

My joke had hidden the truth—I had no idea what to say to my classmates. I'd never been a leader and everyone knew it, whatever Tack might believe.

How was Melinda Wilder supposed to unify a resistance?

What did I have to offer anyone?

4

NOAH

Gears groaned after being dormant for so long.

The ski lift rumbled to life, painted green chairs cycling through the station like toy soldiers before floating up the hill in a steady line.

I let a few pass as the motor settled into a steady purr. This lift climbed the longest run in the resort. It hadn't been fired up since the slopes closed in May. Then I shook my head. Stepped into position and let a chair scoop me, keeping the bar raised as I arced gracefully into the cold gray sky.

This lift had *never* been turned on, because it wasn't real. It was a mirror image—a reflection of what had existed on this spot in the real Fire Lake valley, before it burned. But that was all gone.

As the chair rose, I marveled at the complexity of the Program's simulation. How could the architects have gotten every tiny detail correct? I knew these chairs. Had ridden them my whole life. The paint was peeling in all the right places, the white seats slightly browned by weather and hard use.

Whoever designed the Program had been geniuses. They'd known what they were doing.

The chair glided above the tree line. I glanced back over my shoulder at the wide lake in the center of the valley. The surface had a leaden gleam—the ice was thickening, though not enough to walk on yet. Fire Lake was beautiful this time of year. A white carpet of snow made everything look pure and wholesome and safe.

Something moved on the waterfront docks. My eyes focused instantly—Vonda Clark was strolling along the wharf, hand in hand with that big blond Thor look-alike, Finn Whitaker. Interesting. Before the Program, those two probably never would've spoken.

Then I started. They were miles away, yet I had no trouble making out their faces.

I jerked back around to face the mountains. Stared at the craggy peaks encircling the valley, locking us in. This was getting scary.

The lift rocked gently in an icy breeze, but I ignored the cold. If I concentrated, I could detect individual stitches in my jeans as they pressed against my legs. My senses had been electric since the cabin raid. I could smell a fire burning in the ski village hundreds of yards away. I could hear the whine of the lift's engine powering me up the mountainside even as I lofted well beyond sight of the station.

I didn't worry about someone stopping the works and

stranding me up there. If necessary, I could drop down to the snowpack and be fine. No reset needed.

The chair approached the halfway pole. I reached out, idly slapped it with an open hand. A sound like a warlord's gong reverberated up and down the slopes. I sat back and flexed my fingers, amazed by their strength.

Something had happened to me during the raid. Some kind of . . . evolution.

I was stronger. Faster. Barely slept. I still ate regularly, but only to avoid drawing attention. I didn't want the others to learn my secret.

Because the truth had become plain—kills in the Program gave you something. I recalled the flood of energy I'd experienced after firing into the cabin as it burned. As lives blipped out, flying back into the Program's circuits to be reborn. But that wasn't the half of it.

I'd felt an *avalanche* of power when Piper stopped twitching in the snow. And I knew what it meant.

I'd been right. The truth was terrible, remorseless, and cruel. But I'd been right and Min was wrong. Piper proved it. There was only going to be room for so many.

I hadn't worked out all the details yet. *Why* had Piper failed to reset? If kills gave you power, did deaths take something away? Had I experienced that final influx as an accumulated effect, or was killing a person who *stayed* dead worth more?

God, listen to yourself. What was Piper *worth?*

I creaked higher up the mountain as frigid gusts swirled around my chair. The ground momentarily rose to nearly touch my feet, rife with the smell of moss and rotting logs. Then it dropped away again as I was carried over a shallow ravine.

It was insanely peaceful. So nice to be alone, without eyes on my back.

I'd tried to keep my new abilities from the others, but nature had betrayed me. Or the simulation did. Whatever. It was all the same now.

We'd been scouting a rough patch of country behind the chalet the day before—me, Akio, Richie, and Leah—trying to locate a cell tower, when a dragon's roar froze everyone in their tracks. A tidal wave of white was tearing down the mountainside. We'd barely had time to cower behind our SUV before it struck. The avalanche hit like a giant's punch, and the SUV tipped, threatening to crush us beneath it. But my survival instincts kicked in and I caught the vehicle on one shoulder, then pushed it back upright.

I should've let the damn thing crush us. Taken the reset. Now the others watched me cautiously as I patrolled our domain— the ski chalet and a little mountaintop shopping village beside it. They knew I was different, but did they know why? Had they put it together?

I'd sworn Akio and Kyle to secrecy about what happened to Piper. Or rather, what *didn't* happen. Right there in the frigid night, next to the blazing ruin of the cabin. I wasn't sure what to do yet, and didn't need my whole team freaking out. I knew I shouldn't trust anyone, but they'd seen Piper die with their own eyes. There was no other option.

The wind picked up, rocking my icy perch. Pregnant storm clouds crept over the horizon, swirling like ghosts, promising darkness and loss and pain. Jesus, why was I up in a damn ski lift? I was going to freeze to death.

Akio had gone patrolling last night and never came back.

I felt tightness in my chest. Maybe I'd been too aloof? Or maybe I should've *deliberately* scared the others with what I could do, to keep them in line.

Alone in this chair, a mile removed from everyone else, I could admit things.

I was terrified the others might see through me. That they'd sense I wasn't really a leader, even with this new . . . whatever it was. God, what did they think of me right now, riding a freaking ski lift all by myself. I was acting like a weirdo.

I had to give them something. Some new reason to support me. If not they'd slip away and join my enemies. Like Akio had?

A knot hardened in my stomach. *Had* he abandoned me? Did he blab? Why didn't I see it coming?

I slapped the lift bar down and leaned my elbows on it. I needed a win. A reminder to my team of why they were up here with me, and not lounging in town eating Fritos. Which meant I had to make Ethan look weak. But how?

The mountaintop station hove into view. My chair pulled in and I raised the bar, hopped off, then jogged a few steps to avoid the next one. I was several klicks east of the chalet, but my feet took me in the opposite direction. The trees opened up and suddenly I was staring down at the whole basin.

Fire Lake valley is a steep-sided bowl surrounded by white-capped peaks on three sides, with its signature lake directly in the center. The western edge drops hundreds of feet into Gullet Chasm, uncrossable with the bridge down even if there was

43

something left on the other side. Which I doubted. All exits from the valley seemed deliberately blocked, and the Program had to be finite. For the sixty-four of us, this was our entire world.

Sixty-three. Piper is gone, and you sent her packing.

My eyes strayed east. To the fenced-off woods, where the silo was hidden.

Min.

Was she there? Her trailer park hid behind Miner's Peak in the opposite direction, but I was sure she'd gone to ground at the heart of Project Nemesis. It was the smart move, and Min was the smartest person I knew.

I rubbed my chin, let the cold outside fill me within.

Was she in the control room right now, scared and alone?

Then I chuckled without humor. Min hiding? Weepy and sad? No chance. She'd be furious. Out for my blood.

And not alone. Tack was always with her, like a virus you couldn't shake.

Acid filled my mouth as I pictured Min and Tack way down in the silo, lying in each other's arms. Giggling together as they plotted my downfall.

Fire exploded in my chest. My arms tingled. My lips curled into a snarl as I tried to banish the taunting image. I turned and started back toward the chalet. I was wasting time. The others would wonder.

I kicked myself for not going to the silo first thing, weeks ago, but I'd been too afraid to leave my people alone without me. When I'd finally had the chance to sneak away, I'd found the outer door locked and tracks all around the gravel lot.

Someone had been there. Was probably still inside. It didn't

44

take a genius to figure out who—Min and Tack were the only other people who knew the silo existed. I'd retreated quickly before being noticed. Wasn't ready for that fight.

Honestly, it was better this way. I didn't want a real threat like Ethan or Sarah to learn the secrets hidden there. Min and Tack had probably gone in right after the Town Hall massacre, and would never come out. That worked for me. They could be my guard dogs for now. I'd deal with them eventually.

A twig snapped and I froze. I was still a couple hundred yards from the chalet. Not quite no-man's-land, but who knew what the townies might try after the cabin bonfire. And for the last fifteen minutes I'd been winging through the sky like a clay pigeon.

I reached for my Beretta just as Kyle jogged from a thicket of longleaf pines. He saw me standing there, pistol in hand, and skidded to a stop, throat working as his hands flew up. Good. Be afraid.

"Yes?" I asked in my coldest voice. *Can I trust you with our secret, Kyle?*

Kyle swallowed again. He was sweating. "We, um . . . we have a problem." I could tell he wanted to be anywhere but there.

I declined to speak.

"At the chalet," Kyle continued, expelling a misty breath as I shoved my weapon back into a jacket pocket.

"What kind of problem?" Voice flat, but my heart began racing.

Kyle looked like he was about to throw up.

"There's been an accident. I'm so sorry, Noah, but I think we're screwed."

5

MIN

"Why do you think we have to eat?" Hamza Zakaria said.

"Because we're hungry," Floyd Hornberry replied. "Same as always."

I could barely see their faces as I squinted into the afternoon sunshine reflecting off the snowy peaks behind them. Tack and I were crouched behind an outcropping twenty yards from the quarry gatehouse, uncertain how to make our approach. Floyd and Hamza each had a rifle slung over one shoulder, but they were sitting on wooden stools and drinking from soup cans. They didn't seem on particularly high alert.

"The MegaCom's OS must require it," Hamza continued, pausing briefly as he chewed. "A need for virtual sustenance is probably embedded into our basic programming."

"You think too much."

"We're currently dead and bodiless, living inside a digital reality. That doesn't interest you?"

I could almost hear the shrug in his companion's response. "I don't feel dead. So I eat. What's the difference?"

"You're a real scholar, Floyd."

"I'm trying to have lunch, Hamza. Lay off."

We ducked back down. I glanced at Tack, who shrugged. Floyd and Hamza were clearly bored, and doing a terrible job. We'd managed to sneak over the perimeter fence and up the access road without being spotted. But we could go no farther in good faith without announcing ourselves.

"You ready?" Tack whispered. "Try to be charismatic when we talk to them. That's Chunky soup, and I really, really want some."

"This isn't going to work," I answered, shaking my head. "They seem to be doing fine without us."

"That's the spirit. You've got a great soup-acquiring attitude going right now."

"Shut it." Taking a deep breath, I rose and stepped onto the frozen gravel road.

Five steps.

A plume of white exploded beside my left foot.

Hamza and Floyd looked up from their cans in surprise. Neither had touched his rifle.

"Down!" Tack tackled me by the waist, driving me behind a cluster of shattered boulders beside the road. I hit the ground hard, scraping my elbow, dirty snow smearing my mouth and nose.

I coughed and spat. "What the—"

Silver streaks pinged off the stones around us.

"Someone's shooting!" Tack hissed, driving home the obvious. "From farther up the road I think."

Great. We hadn't even made contact yet, and already my plan was in shambles.

"Why would they . . ." I peeked over a jagged boulder. Hamza was now on his feet, soup can capsized on the ground as he pointed his rifle in our general direction. Floyd had turned, was staring up the access road at a low warehouse fifty yards deeper into the quarry. Then something ricocheted an inch from my ear and I dropped with a yelp. "They don't even know what we want yet!"

"Or care, obviously." Tack chomped his bottom lip, thinking hard. "Hold on."

Griping quietly to himself, he tore off his hoodie and the white tee beneath, goose bumps erupting along his pale arms and chest. Spotting a long stick a yard away, he scampered out and snagged it. A line of pulverized ice puffs chased him back to cover. "Just hold on a minute already!" he shouted in annoyance.

Tack tied his T-shirt atop the stick, then slowly raised it above the boulders and waved the makeshift flag back and forth. At first, nothing. Then the shirt jerked backward as a bullet tore through the fabric.

"Oh, real nice!" Tack yelled. "That's my best undershirt!"

Silence. A full minute passed as we cowered behind our meager concealment. I couldn't think of what to do next. There wasn't even a line of retreat. We were trapped behind a narrow cluster of broken stones, pinned down and outnumbered. We'd debated whether to bring our guns with us, but had elected not to, hoping to appear nonthreatening. Certain resets seemed in our future.

"What do you want?" a voice demanded. Neither Floyd nor

Hamza. My eyes darted to Tack, but he shook his head, eyes wide. Neither of us had seen a third person.

"Not to get shot!" Tack called back. "Let's start with that!"

"It's Min and Tack," I shouted. "We just came to talk. That's it. We promise."

A tense moment passed. Then, "Come out with your hands up."

Tack giggled nervously. "What are you, an old-timey sheriff? Should we reach for the sky, too?"

"Shut up, Tack," the voice snapped. "Do it or we'll send you both back into the mixer."

"Okay, okay!" I said, trying to keep my voice firm. "We're coming out. Do *not* shoot us."

I caught Tack's eye and nodded. What choice did we have?

Tack shook his head, eyes askance. "Stand up like target dummies for these guys? No way, Min. We should run for it."

"Then why'd we even bother? Come on, I didn't walk all the way up here for nothing."

Tack ran a hand over his face, then shot a quick glance to the heavens. But he popped to his feet before I could move, hands above his head as instructed. I couldn't help but smile, even as I cringed. Tack thought I was making a mistake, but if this was a trap, he wasn't letting them get a shot at me first. My maddening and wonderful best friend.

I rose quickly beside him, ignoring his warning scowl. We'd share the risk together.

Carl Apria was standing next to a shamefaced Floyd, holding a sleek bolt-action hunting rifle equipped with an expensive-looking scope. I saw Hamza sprinting up the road, probably to alert Sam Oatman, Carl's cousin. Carl's thick black brows were knitted in suspicion above dark eyes. A descendant of the Nez Perce tribe native to Idaho, his copper-tinged skin gleamed in the sunlight.

Carl's face was sweaty despite the frigid alpine breeze, as if he'd run a short distance. He spat sideways into the dirty snow, then rubbed his snub nose. "You two can't stop causing trouble, can you?"

"Great to see you too, Carl," Tack quipped, hands still sky-high. "Nice place you've got here. Okay if I stop showing you my abs?"

Carl's frown deepened, but he nodded and we lowered our hands. "Our camp isn't a resort, but it's secure. Or was before you guys showed up."

"Ethan and Sarah might do worse," I said, attempting to steer the conversation to a productive place. "They've got a lot of people, and control the supermarket. We need—"

Carl held up a hand to stop me. "Wait for my cousin."

So we stood in awkward silence until Sam strode down the gravel road, shaggy black hair curling over his ears. He was shorter than Carl, with a wider mouth, but they were both built like tanks. The cousins used to have matching faux-hawks, but strict personal grooming must be tough in an abandoned quarry. Sam had always been the more talkative of the pair.

He examined us with distrustful eyes, then turned to Carl. "Why didn't you shoot them?"

Carl shrugged. "It's windy. I missed. Then Tack waved a white flag."

"My shirt, actually," Tack said. "Which you put a bullet through. Thanks a bunch."

Carl offered a half smile. "Had to hit something, Thumbtack."

"Tell us why you're here," Sam insisted. "Why'd you come up to the quarry?"

"We've been neighbors for weeks," I said, trying to keep my voice light. Though we'd never been close, I'd known these boys for years. I was secretly unnerved by the reception we were getting, but was determined not to show it. "Tack and I are living in the trailer park. He spotted you a few days ago."

Tack winked, flashed a thumbs-up. The boy can't help himself.

Sam looked to Carl, who shrugged again. "It's a small valley."

"Which is why we should work together," I said, hoping to wedge something open. "Before the food runs out and Ethan really has a rope around our necks."

Sam shook his head. "It's every man for himself. We have food. Shelter. Firewood. A building full of camping supplies. Weapons. And all the ammo we need," he added significantly. "Tell the others that. Tell everyone you meet to stay away from here."

I shifted my weight, growing frustrated. "You'll run out, eventually. Ethan and Sarah have more of everything, including people. How many of you are there? How long can you guys squat inside a cave?"

"As long as we have to." Sam's voice was as hard as the granite slabs surrounding us. "We're not living in a fucking mineshaft,

Min. Give me a little credit. We have a warehouse and three outbuildings with solid roofs. And a damn good place to fall back on, if pressed. Unless you're offering something better?"

I glanced at Tack, who nodded eagerly for me to continue.

I hesitated. "An alliance has its own rewards. If we unite everyone who opposes Ethan, we can—"

"Unite under who?" Carl said, his mouth twisting into a knot. "You?"

"No!" I answered sharply, just as Tack piped, "Of course. She's a beta."

"I'm not trying to run anything," I said quickly, avoiding Tack's gaze as it bored into the side of my head. "I just think we need to show Ethan we aren't afraid. That we're not going to let him push us around."

"*We* did that already," Sam countered. "Ask those thugs we stopped with bullets in their chests."

"But that's stupid, too!" I snapped, unable to hold my tongue. "Meeting their violence with your own is just as bad."

"When Min says 'stupid,'" Tack cut in, hands fluttering up from his sides, "what she really means is . . . *counterproductive*." He smiled encouragingly at the cousins, then shot a what-are-you-doing-get-it-together glance at me.

I faltered, unsure what to say next. Realized I didn't even know what I wanted.

Sam shook his head with finality. "There's no way out of the valley, Min. Right now Ethan is leaving us alone. And you said it yourself—he's got more people, more guns, more everything. Why should we pick a fight with him? He hates you guys, not us. If he stays away, we'll mind our own business, too."

I pounded a fist into my thigh. "That won't last. You have to see that! And what if Ethan *does* make a move? We're better off together than splintered into tiny factions. You're being incredibly naive."

"And you're a guest here," Carl shot back. Floyd's expression had darkened. I was being too impatient, too bossy. Blowing this with my big mouth.

I took a calming breath. "I just think we're stronger as one group. Everyone outside of town needs to rally against Ethan and Sarah. We'll *choose* a leader, then force those assholes to negotiate with us on even terms."

"Everyone?" Sam said. "Even Noah?"

I hesitated, momentarily thrown. Why were they throwing *him* in my face?

"That dude is *crazy*." Floyd ran a hand through his ragged Afro. A lumbering country boy, he had arms like slabs of beef and a barrel chest to match. "Trent Goodwin was with some of Ethan's people in a cabin up by the black-diamond slopes. Noah and his murder freaks burned the whole place down, with almost everyone still inside. Can you *imagine*?"

I went cold to my bones. Refused to look at Tack, who was trying to catch my eye.

The . . . *brutality* of it.

I thought of the night I'd spent at Noah's house before the soldiers rounded us up. How I'd found him downstairs the following morning, attempting to make me a lavish breakfast even though he'd clearly never cooked before.

I tried to picture that Noah *burning people alive*. I couldn't believe it.

Sam silenced Floyd with a hard look. Turned back to me. "Say what you came to, Min. But know that we can't take you guys in, not with how pissed off Ethan is at you. I'm sorry, but we're trying to avoid trouble here, not throw middle fingers at the world."

I blinked. Tried to focus on the moment. "Your group should move down to the trailer park with us. You've got the supplies, we've got plenty of room for everyone to have their own unit. Then we put out the word that everyone else should join us. If we gather enough people, Ethan and Sarah will have to take us seriously and negotiate. Then we can form a *rational* community, instead of this feudal kill-or-be-killed nonsense."

"So your 'offer' is the chance to live in the worst neighborhood in Fire Lake while also feeding everyone?" Sam's voice dripped with derision. "Pass. The trailer park sucks, and it's less defensible than the quarry. We're doing fine. And if we ever *do* want those trailers, we can take them."

Carl turned to his cousin. Lifted an eyebrow in silent question.

My palms began to sweat.

"What's the point?" Sam said, scratching his cheek in irritation. "They'll just reset, and still know where we are."

Carl crossed his arms. "Prisoners, then. Tack's been sniffing around. If Ethan captures them he might learn more than we want him to know."

"Who cares what he knows. Plus, you want two more mouths to feed?"

"This is fun." Tack hooked his pockets with his thumbs, whistled like he didn't have a care in the world. "Should Min and I move down the road a bit while you guys decide whether to kill or imprison us?"

My temper slipped its leash. I lurched forward a step, fingers balling into fists. "Stupid macho *bullshit*. You're making a mistake, Sam. They'll come for you eventually, and you'll be cut off and alone."

"Let 'em try." Sam pointed back the way we'd come. "Go. Now. Before I change my mind. Tell everyone you see that the quarry is closed."

"For how long?" I caught and held his eye. "You plan on hiding forever?"

"We don't know any better than you." Some of the ice left Sam's voice. "But with the Plank down, the valley is sealed. Everyone has to make a stand somewhere. This is our place." The hint of a plea crept into his dark brown eyes. "If you know what the point of all this is, I'm listening. Tell me that and we might have something to work out."

My mouth opened. Then closed. I didn't have an answer, and we both knew it.

Sam pulled a Colt 1911 pistol from his waistband, thumbed off the safety, and racked the slide. "We're done. Get lost unless you want another trip through cyberspace. Death might not exist anymore, but getting shot still hurts like hell."

There was nothing left to say.

I turned and stomped down the road, half expecting to catch a bullet between my shoulder blades. But no shots came. I heard Tack's voice floating on the wind. "Thanks for nothing, jerks. We'll remember this. Don't forget, that's a *beta* you just told off." Then his boots pounded after me in the hard-packed snow.

Tack's words rang hollow, as I'd known they would. How was I special? Because the government started killing me first? All being a beta patient had brought me was more death. A savage childhood of fear and misery.

It took us ten minutes to get back to the trailer park. I was silent the whole way, stewing, angry at Tack for suggesting the effort even though I knew the failure was mine. *I'd* lost my cool. It was *me* the cousins didn't believe in. Tack was just too blind to see.

He was right about one thing—people had to rally against Ethan. Arguing with Sam had convinced me, even if the cousins weren't buying it. But what message would get through to the others?

The Guardian had left chaos in his wake. Everyone was flying blind, making up the rules as we went along. No one felt safe, so how could anyone work together? We didn't know what we were supposed to be doing.

Then figure it out. Get answers.

Find out what the Program wants.

And just like that, I knew where we had to go.

6

MIN

"We could shoot them?" Tack said casually.

I gave him a scolding look. "We don't even know who they are." I released the branch in my hands, pine needles smacking Tack across the face as we stepped back from the tree line.

"Ow!" Tack rubbed his cheek.

"Serves you right." We were too far away to be spotted or heard, and I hadn't liked his violent suggestion. "We need to get to the silo as quickly as possible. That's it. We *don't* need to leave a trail of dead in our wake."

"Not dead," he corrected in the same airy tone. "Just . . . temporarily gone. And who knows, maybe we get Skee-Ball tickets for every kill? Redeemable at Town Hall for delicious cotton candy!"

I spun, mouth a hard line, but Tack already had his hands up. "Jokes, Melinda." Then his shoulders rose to scrunch around his neck, his hands swinging down, palms up, wrists tight to his chest. "But also . . . kinda not. Don't act like blasting everyone in our path isn't the safest way to travel right now. They all come back fine. I'm just saying."

"Well, you can *stop* saying. We're not gonna win people over by murdering them."

Down below us, on a lakefront pier, two huddled figures were fishing. The ice was still paper thin and they'd smashed a hole through to open water, dropping hopeful lines into the sapphire-blue depths. The morning was cold and miserable, with one of those awful thirty-eight-degree drizzles that turns snow to slush and steals the warmth from your limbs, making everything you wear sodden and heavy and terrible.

"Only lunatics would sit out in the open like that," Tack grumbled, picking his way past a clump of grasping ferns. I tended to agree. We were fifty feet up the side of the canyon, in a park area south of the ruined bridge. We'd been following a hiking trail through the woods when I spotted the mystery pair. They had their hoods up, legs dangling from the outermost dock as they fished. In their formless black ski jackets they could've been anyone, though some instinct—perhaps the way they were sitting—made me think they were girls.

My throat had gone dry just watching them. "We can sneak by. We'll cut through Lakeshore Estates and go around them."

Tack wiped a gobbet of sap from his pine-slapped cheek as rain droplets tumbled down his parka. With a pout, he held two sticky fingers up for me to see, but I just rolled my eyes. "So we're not seeking converts along the way?" Tack said, wiping his glove on the side of his jeans. "This is the worst mission trip ever."

I brushed past him, crossing the trail and cutting through

a crooked line of Douglas firs, emerging out onto wet pavement. A narrow side street wound up into the valley's swankiest neighborhood. "Sam's being stubborn, but he won't be the only one," I said over my shoulder. "Without something concrete to offer, no one's going to listen to us. We need to exploit our one advantage."

"No argument here." Tromping after me. "We should've raided the silo weeks ago."

I resisted the urge to bite him. We'd had this fight a dozen times, too.

"It wasn't safe before," I said in a flat tone, patience strained to the breaking point. "You know Noah must've gone straight there after the shootout. He's probably got people watching the place, or hauling out all the useful stuff. That's what I'd have done in his shoes, and he has too many followers for us to take on alone."

Tack snorted. "So what changed? Last I checked, Noah is still closer to the silo and knows everything we do. We're walking into the same situation you wanted to avoid."

I shot him a dirty look, but then sighed and nodded tartly, conceding the point.

"Our situation changed." I waited for him to join me on the blacktop. "A few weeks ago we had food for a few more weeks. Plus, I didn't know how bad the fighting would get." I leveled a finger at him. "And you agreed we might accidentally lead Ethan and Sarah to the supplies and Nemesis files, which was too big a risk. That stuff is our only advantage."

"Yeah, yeah," he muttered as we set off toward the first row of houses. "I'm just glad we're finally going. Maybe Noah never even bothered. Too busy roasting people like marshmallows, or making out with his hunting knife. If we can sneak inside the silo somehow, we could hide down there for months. It's a hoarder's bonanza."

"*If* Noah hasn't cleaned it out already. Or blown up the entrance. And remember, those supplies are boxed for the long haul. We don't know if there's any food beyond seeds. I'm more afraid that he's sitting in the control room right now, studying the Program."

The eastern end of Fire Lake valley was a fenced-off government property that, for decades, everyone had assumed was deserted. Only three of us knew the truth: that the base contained a decommissioned missile silo secretly repurposed to house the world's most powerful supercomputer. Past the rusty gates, deep in the woods and a hundred feet underground, hid humanity's sole remaining lifeboat.

In the real world, anyway. Tack and I were actually *inside* the MegaCom as we argued, arcing through its circuits as two series of ones and zeroes. You could go crazy thinking about it. But the Program reflected the supercomputer itself into our virtual reality, along with everything else in the silo, including dozens of crate-filled alcoves lining the missile shaft.

The silo also contained a set of Project Nemesis files at the base of the structure. I'd only been able to skim them before we were forced downtown by the Guardian and all hell broke loose. It was those records that interested me now. They might reveal the true purpose of the Program.

Only three people knew about any of this. Me. Tack. And Noah.

I felt a heaviness in my limbs. Unconsciously, my gaze rose to the canyon rim. A thick gray mist was seeping slowly over the surrounding mountains, swallowing the southern peaks in wet, hungry jaws.

Though I couldn't see it, I knew we were close to Noah's old home. His neighborhood was one over from here, the priciest set of streets in Fire Lake. I imagined that gigantic house, standing cold and dark on the valley's highest cul-de-sac, abandoned like every moral principle Noah had ever possessed.

Terrible images strobed in my mind.

A smoking hole in my chest. Tack's horrified, blood-splattered face.

Noah standing over me, eyes narrowed and burning, yet at the same time so far away.

The second shot had murdered anything between us. *Everything* between us.

The memory woke me some nights. Sweaty, breathless, bed-sheets snarled in my white-knuckled fingers. I tried to hide the nightmares from Tack, but he knew. And was smart enough not to say anything. Noah's betrayal was the one topic we never discussed.

Before shooting me point-blank, Noah had called me his nemesis. Not the Guardian. Or the Program. Not the twisted conspiracy that had used us both like guinea pigs. Not even the dark star whose return destroyed the planet.

Me. The one he kissed. Comforted. Saved.

I thought I might love him, and he fucking killed me.

What if Noah really was at the silo? He was smart enough to unravel the Guardian's secrets if he put in the effort, but did he have the patience? Did he even care? Then a wave of nausea swept over me.

What if the files proved him right?

The thought jarred me to my core. I'd never considered that possibility before, but now uncertainty stole through me like a disease.

What if violence *was* the purpose of the Program? This whole existence, just a video game loop meant to distract us while the world burned. A pointless cycle to keep us busy until the power ran out and we dissolved into random electrons and nothingness. God, what if there weren't any more phases at all?

No.

I refused to believe that. I would not give in to hopelessness.

Noah might be at the silo, and he might not. We'd know in an hour. If there were answers, we'd find them. I just had to keep moving forward.

Tack was peering down a cross street and had missed my spasm of distress. By the time he looked my way again, I'd carefully blanked my expression. "Let's get going," I said. "I don't like the look of those clouds."

Tack nodded. He led us around a corner, taking a route parallel to the lake but out of sight from it. The rain started coming down harder, and a dark smudge of gray was blowing in from the south with the promise of more. My feet were soaked, my sneakers making disgusting squishy sounds with every footfall. I dropped to a knee for a moment to tighten my laces. Tack halted miserably by my side. He didn't mind the cold, but wet was another story entirely.

I rose, knocking rainwater from the brim of my hood. "At least this weather's good cover."

Tack glanced around as we resumed walking. "For everyone. Keep your head on a swivel."

We kept silent after that, trudging past rows of giant homes, each with a stunning view of the lake. Prices went up the higher you climbed, and this was only the first tier. I wondered again which of our classmates might be living in this area. Tack was sure that at least a few people had avoided the big groups, and it made sense to come here. There were literal mansions for the taking. If you have to hide someplace, why not do it in style?

"What do you think might be in the Nemesis files?" Tack asked suddenly, rubbing his sticky cheekbone. The sap was refusing to come off, and I felt bad about my branch assault. "Like, are you looking for a Program instruction manual or something?"

"That's my hope." I gave a full-bodied shrug, the gesture nearly swallowed by my parka. "We found answers last time. And I feel like, no matter how top secret, a government program would write everything down somewhere, at least once. Isn't that what bureaucracy is all about?"

"Unless Noah's soiled the carpets already," Tack muttered.

I started walking faster.

We covered two more blocks, then cut back downhill to Shore Point Road. The fishing duo were now safely out of view. I couldn't help wondering who they were, and why they weren't being more careful. I looked back at the manicured lanes rising in sweeping tiers behind us. "Do you know who's playing millionaire?"

Tack shook his head, then clicked his tongue as we traversed a sharp bend in the road, the valley floor opening up before us. "I do have theories, though. I haven't seen Anna or Aiken anywhere, and they'd never stick with Ethan's gang. And some of the soccer girls are unaccounted for, but I guess they could be with the cousins." Then he stopped and pointed. "Or they could all be over there."

Dead ahead, a field stretched a few hundred yards to a cluster of squat wooden buildings hard against the lakefront. Starlight's Edge Fellowship Camp, in all its glory. Smoke was wafting from one of the big chimneys, a thin line of charcoal gray barely visible in the soggy gloom.

"Somebody's home." Tack chewed his thumb, frowning as we scanned the acres of open ground surrounding the camp on three sides. "And that somebody shot me like a prize buck when I tried to get close a week ago. I'm still very offended."

The smoke was coming from the centermost building, which I thought was the assembly hall, though I'd never been inside it. "Well, you *were* sneaking through the grass like an escaped convict."

"True. Honestly, I don't even know for sure it was them. I didn't see the shot."

We stood there another minute, examining the exposed approach. There was no way past the camp without being seen, not unless we wanted an afternoon-long detour hacking through scrub forest or an even longer climb up the canyon walls.

"We could steal a boat," Tack offered. "Break through the ice and paddle around."

I grunted. "It's thick enough already to make that tough

going. We'd leave a trail, too, and anyone looking at the lake would see us. Plus, the closest boathouses are behind us, right where those friendly fisherfolk happen to be."

Tack sighed. "Stick to the road, then?"

"I guess. Maybe we can parley with them, like we did at the quarry."

"Because *that* went so well." But he held up a hand to cut off my nettled response. "You're right, you're right. There's no other way to the eastern woods from here. Not unless we go all the way back around and through town."

"Not an option."

"Fine. But if they shoot me again, I'm going to be super-pissed." Tack pulled out his father's Glock 17, ejected and checked the magazine, then slammed it back home and shoved the pistol into his waistband. He gave me a significant glance.

"I have it," I said irritably, running a finger over the bulge in my jacket where the revolver lurked. "But I don't need to whip it around like a movie villain before we cross an empty field."

"You're probably right. If these jackasses shoot first, we won't feel a thing."

I cleared a lump in my throat. "If either of us gets killed, head straight for the silo afterward. No sense meeting anywhere else."

Tack nodded, then flashed a lopsided grin. "Who knows? Maybe we'll get lucky and reset in Sarah's field. That'd save us half the walk."

I chuckled despite myself. "Us. Lucky. Right." But Tack's dark humor was interesting. The idea that a reset might some-how *help* me . . . I'd never considered it. Our whole existence was borderline insane.

Mine always has been.

So far I'd died twice inside the Program, resetting in different places. Never the eastern field, however, where Sarah had returned for so many years. Was that spot on deck for me?

I shivered. Had to remind myself that this situation wasn't novel. Not to me. I'd been executed *five times* before even entering the Program.

Tack could joke about resets because he didn't understand. Not truly. He could never grasp the damage those birthday murders had inflicted on me. The horror of waking up outside in the dark woods, alone, with nothing but a scarring memory to tell me the experience had been real. How every death felt like a violation of my soul.

How could Tack know? He wasn't one of Dr. Lowell's betas. He hadn't been tested, and broken, and used. Only Noah truly understood, and he was my enemy now.

Is that right? Is Noah my nemesis, too? What does that even mean?

Did I have to destroy him? Was that even possible on this merry-go-round?

I still didn't understand why Noah and I had been repeatedly killed back in the real world, before the simulation began. The black-suited man must've had a reason, but what was it? Why do it so many times? And *how?* How did we literally come back from the dead? That was obviously something different from resetting virtually inside the Program, but I couldn't make the pieces connect.

Silo. Control room. There has to be something we missed.

Tack nudged me from my reverie. Left his elbow hanging

out like a chicken wing, a prom date offering me escort into the gymnasium.

"Shall we?" Waggling his eyebrows.

"Doofus." I shoved his arm away, though not unkindly. Tack snorted.

We started forward down the road, eyes scanning the campground, ready to turn and run in an eyeblink. Sweat trickled down my spine. I tried to convince myself it was rainwater. Nearing the outermost building, I felt eyes on me. My skin began to itch. A shot could ring out at any second. I probably wouldn't even hear it.

We passed the first building, then a second.

Nothing. No challenge, no sign of anyone observing us.

Maybe the miserable weather was keeping them inside. Or maybe the fishers by the lake were the ones living here.

We drew even with the assembly hall. I had an urge to sneak off the road and check it out, but resisted. Tack and I had pressing business and didn't need to go asking for trouble. We could always come back by here after the silo.

Then Tack snagged my arm, stopping me short. He put a finger to his lips.

I heard it, too. Boots sloshing through puddles. A second later, Neb Farmer rounded the building in front of us, whistling off-tune, a pump-action shotgun resting loosely on his shoulder as he lumbered through the misting rain.

Tack and I slipped out our guns. The revolver felt cold and heavy in my fingers. I didn't like the feeling. Then I nearly jumped as Tack racked the slide on his Glock.

Neb's head jerked up. He stopped dead. The shotgun's barrel shifted an inch on his shoulder.

"Don't," Tack warned, raising his pistol. "Let it fall, Neb. We're not here to shoot you, so you can relax. Just passing through."

Neb seemed to weigh Tack's words. Tall and skinny, with pale-pink skin and shaggy blond hair, he wore denim overalls and a drenched half-zip hoodie. Quiet by nature, he'd never fought with anyone, as far as I could recall. But he was a stranger now, and armed. I gripped my weapon tightly, ready for anything.

"I'm not getting mud on this thing." Neb carefully set his shotgun against the wall and stepped away. "You better not be lying, Tack." He scratched a freckled cheek, hazel eyes wary. "I've been popped once already, and it sucked."

I started breathing again. Tack hadn't lowered his Glock, so I gently put a hand over his, pushing the barrel down, my eyes flashing in rebuke. "He's telling the truth, Neb," I called out. "We're not here to hurt anyone."

Tack flinched. Frowning, he shoved the pistol back into his jacket. I did the same, sensing a disappointment in my friend I didn't like.

Neb relaxed a fraction, his expression growing quizzical. "You guys are just out walking in the rain? Kinda dumb these days."

"Not exactly," I answered, then changed the subject. "Are you still with Ethan?"

Neb shook his head with a scowl. "Hell, no! He's a jerk. And Toby's gone nuts. We don't want any part of that shit-show."

"We?" Tack countered, tilting his head.

"There's a few of us around." Neb hesitated. I could almost

see his wheels turning. "A lot, actually. Enough to make anyone who messes with us sorry."

Tack snickered, shaking his head. "Oh, Neb. Such a terrible liar. Like that time you knocked over the paint station in Mrs. Dixon's class, and said a bird did it."

Neb's face flamed scarlet. "Shut up, Tack. That was third freaking grade. Plus, the window *was* open, so nobody can say—"

"Let me guess." Tack rolled right over him, scratching his chin as he thought aloud. "If you're here, that means Corbin and Isaiah must be too, right?"

Neb shifted, looked away. He really was a terrible liar.

"Thought so. That means we can safely add Liesel to the list. Anyone else?"

"Emma Vogel," Neb growled through clenched teeth. "And, like, ten others."

Tack looked hard at Neb, then wagged his head again. "Nope. I think five is the number." He nodded to himself, no doubt mentally updating his crappy map. Then Tack jerked a thumb back over his shoulder. "Who's fishing down the road? Is that some kind of trap?"

Neb's brow furrowed. "Fishing? In freezing rain? Not us." He glanced at the assembly hall, eyes suddenly anxious. "I better tell Corbin."

Neb scooped up his shotgun, took two running steps, then stopped. He turned and sized us up for a moment. Seemed to make a decision. "You coming? We're not hurting people, either. Not if they don't make us. But it's hard keeping watch with just five."

I considered the offer, but the silo was drawing me like a lodestone.

We can always come back.

Then Neb spun sideways as a dull crack reverberated across the camp. He dropped to his knees, gaping in confusion as a red bloom spread across his chest.

Tack and I bolted to the closest building as another shot rang out. We flattened against its weathered brown timbers, eyes darting in all directions.

"Lying bastards!" Neb cursed, crawling in the muck. He made it two yards, then collapsed.

"It wasn't us!" I shouted, but he'd already lost consciousness. I watched in silence as his body sagged, then disappeared.

"Neb got it in the chest," Tack panted, ripping his Glock back out. "That means the shooter is behind us somewhere, back the way we came."

I ran a palm over my mouth. Tried to slow my drumming heartbeat. "The fishermen?"

"Yes. No. Maybe!" Tack yanked at his hair with his free hand. Rain and sweat mixed on his forehead, plastering it to his flushed skin. "I have no idea. Where the hell are Neb's people? *Man* am I tired of getting shot at."

I squeezed Tack's shoulder, my breath still bursting in and out. I shared his frustration, but mostly I was furious. Who was out there randomly picking people off with a rifle? It was insane! It was *pointless*.

Tack edged to the corner of the building and peeked around, then whispered back at me. "We need to keep moving. Let's sneak to the other side and bolt down the road. We can still reach—"

Boots on gravel. A shout, answered by another.

I glanced toward the center of camp, spotted a window inching open on the second floor of the assembly hall. The barrel of a rifle poked out. It fired twice, and there was a yowl of pain from the other side of the building Tack and I were cowering behind.

"One for the campers," I hissed.

Tack retreated from the corner, mild panic in his eyes. "It's the twins. Ferris and Cole too, but Cole's down. We gotta go!"

Shit. Ethan's goon squad had chosen *this* exact moment to attack the summer camp. Of course they had. But why bother? What could they hope to achieve? Anyone the twins killed would just disappear and reset, waking up somewhere else in a couple of hours.

"Min!" Tack was tugging my forearm. "We have to bail. *Right now.*"

He was right. Locking fingers, we ran to the shadow of the next cabin, following Neb's sodden footprints from moments before. The sky opened into a downpour, soaking us as we slunk from building to building, hugging slick hewn-log walls until we reached the field on the opposite side.

Tack pointed fifty yards down the road, to where tree cover resumed. "Ready to run?"

I nodded, wiping my eyes. "Don't stop for anything. No matter what. Just get to the silo."

We bumped fists. I tensed, preparing for an all-out sprint.

"Hey, guys."

I recoiled like a startled cat as a silhouette materialized in the rain. Toby Albertsson was straddling the road like a Tombstone gunslinger. He wore tactical gear, held a sleek black assault rifle that looked modern and deadly and final.

No point talking.

I jerked up my revolver and squeezed, firing wildly. Slipped and fell in the mud.

Tack aimed his Glock with both hands.

Bang. Bang.

Crack. Crack. Crack.

Crack. Crack. Crack. Crack. Crack.

Bang.

The world went black.

7

NOAH

Tepid water sloshed over my ankles.

I stepped out of the walk-in freezer in disgust.

"How long has it been like this?" I demanded.

Kyle took an involuntary step back. Jamie kept her eyes on the floor, short chestnut curls creating a curtain across her face. "We're not sure," she said. "Two, maybe three days to melt all the ice. We don't come down to this level every day because the restaurant kitchen is easier to use."

I put a hand to my face, trying to keep my temper in check. "Damage?"

"Some of this we can salvage," Jamie said quietly. "The sealed food we can put outside in the snow and refreeze. But the unpackaged stuff, like the meat . . . I don't know." She swallowed. "And everything in the refrigerators is ruined."

I blinked, the magnitude of the disaster setting in. "What's wrong with the refrigerators?"

"Whatever popped this circuit shut everything down." Jamie fidgeted with her zipper, unable to keep her hands still. "It's crazy, I know, since it's freezing outside, but the furnace is right below us. This room heats up pretty quick if the power fails. And . . . it did."

I choked back a caustic reply—I could damn well see the electricity was dead, and I was sweating in my jacket. The question thundering inside my head was *why*. The power upstairs was working fine. It wasn't until this basement level that we'd needed flashlights.

"We just stocked this kitchen. We put everything down here because it was safest."

Neither Jamie nor Kyle replied. The tension level rose like mercury.

I'd ordered everything gathered from the main resort at the bottom of the slopes, and the ski village on top, cobbling together a fairly solid food supply. Then we'd augmented our stores by raiding outlying houses. I'd insisted everything be kept *here*, in the depths of the chalet, at the heart of our main encampment. Now all of our perishables were gone.

The waste was sickening. Nothing Sarah or Ethan could've done would hurt half as much as this power outage. Our mountaintop fortress was amazing for defense, but we were miles from everything else in the valley. Without food, this might as well be a crypt.

The lights suddenly flickered back on. I glared a question at Kyle.

"I sent Richie to check the breakers," he answered, rubbing

his palms on the sides of his jeans. He tried on a shaky smile. "Guess we're lucky nothing's busted for real."

Lucky. Or something else?

"Who's been down here in the last three days?" I asked.

At first neither answered. I looked at Jamie, and she shrugged helplessly. "I don't know. Anyone who felt like it, I guess. Richie and I have been using the restaurant to prepare meals, and keep what we need for two or three days up there. I came down here a half hour ago and found the room pitch black."

I stared at Jamie until tears formed in the corners of her eyes. Was she lying? Was this an act of sabotage?

I pressed my lips together. Felt a quiver in my stomach. I coughed into a fist, then thrust a finger at Kyle without looking. "I want to know who's used this kitchen in the last forty-eight hours, and I want to know why the power failed. Go."

Kyle opened his mouth to say something, then thought better of it. He scurried from the room. Jamie hesitated briefly, and I nodded toward the door. She bolted out behind him.

Alone, I unzipped my jacket and ripped it off, then threw it on the ground and kicked it. This was a disaster. Worse, it made me look like a fool. Like I was too incompetent to protect our most valuable assets. Too stupid to live.

What would the others say? What would they think?

A cold fist squeezed my heart. Why would a breaker flip? With so few people staying at the chalet, power usage must be way below what the grid could handle. A surge seemed incredibly unlikely.

Which meant someone did it on purpose. But who? Including

me, there were eight people staying at the resort. Which one couldn't I trust?

Seven people. Akio is gone.

My lips began to tremble. Then my hands. I took a shaky step backward as my breath broke down into rasps. I leaned forward, hands on my knees, then my body went rigid, muscles freezing in place as my pulse accelerated like a runaway train.

Oh no.

No no no no no.

I was having a panic attack, my first since the Town Hall massacre.

My jaw clenched. I began to hyperventilate. I dropped unsteadily to sit on the floor, pulling my knees up to my chest and curling into a ball. My eyes squeezed shut as the walls closed in around me. I felt a streak of terror at being alone so far underground.

Relax. Breathe.

But my thoughts were spiraling out of control. I imagined Kyle whispering to the others about Piper's scorched body. Zach telling them I was losing it. That I was weak and needed to be replaced. I pictured Akio sneaking down here and jamming a fork in an outlet while Richie and Leah cheered him on.

Stop. Stop it.

I forced my hands to stillness. Measured the rhythm of my lungs. Slowly the pressure eased. I opened my eyes and wiped them. The crushing anxiety had passed, but the fear lingered. I'd thought I was past this.

I had to remain cool. Calm. Scary. They only followed me because I had answers, so I had to give them some, *now*, or they'd turn on me like jackals. That was the world we lived in. Crying on the floor like a baby accomplished nothing.

Min has a different way.

I jerked to my feet, ignoring a mind I couldn't trust. I'd wallowed enough for one day. The Program had no time for self-pity.

The Program.

I froze. Could the system itself have thrown this curveball? Shut down my freezers to observe how I'd react? The thought was strangely seductive. Maybe the Guardian was testing my will. Seeing if I could handle it.

Game on.

Suddenly I felt rejuvenated. I scooped my jacket off the tiles and headed out, mounting the stairs two at a time up to the lobby. I chastised myself for losing sight of what matters. The others wanted to see me take control? Fine. I'd take things to the next level.

I stepped outside, took a deep cleansing breath. The crisp mountain air burned my lungs, but I didn't care. Didn't even put on my jacket. I'd conquered my demons and finally knew what to do.

We needed food. So we'd go get it.

Breath misting like a dragon, I was working out the details as I reached the ski village, a tiny collection of faux-log-cabin shops surrounding a central courtyard. The village and the chalet were the only two structures atop the slopes.

I found the others where I'd suspected they'd be—in the large cafeteria-style eating hall at the far end of the complex. The group was sitting at one of the long bench tables, whispering quietly to each other. They fell silent at my approach.

I didn't speak at first, taking the time to glance at each of them in turn. Inviting challenge. But all eyes dropped as they met mine. Kyle. Leah. Jamie and Richie. Zach and Morgan.

No weakness. No fear. King Kong ruled the jungle for a reason.

Then I noticed someone new in the room, sitting beside Kyle and watching me with calculating eyes. The visitor nodded slowly in greeting. I nodded back.

"You come to join us?" I asked, in a voice so hard I barely recognized it.

"Yes."

"Does anyone else know?"

"Not yet. Ethan doesn't notice people he considers beneath him."

I smiled, the last piece of my plan falling into place.

See? The Program might be testing me.

But it provides, too.

8

MIN

I awoke in an unfamiliar spot.

A rocky hollow, high among the southern cliffs, near the canyon rim and its two-hundred-foot drop into river country. An icy wind knifed through a ring of boulders surrounding me, chilling my nose and ears. I was wet and exposed, storm clouds close enough to touch.

Ethan's spot. I'd never seen it before.

For some reason I'd expected the eastern field, or maybe I'd just been hoping. The reset points truly were random now. A pattern would've been helpful, but what about the Program had been so far?

Dead again. Three times since being uploaded. Twice in the last forty-eight hours. No matter what I tried, nothing seemed to work. My failures were piling up, and I'd come no closer to learning anything about the Program.

I choked back hot tears of frustration. The rain had stopped, but the thin grass was soaked and my butt was getting there. I stood, abruptly realized my head was pounding. My nose was a snotty mess, and I wiped it absently, felt heat radiating from my cheeks.

This was new. I'd never come back with physical discomforts before.

Dying hurt, certainly. Getting shot, or crushed, or drowning in a flash flood—those things felt as excruciating as you'd expect. But once it was over . . . it was over. You reset back to normal and everything was fine. So what was happening now?

I coughed into a fist, thrown by the change. Took stock. My limbs felt weak and rubbery. My stomach roiled. I brushed stray twigs from my hair, then ran both hands over my body. No injuries. My jeans and shoes were intact. I still had on my ski jacket, but with a twinge of panic I realized the gun was gone.

Huh.

Did it disappear, or had I dropped it? Was it lying on the road where I'd been shot? I'd never died holding a weapon before, so this was uncharted territory.

I rubbed my forehead, trying to focus. I knew that somewhere else in the valley, Tack was doing the same things. Toby had gotten the drop on us and we hadn't stood a chance.

The sun was a hazy blur behind the clouds, lower than when we'd reached the summer camp. I'd been gone for a couple of hours at least, maybe more. I was cold and wet and alone, surrounded by leering stone sentinels that seemed to mock me. This reset zone had an unfriendly vibe. All at once, I wanted out of Ethan's old territory.

I took a shaky step, dizzier than I'd thought. My knee banged against a knob of solid rock and a hiss escaped my lips. I stumbled back against a pillar, holding my leg and swearing with impressive foulness.

A memory flashed in my mind—Mom's hands, gently applying a Dora the Explorer Band-Aid to my skinned knee, the two of us tucked away safe in our little trailer as a thunderstorm raged outside.

My shoulders heaved. Tears streaked down my face as a strangled sob escaped.

I was tired. So tired of the cycle. Tired of waking up outside with no one to comfort me. Tired of struggling against things I didn't understand.

The sky rumbled overhead with the threat of more rain, or a flurry if the temperature continued to drop. My hands balled into fists, fingernails digging into palms. I didn't have time for this. My mother was dead. There was no warm, safe place for me to hide.

A storm was coming. I needed to get down the mountain before the lightning struck.

I swatted tears from my checks. Shook out my limbs. I'd told Tack to head directly for the silo if we were separated, so that's what I'd do. Spotting what appeared to be an old deer run, I began zigzagging downslope, careful not to step on any of the loose pebbles littering the mountainside. I was only a few miles from where I'd been gunned down, and didn't want to attract attention. The lack of birdcalls was unnerving, though I'd grown used to silent forests.

I rounded a switchback, spotted a pitted granite pillar ahead that reared ten feet and overhung the path. I slowed, stopped.

Something about it made me anxious. I looked left, then right. Jagged rocks on both sides funneled the trail directly past the pillar, which perfectly concealed the next bend.

My instincts hummed in warning. I didn't want to go that way.

I turned to a boulder on my right—weathered and creased, it was riddled with easy handholds. I decided to climb it, pulling myself halfway up in one go, then reaching for the top and hauling my body to where I could stand. From this vantage point I saw that the rest of the boulder field dropped twenty yards straight down the mountainside to where the path swung back around below it.

Shortcut, but a tricky one. Why not use the trail? Was I being paranoid?

Safety first, right? Hands extended, I began walking across the uneven rocky points, ready to leap backward if any proved unstable. By the third boulder I was able to see around the pillar that stood beside the path.

Derrick Morris was crouched behind it, gripping a burlap sack.

For a moment I just blinked. It was comical. Why was Derrick lurking in the shadows with a bag in his hands, like a hungry troll stalking hobbits?

Eyes glued to his back, I hopped to the next boulder, craning my neck to see if he was alone. I didn't spot anyone else, but the trail was crisscrossed with pools of darkness. I inched forward, eyes straining, praying Derrick wouldn't feel my gaze digging into his back. Was Ethan here? Why were they guarding the path?

The rock beneath my feet slumped left.

I toppled sideways with a silent curse, slamming against the next boulder and falling gracelessly between them. Then I slid headlong down a short scree slope, coming to a halt in an abraded tangle of arms, legs, and bruised ego. I'd felt an icy tingle as I plummeted, and knew I'd crossed through the reset zone boundary.

I'd tumbled nearly all the way to the lower section of trail. Scrambling to my feet, I turned to run, but Spence Coleman and Leighton Huddle were standing ten feet away, gaping at me like I'd fallen from a spaceship.

Derrick appeared around the bend. "Grab her, you idiots!"

There was nowhere to run. Spence reached for my shoulder and caught a fist in his teeth for his trouble. He howled, staggering backward, but Leighton grabbed my forearm and wouldn't let go. Then something rancid and slimy slammed over my head, smothering me.

I toppled to the ground with a garbled shout. Felt a heavy weight press down on me as my arms were wrenched behind my back. Someone was tying my hands. The whole thing felt like a Bugs Bunny cartoon.

"What the hell!?" I snarled, panicking, choking inside the filthy bag. I jabbed my elbow backward and was rewarded by a yowl of pain.

"We've got a live one!" someone joked. Leighton, I think. I could hear Spence spitting and cursing somewhere close by. Then I was yanked roughly to my feet.

"You gonna calm down, Melinda?" Derrick's voice boomed through the itchy burlap. "That can stay on, you know. You look great."

I seethed like a cauldron, but quit struggling. Moments later the bag was removed.

Derrick was facing me, looking pleased with himself. He was tall and lean, dark skinned, with a short, tight Afro and gleaming white teeth. "Oh man! Ethan is gonna be stoked. You're at the top of his wish list."

I glared a hole through his forehead. "Damn it, Derrick. Let me go!"

"Now why would I do that?" Derrick turned to his companions. "Y'all take Melinda over to the jail, then run tell Ethan who we bagged."

As I listened to Spence and Leighton grumble, the strategic situation snapped into focus. Ethan must've set up ambushes at all four reset points.

Heat rose to my face. The raid on the summer camp? Not so pointless after all. Toby and his team weren't randomly killing people. They were *herding*. Funneling holdouts through the reset points so they could be taken prisoner.

The scheme was . . . brilliant. It had Sarah's fingerprints all over it.

"Why do *we* have to go?" Leighton whined. "I just got out here, and haven't even eaten lunch yet. Plus, Spence already went into town once this morning."

Derrick smiled, clicked his tongue. "Because *I'm* in charge, not you. That's how it rolls, kid. Downhill. You're not class president here in Ethanland."

Leighton's pale blue eyes narrowed, but before he could respond, there was a disturbance up the path. Derrick clamped a hand over my mouth.

Tack is coming. Do something!

But my hands were literally tied and Derrick was twice my size. I tried yelling into his palm, but only a wheeze escaped.

"Hush now," Derrick whispered, dragging me behind a boulder and motioning Spence and Leighton into ambush position. "We've got another customer."

A shadowy figure appeared on the trail above, but the person stopped and called out before crossing the reset boundary. "It's Toby, you jackasses. Don't touch me or I'll slug you. I'm not in the mood."

Derrick released me and stepped into view, a smile appearing like magic. "Who gotcha, champ? One of those soccer girls?"

Toby trudged down the path, looking sheepish as he rubbed his shaved head. Short and squat, he resembled a fairy-tale gnome escaped from some old lady's garden. Toby had made the worst grades in school, but he'd always possessed a base cunning. Since the fighting started, I thought he might be the most dangerous kid in Fire Lake.

"Naw, I don't think those chicks are with Corbin." Toby glanced at me with a lopsided grin, though it didn't sync with his watery eyes. "I got Min and Thumbtack easy enough, but the little bastard got a lucky shot off before fading out. Sumbitch hit me right in the neck. I'm gonna pound him into the ground when I see him."

My heart sank. Tack was resetting, too. Walking into a similar trap.

Toby put a hand on my shoulder, squeezed it in a friendly manner. "Hey, Min. Were you two crashing at Starlight's Edge the whole time? I was sure you guys were hiding in the trailers, but we never spotted you. I might owe Charlie a condo."

His touch burned like acid. I shrugged his hand away. "Screw you, Toby."

"You offering?" He turned to Derrick before I could spit back a heated denial. "I'll walk her in. Lost my AR-15 on the raid, damnit. That one stings—I loved that piece. Gotta hit the armory before I head back out."

"Cool." Derrick glanced at Spence and Leighton, who were bumping fists at having avoided the trek. "Don't celebrate too hard—we're still stuck out here another hour. Now y'all get back in position. That firefight at the camp might keep us busy."

Toby reached for me, but I stepped in front of Derrick before he could lope away. "Why are you doing this? When'd you become Ethan's errand boy? Or a mass murderer?"

Derrick's shoulders bristled, but when he spoke, his voice was calm. "I'm nobody's errand boy. I just like being on the winning team. And stop it with that 'mass murderer' nonsense. Are you dead? Is Toby?"

I looked away. Toby waggled his fingers at me in a silly wave.

"It's just a game, Min. Can't you see that?" Derrick gathered my elbow and, not ungently, started me along the path. He and Toby exchanged five as I began picking my way downhill.

"Nobody's getting hurt," Derrick called after me. "Everybody comes back. Me? I prefer to eat well. If Ethan wants to set up water usage committees and count batteries, that's all right." He chuckled. "I'm sleeping in a penthouse."

"Come on, Min." Toby had caught up, put a hand to the small of my back. He left it there for a few paces, then ran his fingers up and over my bra strap, making my skin crawl.

"Watch it," I warned.

Toby giggled, removed his hand. "Just trying to help, Wilder. Wouldn't want you to face-plant with your hands tied."

I ground my teeth. Refused to respond.

As we followed the trail down to the valley floor, Derrick's words gnawed at me. A voice in my head worried he was right. Why *was* I so opposed to Ethan and Sarah being in charge? Those two had run Fire Lake High School like dictators before all this happened anyway. So why did it bother me so much now? Was it pride? Jealousy? Should I just fall in line, and leave it alone? Derrick's voice echoed in my eardrums. *Everybody comes back.*

A vision of Ethan stabbing Tack flashbulbed inside my head.

Ethan hadn't known about the resets then. He'd thought he was actually killing Tack—murdering my best friend in front of everyone. *That's why. Ethan's psychotic, and Sarah makes him smart.* Whatever this game was, those two couldn't be allowed to control it.

Not that *I* wanted the job. Tack might think I'd be a good leader, but he was the only one. People who ignored me in high school weren't suddenly going to listen now. Being a beta didn't change facts on the ground.

What was a beta anyway? A prized lab rat, and nothing more. The project could've picked anyone to run their initial experiments on. They chose me because of a fluke of my birthday, a trailer-trash nobody who wouldn't be missed if things went wrong. Someone no one would believe.

Overworked mom. No dad. Disposable. Replaceable. Disappearable.

Leader? I was practically a ghost. I'd never liked being out front. Never wanted the spotlight. Even the *idea* of trying to solve this mess made me shudder. No thanks. Being completely honest, I didn't like most of these people anyway.

We reached level ground. Toby guided me west around the lake, reversing the route Tack and I had taken hours before. We passed the waterfront neighborhoods and fairgrounds, rejoining the highway where it became Main Street as it headed into town. The whole trip, we didn't encounter a soul.

"You're awfully quiet." Toby was pacing along, pulling bark off a stick, a little boy on a nature walk without a care in the world. He had a pistol tucked into his waistband—commandeered from an annoyed Leighton as we left—but he didn't seem worried about any possible attack. "You look kinda pale, too."

"Sorry. Being shot to death makes me terrible company." I didn't want to admit that my head was throbbing, or that I was tiring quickly from the long hike. It felt like I was coming down with something, but could you really get sick inside the Program? There were no animals here, but did pathogens exist? That seemed illogical, but what did I know.

I've got a computer virus. Ha ha.

Still, it was troubling enough that I decided to probe what Toby knew. "I'm actually not feeling very well. I might have a fever. Has anyone else mentioned being sick?"

Toby gave me a strange look, perhaps surprised I'd responded. "Not that I've heard." Then he smirked. "Honestly, I've never felt better. I hardly even have to sleep anymore. This place is great. No one's around to tell us what to do, we can't die, and I get to shoot people." He waved a hand extravagantly as we passed the deserted marina and its cluster of empty restaurants and shops. "If this is a dream, I hope I never wake up."

"You're sick."

"*No*, but you seem to be. I'm in the best shape of my life."

I didn't reply. Didn't want to talk to him ever again. Toby was one of *those* kids, the ones who relished the total freedom. He *preferred* living inside a circuit board.

Like Noah.

My throat clenched. My hands flexed against their bonds, increasing my frustration. Why did I feel the need to rehash this so often? I was sick of agonizing over Noah. Wondering how he could bring himself to do it. Feeling miserable he'd chosen the Program over me. It was worthless. Done was done.

Noah had made his choice. So why was I having such a hard time moving on?

Because you know he didn't mean it.

I stumbled, nearly fell.

"Watch your step," Toby admonished, but I barely heard.

Is that what I believed?

My lips curdled.

Was I really that stupid?

I squeezed my eyelids shut, then snapped them open again. This was *exactly* the kind of distraction I couldn't afford. We reached the first row of businesses and continued on toward town square. I knew where we were going—I'd been held there once before. And this time Noah wasn't hiding in an alley, plotting to break me out.

Stop it. Stop thinking about him.

89

But my mind betrayed me. I remembered Noah vaulting the counter. Slugging Toby across the face. The desperation in his eyes as he looked for me. The softness of his hands as he reached through the jail cell bars.

I felt a tightness in my chest I couldn't dispel. An emptiness in the pit of my stomach.

Suddenly Noah was all I could think about. His scent. The heat from his arms when he held me. The way his lips trembled when he was worried. The way he cupped my face when we kissed.

How scared he'd been that night in the trailer. How safe he'd made me feel.

For a moment, I missed him so badly I couldn't breathe.

Then I cursed myself for being so pathetic. *He. Shot. Me. Threw me away like garbage.*

"Easy, killer." Toby was eyeing me with a bemused expression, mistaking my emotional panic for fear. "Almost home."

I sniffed, rubbed my cheek against my shirt. "Shut up, Toby."

Entering the sheriff's office, Toby marched me around the counter to the cells in the back hallway. Tucker Brincefield and Josh Atkins were on guard duty, a pair of red-faced meatheads who had anchored the football team's offensive line. They'd gone over to Ethan and Sarah early, seduced by cushy spots on Toby's goon squad. Both looked incredibly bored.

"Welcome back to your luxury suite, Melinda." Toby lifted a key ring off its hook and unlocked the left-hand chamber. "You've got some company this time around."

There were two cells divided by a line of unpainted steel bars. Both were stark and dreary, sharing the same naked concrete floor and white cinder-block rear wall. More exposed bars formed the other three sides of a long rectangle, allowing a view inside from all angles.

"Girls in this one." Toby opened the door and bowed, sweeping his hand like a hotel valet. Tucker and Josh watched with satisfied smirks. I had no choice. I stepped inside.

Colleen Plummer rose from a bench and hurried toward Toby, stopping short at his sharp look. She had frizzy black hair and a frowning mouth.

"This is crazy, Toby." Colleen's voice was pleading, her red-rimmed eyes tinged with panic. "Just let me out now, okay?"

Toby shook his head like a disappointed father. "Can't do it, CP. Hiding food is like our number one no-no. You've got two more days to go."

Her simper morphed into a snarl, an index finger jabbing at Toby's face. "My father *owns* the marina, you snotty little shit. Anything left inside it belongs to *me*, not Ethan, or Sarah, or you! Now let me out of here, *right now*, or . . . or I'll—"

"You'll what?" Toby leaned an elbow against the bars, seemed genuinely amused. "Do the crime, do the time. It's not that hard, kids."

Colleen actually stomped a foot, but Toby just giggled. Then he straightened, closed the door in her face, and strolled away down the hall, whistling tunelessly as he spun the key ring on his index finger. Colleen retreated to her seat and sat hard, seizing her hair in her hands as she unleashed a high-pitched screech. But when our eyes met, she sneered at me, before deliberately looking away.

We'd never been friends at school, and that clearly wasn't

going to change. Colleen might be a prisoner, but she still considered herself teen royalty in Fire Lake. She'd rather sulk alone than talk to me.

Sighing, I took a seat on the back bench. Rested my head against the cool concrete wall. I felt drained. Wrung out and overused, like an old dishrag dried to a hard shell.

Three other girls occupied the cell with Colleen and me. Fox-faced Susan Daughtridge hid behind a curtain of glossy black hair. She was popular and a cheerleader, but that clearly hadn't saved her from Ethan's kangaroo court. Cenisa Davis was short and prim, with big blue eyes and light brown skin. Beside her, Maggie Knudson was crying softly into her hands. There were boys in the other cell, but at the moment I was too tired to turn and look.

"Is she okay?" I asked, wriggling out of my winter coat. The bench was chilly and hard. The cell smelled like wet metal and cracked paint, felt antiseptic and grimy at the same time.

Cenisa shrugged. "Neither of us have been murdered before, so who knows."

I tried to be sympathetic. "First reset?"

Cenisa nodded. "Maggie and I were picking berries on Miner's Peak. Then that bastard Ferris showed up and blasted us with a shotgun like we weren't even people." Her bottom lip quivered, but no tears fell. "I knew things were bad, but . . . *damn*."

I sat forward. Miner's Peak bordered the trailer park. "Were you guys with Sam and Carl? What's it like at the quarry? Tack and I tried—"

Cenisa lifted a hand, cutting me off, then rubbed it over her face. It was long moments before she spoke. "It's a mess, Min. This whole world is a mess. And there's no way out of it for anyone." She sighed deeply, then reached over and pulled her weeping friend's head into her lap, closing her eyes as she stroked Maggie's pale red hair.

I opened my mouth to . . . what, I wasn't sure. Protest? Sympathize? Buck her up?

In the end, I stayed silent.

I was trapped in the same cell she was. Who was I to argue?

9

NOAH

It was almost too easy.

"Get ready," I whispered, peering through my binoculars. A misty rain was falling and kept fogging the lenses. Not that I needed them, but appearances still mattered.

Our new best friend was standing in front of the grocery store, on guard duty, looking nervous as hell. Leighton Huddle wasn't used to taking risks. He stood rigidly beside Cash Eaton, his curly blond hair frizzing like a chia pet in the damp afternoon air. Leighton kept shooting glances over to where my team and I were hidden in the woods across the street. But Cash was oblivious, earbuds in as he nodded along to some beat.

Leighton double-crossing Ethan was a surprise, though maybe it shouldn't have been. He'd never been close with those guys, though they'd never had problems that I knew of, either. But Leighton had been elected sophomore class president just before the shit hit the fan—mostly because he'd promised to get more junk food into the cafeteria and nobody else wanted the job. I guess he still thought of himself as someone important.

I said a silent prayer of thanks to those jerks for making Leighton feel small. He'd stewed about it for weeks, then finally come looking for me that afternoon. I'd quickly added him to my plan and sent him back to take his normal shifts. No one appeared to have noticed. And now, it was time.

I'd never trust him, obviously. Once a traitor, always one, in my book. But I'd told Leighton what he'd wanted to hear. Because having him in the fold made things *a lot* easier—now we knew when their guard was weakest, and where people were positioned inside the store. Upon my signal, Leighton would take out Cash, and the others wouldn't even have the benefit of a warning. It was perfect.

Kyle bumped his shoulder against mine, and I shot him a cold look. He shied back, his face reddening. Too familiar. I couldn't let anyone get that close.

I let an awkward moment linger, then whispered, "Everyone in position?"

Kyle nodded eagerly. "Zach and Leah are in the drainage ditch on the far side of the road, next to the store. Jamie and Richie circled around to cover the back door. Morgan is with us, tucked into the bushes with her rifle." He licked his lips, and I could see the anticipation building in his eyes. Kyle lived for this stuff now. "Just say the word, boss."

"Okay. Get Morgan up here."

Kyle scampered back to his partner. I took a deep breath. Unleashed my senses, and drank in the fading light. I could feel tiny droplets of water condensing on my scalp. Could smell wet garbage in the gutter of the grocery store parking lot. I heard Kyle's hands flutter as he motioned Morgan into position. Power flowed through me, infusing my limbs—so emphatic, I bit my tongue. I tasted hot blood in my mouth.

I felt godlike. Like I could take on the whole town by myself. I raised a flashlight, preparing to signal Leighton and begin the carnage. But then I froze as someone appeared from the gloom, strolling down Main Street toward the grocery store.

Toby. He ignored a guilty-looking Leighton and pushed inside.

I hesitated. Toby being there wasn't part of our plan. I didn't like surprises, but maybe this was an opportunity? Toby was no match for me now. Nobody was. And if I got him here, he couldn't pop up later as we pushed deeper into town.

"Nothing changes," I said to Kyle, who grinned. Muscles tensing, I crouched, ready to charge, when the front door flew open and Ethan, Toby, and three others burst outside. Ethan barked something at a red-faced Leighton, then he and the others strode up the block, smiling and laughing.

I blinked. "How many did you count leaving?" I asked Kyle, just to be sure.

"Toby plus four." His voice thrummed with excitement.

I shared his glee, though I didn't let it show. According to Leighton, that meant *no one* should be left inside. I glanced at our turncoat, found him literally staring at my hiding spot. Where Cash couldn't see, Leighton spun his index finger in a clear *come on come on come on* gesture.

Don't look a gift horse in the mouth.

I thought of Min and Tack, but quickly banished the distraction.

"Let's go."

I raised the flashlight and clicked it on and off twice. That caught Cash's eye. Squinting, he pulled his earbuds out and turned to Leighton, only to find Leighton's gun pointed at his face. Cash threw his hands into the air and started babbling. Whatever he said must've convinced Leighton, or perhaps my new best friend lost his nerve, but in any case Leighton didn't shoot Cash like he was supposed to. With a snarl, I fired out of the trees, Kyle trailing, Morgan covering us from the woods like we'd planned.

I darted across the parking lot, approaching the entrance at a fast trot. Zach and Leah scrambled up from the drainage ditch and soon the four of us joined Leighton, surrounding Cash, whose hands were still up.

"Hey, man, take whatever you want!" Cash's wide-eyed stare swiveled from face to face before latching on to me. "Seriously, I don't care. I'm not getting shot over Ethan's fucking Eggos."

"Who's inside?" I demanded.

Cash shrugged helplessly, seemed overwhelmed by our sudden invasion. "I wasn't really paying attention. I hate it here, dude."

"No one." Leighton was breathing hard, cheeks dotted with crimson blooms, but he wore a satisfied smirk. "The others all went to the sheriff's office. Amazing."

I thought for a moment, then started giving orders. This was going better than my wildest dreams, but we could still push our advantage. "Kyle, run tell Morgan to pull the van around back. You drive the SUV. Then you two help Richie and Jamie load the vehicles. The second they're full, have the girls drive them up the mountain. Then you and Richie find another vehicle and keep at it."

As Kyle ran off, I turned to Cash, removing the Beretta from my jacket. "We can't spare manpower to keep you prisoner." I chambered a round, then met his eye, holding the pistol loosely at my side. "Would you like to join my team, Cash, or should I send you along to the reset lottery?"

"Hey, I'm with you!" Cash said quickly, nodding like a bobble-head, a line of perspiration dampening his forehead despite the chill. "Just tell me what to do, Noah. Seriously. Ethan and those pricks mean nothing to me."

I held his gaze a second longer, then nodded. "Go around and help with the loading. Send Richie back in your place." It'd be better to keep Cash on the door with Leighton, like nothing had happened, but two traitors as my lookouts was far too big a risk.

Cash blew out a relieved breath and lowered his hands. He took a step into the parking lot, but I stopped him by the arm as he drew level.

"You wouldn't double-cross me, would you, Cash?"

Cash shook his head like wet dog. "Swear to God, man. I only stayed in town for the food, and you're taking it. Works for me."

"For your sake, I hope that's true."

I released him. Cash wasn't the hero type and would do as told. Dismissing him from my thoughts, I led the others inside.

The place smelled amazing, like Frosted Flakes and chocolate brownie mix and everything else we didn't have. Though all the fresh food was gone, rows and rows of packaged delights spread out before us. I'd never thought about how magical a grocery store truly is.

My team was wide-eyed—we hadn't seen this much to eat in weeks. I was tempted to let them gorge for a bit as a reward, but I remembered the mission. This was only the beginning.

Richie Lopez joined us a second later, a quiet, slender kid with pale yellow eyes. We exchanged nods. "On me," I said to everyone. My team huddled quickly, all but Leighton with their game faces back on.

Leighton. He'd hesitated outside, and that wouldn't do.

"We're not done." I kept my voice cool. "No one knows we're here yet, so Leighton is still technically on guard duty—he'll stand outside like nothing is going on. Richie, you stay right here by the door, ready to back him up if necessary." I held Richie's gaze a beat, and he gave a slight nod. He knew his job was also to watch Leighton, just in case. "Kyle, Zach, and Leah will come with me."

I'd prefer to take Richie over Zach, given their relative intelligence, but Zach was better in a fight and had been hit a few times, so he wasn't afraid of resetting. Akio was light-years better than both, but he wasn't here. I had to make do.

"Where we going now?" Zach asked, racking his gun dramatically and unnecessarily. A round had already been chambered and flew out, unused. Red-faced, he scurried over to pick it up and stuffed it into his pocket.

"The sporting goods store," I said, as patiently as possible.

We'd discussed this at length in the ski village hours ago, but Zach obviously hadn't been paying attention. "Where guns and bullets are. We're going to grab whatever we can, then turn over the kerosene canisters and torch the building."

Kyle elbowed Zach. "Burn baby burn, remember? Then BOOM!"

Zach's face lit up like he'd just remembered something. He and Kyle bashed forearms like a couple of dopes. "Right," Zach crowed. "If we can't have it, *nobody* can!"

"Just stick to your assignments," I scolded. "Leighton said at least one person is always stationed there, but never more than two. It's on the far side of town, so they won't expect any-thing. We'll creep down Main Street and bum-rush the door. Remember—it's more important that we destroy the place than get anything out."

We already had a decent supply of weapons and ammunition stockpiled at the chalet. God bless Idaho's love for the Second Amendment.

"Are you sure this is a good idea?" Richie asked quietly, rubbing his knuckles along the underside of his chin. "Why not stay here and take everything?"

I regarded him silently. Decided it was an innocent question. "Right now, Ethan controls the two biggest arsenals in town—the sporting goods store and the sheriff's office. We'll always be outgunned until something is done."

Richie's lips puckered, but he nodded.

I bristled, had to remind myself to stay focused. Later, however, we'd have a talk.

"You want me to just stand outside like nothing's going on?"

Leighton said, face sour, pale fingers worrying the back of his neck. "What if Ethan and those guys come back?"

"Shoot them. Then run." I beckoned my three-man strike team. "Let's go."

Kyle grinned, pulling a pistol from his waistband, a giant Desert Eagle .50 caliber hand-cannon he'd stolen from somewhere. Zach nearly racked his gun again before remembering he'd already done it twice. Leah's jaw made a hard line, but she cocked the hammer on her Browning semiautomatic and thumbed off the safety, gripping it at her side.

They were ready. This would work. The four of us slipped outside, followed by a reluctant Leighton assuming his lookout position. "Hurry back," he whispered.

I cast my senses in a wide net. Didn't see a soul, but that didn't mean no one was there. The supermarket sat on the eastern edge of town, close to the slopes, but the sporting goods store was on the other side. We had several blocks of enemy territory to cross, including town square.

The hairs on my neck stood, but I shook it off. No one knew we were coming. The sheriff's office might be packed with Ethan and his people right now, but then they couldn't be watching the sporting goods store. We could pull this off.

"Zach, you're with me. Leah and Kyle, trail us by a block. Anyone sees you, shoot your way free, but don't let them know we're ahead. We just need one team to get the job done."

Nods. Leah bounced her shoulders, shaking out nerves. She hadn't spoken since we'd come down the mountain, but I knew she was locked in. I wished for a dozen more like her.

We moved out in pairs, hoods up against the misty drizzle. One block. Two. A third. I held my breath as we reached Town Hall, its white pillars wet and glistening. The Guardian had gone inside there weeks ago and sealed the doors, and hadn't been seen since. As we passed, I spotted a bright red light gleaming from the keycard port. Still no entry.

The sheriff's office was the next building up. I tapped Zach's arm and we crossed the street. The sporting goods store was on the other side anyway. No reason to tempt fate. I resisted the urge to glance back at the team following us, trusting they'd obey my instructions. Zach was glued to my side and seemed relaxed, a secret smile on his lips. I guess he just wanted to burn something.

Still no people. Another block and I spied the store's front door. An electric thrill swept through me. We were going to walk right inside, unchallenged, just like at the grocery store.

My winning streak knew no bounds.

10

MIN

A sharp clang jarred me in my seat.

Incredibly, I'd drifted off for a moment. I looked up with fuzzy eyes to find Ethan Fletcher standing outside the bars.

"Damn! If it isn't Min Wilder. Looks like your luck finally ran out."

Big and blond, with sharp features and cruel blue eyes, Ethan had a face like an eighties movie villain. He was decked head to toe in pricey Arc'teryx gear, like he'd just robbed a ski shop, which he probably had.

My hackles rose. I could barely stand him growing up, and despised him now. Every high school has an aspiring dictator, but Ethan Fletcher was getting the chance to actually live out his dream. It made me sick.

My headache swelled, hammering at my temples. Maybe the feeling of helplessness fed it. Ethan had me trapped in a jail cell, and there was nothing I could do about it.

He put an elbow against the bars. "Did you miss me?"

Insults jockeyed inside my mind, but my tongue couldn't pick one. So I ignored him. More than anything, Ethan hated being ignored.

Turning away, I examined the other cell. Three boys were inside—Akio Nakamura; Greg Kozowitz, the school's tech geek; and skinny Jacob Allred. None of them had gotten along with Ethan in school, so I doubted they'd stuck around after the Town Hall massacre. They must've been "collected" like me. Greg and Jacob were slumped on a bench side by side, staring sullenly at the floor. Akio was watching Ethan.

Ethan cleared his throat. I still didn't react. Normally that would drive him nuts, but today his good mood seemed irrepressible. "I knew you'd come out eventually," he said, bumping a fist against hardened steel. "It was food, wasn't it? Tired of trailer-park fish sticks? Literally *dying* for a Diet Coke?" Ethan giggled at his own wit. Insufferable.

"Why aren't you out shooting people?" I snapped, my ability to ignore his taunts depressingly short-lived. "Afraid of your own dirty work? Or did Sarah not give you permission?"

That wiped the grin off his face.

"Sarah's plan is good, but *I'm* running things."

I nodded, wide-eyed. "I'm sure she prefers that you think so."

Ethan's nostrils flared momentarily, then he waved a dismissive hand. "I put Toby and the twins in charge of the roundup. They answer to *me*, and no one else. Plus, I've got *these*." He dug into a pocket and pulled out a set of keys. "It's kind of a big deal to own a grocery store right now."

Despite myself, I took the bait again. "You don't own anything, Ethan. You only control that store for as long as other people let you." Rubber soles squeaked on concrete—my cell-mates, shifting to listen. Encouraged, I plowed ahead. "I don't think you get it, Ethan. There's no reason for anyone to be scared of you." A bitter laugh escaped my lips. "What are you gonna do, kill us?"

Ethan gripped the bars, eyes going dead in a way that scared me. There was an emptiness to them, as if his humanity had been sloughed to the floor like a discarded cape.

"How about I keep you locked in this cage?" he said softly. "With only enough food not to starve? Or maybe Toby could practice his branding technique." He stared into my eyes, his face devoid of expression. "Not everything unpleasant is fatal, Min. You should remember that."

I found I was holding my breath.

He'd do it. He'd hurt me—or worse, if it suited his purposes.

Then Ethan stepped back and crossed his arms, the superior smirk returning. "Besides, we're not killing our enemies any-more. That obviously doesn't work. But how does prison feel?"

My lips pressed together in a thin line.

"Things are changing," Ethan continued, leaning back against the rough cinder-block wall. "Sarah's new strategy is damn-near perfect. Did you know weapons don't reset? Every-one comes out of the death zones defenseless and stupid, blink-ing like a newborn calf." He winked. "Until my guys grab 'em. It's just a matter of time until we've got everyone, and there's plenty of room in these cells."

I couldn't hold my temper. "Then what? Why even bother, Ethan? What's the point?"

"Dr. Fanelli told me I was supposed to take control," he answered calmly. "The Guardian said the stronger sequences have to dominate the weaker ones. So *I* will, and *we* will."

"But *then* what?" I practically shouted, my hands flying up. Grumbles of agreement wafted from my cellmates. Even Tucker and Josh looked thoughtful.

"We have to complete Phase Two," Ethan insisted doggedly. "The Guardian will tell us what comes next." He was trying to sound confident, but his restless eyes betrayed him.

He doesn't know, either. None of us do.

I rose and walked to the bars. Caught and held Ethan's gaze. "If you really want to be a leader, open these cells. Put the guns away. Invite everyone back into town to decide as a group how we're supposed to live. Stop *forcing* things." I exhaled deeply. "Do those things, and even I'll follow you."

For a few heartbeats, I thought he was actually considering it. Then Ethan snorted, shaking his head with a wry smile. "You'd like that, wouldn't you? Now that we've taken you off the board. No thanks, Melinda. In case you haven't noticed, I'm winning. We'll get everyone eventually."

I wanted to yank out my hair in frustration. Scream at him for being such an idiot. But a voice from the other cell spoke first.

"You won't get Noah."

Heads turned. Akio was sitting back with his legs pulled up beneath him, regarding Ethan with serious eyes. "He's coming for you, Fletcher. You have no idea what he can do."

Icy fingers walked down my spine. What did *that* mean?

"I've got three times as many people," Ethan shot back. He

seemed rankled at having his victory dance over me interrupted. "The only reason Noah isn't sitting next to you is that I haven't gotten around to him yet."

Akio smiled, but it didn't touch his eyes. "You tried him once, though, didn't you? How'd that work out? When Noah torched your friends at the cabin, was that part of Sarah's master plan?" Akio shifted to address the other prisoners. "And we took all their supplies. Our camp had been running low on ammo, but Ethan's team of geniuses hadn't even bothered to unpack their van before we moved in. Now we have enough to last through winter."

A pink flush began creeping up Ethan's neck. "I got *you*, didn't I, Akio? You're in a metal box just like Min. So maybe don't worry about how long it takes me to gather those other losers. You'll be here, waiting. You'll get to see it all."

Akio's face was etched in stone. "Noah's gonna carve up your whole world, Ethan. You don't understand." He rose and walked to the bars, dropping his voice to a stage whisper that everyone could hear. "I know you're scared. You should be." Akio made a gun with his fingers and pointed them at Ethan's head, then mimed the hammer dropping. "Noah already got you once. In front of everybody. Remember?"

The sickly flush leaked onto Ethan's cheeks. He strode to the barrier and stuck his nose an inch from Akio's. "You're lucky these bars are here."

Akio blinked. Then spat full in Ethan's face.

Ethan's hands rammed through the bars, grasping, but Akio darted back out of reach. He smiled darkly and gave Ethan the finger.

Ethan pulled back. Went still. Then he slid a pistol from his jacket and racked the slide.

Akio licked his lips. "You don't have the balls."

Ethan lifted the weapon. Took careful aim. "Good night, asshole."

"Stop, you idiot!"

Tucker and Josh flattened themselves against the concrete wall as Sarah Harden stormed past them. Thin and beautiful, with strawberry-blond hair and sparkling white teeth, she arrowed straight for Ethan, glaring like an angry nanny. "What are you doing?"

Ethan's cheek twitched. He was still aiming the gun. "I'm teaching Akio a lesson."

Sarah pinched the bridge of her nose. She took a deep breath, then continued in a forced-patient voice. "And then what happens?"

Ethan faltered. The pink stain on his cheeks deepened to scarlet.

Sarah spoke in that voice of hers that makes everyone feel small. "Shoot Akio and he goes from being *inside* the cell to *not* being inside it. He also knows our plan to grab people at the reset points. He could slip away and tell everyone, which would eliminate the element of surprise that's worked so well for us."

Ethan's face now blazed like a torch. Jaw tight, he didn't speak.

"So . . . is murdering Akio a good idea?"

Ethan lowered his weapon, then muttered at the floor. "I wasn't really going to do it."

Yes you were. I glanced at Akio, saw naked frustration flit across his features.

Sarah turned to the two linemen, who were eyeing her warily. "Does everyone understand that killing a prisoner is the same as *releasing* a prisoner?"

Tucker and Josh nodded in tandem, eager to please. Ethan was pretending to ignore the whole scene, and Sarah didn't push any further. The point was made. Then her piercing blue eyes found me.

I held Sarah's gaze—determined not to back down first—even as the weight of her attention unnerved me.

"Hello, Min. Sorry about this."

"Then let me out."

"No."

The clink of glass carried down the hallway. Devin Carver entered the now-somewhat-crowded corridor, balancing a tray in his beanpole arms. I was surprised to see him. Timid by nature, he'd never been popular with Ethan's crew. Too bookish. Too into *ALF* reruns and Lego *Star Wars* figures. Devin had likely stayed in town assuming it was the safest move. So Ethan had him serving meals, of course.

Shoulders hunched, Devin made himself small, shying from the larger boys as he spoke in a soft mumble. "Lunch. I didn't know so many people would be here. The lobby is full. I'll go back upstairs and make more."

Tucker and Josh snagged Hot Pockets off the tray, causing the smaller boy to flinch. Tucker frowned at the two bottled waters Devin provided. "Bring beers next time," he warned, smacking the back of Devin's head. "Guard duty sucks enough as it is."

Devin shrank back, eyes glued to the floor. My heart went out to him.

"Not a chance." Sarah didn't bother looking at Tucker. "No drinking in here. *Honestly.* Sometimes I feel like you guys are trolling me."

Tucker pouted but didn't protest. The more I observed, the more convinced I became that Sarah was really running things.

Devin gathered himself and brought the tray over to Ethan. Ethan's head jerked up, as if just noticing his presence. Devin cringed in alarm, one hand rising as if to ward off a blow. The tray wobbled and Devin scrambled to steady it, but his heels caught together and he lost his balance, stumbling sideways into the bars.

A Hot Pocket flopped to the floor.

Ethan looked down.

Devin's face blanched. "Sorry, man. I'll eat that one."

Ethan stared at the Hot Pocket on the concrete. Then he raised his gun and shot Devin in the stomach.

The report echoed like a thunderclap in the enclosed space. Everyone ducked, hands flying to their ears. My eardrums throbbed with pain. For several seconds, I couldn't hear a thing. The muzzle flash had seared a jagged, blurry line across my retinas, making everything hazy and dreamlike. The smell of gunpowder filled the room.

Regaining my senses, I saw Devin lying on his back, gasping, the tray's contents scattered and broken on the floor around him.

"What the hell?!" Sarah shouted, still shielding her ears. "Damn it, Ethan!"

The other prisoners fled to the rear wall, shouting, all but Akio looking terrified.

"Oh shut up," Ethan growled.

Silence fell like a scythe. No one said another word.

I stood rooted in place by the bars, too stunned to move.

"You wasted food." Ethan leaned over Devin and spoke matter-of-factly. "I told you what would happen if you kept screwing up. How many times is that? Three? Four? Now get back here right away and clean this mess up."

Devin nodded through clenched teeth, face drenched in sweat. Blood bubbled on his lips as he panted like a dog. He was in agony, but choking back his wails. Ethan sighed dramatically, then knelt and put his gun to Devin's heart.

"Ethan, no!" My hand shot forward between the bars.

Ethan fired again, eliciting another round of screams. Devin stopped moving. My eyes jerked away.

"You incredible asshole," I hissed. Then I dropped to my knees and reached for Devin's hand. It was slick with blood, but I gripped it anyway, hoping he might feel some tiny comfort before slipping away.

Sarah slapped her hands down to her sides. "Complete waste of time!"

The linemen actually started laughing. Tucker elbowed Josh, spoke in a whisper that carried right to me. "Last week, Toby got bored and shot Devin with a sniper rifle from the bell tower. It was *hilarious*."

Josh chuckled, didn't even bother lowering his voice. "Charlie pushed him off a roof two days ago. I swear that dork's died more times than anyone."

Sarah began laying into Ethan about gunshots in enclosed spaces. Tucker scooped the fallen Hot Pocket off the floor and split it in half, handing one side to his partner. Cenisa and Maggie were crying softly in each other's arms. Susan and Colleen appeared to be in shock. In the other cell, Jacob had been sick on his shoes, while Greg had his head buried in his hands. Akio was watching Ethan like you would a wild animal loose in the building.

Devin's hand had grown cold, and I released it, standing and squeezing the bars in my fists. Anger and sadness and fear bubbled up inside me. This could not stand. I couldn't allow these monsters to dictate our future.

We can't live like this. It has to stop.

But I was helpless. Trapped inside a jail cell with no way to escape. I'd well and truly lost this time. It took everything I had not to break down and cry. Then I noticed Colleen. She'd risen to her feet and was slowly approaching the bars, eyes glued to the hallway floor. "Guys?"

No one responded. Colleen cleared her throat.

"Guys?"

Ethan and Sarah glanced over in annoyance. Swallowing a lump in her throat, Colleen extended a finger.

I looked to where she was pointing.

Felt goose bumps erupt all over me.

Devin's body.

It was still there.

11

NOAH

The store's windows were dark and glaring, its brick exterior soaked to the color of dried blood.

Was it empty, too? Could I be *that* lucky?

I glanced at Zach, unable to keep a grin from splitting my face, but as I turned, something glinted on the rooftop. I squinted up in the dying light, then my eyes widened as I spotted a gun barrel, followed by a gleaming scope and a shock of red hair.

"Down!"

I tried to drag Zach with me, but a line of bullets ripped into his jacket, scarlet-tinged feathers ejecting skyward as he collapsed like a balloon with the air let out. I rolled to my left on the sidewalk and wriggled under a bench. Wood chips exploded all around me.

Shouts behind us. Kyle and Leah were cowering behind a mailbox as someone on the roof of the bank across the street opened up with automatic fire. Whoever was up there had let me and Zach stroll by unchallenged.

Ambush. I walked right into it. Not so slack about defense after all.

Kyle rose to his knees and tried to throw something, but before he could release it, his head jerked sideways. He keeled over, a green oval spilling from his hand.

Oh no.

He brought them.

Leah scrambled back from Kyle, diving into a storefront alcove. I flattened myself to the ground and covered my ears with my forearms. Seconds ticked by and I grimaced, eyes squeezed shut as I waited for the explosion. But nothing happened. Unsure, I peeked from cover, watched as Kyle's body stopped moving and disappeared.

Never pulled the pin?

I cursed him even as I scrambled forward to drag Zach behind the bench.

Weeks ago, Kyle had shown me a box of vintage, Vietnam-era hand grenades he'd found in a locked chest in his father's garage. Unsure if they were even live, I'd stashed the relics in our armory and forgotten about them. Obviously, Kyle hadn't. I thought back to him elbowing Zach at the grocery store and ground my teeth. Kyle must've thought to use one on the raid, but never got the chance. Or maybe he'd pulled the pin after all, but the grenade was a dud.

More bullets danced around the bench. One struck Zach in the leg. With a snarl of rage, I rose to a knee and scanned the rooftop for a target. Someone was standing near the edge. Red hair. That's who got Zach.

I drew a bead, pulled the trigger four times. Was gratified to see Mike Nolan's mouth form a surprised O, his hands converging on his chest. Then he toppled forward and fell to the sidewalk with a sickening crunch, vanishing seconds later, but not before leaving a wide smear on the icy concrete.

My head snapped around. Leah was racing back down Main Street in full retreat. Fine. Good. Maybe she'd draw the other sniper away with her. Then I heard a crash from within the sporting goods store.

Shit. If more people were in there, Zach and I were in deep trouble.

I grabbed him by the front of his jacket. "Hey! Can you hear me? How bad is it?"

His neck flopped, and I spotted a neat red hole in the center of his temple. Dread coursed through me. Zach was gone, but he also wasn't. I wanted to thrust his body away, but my fingers refused to let go of his jacket. With a spasm of anger, I shook him instead.

"Damn it, Zach! *How many lives was that?*"

Zach slumped bonelessly to the snow, his mouth lolling open. He wasn't going to reset. This assault had been a disaster, and now I'd lost a man for good.

I started sweating like a convict, knuckles white against Zach's jacket. What would the others say? They didn't even know this was possible. Richie had questioned my plan back at the store, and now it had failed spectacularly. Zach was dead. Everyone would know I'd made a disastrous mistake.

I had to hide his body.

That's insane! This isn't you!

I scrambled to my feet, lifting Zach's body and slinging it over one shoulder. The ease with which I could carry him calmed me, quieting my doubts. No need to panic. I could handle this. With what I was becoming, I could handle anything.

I darted across the street and begin hoofing it down the block.

No one fired. Maybe the other shooter had gone after Leah. I prayed that was true.

I'd dump Zach in the lake. No one would know.

But as I drew level with the sheriff's office, Toby stepped out the door. For a hot second, we just stared at each other, Toby's eyes widening at the limp form draped over my shoulder. Then I had my Berretta out before he could draw and lit up the doorway. Toby dove back inside. Zach's body fell to the ground.

I was breathing heavily, fingers burning from the cold. I reached down for Zach and felt a bulge in his jacket. That elbow from Kyle. I dug into Zach's pocket and found another hand grenade.

"Morons!" I hissed. He and Kyle had clearly planned this without me. The notion chilled my blood. Did Leah know? The others? How many little plots was I in the dark about?

Later. I had to ditch Zach's body before anyone saw it.

Listen to yourself!

I was stuffing the grenade into my jacket when the door to the sheriff's office rattled. My rage exploded all at once. *Suck on this, Toby.*

I pulled the pin and lobbed the grenade, then seized Zach by the shoulders and dragged him away as fast as I could. The grenade bounced, rolled to a stop by the door, then exploded, ripping the facade of the sheriff's office to shreds and knocking me on my butt. If Toby hadn't moved, he was toast.

Pinpricks of energy raced along my limbs. My emotions felt wild and raw, thundered unchecked. The weather picked up as if in response, the rain transforming into tiny needles of dagger ice that stung my nose and cheeks. Cackling like a maniac, I lifted Zach again and hurried down the block, but then a line of sparks cut across my path. Lips forming a snarl, I ducked behind a column at Town Hall.

I peered back toward the sheriff's office. Chris Nolan, Cole, and two others were slinking up the block. Looking to my right, I spotted Derrick and Spence closing in. I'd never get away while carrying Zach's body. More bullets tattooed the sidewalk, forcing me up the steps toward Town Hall's front door. If I didn't move soon, I'd be trapped.

I shot a desperate glance behind me. Nearly dropped my awful cargo.

The keycard port was blinking green.

"What the—"

I dragged Zach to the entrance and tested the handle. The door swung open easily. My eyes nearly popped from my head.

Pounding feet. Shouts.

I pulled Zach inside and slammed the door.

12

MIN

For several heartbeats, no one spoke.

Devin was sprawled on his back, a black, bloody stain running from the holes in his sweatshirt to the concrete floor beneath him. His chest was still, his eyes fixed and glassy. No spark of life lingered within them.

My lips and chin trembled as I covered my mouth. The sound of my heartbeat thrashed in my ears. Foggy lights bolted to the ceiling bathed the scene in a harsh hospital glow, leering down with fluorescent judgment at the unmoving form in a widening circle of glossy, wet scarlet.

Ethan stepped closer and nudged Devin with his foot.

"What the hell?" Tucker whispered. "Is he still alive?"

Ethan knelt and checked Devin's pulse, being careful to avoid the pooling blood. A pointless maneuver—Devin was quite clearly dead. But his body was still lying there.

Sarah licked her lips, scraping a hand through her hair. No

one else moved. I waited, staring, *willing* the body to shimmer and disappear like everyone else who'd died since entering the Program. More seconds passed, and it became clear that Devin had no intention of doing so.

"Oh my God." Colleen backed away from the bars and began rubbing her hands on her jeans. "Is he dead? Like, *for real* dead?"

No one answered, but the question hung in the air like a guillotine.

My mind raced, one step ahead of melting. Devin was breaking the rules. When you were killed in the Program, you reset. The process of dying was painful and awful and felt completely real, but it wasn't. Your body vanished, and you came back to life unharmed in one of the four reset zones outside of town.

So why is he still here?

The implications were staggering.

My knees nearly gave out. I felt the walls closing in around me as facts slotted together in my mind. Devin had been picked on. Brutalized. Tucker and Josh had just been joking about how many times he'd been killed for other people's amusement. Devin might've racked up more deaths than anyone in our class.

But how many? Oh God. How many times had Devin died?

My gaze shot to Sarah, who glanced at me, the same realization dawning in her eyes. She stepped over Devin's body and grabbed Tucker by the shirt, spoke in a low, urgent voice. "You said Toby shot Devin, and somebody else pushed him off a roof, right?"

Tucker nodded nervously. Sarah spun to face Ethan. "You've obviously shot him before. How many times?"

Ethan was still staring at Devin's body in befuddlement. I

noticed he was sweating profusely. Ethan cleared his throat. "I don't know. Two, maybe three times."

Sarah stepped over Devin again, ignoring the puddle of blood. She grabbed Ethan's arm. "Two *or* three times, Ethan? Which is it?"

Ethan rubbed his mouth, still unable to look away. "Three. I mean, this was the third, I think. Or maybe fourth. I . . . I just got mad he dropped our food. The walk back would . . . It'd show him . . ."

He trailed off. Devin was dead on the floor. He wouldn't be walking anywhere.

Sarah ran both hands down her face. Her eyes flicked back to me. "There's a limit," she said softly, as if we were having a private conversation. I nodded, in that moment not caring about the bars separating us.

"What do you mean?" Ethan demanded. "What limit?"

Sarah seemed to remember herself. She straightened. Turned to Ethan.

"We should talk privately. Now."

But Ethan was too wired. "Why's he not resetting, Sarah?" He jabbed a finger at Devin's body, then shuddered as if snow-melt had slid under his collar. "What the hell is going on?"

My cellmates were backed against the rear wall, putting as much distance between themselves and the murder scene as possible. Colleen had both hands pressed to her cheeks. The other girls seemed on the verge of panic. Jacob and Greg looked like they'd seen a ghost, which was an odd way to look at it, since the opposite had happened. Akio had moved to the far corner and sat, watching everyone, his knees pulled up into a ball.

Tucker and Josh still seemed lost, but everyone else seemed to get it.

Devin wasn't going to reset.

He was dead inside the Program.

Ethan reached down and grabbed Devin by the shirt, pulling him halfway to a seated position. "Stop messing around and get up! Now!" The pale body sagged in his grip.

"Stop it!" Colleen screeched.

Ethan dropped Devin and removed his gun. Aimed it straight at her. "You telling me what to do?" he asked in a high-pitched voice, pupils dilated.

Colleen froze in animalistic terror. "No. Please. I'm sorry."

Ethan stared at Colleen, panting, the gun quivering in space. Not even Sarah spoke. Then he noticed blood on his fingers. Ethan dropped his pistol and began spastically wiping his hands on his jacket. Red streaks smeared across the waterproof black fabric. With an inarticulate howl Ethan turned and punched the wall.

The building groaned. Spiderweb cracks spiraled from where Ethan's fist was buried to the knuckles in a cinder block. He ripped his hand backward with a yelp, eyes wide, staring at his fingers as he flexed them for damage.

My heart froze, then started thumping. That swing should've broken every bone in Ethan's hand.

A strange look stole over his face. He closed his eyes. Then Ethan sighed, rolling his head on his shoulders. "I feel . . . I feel *amazing* right now."

In the corner of my eye, I noticed Akio squirm in the other cell. He was staring at Ethan with a hunted expression.

He's scared. Really scared, for the first time.

But why? What did Akio suspect? I recalled his earlier taunts about Noah. His claim that Ethan "didn't understand." Had Noah's group discovered something about the Program that the rest of us didn't know? Did Akio know why Devin didn't reset?

"Ethan?" Sarah said, eyeing her companion warily. "Tell me what's happening."

He shook his head, blinking stupidly. "It's . . . this incredible rush . . . I'm not sure . . ."

Before he could say more, a boom carried down the hallway. The whole building rattled, a cloud of dust dropping from the ceiling. The lights flickered.

"Earthquake!" Tucker yelled, but I knew that wasn't it. Seconds later Toby appeared at a dead sprint, scraped up and bleeding, covered in what looked like ashes. "Trouble outside!" he shouted, skidding to a stop just before tripping over Devin's body.

Ethan's gaze snapped to his lieutenant. "What is it?" A spasm of gunfire echoed down the corridor, followed by the crash of breaking glass.

"It's Noah!" Toby answered, though his eyes were glued to the motionless form on the concrete. "His team is attacking Main Street and they've got *explosives!*"

Ethan growled deep in his throat. He scooped his pistol off the floor and started down the hall, but Sarah froze him with an upraised hand. "Stop."

Ethan glared a hole through her head, but did as instructed.

She didn't seem to notice. Eyes narrowed, Sarah was chewing her bottom lip, seemingly staring at nothing. But that was only if you didn't know her.

"Why is Devin on the floor?" Toby asked. "He knocked out?"

"He's dead," Sarah stated absently.

"Dead?" Toby kicked the body, gaping in surprise. "What do you mean, dead?"

"Dead. He isn't coming back."

The truth finally seemed to register. Toby staggered back against the bars, a hand rubbing his bald head in astonishment. "Oh, shit!"

"Exactly." Sarah's cool was returning, though a tremor thinned her voice. She finally turned to Ethan. "We have to reconsider our plans. This changes everything."

Toby was staring at Devin in disbelief. A trickle of blood ran from a cut above his ear.

His back was to my cell.

A small, snub-nosed revolver was tucked into the rear waistband of his jeans.

I thought about Akio's attempted trick with Ethan. It wouldn't work with Sarah around, but that didn't mean I was helpless.

More gunfire carried from outside. Closer this time, riding a wave of raised voices.

Toby stepped back. His shoulder blades kissed the steel between us.

Cat quick, I reached between the bars and snatched the gun from his jeans. Toby spun, grabbing for my arm, but I'd already leapt out of reach. Then I aimed the revolver squarely at his round head.

Toby huffed an exasperated breath, rolling his eyes. "What are you doing, Min? You gonna shoot me? Go ahead. You'll still be in there, and I'll be back in an hour."

I nodded at Devin's body. "You sure about that? Now open these doors and let us out."

Toby's smirk faded, but Sarah spoke quickly to reassure him. "Devin's been killed more times than anyone. This must . . . must be the . . . end result. But Devin not resetting doesn't mean the rest of us suddenly won't. There's no reason to believe that."

Toby nodded thoughtfully, then stepped back and crossed his arms. "Nobody's letting you out, Min. You *know* it, too, so stop playing around and give me back my gun. You won't get a damn thing to eat until you do."

Okay. Fine.

Plan B.

I turned the gun on myself. Placed its barrel against my temple.

Sudden understanding flashed in Toby's eyes. "No! Stop!"

Sarah surged forward, a hand outstretched. "Wait! You don't want to do that."

I hesitated, the revolver's round muzzle denting a circle in my bare skin. I couldn't stop thinking about what a bullet would do as it tore through my skull. My arm began to shake.

Glass shattered out in the office lobby. Someone screamed as the buzz of automatic gunfire echoed down the corridor.

"That's *it*," Ethan hissed. "I'm *done* standing around." He shouldered past Sarah, signaling for Josh and Tucker to follow.

Toby glanced at the trio disappearing down the hallway, then at the gun in my hand, his face scrunched in frustration. "Whatever," he grumbled. "I've got plenty of guns." He turned to Sarah. "You deal with this bitch." Muttering darkly about trailer-park trash, Toby hurried after the others.

Sarah ignored him, her whole focus on me.

"You could die," she said calmly, looking me directly in the eye. "I could be wrong about why Devin didn't come back. What if you end up on the floor next to him? We can't take that risk."

My heart was pounding. Black spots danced at the edge of my vision.

"We?" I rasped, throat as dry as sandpaper. I was oddly touched by her concern.

"I'm not a monster, Min." Sarah smiled weakly, eyebrows drawn in. She gave a light shrug. "We might have our differences, but we're all in this together."

We're all in this together.

My mind flashed back to seventh grade. The prank.

The popular girls had planned to sprint out from the locker room in their bras and water-balloon the boys at football tryouts. Impossibly, Sarah approached me about it, and somehow talked me into joining the madness. *It'll be fun,* she said, tugging my arm. Pulling me along until I agreed to go with her. *But I need* all *the girls. We're all in this together.*

I'd stupidly taken a place in front. Ran out screaming, balloon held high, only to hear the door click shut behind me with no one following. The football team had collapsed in hysterics as I'd scrambled around the building, trying to get back inside.

I remembered Sarah's wicked laughter through the door.

We're all in this together.

A whole hour of scheming, just to humiliate me. She never apologized. I doubt it even occurred to her.

"Wow." I snorted derisively, wiping the sympathetic mask from her face. I'd been her fool once, but never again. "You *really* don't want me to escape, do you, Sarah? Since I'll tell everyone what happened to Devin, and ruin your kidnapping plan, too."

Sarah's eyes went cold. "You can't beat me. You know that, right?"

I glared right back at her, anger outstripping my fear. "I'll take my chances."

The gun steadied in my hand.

Had Sarah been right the first time? Was Devin an anomaly, or was I about to join him?

Only one way to find out.

Sarah grabbed the bars, her nostrils flaring. "Min, I'm warni—"

I closed my eyes and pulled the trigger.

PART TWO

AGGREGATION

13

NOAH

Darkness filled the office of Principal Andrew T. Myers.

I slumped back in his creaky rolling chair, rubbed my face with my palms. Outside, the halls of Fire Lake High School were deathly silent, empty except for the ghosts of all those kids who hadn't been chosen for the Program. I closed my eyes and tried not to see their faces.

I wasn't sure what I was doing there. School had never been my happy place, but I'd needed a quiet corner in which to be alone. Space to relax for a moment and think, where the others wouldn't see me worry.

After I'd left the Guardian, gun battles had erupted all evening as my team clashed with Ethan's thugs in the streets. Chaotic, disjointed death matches that piled up resets on both sides. The fighting had finally broken off after full dark, and I'd taken the opportunity to slip away.

I'd had no time to consider what the Guardian said to me.

He was there. I spoke to him. I still can't believe it.

I closed my eyes. Tried to remember the last time I'd slept. Two days? Three? I'd lost track.

Was I finally tired? I didn't feel it, despite racing all over town—barking orders, checking our positions, even hiking back up the mountain once to make sure the vans had arrived safely and were being unloaded.

The others couldn't keep up, though they refused to admit it, or look me in the eye when I lifted something too heavy for one person alone. They were still afraid of me. And best of all, word about Zach hadn't spread.

They asked where he was, though, didn't they?

I flinched, then scolded myself for jumping at shadows. The situation was under control. Leah had escaped the ambush on Main Street and rejoined our team at the supermarket. Kyle had reset like usual, fortunately right above town, stumbling back into the store a half hour later. I showed up moments after Kyle, avoiding questions about where I'd been. Where Zach was. Just in time to mow down Ethan, Toby, the twins, and three others when they came charging through the parking lot. We repulsed them easily, sending them wailing back to the reset points.

Then, after sunset, everything had gone quiet. Both sides needed to recover people spread out all over the valley.

No one mentioned my failure at the sporting goods store. No one had seen me drag Zach's body into Town Hall, or leave without it. No one sensed how shook I was the rest of the afternoon, locked up with my head spinning during Ethan's attack.

I'd masked it. And once we'd shot them all to hell, I'd grabbed Kyle by the throat and demanded to know about the grenades. Legs trembling, he'd confessed to a plan he and Zach had cooked up to blast more targets. They'd thought I'd be impressed. Kyle swore that no one else had known, said I could ask Zach when he reappeared.

I'd stared at Kyle without speaking until he could barely breathe, watched him wilt like a flower. *He should worry.* But I was worried, too. On my whole team, only Kyle and Akio knew about Piper not resetting. Now one had ghosted and the other was scheming behind my back.

Kyle apparently had secrets. Had he told Zach the biggest one? If so, it wouldn't travel any further that way, but what about the others?

Enough. I rocked back in Myers's crappy chair, tried to clear these nagging worries from my head. I'd settle with Kyle later. At the moment I had more pressing concerns, like how to play the next few hours.

We held the grocery store and the eastern end of town. For some reason Ethan and his cronies seemed reluctant to attack again. The question was for how long.

No one knew about Zach. I'd shot Mike Nolan off the roof, and I don't think anyone else had seen how bad Zach was hit. His body was stashed in the one place where no one could find it. My team wouldn't learn he was gone for good unless I told them so.

Is that all that matters to you? Zach is DEAD.

"Yes," I hissed, angered by the thought. I kicked the desk for good measure.

It *was* all that mattered. I'd been told so directly by the only person who knew.

The Guardian had been waiting inside Town Hall. I shifted uncomfortably in my seat, the memory sending shivers down my spine. What I'd learned changed the game. I had an advantage over everyone now, if I played my cards right.

I replayed the scene in my mind. Gruesome red streaks on the marble floor as I dragged Zach into the domed foyer. The keycard port blinking from green to red as the door silently closed on its own, sealing the building once again.

I'd barely been able to think, panting like a hunted animal as I towed the dead body of—what . . . a friend?—deeper inside. Zach's head had lolled against my arm and I'd dropped him, skittering back with a childish moan. Bile rose in my throat and I nearly puked on the floor tiles.

It was just like with Piper. Zach was definitely dead, and just as definitely not resetting. Sweat erupted from all my pores. I feared another panic attack. Then a wooden door to my left creaked open, revealing a large office beyond.

Soft orange lamplight spilled from within. I was drawn like a moth. Stepped inside.

He was there.

The black-suited nightmare of my childhood—a man who'd brutally murdered me *five times* in the real world—was sitting behind a wide mahogany desk, calmly smoking a cigarette. He regarded me for a moment, then pointed to an overstuffed leather chair. Like a robot, I sat. Or maybe he'd done something to dull my senses. This was *his* world, after all.

My heart thudded in my chest just thinking about it. I'd gone numb upon seeing the bastard. He'd always had that effect on me, both as my executioner and in this new iteration as the

Guardian. His mere presence invoked a terror inside me. Made me feel like prey.

I rose in the dark, shying from the memory, but his words were seared into my brain. We'd spoken for less than a minute. Barely a conversation. Yet in a few clipped sentences, the Guardian had confirmed everything.

Fact: kills increase your power.

Corollary: deaths sap your strength.

Bottom line: eliminations occur when the balance tilts too steeply.

That was the secret. *That* was the point. I was right and Min was wrong.

He'd shown no warmth or humanity. Didn't explain why I'd been allowed inside. He didn't even tell me what the limits were. He'd simply said he was counting on me, then told me to leave. I'd risen and hurried out like a frightened child.

I couldn't handle being close to the Guardian, even if he was only an avatar. That face had been the last thing I saw too many times. More, though, I'd been strangely . . . proud of myself. Like a dog who'd done a trick properly for its master. I'd left feeling renewed. Filled with fresh purpose.

You left Zach on the floor like garbage. Is that why you need to be alone?

I rubbed my temples, as if to physically wrest the doubts from my head. Myers's office was windowless. The door was closed, and no lights burned in the outer suite. There was no one to witness my moment of weakness. No one saw the tears on my cheeks.

The Guardian had said he'd take care of Zach.

I blew out a sigh. Took a moment to recover. Idly, I sparked a cigarette lighter I'd found in the desk drawer. Who knew Peg-Leg Myers smoked? I hadn't thought of him in weeks—big and brooding, with a laser stare over the rim of his bifocals that could freeze a truant in place. He'd patrolled these hallways like an angry father on prom night, one knee unbending as he stalked our every move. I'd thought he was a monster, but he'd been a saint instead. I said a silent prayer for his soul.

And wondered. If Myers had known the truth about the Program, would he still have agreed? Is this the existence he wanted for us? Running a hand over my face, I dismissed the question. Too late now.

I circled the desk to stand before the door. I'd needed a moment to gather myself, but that was over now. The Guardian had given me answers. To ignore his instructions—to go against his wishes—was insanity. I was a part of the Program, not separate from it. It was time to get back to the task at hand.

I ignited the lighter one last time. In a total blackout, I was as blind as you'd expect. But add just a *sliver* of light—the tiniest flicker—and I could make out almost anything. My night vision had become scary good. And now I knew why.

Had Ethan figured it out yet? I hoped not, but Sarah would catch anything he missed. It boiled down to whether they had a body on their hands that hadn't winked out of existence, its owner waltzing down the mountain an hour later, with an aw shucks, you guys, I'm fine, here I am.

Footsteps echoed somewhere outside the suite. Not close, but I heard. Kyle was overdue with a report, but these treads were heavier.

My mask fell back into place. I silently opened the office door. Strolled through the lesser darkness of the hallway to the suite's main lobby. At the counter, I paused to listen. Clomping feet. Lazy gait. Enough noise to shame an elephant.

I had my gun, but ignored it. No single person was a threat to me. Not anymore.

Still cloaked in darkness, I slipped to a corner beside the door. A skinny boy pushed into the room, squinting like a mole. "Hello?" he whispered, taking a hesitant step inside.

"Cash."

Cash Eaton jumped, startled to find me right beside him. I flipped a light switch, watched him edge back a few paces, unable to meet my eye.

"Yes?" I said softly.

Cash swallowed. "Kyle is back from scouting. Says he got three kills."

Three? He would need watching.

"Akio?"

Cash shook his head, worrying a freckled cheek as he cleared his throat. He'd switched to our side during the grocery store raid and didn't seem comfortable yet, maybe because his choice had been made at gunpoint. I was surprised he'd been entrusted with a message so soon, and planned to have a word with someone about it. Discipline was getting lax.

"Kyle thinks they have Akio in lockup," Cash said, fidgeting like a convict in a lineup. "He said Ethan just moved his whole headquarters over to Emerald Tower, and that he also saw some guys on the library steps. Said he caught Tucker and one of the Nolan twins napping."

"Why didn't Kyle report here himself?"

Cash shrugged like he might be the one in trouble. "He's at the supermarket. I think he's just hungry, to be honest. He and Richie were out for hours." Cash's eyes found his shoes. "The rest of us still need downtime now and then. Almost everyone took a reset today but you."

I nodded, kicking myself. I'd given too much away. I didn't want people sensing my advantages, or wondering how I got them. Kyle knew too much already.

My last meal had been yesterday. Food was another thing that applied less and less.

Our initial raid had been an unqualified success. We'd captured the grocery store, which must be driving Ethan insane. My team had literally walked right in behind him. Only my assault on the sporting goods store had failed. But after wiping out Ethan's counterattack, we'd pushed deeper into town, taking the whole eastern quarter.

Ethan now seemed reluctant to commit more lives. That surprised me. I'd expected him to hit back repeatedly, wasting his strength and building ours. I'd counted on it, actually. The sudden caution made me wary. Ethan should've spent dozens of resets trying to retake his father's store. It was a serious matter of pride. Plus, we'd taken all the food.

The explanation seemed inescapable: they'd learned the real stakes.

Did Ethan know he'd make our group stronger with each person we gunned down? The grocery store had only two doors and was easy to defend. It must be *killing* him that we'd stolen something he considered his, but he'd stopped fighting, leaving the place in our hands.

Which meant *I* had to adapt, too. After some intense grilling of Kyle, I'd devised a whole new plan. When they finally came again in force, they were in for a nasty surprise.

I knew we couldn't hold the store indefinitely. Not without a dozen more people. Cash and Leighton joining us gave me eight foot soldiers total. Not enough. I risked getting most of my people trapped in a siege, on low ground, while simultaneously exposing the chalet to attack. It wouldn't do.

I felt a quiver of unease in my gut. If Ethan were smart, he'd hit us *now*, while we were overextended. But most bullies are cowards, and he was no exception. Sarah was smart and fearless—bloodless, if you asked me—but also the cautious type. She might see the opportunity, but perhaps wouldn't risk it.

Don't underestimate her. Everyone who does gets buried.

Sarah and I had dated for a few months during freshman year, a terrible match from the start. She'd had trouble seeing it for a while—I'd spent my last weeks alive avoiding her attentions while trying not to look like it—but Project Nemesis had clarified things. She'd called me a fool. Said I was weak. A child. All true at the time, but that didn't make the insults burn any less. Did she know that right now I'd gun her down as soon as look at her?

Cash coughed. Scuffed a shoe on the linoleum. How long had I been lost in thought?

"I'm pulling everyone back to the store." I walked past him out into the hall, knowing he'd scurry after me. Town had no strategic value, I decided, now that we'd stolen so much. But I could send one hell of a message. I didn't need territory. Not the way *I* wanted to play it.

Bait the trap.

Hit them in the mouth, then ghost.

Wait for mistakes.

Pick off their leaders one at a time.

Don't give up any cheap kills.

Make the bastards bleed until they stop coming back.

Min would be ashamed.

I paused at the doors leading outside. "She's wrong," I mumbled, then cursed myself for speaking. Cash glanced at me and I turned away. I had to stop thinking about her. Maybe one day I actually would.

Flickering images in my head. The silver melted around Piper's finger. Scarlet blood pooling on a white marble floor.

I shuddered. Blinked hard to clear my head.

God, what was happening to me? Weak thoughts were popping up too often.

Doubt was poison here. Worrying about the old morality, when I was nothing more than ones and zeroes? Nonsense.

The Program had been crafted by greater minds than mine or Min's. Black Suit had known what would happen *years* in advance. He must've had a reason behind every decision, including the harsh ones. Logic too complicated for teenagers.

Questioning those choices? Lunacy. Worse, it was incredibly ungrateful. We were alive only because of what the Project had built for us down in the silo.

The silo. Another loose end. I needed to secure it, *especially* if I pulled off my new plan. Min might be hiding there—the thought thrilled me, even as it made me queasy—but I couldn't ignore those supplies any longer. Couldn't let them fall into the wrong hands.

After. For now, I had to focus on hurting Ethan.

I pushed through the double doors and walked into the courtyard, Cash a step behind. The frigid air bit at my ears and nose. The moon was a pale yellow disk hanging in the night sky. Or a high-res graphic on the roof of our game-world simulation. I wasn't sure how to think about it. But my vision cut through the darkness anyway, my ears catching the slight whisper of rubber on pavement.

Which is what saved me.

I froze. Bushes rustled to my left. Three pops in the darkness. I felt something sizzle by my ear.

Cash wasn't so lucky. He fell and didn't move. I dropped to a crouch, holding my breath as I watched his prone form. Then Cash's body vanished and I dismissed him from my mind. Still in the game.

I dashed to a low stone wall bordering the senior lunch patio and snaked over it, taking cover on the other side. Then I craned my neck and peered across moonlit grass. Watched as Derrick and Chris Nolan crept up the covered walkway from the parking lot, trailed by Sarah, of all people. *Not so cautious after all.*

Removing my Beretta, I threw a glance in the opposite direction. The hairs on my arms stood. Tucker and Lars were creeping up the opposite walkway.

I wasn't scared. My senses were sharp, and I could feel added power flowing through me. My worst case was a quick trip through one of the reset zones. But I *was* outnumbered. They had me boxed in.

If killed, what happened to the energy I'd acquired? How much was it reduced? Removed? I didn't know, and wasn't looking to find out.

Sarah's voice drifted across the courtyard. "Come on out, Noah. We won't shoot."

"Can't hear you over the gunfire," I called back, stalling for time. The patio was small. If they charged as a group, they'd get me easily.

"We just want to talk. You have my word."

"Did Cash have your word, too?" I shifted onto the balls of my feet, preparing to sprint back to the building, but then a thick blur darkened the window of the center door. *Damn it.* Someone was lurking inside. All their bases were covered.

"That was Cash?" Sarah laughed softly. "Good. Don't forget, he was supposed to be guarding the store for *us*. He doesn't get a pass after that."

"But I do?" I eyed B building directly across from me, its outer wall bounding the far side of the courtyard. Twelve feet high. Fifty feet away.

"Of course, silly." Sarah's playful tone floated on the wind. "You have special privileges."

Movement to my right. Tucker and Lars were sneaking into the courtyard. They didn't know I could see them. Didn't understand how much power I'd absorbed.

She's distracting me.

"Careful, Sarah." I slid back over the wall, off the patio, and pressed my back against it. "Shoot me here and I'll just pop up somewhere else."

Several heartbeats passed. "Maybe."

She knows. That changed a lot. But did she know everything?

"How many times have you died, Sarah?" I pulled the slide on my pistol, chambering a round. The click carried through the air as I'd intended. Lars and Tucker froze, roughly halfway to my position. "How many resets for the boss lady?"

There was a long silence.

"None yet, Noah. At least, not in here."

Not inside the Program, she meant. Like me and Min, Sarah had been murdered five times during the Project Nemesis beta phase, before our class was digitized and inserted. Did any part of that number transfer? I doubted it. Which meant she wasn't at much risk. Which meant she was dangerous.

Derrick and Chris began fanning out across the grass. They couldn't see me yet, but I had a clear shot at both of them. I kept talking, trying to throw Sarah off balance. "How many lives have you taken? Think carefully."

"Why does that matter?"

I forced a chuckle, pushing one of her buttons.

"If you have to ask . . ."

"Don't play games with me, Noah. If you know someth—"

I rose smoothly, fired four shots to my right. Tucker dropped to the ground, holding his neck. Lars retreated like I'd hoped, but he didn't panic. He stopped at the edge of the courtyard and took cover behind a trash can, weapon up as he peered back down the walkway.

Damn.

Sparks erupted off the patio wall, but I was already gone, streaking for the lone tree at the center of the courtyard. I fired twice to the left, watched as Derrick and Chris dove for cover.

"He's by the tree!" Lars yelled.

I felt a bullet whiz by me. I spun and fired at Lars. Heard a satisfying howl of pain as I sprinted the last stretch toward B building. I leapt, took two running steps up the brick wall, then grabbed the roof's edge and pulled myself over in one fluid motion.

Feeling cocky, I rose and glared back down at the courtyard. Tucker had vanished. Lars was down and moaning on the walkway. Sarah was nowhere to be seen, of course, but Derrick and Chris were standing beside the tree, staring up at me in shock. In the pale moonlight I could see the whites of their eyes.

"You're lucky I'm in a hurry," I called down, giving them a one-finger salute. Then I whirled, jogged across the roof, slid down a drainpipe, and melted into the night.

There were no sounds of pursuit.

I knew there wouldn't be.

14

MIN

I woke up gasping to the memory of cold metal pressed against my head.

I did it. I pulled the trigger.

I turned and threw up on the grass, my stomach heaving until nothing else would come up. Then I rolled over and curled into a ball. Lay there, shaking, listening to the gunshot echo over and over in my mind. Stomach acid burned my nostrils and gums. My eyes stared blankly, unfocused.

This is no way to live.

Several minutes passed before I could pull myself together.

I knew where I was. The northern woods. This clearing was as familiar as loneliness. The stars were out in force, shining down like tiny flashlights of concern.

Finally, my pulse slowed. The cold caught up to me, wrapping my body in an icy cocoon. I sat up, brushed pine needles from my sweater and jeans. Goose bumps erupted up and down my arms—I realized my jacket was still resting on a jail cell bench. I'd need a new one, and fast.

My headache had intensified to a constant pounding behind my eyes. My limbs felt weak and rubbery. I coughed and spat, felt a friction in my lungs. I wanted to sleep away these feelings and forget, but I knew that wasn't possible. Outdoors at this altitude, a nap would be fatal.

A second chill ran through me.

Devin.

I pictured his body in a pool of blood on the concrete floor. Nearly got sick again. I hadn't known him well, but we'd gone to school together for years. He was kind, and sweet, and didn't deserve to be gunned down like an animal. And now it seemed like he was really dead.

Ethan and Sarah had been as shocked as me. Everyone had, except maybe Akio—a fact to consider later. In their frantic argument, they'd guessed that Devin had died five times, but hadn't known for sure. While they'd fought, I'd quickly tallied up my own deaths since insertion.

Noah shot me outside of Town Hall.

The elevator crash squashed me like a bug.

Toby mowed me down at the summer camp.

Three since the Program began. When I'd grabbed Toby's gun, I'd known a jail-cell suicide would make four. I'd gambled, and here I was. Yet my hands wouldn't stop shaking.

What's the magic number? How many lives does this cat have left?

I stood up. Bounced my shoulders, trying to relieve the tension. I sucked in a mouthful of bitingly crisp air and sputtered a shallow cough. Pressing my palms together, I brought my hands to my lips and closed my eyes.

I'd been certain I'd reset in the eastern woods this time, within the fenced-off government land where the silo was hidden. Which would've been great, since I was still determined to get there. But instead I'd landed in my usual place. I guess random really meant random.

The forest around me was unnervingly silent. Dark as a crypt, though the moon above was high in the sky. I could tell it was much later in the evening. I knew Ethan and Sarah had a goon squad hiding somewhere in these woods, waiting to drag me back to the jail. If they caught me again, I'd never get out.

I wondered what Sarah and Ethan were thinking at that moment. Would they bury Devin's body? Or were they too busy counting up their own resets?

There was a crack behind me, then a dull roar as snow slid down from one of the peaks. I shivered. I'd been killed three times in less than twenty-four hours. I was unarmed and alone in the wilderness. There was no telling where my enemies were lurking.

Keep moving forward. Get to the silo. Find Tack.

But would he be there? Or had Tack been marched into a jail cell moments after I pulled the trigger? There was no way to know. The timing of resets seemed as arbitrary as locations. Did it matter *how* you died? What number death it was? Searching for a pattern felt hopeless.

Get it together. Wherever Tack was, I'd clearly been off the grid for a while. Runners could've been sent to warn the kidnap teams of my "escape," and that I knew about their plan. They might suspect I'd avoid the main trails out of the reset zones.

But there'd also been an attack. Ethan might've pulled people back to deal with Noah—he didn't have *limitless* numbers—or the team stationed here might've heard the gunfire and gone to help, leaving the way clear. If I was careful, I might slip the trap unnoticed.

To the north were the steepest peaks encircling the valley, with a dense forest standing between them and me. I could beat a trail through it to the base of those mountains, then work east across the ski slopes to the military land. A long walk, but nearly certain to avoid Ethan's people.

Of course, I'd be traveling straight through Noah's territory.

An icy gust swept the clearing, stirring broken sticks and dead leaves. I blew into my fists. Stomped my feet to restart the blood flow. I couldn't just stand here freezing to death.

Considering my other options, there wasn't much choice. The trails were out, and I couldn't head directly south—I didn't know who might be roaming the upper neighborhoods. West was the wrong direction. To avoid both downtown and the ski resort I'd have to go all the way around the lake counterclockwise, but Tack and I had tried that route and gotten shot for our trouble, which was how I'd landed in this mess in the first place.

No. There was no choice. I had to head north, then take my chances on the slopes.

After a deep breath, I began picking a path through the tangled undergrowth, moving upland as quietly as I could. Moments later I felt the familiar tingle of leaving a reset zone. Exposed and weaponless, I was now an easy target, though one traveling deeper into the woods under the cover of darkness.

The trees were tightly packed, and soon my hands were covered in sap. I could barely see five paces in front of me. Vines and clinging creepers kept pulling at my hair and jeans, rubbing against my neck and causing me to flail. But after a few labored miles I reached a higher elevation. The way opened up and I turned east.

I kept straining to hear a bird, or chirping cricket, but I knew it was a waste of time. There was no more mystery to the ghostly silence. The valley contained no wildlife because none had been programmed for it.

It did feel good to be outside and walking, even though my hands were numb and my toes felt like ice cubes. My headache had receded a bit, and I could breathe easier. After so many days skulking around the trailer park, I needed to get my blood pumping again. I was surprised to discover that I was enjoying myself, my body responding to the environment as if this were a real place. Whoever coded the simulation had done incredible work. No matter how hard I tried, I couldn't distinguish anything fake about it. The moss on the wind tasted real. The scratches on my arms felt real.

I reached the first ski slope and began angling back downhill. The moon was hanging right over my head, reflecting off the snow in a thousand dancing winks. The lake was as still as glass in the valley's center. It was a magical autumn night, or would've been if I hadn't been slowly glaciating.

I was debating a quick detour into town to raid a closet when an acrid scent infested my nose. I paused, inhaling deeply. It smelled like wood smoke, but not quite. Another big whiff and I had it: a campground pit, doused by heavy rain.

Somewhere up ahead, a large fire had burned.

I moved forward carefully, senses on high alert. It was probably a lightning strike, but I couldn't take any risks.

My feet found themselves on a trail cutting through a stand of evergreens. I emerged into a man-made clearing that surrounded the charred remains of a log cabin.

I scanned the area. No one in sight. So I crept forward to examine the scene.

The fire had burned hot, scorching a black circle of dead grass around the crumbling, blackened foundation. The trees had been cleared back twice as far, thankfully, or else this entire section of forest might have gone up. Maybe even the town.

Though rain had washed away some of the debris, the fire was clearly recent. I chewed my bottom lip, thinking. This didn't look natural. The damage was too complete, with foot-thick oak logs burned completely to ashes. Lightning *could* do it, maybe—and last week's storms had seen their fair share—but my gut said otherwise.

I felt a spike of adrenaline, my thoughts zipping back to the confrontation at the quarry. Floyd had said Noah torched one of Ethan's outposts, with people still inside. And Akio had confirmed it, back in the cells.

I backed a few steps, nearly tripped over a fallen tiki torch. The ski chalet topped these runs. My teeth began to chatter as I turned and hurried from the clearing, blackened grass crunching beneath my soles.

How? How could Noah do this?

Because he's crazy now. Why was that so hard to accept? The boy I knew was gone.

I strode away without looking back. I had somewhere to be. A real friend might be waiting for me, and getting sidetracked could get me killed. Maybe for good next time.

I started downhill again, but after a dozen yards, something else stopped me short.

Beneath my feet was a rectangle of bare earth. Frozen grasses surrounded it, covered in frost, but this ground was clear and exposed. I knelt, dug a finger into the soil. It was soft and crumbly, as if recently turned. Then I leapt up, abruptly realizing what it was.

Grave.

I was standing on a fresh grave.

Questions battled for position in my head. Who died? How did it happen? Who buried them? Was this grave here before the Program engaged—and therefore mere scenery, captured within its pixels—or had something happened to *another* classmate?

How many people are gone already?

Suddenly, it was all too much. I was shivering nonstop. I needed warmth, a release from the unbearable tension, and a safe place to think.

I peered across the slope, then down at the crust of white covering it. The snow was thin and patchy, eroded by freezing rain. Slick, but soft enough that my shoes wouldn't slip. However, I'd leave a trail of muddy footprints like a calling card, and three more runs like this one cut across my intended path.

I changed my mind. I'd head for town instead, steal a jacket, then cut east below the main ski lodge at the foot of the slopes. Noah and his killers were on the mountaintop. With luck, I'd slip by them unnoticed. This route would bring me closer to Ethan and Sarah's domain, but I had to thread the needle somewhere. I prayed for an opening between the two groups.

Because I was more worried about getting caught than I wanted to admit. Escape through suicide was an option of last resort, but Devin's failure to reset had shaken my faith in my own indestructibility. Plus, I really didn't want to get shot again. I just wanted *past* all these bloodthirsty bastards, so I could disappear beyond the eastern fence.

Find the silo. Find Tack. Find answers. Pray to God Noah isn't sitting there waiting for me.

Pray to God? Or the Guardian?

"Not a chance," I muttered. No matter what this existence was, I'd never give him that much credit. I wasn't even sure I was thankful.

To still exist was . . . a gift. It felt like a moral imperative to appreciate it. But this virtual world was ugly and cruel, and the Guardian had designed it that way. Or rather, the black-suited monster whose face he wore had done it.

And for what? I still didn't know. But I was going to find out.

I began angling southwest. After a few hundred yards I reached the first line of houses. I crept over a backyard fence, alert for any sign that the property might be occupied. But the windows were dark, and no smoke rose from the chimney. There was a little garden to my left. A child's swing set rose just beyond it, a miniature black tower in the gloom. Plastic deck chairs faced off on a rickety wooden deck, one tipped over onto its side.

I couldn't help wondering who'd lived here before the end came. How many dead people had called this place home. Shaking off the bitter thought, I stole over to the back door and tried the knob. It opened without resistance—Fire Lake was that kind of town.

This reminder of the past almost brought me to my knees. I missed home more than I could say. My mother, warts and all. The stupid Jenkins brothers, passed out drunk by the community fire pit. Sunburned tourists, filling the cafés with laughter and strange accents.

Would I never see another stranger's face? Would I ever have a home again?

Inside I located a hall closet filled with winter coats. I took a blue North Face, whispering a silent thanks to whomever had owned it. I stuffed gloves into its pockets and jammed a hat down over my ears. Then I zipped the jacket tight, purring like a cat in a sunny spot.

I debated hunkering down for the night, but I knew that'd be foolish. I had to move under cover of darkness. If I stayed in the house past sunrise, I'd burn the whole next day hiding there. So after a few minutes recharging—checking the fridge and finding it depressingly empty—I slipped out a side door and crept onto High Street, then snuck along the road to where it turned ninety degrees and dropped toward Main. Small cottages lined the left side of the street, backing up to the woods. A handful of shops marched downhill along the right.

At the bottom of the hill the two streets formed a T-intersection with the supermarket parking lot straight ahead. Streetlights burned on the corners. There was no one outside the store that I could see, but it was a lock that people lurked within.

I scurried back off the road and began working my way down-hill through the cottage backyards, scaling a few fences, the last nearly toppling over with me aboard. As I hit the ground, I paused, listening, my heart bouncing inside my chest. When nothing happened, I snorted in relief, then continued until I reached a back porch twenty yards from Main Street.

This was where my cover ended. I had to follow the road for at least fifty yards until it linked up with Old Fort Run, where I could disappear into the darkened thickets safely out of range of the streetlights. I scanned the block, suddenly impatient. The thought of Noah inside the silo was gnawing at my brain. I glanced at the grocery store. Still no one. The road was dark and empty in both directions.

A twig snapped. My head swung left.

Twenty feet from me, in the woods beyond the cottage, something glinted.

Holding my breath, I eased back into the shadow of the porch, zeroing my eyes on the woods.

There. Two outlines in the gloom. They were in the bushes where the forest stretched closest to the road, just beyond the pools of orange light. One had binoculars up and was watching the store.

Noah's people? Maybe *him*. I'd nearly stepped right out in front of them.

Before I could digest this threat, shouts carried from deeper into town, followed by the clatter of gunfire. With one eye on the woods, I peeked around the deck. Two figures came barreling out of the grocery store, bullets skittering off the pavement around them. They ran directly toward me.

I dropped to my stomach and crawled under the deck. Held my breath. Sneakers pounded past me as the pair dove into the woods, rolling into positions beside the two silhouettes I'd spotted.

All four began shooting down the street at once. I dragged myself deeper into the shadows and covered my ears. Waited. Sweated.

The quartet abruptly ceased fire. They slipped into the forest and were gone.

More yelling down the street. I slithered back to the edge of the deck and peeked out. Ethan and a dozen others were now milling in the grocery store parking lot. Two bodies lay in the gutter. One disappeared, but the other didn't. Several people were staring at the remaining corpse, gesturing wildly and freaking out. Ethan was pointing toward the trees. Toward me.

I scurried back under the deck a second time, my pulse pounding in my ears. Ethan and his guys would be more careful now. They might check my hiding spot.

Suddenly a scream of warning cut through the still night air. I froze.

A blast of light.

A boom like breaking the sound barrier.

I felt a wave of heat envelop me as the ground shook. Wooden timbers heaved and groaned. Covering my head like a tornado drill, I prayed the deck I was hiding under wouldn't collapse and crush me. Smoke and dust filled my lungs, choking me.

When I could finally see again, I crawled forward on shaking knees. A thick black plume was pouring across the road, swallowing the streetlights in a hellish maw. I buried my mouth and nose in the elbow of my sleeve. The heat baked my eyeballs, and they began to water.

The supermarket was a mammoth fireball. I gaped, shell-shocked as I watched it burn, red and orange tendrils arcing into the sky and reflecting off the lake. Everyone who had been standing in the parking lot was gone.

The street was empty now, except for the body, which had been tossed face-first into the gutter and was smoldering with tiny flames. The victim, a girl, lay unnaturally, her neck twisted too far around. The only sounds were the inferno consuming the store and a high-pitched ringing in my ears. Soot began raining down like tiny black tears, matching what I felt inside.

The explosion was a horror show—a crime against humanity. Ethan and his friends had been lured in and then blown straight to hell.

So many killed at once. Monstrous.

But the carnage gave me the distraction I needed.

I dragged myself from the muck and bolted down the road.

15

NOAH

It went perfectly.

Ethan had attacked with twice as many people as I'd hoped, and after some well-placed gunfire by my team in the woods, they'd bunched up around the store entrance like scared puppies.

Ten minutes beforehand, we'd sealed the doors and ruptured the main gas line. When Kyle's pipe bomb went off, not a single one of them escaped.

Amazing.

Appalling.

I shook my head bitterly, ignoring my own weakness. Sarah's ambush at the high school had taught me a lesson. We couldn't hold ground. Not in town, not when they had so many more people than I did. Until we chipped away at their numerical advantage, the best we could do were blitzkrieg attacks.

But that didn't mean we couldn't hurt them. Break their spirits. I'd given my followers an emphatic victory. Shown them

I was resourceful and remorseless. They'd stick with me now, both out of fear and in their own best interests.

Everything I'd hoped for. The Guardian would approve.

I was perched in the bell tower of Sacred Heart a half block away, watching flames lick the sky. The fire wanted to spread, but there wasn't anything close enough to dig its fingers into. It occurred to me that burning down the whole town wasn't the worst idea, but I wasn't sure we could pull it off. This only worked because we'd been able to set things up precisely.

Plus, they'd never suspected we'd torch all that food. Ethan didn't know we'd been ferrying groceries out the back door by the vanload for almost six hours.

Something boomed inside the ruins of the store. A ball of yellow arced skyward, lighting up the horizon before landing with a sizzle in the lake. Two more makeshift rockets followed in quick succession, though neither cleared the parking lot.

I grinned at the impromptu fireworks. Oil canisters? Propane tanks? But the smile died as I spotted someone lying facedown in the gutter.

I sat forward and brought up my binoculars—with the added firelight and my enhanced vision, they were more than enough to see. The body was crumpled like a balled-up newspaper, hanging backward over the lip of the curb and into the street. I swallowed. Felt my jaw tighten. I took deep breaths through my nose to slow my heartbeat.

A slack face, wrapped in a wavy tangle of scorched brown hair. Eyes staring up at the heavens, unblinking. She wore a melted letterman's jacket and tight black jeans. The girl could not have been more dead.

No. Not "a girl." Her name is Melissa.

That's Melissa freaking Hemby dead in the gutter.

"So what?" I growled, infuriated by this nagging voice I couldn't silence. "You heard the Guardian. Eliminating people is the *point*." Then I clamped my lips shut and stopped talking to myself like a crazy person.

Melissa's body was lying in full view of anyone who might look. The secret wouldn't keep anymore.

Sure, I felt sorry for her. She was on the cheerleading squad. Sat at the table across from me and my friends during lunch. She'd always been nice. Melissa dressed as Black Widow once for Halloween, and all the guys noticed.

But it wasn't my fault. Not completely. I only killed her this once.

Then my blood turned to ice. *I* didn't kill her at all. Someone on my team did. Which meant they'd just powered up.

A rival. But who? Did the bomb blast kill Melissa? I wasn't sure who the Program would credit for something like that. Or did she get hit during the shootout? If so, which of my teammates had made the fatal shot?

I turned my binoculars east, located the two vans inside the ski resort gates and speeding up toward the chalet. Each was stuffed with the last of what we'd had time to loot before setting our trap. That made eight trips total. Incredible.

I regretted incinerating the rest of the food supply, but the move had to be made. I needed to break Ethan's hold over our weaker classmates, and his strength was mostly based on cereal boxes and mac and cheese. Without that, how long would people listen to him? Ethan was gone on a reset right now, while his leverage burned. I bet the smarter kids were scrambling, grabbing what they could while the cat was away.

Idly, I wondered where Ethan was at that exact moment. He was going to be so pissed.

I swept the binoculars back to the store, careful to avoid the body. I didn't have time to fall apart. This was the way it was. No sense crying about it, even if I felt bad.

There wasn't much else left to see. The destruction we'd wrought was total. I was about to climb down and start hiking home when movement in the road caught my eye.

A girl, running.

I couldn't see who it was, but she definitely wasn't with me. I knew my people inside and out—what they wore, even how they moved. This girl had on a blue North Face that wasn't familiar. I lifted the bolt-action rifle sitting on the ledge next to me and drew a bead on the moving target.

I hesitated. The girl was heading east, not west. *Away* from town.

Interesting. Going AWOL? Now was the perfect time to jump Ethan's ship. I didn't see a weapon in her hand, but that didn't mean much.

Something . . .

The girl's flight. It didn't feel normal. She ran with purpose, but there was nothing over that way. At least, nothing *I* knew about. Or, rather, the only thing over there was something no one *else* knew about.

Unless . . .

I made a decision. Taking aim, I fired a shot at the ground

a dozen yards in front of her. She stopped dead. Working the bolt, I fired twice more, walking the rounds back in her direction. The girl swerved, dove into the drainage ditch next to the road.

Perfect. I slung the rifle over my shoulder, grabbed the rope I'd tied to the side of the building, and rappelled to the ground.

Stay put. I'm coming.

I jogged down to Main Street and cut left, slipping past the girl and worming into the bushes beyond where the ditch ended. Clawing through the muck with her head down, she didn't see or hear me. I lay down on the ground and flipped open the rifle's bipod kickstand. She'd have to climb out right in front of me; I could pick her off, then stroll upslope in time for fourth meal.

I squinted through the nightscope. Seconds ticked by, then a dirt-caked head emerged in the crosshairs. She swiveled and peered back toward the inferno, oblivious to my presence. I had a clear shot.

To murder someone.

I slapped an itch by my ear. Hesitated. Where was she going? There was nothing east of here but the government land. Was she running blind? Or did she know what was hidden in the woods behind me?

Stop playing stupid. Stop ignoring the obvious.

The figure turned back to face me.

The jut of her chin. The set of her shoulders.

My heart stopped beating. I stopped breathing.

159

It was her.

My fingertips burned with electric fire. I felt a spike of panic at what I'd nearly done, then one of terror at her possible approach. Everything shut down, like a frozen hard drive needing to reboot.

Mind gone numb, I watched Min slither from the ditch and break into a run, heading directly for me. Filling my scope. She had no idea I was there. The rifle was in perfect position. A flick of my finger and she'd be gone.

I had seconds to react. Heard a cold voice inside my head.

Do it. Shoot. Send her away. Never let her get close again.

My knuckle whitened on the trigger. The tiniest pull was all it would take.

A scene emerged from somewhere deep inside. Christmas. Sixth grade. The elementary school gymnasium. Principal Myers was dressed up like Santa Claus and not enjoying it. Min was wearing a purple dress with sleek black buttons. I had on that awful red Rudolph sweater my dad's secretary had given me.

My father was there, red-faced and owning the room, loudly joking to the other parents that the punch was too weak. Their forced, nervous laughter echoed to the rafters. His new wife clung awkwardly to his arm, my mother barely six months gone.

I'd retreated under the bleachers as soon as the party started, not that my father noticed. I didn't want my classmates to see me. Then here came Min, crawling through the forest of steel girders to sit with me, smudging her white tights on the dirty hardwood floor. She handed me a sketch of a cartoon Death Star making out with Taylor Swift. I snorted despite myself.

I knew it was supposed to be a present for Tack, but I took it anyway. We sat together silently, eating chocolate snow globes. She didn't make me tell her what was wrong.

I slid the rifle into the bushes beside me, concealing it. Then I rose, drew my Beretta, and stepped from the woods into the moonlight.

Min saw me in the next moment and skidded to a stop. Her eyes darted left, then right.

"I'm alone," I said softly. Why did my voice sound so strange?

Min licked her lips, still crouching like a coiled spring. "So am I."

"I know."

We stared at each other across fifteen feet of snow-covered pavement.

I found I had nothing to say. What could I? The awkward moment grew and stretched, swallowed the whole valley. I began to sweat. Why hadn't I just shot her and been done?

"That your work back there?" Min said finally, jabbing a thumb back at the flames.

I nodded. "Ethan's leverage is gone."

"With most of the food in the valley, I'd guess."

"Small price to pay."

The inferno raged behind her, tossing long shadows, creating a mishmashed tangle of dark and light. The fire backlit Min's face, and I couldn't see her eyes. But she could see mine. I could feel the weight of her judgment.

I felt exposed before her. The fraud again. A little boy caught being naughty. My anger erupted like a Pavlovian response as harsh truths whispered in my ear. No one had the right to judge me but the Guardian. I didn't have anything to prove to this girl. She was lucky to be standing there.

You're stronger without her. She's your nemesis.

"Where are you going?" I demanded raggedly, though I could guess.

She didn't answer, all but confirming it.

The silo. I'd caught her sneaking home, which meant Tack must be there.

I'd ignored this issue for too long. There were useful things in those alcoves. Fuel. Vehicles. What about weapons? I hadn't seen any the first time, but we hadn't explored the place in depth. Min must've by now. She might be sleeping on a crate of bazookas.

I'd been ignoring a potential treasure trove. Once again, Min had leapt to the right answer while I flailed about like an angry toddler knocking over sand castles. Shame burned my ears. But it was okay. I could fix this.

Only two other people knew about the silo, and I had one at gunpoint.

"Where's Tack?"

A slight hesitation. "Waiting for me."

I hid my dismay. They'd had weeks. Tack probably knew how to operate the blast doors. He could keep me out indefinitely.

Then I nearly kicked myself for being an idiot. I had Min as my prisoner. The one thing Tack cared about more than hating me. She was all the leverage I needed to get inside. I just had to bring her.

Why did that realization feel like . . . relief?

"So are you going to shoot me?" Min said coldly, but I heard a tremor in her voice.

I flinched. Couldn't help it.

She didn't miss my reaction. "What? Suddenly feeling guilty? Didn't stop you before."

"That was different," I stammered, cheeks burning in the darkness. Somehow she'd taken control of the encounter and put me on my heels. "I did what I had to."

Min shook her head in disgust.

"You don't know everything!" I shouted, my temper slipping. "I could've shot you as you crawled from that ditch. But I didn't. There's more going on than you realize, Min. This game *isn't* pointless."

She looked away. Did she know the truth?

Then her gaze sawed back into me. "Why *didn't* you shoot, Noah?"

Words escaped before I could vet them. "Maybe I don't want to be the one who puts you out."

A definite reaction this time. Had she seen Melissa's body in the street?

An icy breeze swept off the lake and stirred her mud-caked hair. Min hugged her sides and shivered. She looked ridiculous, standing in the gloom, covered in drying sludge from head to foot. Except she didn't look ridiculous at all.

Something stirred inside me. Feelings I'd thought murdered for good on the steps of Town Hall.

"It doesn't have to be like this," Min said suddenly. "You're not a machine."

I shook my head, annoyed. "This crap, still? Let's just lay our cards on the table, okay?"

"Fine," she spat through clenched teeth. I realized she was furious, and barely holding it in check.

You shot her in the back, you moron. Did you think she'd forget?

I hardened my emotions. I was facing an enemy, and had to act accordingly.

"Who didn't reset?" I demanded, hoping the question would throw her off balance.

Min hesitated a moment, then, "Devin Carver. Those bastards had been shooting him for sport. But the last time his body didn't disappear."

My eyebrows rose in surprise. "How do you know? Did you see it?"

Crossing her arms, she didn't say more.

I tried to hide my confusion. And alarm. Devin had been part of Ethan's gang—was Min working with them somehow? The idea seemed impossible, but . . . who could you really trust?

The question rose to my tongue, but I found I couldn't ask it. I didn't want to hear the answer. The idea of Min working with Ethan bothered me so much, I didn't want to test whether it was true. What was wrong with me?

"Now you," Min said coldly.

Still thrown, I hedged. "You must've worked it out already."

"I want to know what you've seen."

I swallowed. This was stupid. I was the one holding the gun. But then I heard myself say, "Piper Lockwood didn't reset a few days ago. I buried her in the woods."

Min's hand shot to her mouth. She took a step backward. I still couldn't see her eyes. Why had I told her the last part? But I kept talking, only half aware of my words. "So I guess we're down to sixty-two. Sixty-one, actually. Melissa Hemby didn't reset after the blast."

Sixty. But Zach was my secret alone.

"Listen to yourself!" Min exploded, storming a step closer. A sliver of moonlight caught her face, electrifying her gray eyes. They glistened with rage, and horror, and unshed tears. "We went to *preschool* with Piper, for God's sake! You kissed Melissa at the eighth-grade dance. But now you're talking about their deaths like it's a fucking video game!"

I stared at her in honest bafflement. "It *is* a game, Min. Melissa died five weeks ago, same as you and me. We were gassed by men in Hazmats suits, remember? We live inside a computer program now, which means we have to follow its rules. Why is that so hard for you to accept?"

"Why is it so *easy* for you?" she fired back, chest heaving, her hands balled into fists. "Killing for sport! Hunting people you've known for years. *Friends.* It's disgusting! *And you don't even know why you're doing it.*"

My anger erupted to match hers. "You don't know everything, Min! Jesus, it's like you want to just ignore what the Guardian told us, and hope it all goes away!" I almost screamed that I'd *spoken* to the Guardian only hours before, but managed to hold off. Instead, I took a deep breath. "Don't you get it? *There's limited space for the next phase.* Do you want to make it or not?"

For a minute, Min said nothing, but her shoulders quivered.

Then her head dropped and she spoke in a low, shaky voice. "Maybe not. Not like this. I don't want to become an animal just to survive. That's the difference between us, I guess."

I stared. Felt my resolve crackle and break apart inside me. I tried frantically to stitch it back together, but the pieces melted in my hands. God, was she right?

Then Min's head rose, her smoky eyes flashing like chips of ice. "Sarah was right about you. You *are* weak. It wasn't your fault growing up. I know that. But you shook free of Dr. Lowell and had a chance to find your own way." Her lips formed a sneer. "A handful of words from the Guardian was all it took to enslave you. You're a coward. You really do need someone to tell you what to do. I don't know what I ever saw in you."

"*Shut up.*" The barrel rose. One squeeze would banish her to a far corner of the valley. "Just shut your mouth. You have no idea what I've been through."

"Don't I?"

And even that was true. With her, I had no defense.

I racked the slide. Her legs began to shake, but she didn't run. Or cry out. Or curse me. She just stared a hole through my head until I wanted to hide.

The gun lowered. I wiped my eyes, disturbed to find my cheeks wet.

"Let's go," I ordered.

"I'm not going anywhere with you," Min snapped.

A harsh little laugh. "I doubt that's true. I really will shoot you if I have to."

"Shoot me if you want, Noah, but I'm not going with you. I'm headed for the silo. To see Tack," she added awkwardly.

166

His name burned like acid, killing something inside me. I shoved my emotions into a box. Schooled my face to stillness. When I spoke again, it was like a different person stood before her. "A task I've neglected too long myself."

Her eyes narrowed. "What do you mean?"

I stepped aside. Pointed the gun at her chest, then motioned into the eastern woods.

"You're in luck. We're headed to the same place."

16

MIN

The forest was dark and silent.

I wasn't sure of the time, but it had to be nearing midnight. I was cold, tired, covered in mud, and intensely aware of the gun at my back. A gun held by Noah.

Noah.

He walked behind me, saying nothing. Hadn't spoken since we set out. My insides roiled from the intensity of being so near him again after all this time.

He looked different, at least from what little I'd seen before we entered this pitch-black forest. Still tall and beautiful, with piercing green eyes. But his posture radiated tension. Noah's mouth was baked into a frown that never faltered. He'd lost weight, something I found curious. Could you die of natural causes inside this fishbowl? What would happen if I decided not to eat anymore?

Focus. Technically you're being kidnapped.

We'd crawled under the fence at the usual place. Not sure why we bothered—with the soldiers gone, we could've just forced the gate. But on second thought, not advertising our presence was smarter. I still didn't know who else had learned about the silo.

Noah believed Tack was already inside, awaiting my return. Something I desperately hoped was true. I was angry with myself for being so timid, and not securing this place weeks ago. Noah obviously hadn't, like I'd assumed—he must've thought the same thing as me. It'd be funny, if it weren't so pathetic.

Only three people knew that the secrets of Project Nemesis were buried in these woods, and none had bothered to check on them. A sad reminder that we really were just kids with no idea what we were doing.

Noah flicked on a flashlight, then waved me forward with his stupid gun. It was ridiculous he still held it, but I didn't press the issue. I'd pushed him earlier and he'd almost lost control.

The forest was ghostly, an army of slender pine sentinels that regarded our presence with silent disapproval. Freezing rain began to fall, slushy drops tapping the canopy in a sporadic drumbeat. My breath misted as the smell of decomposing wood enveloped me.

The moon slipped behind a bank of clouds, shrouding the way forward in near-total darkness. I tried to move quietly, but my sneakers kept sliding on the rain-slicked leaves and dead pine needles lining the forest floor. After my third stumble I turned and snapped my fingers at Noah. He hesitated a moment, then reluctantly handed over the flashlight.

We worked deeper into the woods, perhaps another quarter mile, until I actually bumped into the invisible barrier surrounding Sarah's reset point. I'd forgotten it was now off-limits. I still thought of that space as hers, even though it was a random function of the Program now. Then, in a panic, I remembered the kidnap teams.

I turned to Noah and put a finger to my lips, then switched off the light. He lurched forward and grabbed me by the arm, but I hissed at him to be quiet, pulling his ear close to my lips. "They have people watching the zones," I whispered.

Noah released me, but didn't step back. The tension never left his shoulders. He was standing so close, we were almost touching. I could feel heat pouring off his body. Like a dirty traitor, my body responded in kind. Breath short. Heartbeat up. I wanted to lurch away and melt into his side at the same time. *What is wrong with you?*

We stood like that in the darkness for several minutes. Then, finally, I flipped the light back on and stepped back. A twinge of regret? Then I noticed he was still holding his gun.

"Well?" Noah whispered, a looming form in the black.

"Sarah persuaded Ethan to capture people as they come out of the zones. They're throwing everyone in jail now instead of shooting them. That's how they got me." Then I cringed at having told him I'd been caught. For some reason, it embarrassed me for Noah to know. "I escaped, obviously," I finished like a dunce.

I sensed him nodding in the gloom. "Smart plan. But we spotted most of their people during our attack. I bet Ethan called everyone back to focus on the store." He took a step, then stopped. "Was Akio in the cells with you?"

I debated whether to answer. Then, "Yes."

"Thanks," was all he said, but some of the tightness had left his voice. He stood still for a moment, then I heard his jacket unzip. Curious, I lit him up with the flashlight. Both his palms were now empty.

"It's still handy. Move."

I grunted, but a tiny part of me unthawed. Noah was still Noah, no matter how hard he tried.

We circled the barrier to the base's dilapidated access road, then followed it the rest of the way in. If anyone was resetting in those woods, we never heard a sound.

Quite deliberately, the silo building wasn't much to look at from the outside—a squat, one-story structure with cheap vinyl sides and a patchy tin roof, surrounded by a gravel parking lot. It looked more "abandoned airplane hangar" than "top-secret military facility." No lights burned.

I illuminated the dented metal door, its paint chipped and peeling, looking for all the world like no one had opened it in years. If Tack was inside, there was no sign of him.

I felt Noah's breath on the back of my neck. "No tricks," he warned. "If Tack gets cute, we'll all go down together." Then he stepped back and I heard his pocket open.

I resisted the urge to turn around and slap him. "You don't need the gun out, okay? I get it. You'll shoot me. It's tired."

A silent moment. I didn't move. Finally, the zipper sounded again.

"Okay, Min. We'll keep this civil. But you better keep a leash on your·. . . friend."

My eyebrows rose where he couldn't see. Had he stumbled on the last word? What did *that* mean?

I tried the handle but it wouldn't budge. I felt a flash of hope—Tack *is* inside!—before remembering that we'd locked the door behind us last time.

"Open it," Noah said impatiently. He obviously thought I could.

"I can't. Tack's the one who knows how to pick this lock. I don't have a key."

"Well, I've got one. Give me space."

I stepped away, watched as Noah shoulder-charged the door. With a satisfying thud, it declined to open. Noah stumbled backward, hiding a grimace, working his arm as he pretended the failure hadn't hurt him on several levels.

"Nice job, Hulk. That's a military-grade door."

Hands on his knees, Noah coughed into a fist. "Just get Tack to open it," he wheezed.

"How? He's probably a hundred feet below us right now." A stall, but possibly true. We couldn't just knock, and covert defense installations don't come with doorbells. I didn't have the first clue how to get inside.

"You never planned for this?" Noah's eyes narrowed. "Is Tack even in there?"

I chewed my lip, thinking. If Tack wasn't languishing in one of Ethan's cells, he'd have come straight here, arriving hours ago. Logically, he *would* have tried to leave me a way inside, but we hadn't planned one.

I stepped back and examined the entrance with the flashlight, then scanned the immediate area. A loose brick was propped against the building six feet to our left. Had it been there the last time? Fingers mentally crossed, I walked over and lifted it, illuminating the exposed ground underneath. Nothing. But then something on the brick's underside winked in the flashlight's beam. I knelt and aimed the light.

Two words had been scrawled there in silver Sharpie. *Valley Grounds.*

A huge weight slipped from my shoulders. I straightened, grinning like a lunatic. Tack was here. I wasn't alone.

"Well?" Noah said.

I swung the flashlight in a wide arc, probing the area with fresh eyes. Valley Grounds was our favorite coffee shop. Tack *loved* caffeine, and had an affection for tiny cups. His order never varied: double espresso with a shot of chocolate milk. They called it the Double Dirt.

There. A bag of compost was resting in a heap a dozen yards away. The packaging looked cleaner than you'd expect for something outdoors, and there was a fist-sized rip in its side. I walked over and dug my fingers in. Found the key almost immediately.

I stood and waved it innocently at Noah, making sure the flashlight beam blinded him.

Noah scowled, shielding his eyes. "You had to let me try first?"

"I don't remember you asking."

He sighed audibly. Pointed at the door.

I strolled past him with perfect nonchalance, inserted the key with a satisfied smirk. It turned. I barely suppressed a squeal of delight, but then my smile evaporated.

What was I doing? Joking with Noah like we were buddies on a road trip? God, was I *flirting* with him?

He murdered *you. Called you his nemesis. Never forget.*

173

The door opened smoothly. Feeling a spasm of fury, I shot forward down the dimly lit corridor to a steel blast door at the opposite end. Solid and imposing, it was equipped with a shiny electronic keypad, which, in turn, had a small black circle I assumed was a camera port. I heard Noah relock the outer door and hurry after me.

I tried to calm down. I was finally back inside the silo. Now was not the time for runaway emotions. By the time Noah reached me, all traces of my anger had been masked.

He was irritated I'd taken off, but didn't mention it. "Well?" he said, nodding at the door.

"Just hold on a second."

I had no plan whatsoever. The key in my hand wouldn't get us into this freaking bank vault. But as I stared at the keypad, wondering what code Tack might use, there was a clicking sound, followed by a dull rumble ending with a clank. The sensor flashed green and the door swung inward.

I nearly groaned in relief. Tack must be watching the surveillance feeds.

Noah came to the same conclusion. "So he can see us right now?"

"Yes. Worried?"

He glanced at me and I felt a jolt from his eyes. "Just keep moving."

We entered the missile silo itself, a wide, cavernous shaft stretching thirty yards across and dropping hundreds of feet straight down. A slender catwalk was bolted to the granite wall and circled to a miner's cage on the opposite side. Noah followed me around the circuit, breathing heavily by the time we reached the cage. He really didn't like heights.

We opened the sliding gate and entered the cage. The control box had two yellow buttons—arrows up and down—with only the down arrow illuminated. Noah pressed it, and we started rolling down the vertical track.

Noah refused to look into the inky depths of the shaft. Instead, he caught my eye again and held it. "I'm going to trust you. I won't keep waving my gun around like a desperado. But you'd better have Tack under control. If he shoots me, I'll make it my mission in the Program to eliminate him next. Got it?"

I bit back a caustic reply. Noah was being reasonable, so I would be too. "I'll handle it."

I turned away. Talking to him was . . . hypnotic. I had to remind myself that I hated Noah after every exchange. What was it about being near him that confused me so much? I didn't even know why he was there. What was *he* looking for at the bottom of this well?

As we descended past a series of identical catwalks, I stared into the crowded alcoves on each level. They contained mountains of supplies—seeds, vehicles, fuel, batteries, and thousands of other essentials. Project Nemesis had prepared for Armageddon by stuffing these bays with everything conceivably useful to restart society, though none of it was unpacked or ready to use. The stockpile's immensity was just as impressive the second time around.

Then, with a start, it occurred to me that none of this was real. These supplies were graphics in a computer program. I'd never actually been inside the *real* silo, back in the real world. Did a massive survival cache like this truly exist, buried deep underground on a ravaged planet, with only a supercomputer for company?

If so, why bother? Why build a secret doomsday bunker stuffed with everything necessary to rebuild when no one would be left alive to use it? And why re-create those supplies here, inside the Program? The Guardian could've given us a giant refrigerator filled with waffles, or a never-ending taco bar.

Nothing about this made sense. There was still so much I didn't understand.

The cage reached the concrete floor and passed through it, descending down a narrow chute to the operating level twenty yards farther below. It stopped before a pair of elevator doors bolted into solid rock. Noah yanked open the gate, the barrier whisked apart, and we stepped into a short corridor. The control room was dead ahead, beyond a set of gleaming glass doors, one of which had been wedged ajar.

Someone was standing in the shadows.

17

MIN

"Bastard!"

Tack charged past me and launched himself at Noah, who'd clearly anticipated such a greeting. He caught Tack midlunge and slammed him against the wall, holding him pinned there kicking and squirming like a child having a tantrum.

Noah rolled his eyes. "Calm down, Tack. I don't want to hurt you."

"Min, run!" Tack tried to grapple with his larger adversary, but couldn't get loose. "Lock yourself in the control room!"

"Both of you relax!" I shouted. "Noah, let him go. Tack, don't start a fight."

Tack shot me an incredulous look. "I saw this prick blast a hole through your chest, Min! Whatever he's got on you, you don't have to—"

"It's a waste of time!" I shouted, my frustrations boiling over. "We can't do anything permanent to each other, so why don't we all stop acting like monsters? Enough is enough!"

Noah released Tack and shoved him a few steps back down the hallway. Tack stumbled to a stop against a wall, then looked over at me, eyes hurt and confused.

I wasn't being fair. Noah had technically forced me here at gunpoint, yet I was screaming at my best friend for trying to help. The last hour had made everything blurry and chaotic.

Noah certainly wasn't helping the situation. "Listen to your friend, Thumbtack. She's half right."

Tack glared pure loathing at Noah, putting himself between us. Then he glanced over his shoulder at me. "What's he talking about?"

I barely repressed a sigh. "He knows something about the Program. Big, I think."

Noah smiled coldly. It was like Tack's appearance had drawn out this whole other person. *The type that shoots a girl in the back.* "You saw Devin and Melissa," he said. "You know a secret, too."

Tack backed up until we were shoulder to shoulder. He ran a hand through his mussy black hair, blue eyes never leaving Noah. "What about Devin?" he whispered from the side of his mouth.

This time, the sigh escaped. "Let's talk inside." I turned and walked through the glass doors.

The control room was a towering, open chamber, like a movie theater, with tiers of workstations descending toward three massive panels along the front wall. The two outside screens were oversized video monitors. Previously, the center panel had been a giant window into the MegaCom chamber beyond, but all you could see now was a thick steel curtain sealing the super-computer from view.

Tack hurried in after me, then Noah. I had a sick feeling of déjà vu. The three of us had been here together once before, under very different circumstances.

The entrance was at the highest tier of workstations. I stopped at the closest desk to gather my thoughts. Tack joined me, eyes dripping with questions, though he pivoted to keep Noah in sight. For his part, Noah put his back to a cream-colored wall and crossed his arms.

"Okay, talk." Tack pointed an accusatory finger at Noah. "What's he doing here?"

"We ran into each other in town," I explained. "It's a long story."

Tack grabbed my hand in his and whispered fiercely. "Tell me you're not thinking of teaming back up with this asshole. *After what he did?*"

"Of course not." I pulled my hand away. "This trip is a marriage of convenience."

Tack blinked. "Did something happen?"

"Devin happened."

With Noah observing silently, I told Tack about my capture at Ethan's reset point and the jailhouse shooting. How I escaped the cell by taking my own life.

He whistled at that. "*Damn.* That was good thinking. I reset over here, inside the fence. Charlie and Finn tried to grab me, but I ran and lost them in the woods. They must've thought I headed west, and went that way. They never came close to here."

I nodded, relieved. "We skirted the reset barrier and didn't see anyone. But Noah's group hit town a few hours ago, and then they blew up the grocery store. I doubt Sarah's plan to snatch people is still in effect."

I glanced at Noah, who nodded magnanimously. *You're welcome.*

"Blew up the . . ." Tack trailed off, then his eyes widened. "You offed yourself to get out of jail. How many is that for you? Deaths, I mean."

I swallowed. Tried to hide my nervousness. "Four."

Tack whirled to face Noah, his jaw tightening. "Are you armed?"

Noah tapped his jacket pocket. "Yup."

"Toss it on the ground!" Tack ordered, a vein suddenly throbbing in his neck. His whole body had gone rigid.

Noah chuckled. "No chance. And for the record, I know why you want me to."

Tack flinched. For a second I thought he might actually rush Noah. I put a hand on his shoulder, could feel the tension coiled there. "What is it, Tack?"

Tack's head whipped to me, then back to Noah. His mouth opened and shut.

"I learned a few things out there, through a new friend of mine." Noah spoke casually, taunting my friend somehow, and enjoying it. But his relaxed demeanor felt contrived. Noah's gaze bored into Tack. I could see the hard line of his jaw. "Question is, how did you?"

Tack hesitated, seemed stuck on some terrible decision he couldn't make. He moved another step in front of me. "I found the rule book."

Noah popped off the wall, his relaxed pretense gone. "There really is one? Let's see it."

Tack eyed him like a mouse tracking a cat. "I think we'd all be more comfortable if you ditched the gun," he said slowly. "Right now. As a gesture of good faith."

My focus ping-ponged between them. "Will someone please tell me what's going on?"

Noah tilted his head at me. "Have you killed anyone yet, Min?"

"Of course not!" But the crashing elevator flashed through my mind. Had both Nolans gotten off the roof in time? "At least, I don't think so."

Noah clicked his tongue. "So you're down four lives with nothing to counterbalance. Not a good place to be."

Tack moved fully between us, sweat darkening the hair at his temples. "You need to leave. If you're not going to—"

Noah rolled his eyes. "Oh, God, *enough*. I'm wounded, Tack. Honestly."

He removed his pistol. For a brief second Noah pointed it at us, and Tack threw out his arms, shouting in fear. Noah snorted. "Sorry. Had to." He walked to a nearby station, found a drawer with a key dangling from it, dropped the weapon inside, and spun the lock. Then he shoved the key into his jeans and held up empty palms. "Better?"

Tack sniffed, wiped his nose with his wrist. Nodded. "Just as soon as you move away from there."

Noah took an exaggerated step back with a wry smile.

"I'm running out of patience with both of you," I warned.

Tack whirled to face me. "There's something you need to see." He strode to the back of the room, where bookcases filled with binders lined the rear wall. They detailed the history of Project

Nemesis—we'd spent hours pawing through them weeks ago, before the Guardian appeared.

Noah and I followed, keeping a steady distance between us. Tack was in the far corner. I'd skimmed that section before but had found nothing useful.

Tack pursed his lips. "I don't know how we missed this, but check it out."

He stepped forward and pushed with both hands. The bookcase slid backward soundlessly, rolling three feet before hinging open to reveal a narrow room beyond.

I blinked in surprise. "How did—"

"Relentless ingenuity." Tack looked pleased with himself. "I was messing with the computers when I first got here this afternoon, trying to figure out the doors. I accidentally killed the lights instead. Nearly crapped myself, too—it gets *dark* down here like you wouldn't believe. While I was struggling to turn the overheads back on, I noticed a glow. Eventually I found the right place to push."

"Gold star, Tack." I forgot everything else and stepped inside.

The walls were white cinder block, the carpet industrial gray. A counter ran along one side, loaded with computer equipment, with a rolling chair positioned before each monitor. Three rows of binder-stuffed bookshelves hung from the opposite wall. There was another blast door at the opposite end, leading God knows where.

The room couldn't fit more than six people at once. I wondered who'd been assigned to work in this claustrophobic nightmare—hidden away, even from their co-conspirators—and why.

I examined the binders on the closest shelf. These were slimmer than the ones outside in the control room, with red covers.

"Phase Two: Aggregation" was printed on each spine.

I shivered, even as my heart thudded in my chest. Answers. Finally.

Noah had gone straight for the blast door. Its keypad glowed red like a solid middle finger. "Where does this lead?" he asked.

Tack crossed his arms, deliberately ignoring him. Noah turned, spoke loudly, pointing with both index fingers. "Hey. Thumbtack. Door. Where go?"

I nearly growled with frustration. "Just answer him, Tack."

"I don't know," Tack admitted grudgingly. "I haven't figured out how to open that one yet. It's on a different system than the other doors. I've spent most of my time reading these Phase Two files." He looked at me, and his voice grew small. "I've learned a little. It's not good news."

A spider of worry traveled my spine. "Tell me."

Noah strode to the first computer and tapped a mouse, brushing my shoulder as he passed. The touch set my skin ablaze. I felt a flush in my cheeks. God, would it always be like that? A candle I couldn't snuff.

"Well, you already know the biggest news," Tack said. Then, rolling his eyes, he pivoted to include Noah as well. "You saw that a sequence—I mean a *person*—can fail to reset, and fall out of the Program. It's called an elimination. That must be what happened to Devin. But have either of you figured out why?"

"I have," Noah said quietly. Tack ignored him, watching me. Something in his eyes . . .

I shook my head. "I assume it's too many deaths."

"Yes and no." Tack's gaze flicked to Noah, who nodded. How did he know so much? Or was he bluffing?

"Five." Tack tapped a binder lying open on the counter. Then he ran a hand over his face. "Five deaths and you're bounced. But there's more." Tack split his fingers, peeking out at me. "You're not going to like it, Min."

"Why? What is it?" When he hesitated again, I punched him in the shoulder. "Talk to me, Thomas Russo."

Tack winced, rubbing his biceps. Then he flipped a few pages. "The elimination system runs on an algorithm. Five deaths in a row, and you're out, but you *can* break the cycle. You can pick lives back up."

Tack was right—I didn't like where this was going. "How?" I asked quietly. Noah moved closer to both of us, staring at the page.

Tack took a deep breath, leaning back against the counter before meeting my eye. "Kills. It's a running count. Kills versus deaths. If you've died five times, but killed three, you've only got two strikes against you."

"Neg-two," Noah said softly.

I went very still. "The Program requires you to kill to stay alive?"

Tack swallowed. Nodded. "If you've died a few times, yeah. You have to avoid going down five. Once you do, you're gone."

"Just like the Guardian said," Noah stated with finality, his voice like a thousand paper cuts. "He told us to find the proper population size and alignment. *Size*, Min. That means eliminating people. That's what Phase Two is all about. This has been staring you in the face for weeks—you just didn't want to see it."

Tack put a hand on my shoulder, spoke low and urgent. "You're down *four*, Min. Right? That means the next time you die, that's it." His eyes darted to Noah and back. Now I understood Tack's nervousness about the gun. Noah could eliminate me, right now, and there was nothing we could do to stop him.

I thought back to an hour earlier, outside a burning grocery store. Noah had me in his sights as I'd struggled from that muddy ditch. If he'd pulled the trigger, I'd have been erased. Gone for good.

A sudden coldness swept over me. So close. A knife's edge.

And I'm stuck there unless I kill someone.

The thought made my head jerk. No. Never that. I wasn't going to live that way.

My legs began to shake. I sat heavily in a chair.

"There's all kinds of crazy stuff in these binders," Tack continued, his voice lifting an octave as he read from a page. "'*The Program will manipulate environmental factors if the codes fail to meet certain timing benchmarks.*' Haven't figured out what that means, but I don't like it."

I was numb. Floating. Detached from my body. It was too horrible to be real.

"Don't you see, Min?" Noah sat down in the next chair and spun mine to face him. "Everything the Guardian said was true. We *have* to fight. We have to defeat our enemies before they get us, or we won't make it to the end."

I stared at nothing. Didn't know what to say.

Noah leaned forward, forcing me to look at him. "There's more. Not every lesson comes from a book."

I blinked.

"What do you mean?" Tack asked sharply.

Noah tapped the word *Aggregation* on a nearby binder's spine. "I don't need a classified document to explain what this means. I've *lived* it."

I shook my head. Squinted. Once. Twice. A living, breathing software glitch.

"I know what the word means," I said in a stilted voice, aware I was deliberately missing the point but unable to stop myself. "An aggregation is a group of different things, collected together."

Noah's eyes glittered. "*We* are those things, Min. That's what this is really about."

"No." I had a dreadful feeling I knew what was coming.

"This world . . ." Noah waved a hand absently, every word a dagger. "It isn't real. It's an expression of ones and zeros. Electricity flowing through circuits—a continuous flow of power." His face lit up with almost religious intensity. "Inside the Program, kills *transfer* that power. Killing makes you stronger, while dying weakens you until you run out completely. And *that's* when aggregation happens."

I shook my head. Glanced at Tack, who was staring at Noah, slack-faced, a creeping horror filling his eyes.

"Inside this system, we're nothing but competing digital sequences." Noah's tone was almost matter-of-fact. "It's Darwinian. Victorious sequences absorb the energy of defeated ones, which disappear. It's survival of the fittest. The sooner you accept that, the better off you'll be."

A hand rose to cover my mouth. I didn't want to believe, but knew it was true.

"The Guardian told us." Noah's face was growing red. He seemed annoyed by my obvious distress. "We have to whittle down our numbers until only the strongest remain. *That's* the point. *That's* our purpose."

Tack put his back to Noah, eyes troubled as he squatted down and whispered to me. "You haven't been feeling awesome lately. You said it yourself, and that was two resets ago. I think you're too close to the edge. You need . . . You've lost too much power."

"What about you?" I shot back, refusing to acknowledge what he was hinting at. "You've died the same number of times."

Tack's gaze dropped to the floor. "I've killed. Twice."

"What!? When?"

He rose and stepped away, his shoulders hunching around his neck. "I was scouting. Leighton and Tucker tried to corner me, but I got the drop on them. I never said anything because I didn't want you to worry about it. Or *scold* me, to be honest." I glared at him, and he gave a hopeless shrug. "I thought this was just a big game then."

My mind was on tilt, questions pouring out like pebbles. "But what happens when you don't reset? How long does Phase Two run? What happens when it's over?"

"No idea," Noah said. "But it doesn't matter. We don't have any other options."

I couldn't breathe. Needed space. I whirled and bolted, but I raced the wrong way and ran smack into the blast door.

My eyes filled with tears. I slammed a fist against the keypad as everything crashed in on me at once. Hit it again and again. I needed away from this hateful room and its terrible secrets.

Then I tumbled forward as the door swung open.

18

NOAH

Min was lying in the open doorway.

She didn't get up at first. The truth seemed to have overwhelmed her, but that was *good*. A necessary first step. If she stopped fighting the Program, we could work together again. Things could maybe even go back to the way they were.

"How in the world . . ." Tack hustled to the keypad, then stood there staring and scratching his head. "Huh. So this black square thingie under the digits must be a fingerprint reader. Which means the door opened specifically for you."

That got my attention. I strode to stand beside Tack. "It let her through? Why?"

Min was slowly getting to her feet. Her eyes flicked my way, and there was no warmth in their wintry depths.

No. Never how things were. A shot in the back had killed that possibility forever.

"You okay?" Tack asked her softly.

Emotions warred on Min's face as she stood. She still wasn't ready to accept what the Guardian demanded. I worried she might never get there. What then? I knew firsthand that she made a terrible enemy.

My gun was in the control room. Min was on the brink. One push, and she'd be gone.

I could take her power. Part of her would become me. The thought was horrifying, yet strangely alluring. Was *that* the way to save her?

PSYCHOPATH TALK.

I shivered all over. Awful. I'd never admit to the thought. Sometimes I scared myself.

"What do you think is back here?" Tack was saying.

Min was standing in a short, carpeted corridor leading to a pair of massive wooden doors. The narrow space had the feel of a bank lobby. "One way to find out," she muttered, squaring her shoulders. In the time I'd considered murdering her and consuming her life force, she'd pulled it together. I wanted to throw up.

I had no idea what we'd find in there, but this discovery had come at exactly the wrong time. I needed to press my case. Make Min see that we *had* to fight for our position inside the Program.

"OMG, look at that." Tack bounded to the doors and tapped a black starburst engraved into the wood—the symbol of the covert military unit assigned to Project Nemesis. "Is this where those bastards hid out?"

"Only the top people, I bet." Min's eyes were gleaming. I knew she was still hunting for an escape route—some way around the truth—and this place must've felt like a jackpot.

The doors were unlocked. In fact, they didn't even have one. Beyond was what could best be described as an office suite. The carpet switched over to a deeper, more luxurious gray cut. Tastefully bland landscape art adorned wood-paneled walls. We strolled quietly down the wide hallway, muted by the hushed corporate atmosphere.

Doors on both sides led to offices and meeting spaces. There was a communications center, a room filled with surveillance monitors, one that housed computer equipment, even a small theater. "You could run a world war down here," Tack said. He was right. This felt like one of those bunkers built for Congress or the president in case of nuclear attack. A fortress far below ground where hard-faced zealots could manipulate world events like vengeful gods.

At the far end of the corridor we reached a second set of identical wooden doors. "Let's see what's behind number two!" Tack quipped, pushing through.

The next section was like walking into a new building. Gone was the ultraserious business atmosphere, replaced by living space. The walls were muted blue, the floor hardwood. One side of the hall was lined with sleeping chambers, each with its own full bathroom. The other side had a kitchen, dining room, game room, and spacious lounge area with bookshelves and wide chairs.

Tack snorted. "Work. Play. So what's behind door number three?" He pointed to another wooden pair dead ahead.

"How big is this place?" I wondered aloud. Min didn't reply, hadn't said anything, in fact, since we'd entered the complex. Her expression was unreadable.

Tack forgot to ignore me. "I count twelve sleeping quarters. Not enough for an army, but they could keep the bigwigs comfortable if they were stuck down here overnight, planning more child murder. Remember, Project Nemesis operated covertly in the valley for *decades*. Nothing they pulled off surprises me anymore."

There was nothing for it but to keep going. We pushed through the third set of doors and stepped into a corridor of brilliant white. Walls. Tiles. Ceiling panels. Everything glowed harsh and fluorescent, like an expensive hospital. Steel doors lined both sides, but they were locked and wouldn't open. Straight ahead was a pair of glass doors like the ones leading into the control room, but the chamber beyond appeared much vaster. The starburst seal was emblazoned on both sides.

"End of the line?" Tack guessed.

Min arrowed forward, eyes tight, her lips a white line. Something about her focus made me uneasy. Suddenly, I didn't want to go any farther. What were we going to find?

Min pushed through the glass doors with Tack on her heels, leaving me no choice but to follow. We entered a low-ceilinged, laboratory-like chamber that seemed to stretch to infinity. Dimly lit. Cold enough to mist my breath. A counter ran along the walls, interspaced with giant tanks, tubes, computer monitors, and workstations. Bundles of wire and plastic piping disappeared through the floor and ceiling.

In the center of the chamber were rows of low pedestals, each topped by a wide metal tube roughly four feet wide and eight feet in length. For some reason, I thought of escape pods on a lame sci-fi show. The air tasted sterile and antiseptic, like a doctor's office. The chamber was deathly silent except for a periodic hiss, like an air-conditioning unit clicking on and off.

"What in the world?" Tack muttered, stepping deeper into the room.

Min stood in the doorway, staring at the pedestals. All color had drained from her face. Tack walked to a nearby monitor. Spying a keyboard, he tapped the space bar. The screen woke, revealing a stream of letters and numbers.

"Hey, look!" Tack pointed to the monitor. "There's a name here."

Goose bumps erupted up and down my arms. Though he hadn't been speaking to me, I joined him. `Jessica Cale` was blinking at the top of the screen. `Status: 0` was printed beside it.

"Zero?" Tack straightened. "What does that mean?"

I noticed Min was still standing by the doors. Still staring at the pedestals.

Tack stepped back and peered down the long counter, lips moving as he counted. "Sixteen monitors along this wall . . . times four walls. Sixty-four."

I stated the obvious. "One for each of us."

Tack scratched behind an ear, too intrigued to bother hating me. "You think these stations, what . . . track us? Like, we each have one individually? That's so . . . *creepy*. I wonder where mine is." He walked down the row, tapping keys, looking for a screen with his name on it.

I walked back over to Min. "Hey. You okay?"

She swallowed. Didn't speak.

"Guys?" Tack called, his voice tight. "This one's for Piper Lockwood, but there's no status number. It just says 'eliminated.'"

My stomach did a cartwheel. Piper didn't reset. I buried her in the forest.

Min shook herself, as if coming awake. Her eyes darted to me, and loathing filled them. "Because you *destroyed* her, right Noah? Obeying the Program. You stole her power for yourself like a vampire."

My mouth worked, but her fury swept away any defense I might offer. I felt a crushing sense of guilt that quickly morphed to anger. "What was I supposed to do? I didn't know Piper wouldn't reset at the time. Plus, *that's the whole point anyway.* There are only so many spots!"

"The lights," Min whispered, gazing up at the ceiling.

Emotions roiling, I glanced up. Dedicated LED lamps burned directly above every pedestal. Except . . . now that I looked closely, I noticed that a few had gone dark. Three pedestals were no longer bathed in stark white light.

Tack was still circling, looking for his own terminal. I watched Min as her breathing picked up. Her arms and legs began to shake. My heart broke just watching.

"Min, I—"

"Get away from me," she spat. Min seemed on the verge of fleeing the room, but instead she strode to the closest pedestal. I followed, feeling defeated. She'd never forgive me. She'd never accept what was required of us.

You shot her, jackass. When will you get that there's no coming back from that?

Min climbed the two steps built into the pedestal. I inched up beside her, being careful not to crowd. A square of glass allowed a view inside the tube, but it was fogged over. Min reached out a tentative hand, paused, then wiped the moisture away.

Inside the tube was a body swaddled head to foot in clingy white gauze, leaving only the face visible. A ventilator covered its mouth. Its other features were slack and ashen white.

I straightened, confused. Was this some kind of giant morgue? Why keep bodies on ice in a laboratory at the bottom of a well? But one look at Min, and I realized I'd missed something.

"What is it?"

She didn't answer. Min stared, wide-eyed, eyebrows climbing off her forehead.

Sneakers pounded across the floor tiles as Tack ran over to join us. With a grunt, I stuck my nose close to the glass window and examined the body. Then I reared back in surprise. "Oh my God!"

"What's going on?" Tack demanded.

I couldn't form a coherent sentence. "I don't . . . It's not possible . . . What—"

"Sarah," Min choked out. "Sarah Harden is inside this . . . thing."

Tack pressed his face to the glass, then recoiled as if slapped. "Jesus, you're right! What happened to her?" He spun and eyed the doors. "Who brought her down here? Who would even know how to hook this stuff up? How'd they get past the blast door? I was *sure* we were the only ones who knew this place existed."

I was shaking my head, dumbfounded. "But . . . no. Sarah was in town tonight. Like, only a few hours ago. I *spoke* to her, for Christ's sake."

Tack's eyes narrowed. Min's head swiveled to face me.

"You're sure?" Tack said. "And why were you with her, anyway?"

"We were trying to shoot each other, if it makes you feel better," I snapped. "Sarah and some others attacked me at the high school. She was fine! How could someone subdue her, then get her past us, down the shaft, and hooked into all of this crap so soon?"

Tack went pale. "The Guardian? Maybe he, like, *moved* her somehow. Kinda like a reset? Messing with the source code, or whatever."

Min put a hand to her forehead. "Don't you see?" she whispered.

I shook my head, baffled. Saw my confusion reflected in Tack's eyes. "See what, Min?"

She pointed a shaky finger toward the wall. "Did you find your terminal, Tack? Did you see your status?"

"No. But I didn't check them all."

Min swept a hand around to encompass the pedestals. Suddenly, the tubes atop each one looked a lot like coffins. "Maybe you can find your body instead."

I flinched. Then gaped at the orderly rows filling the laboratory. "No."

I leapt down, raced to the next pedestal, climbed up, and rubbed the glass. A body stared back at me. *Lars. Lars Jergen.* His face was barely recognizable without the signature beard, but it was him. I jerked away and ran to the next tube. Sam Oatman lay inside, unmoving.

But he's in the quarry!

I heard Tack gasp, realized he'd done the same thing in the

opposite direction. "Why is Derrick Morris inside this fucking machine?!" he yelled. We glanced at each other, then both looked to Min.

She seemed catatonic, barely able to respond. Min pointed to a pedestal with its light doused. "Check that one, please."

Tack and I met eyes again. The tube was directly between us and we arrived at the same time. I wiped the glass and peered inside. This body was sheet white, eyes fixed open and unblinking. No ventilator or tubes. I recognized the face and flinched as if burned.

"It's . . . it's Devin."

Tack began ripping at his hair. "He's *unplugged*. Because he didn't reset!"

Pieces abruptly slotted into place. Suddenly I understood. "Oh my God. These are our real bodies."

Tack shook his head testily. "We're in a simulation. We don't *have* bodies."

"But the simulation is a perfect re-creation of the old Fire Lake," I said. "They duplicated everything exactly how it was when the Program engaged. Which included the silo, and *this* room."

Tack's eyes rounded. "But why have this coffin party at all, even in the real world? The Guardian said we're all dead. He said they needed our brains for formatting, and that's why they gassed us in town square. If all that's true, why keep our . . . *corpses* in cold storage like this?"

I felt a jolt of hope. "Do you think maybe we're still alive? Like, our bodies are preserved in the real world, in these tubes, and we're just . . . dreaming?"

"But that doesn't fit what the Guardian said. Why would he lie? What would be the point of that?" Tack turned. "Min, what do you . . ."

He trailed off. Min had moved to a new pedestal, was staring down into the tube.

"Min?" I called.

She didn't look up. Tack and I exchanged another glance, then hurried over.

Min had a faraway expression as she gazed within. Tack and I mounted the steps and peered through the glass. She was looking at herself.

I gripped my face, index finger curling over my nose. My stomach churned, and I choked back hot bile. Tack's mouth was working, but no words came out. Then he reached out and tapped something on the side of the tube. A reading appeared on the glass.

Min Wilder. Status: -4.

The number was blinking in red.

She looked up, eyes glistening. "You guys are wrong, you know."

"Huh?" Two dunces at once.

Min sighed, running a finger along the metal cylinder. "These aren't our bodies. The Guardian was telling the truth. He just didn't tell it all."

My jaw clenched. I'd spoken with the Guardian that afternoon, a fact I'd still failed to mention. Yet I had no idea what Min was thinking. I felt a familiar tightening in my chest, something I thought I'd left behind in the real world. "What do you mean?"

"These aren't our bodies, Noah. At least, not the old ones."

"Then what are they?"

Min stroked the glass softly, gazing at her own still form.

"You're looking at our clones."

19

MIN

I couldn't stop staring at my face.

I shivered. Goose bumps covered me from head to foot. The frigid air in the laboratory helped numb my thoughts as I gazed down at myself, terrified those eyes might suddenly open. What would they see? What did *I* see?

The truth.

The final mystery of Project Nemesis was lying inside this metal coffin, wearing my DNA.

"Clones?" Tack eyed me with perfect confusion.

"Think about it." I buffed the glass to get a clearer view. My instincts were certain this time. I didn't need to read it from a manual. "We've spent so much time trying to figure out the purpose of the Program, but we forgot what happened before it."

I glanced up and met Noah's eye. "Black Suit."

He blanched. The old fears were never far from the surface.

"I never understood his role until now." I nodded down at my double. "Until her."

"Well, *I* still don't understand," Tack griped, crossing his arms. "Enlighten me, please."

"What's the biggest question we haven't answered?" I stepped back from the tube, as if gaining physical distance might provide me some clarity. "The one aspect of Nemesis that never made sense, even after the Guardian spoke to us at Town Hall."

Tack's brow furrowed. He looked to Noah, back, then shrugged.

"The murders." I began ticking off fingers, shocked by my sudden cool. The emotional part of my brain had apparently shut down and gone into hiding. "I get the years of planning, and the tests. Isolating our class. Our town. All that makes sense once you understand the threat we faced. They created a way to preserve a group of people digitally because nothing else would work. But it doesn't explain the beta patients. We still don't know why Noah and I were being murdered in the real world, before the end came."

Neither boy spoke, listening intently. The only sounds were the hiss of compressed air and the low hum of machinery.

I sighed. "I was killed five times before town square. So were Noah, and Sarah, and Ethan. Two different methods for two different pairs, but the results were the same. We were killed, then brought back somehow and placed in the woods around town. And we were always one hundred percent healthy upon our return."

Noah face went slack. Moving stiltedly, he retreated down the two steps, then shuffled a few aimless paces, leaning against a pedestal and rubbing his eyes. Then lurched away, no doubt remembering it contained the body of a classmate.

Tack glanced around the room. "So what, then? You guys were . . . cloned?"

I pulled my gaze from Noah. Rapped the tube with my knuckles, startling them both. "Nothing else makes sense. My physical body was repeatedly murdered, but I always came back whole. No scars, no repairs, not the slightest indication of the violence that had been done to me." My gut clenched. "And sometimes, the damage was . . . bad."

"Wait." Tack held up a hand, doubt filling his eyes. "You're saying that every time you were murdered, you came back as a different clone? Not the Min Wilder you were born, but as some . . . re-created version of her?"

I nodded.

"Not possible." Tack shook his head firmly. "I've known you your whole life, Min. We've been best friends since diapers. You're not a series of imposters I've never noticed, like some *Twilight Zone* episode."

"No, no." I wasn't explaining this well. "These clones, they were clearly still me. I mean, I think I'd notice otherwise, you know? They must've found some way to put *me* back into . . ." I glanced down at the girl in the tube. "Into me."

Tack's lips bunched in a disbelieving knot. He looked to Noah for support, but Noah was staring at nothing, having gone somewhere in his mind.

I surveyed the rows of silent pedestals. "This was part of Project Nemesis somehow. They must've been testing a cloning process on the four betas. From the looks of it, they were ready to try it with everyone, back in the real world, at least. I guess they ran out of time or something. I wonder if inserting us as Program codes was Plan B, or if the two experiments tied together somehow."

"How can you know any of this?" Tack glared around the room, angry for some reason but trying to understand. "Maybe these are our regular bodies, frozen in carbonite. Or we could actually be alive, in the real bunker, but hardwired to some bitchin' VR. We could be living *The Matrix* right now."

"It's possible," I said, "but I don't think so. This is what they were testing, Tack. All those times Noah and I were hunted on our birthdays. How else could they kill us and bring us back to life?"

Noah swallowed and wiped his mouth. I noticed he was sweating despite the cold. I couldn't shake a feeling that this discovery had stolen something from him.

"I . . . I think she's right," Noah said haltingly. "I was stabbed, crushed, even blown apart. Some of those injuries . . . they couldn't be fixed. They must've . . . *reintroduced* me somehow. Into something new." He looked down, ran both hands over his chest. "God, how many bodies have I worn? How many different versions of me existed?"

"Stop feeling yourself up, you dope." Tack hopped down and punched Noah in the shoulder. "*This* isn't you, either. You don't have a body at *all* right now, remember?"

Noah winced. "Right." Then he scratched his chin, gazing around the lab. "The next me is somewhere in this room, isn't it?"

"More like the last one," Tack muttered, but then he sliced

202

both hands through the air. "If Min's right, this is pretty intense trivia, no doubt, but it doesn't actually *help* us. That world is gone. Inside the Program, we have to deal with the Guardian and his horror-show clown-house version of Murder Lake."

I shuddered. It was true. Whatever came before didn't really matter. We lived here now, and the Guardian had made clear that not everyone would survive. Three dark pedestals were proof of that.

Yet the enormity of it was staggering. If I was right, my body had been killed *six* times already, my consciousness transferred to a new host after each incident. But what about my soul? How much of *me* was lost when they swapped one Min for another?

I frowned at the darkened tubes. "The Guardian wants a specific number to complete this phase for some reason. But why? And come to think of it, why start something this important with the wrong number of codes to begin with? They spent decades and trillions planning this. They could've inserted the proper group size into the system from the start, then had us sitting around eating doughnuts."

Noah stuck his hands in his pockets. "Maybe they couldn't decide," he said softly. "So they're making us do it."

Tack shook his head in disgust. "A digital death match? You've played too many Warcross missions, brah."

But I shushed him with a look. What Noah was suggesting was awful, but it fit what we'd learned about Project Nemesis.

"This room doesn't change anything," Tack argued, unable to let it go. "We still don't know their plan. The Program is eliminating players, but we don't know why. Until we do, this is all just guessing."

"We agree there." Noah had regained some of his composure. He placed a hand on the tube behind him. "Either this contains a body hauled from town square, or a clone, or whatever. But inside the Program, if whoever's in here dies too many times, that's it." He pointed at the ceiling. "That light goes out and it's game over."

I didn't respond. I couldn't face it before, and wasn't any more ready now.

"Don't you see, Min?" Noah took a step toward me. Reached out a tentative hand, then let it drop. "We *have* to fight. We have to survive this phase. If the Program is whittling down to something, that means there might be a chance at a future."

A future, but only for those who survive. How would I live with myself? And what was this "we" talk? Was Noah saying we should work together? Could I even consider it, after what he'd done? What he was *still* doing, with those other wackos in the ski resort?

"I wanna see Thomas Russo," Tack blurted to no one. He trotted over to the next pedestal, climbed up, and rubbed the glass. His throat worked as he peered inside the tube for a quiet moment. "Hey, Leighton," he whispered, then retreated.

"Tack, don't." Having stared at my own face, I couldn't recommend the experience. "We should go back to the records room. There's nothing for us in this . . . crypt."

"In a minute." Tack sped between the pedestals. I didn't know what drove him, but it was pointless to argue. I walked over to the door to wait.

Noah glanced at me, then away. A moment later he joined me.

"It's freezing in here," he said. Seconds later a small smile stole over his lips. "You think there's food in that kitchen? I bet high-ranking conspiracy guys eat steak every night."

An olive branch statement. I gave Noah a hard look, saw color rise in his cheeks.

I decided to accept it. *For now.*

"I might sleep in a clean bed tonight," I said. "Imagine that."

His smile widened. Some of the tension eased from his shoulders. "I think I saw a pool table on our way in."

I snorted before I could help myself. Then I took a deep breath and regarded him seriously. "I don't know what's going on, Noah. I don't understand why Project Nemesis was murdering us, or raising clones, or how any of it matters inside the Program. I could be wrong about all of it. But I'm not stopping until I figure it out. I'm going to learn what the Program intends for us—*all* of us—before I commit to anything. Do you understand?"

Several beats passed as he stared at the floor, only Tack's sneakers breaking the silence. Then he nodded. "Okay. Before anything else, we make it our goal to find out what the Program has planned." Noah's head rose, his voice becoming low and urgent. "And I think I know a way. I haven't told you everything yet. I was in town square this afternoon, and managed to get ins—"

I held up a hand, cutting him off. Something behind Noah had caught my attention.

A keypad was affixed to the wall beside the doors. On its face, a red light was blinking.

"Tack?"

No response. I swiveled, spotted him across the room. He was staring into a tube, his chest rising and falling rapidly.

"Noah," Tack called in an overloud voice. "If you're interested . . ."

"Not even slightly," Noah replied, attempting to hide his revulsion. He turned back to me.

I pointed to the red light. "That wasn't on a second ago, and now it's flashing. What is it?"

Noah shrugged. "How should I know? You guys are the ones who've been here for weeks, right?"

My face reddened. "Yeah, about that. Tack actually only got in this afternoon. Tonight is the first time I've been in the silo since . . . since the last time we were all here."

Since you shot me.

Noah's eyes widened. "Seriously?"

I shrugged defensively. "We thought *you'd* be here. Guess we're all a little paranoid."

But Noah had gone still. "I did come by once, a while ago, just to see. I found footprints in the parking lot—fresh, deep ones, in a snowfall from the night before. I assumed it was you and Tack, so I took off."

His words jolted me. "Someone else was here? Who?"

Noah shook his head. "Like I said, I thought it was you."

My eyes darted back to the red light, butterflies exploding in my stomach. I cupped my hands to my mouth. "Tack, I need you!"

Tack held up a hand, but didn't look over. Now on the last row, his movements were growing frantic. What if he wasn't in one of the tubes? What would *that* mean? But then Tack jerked to a halt on the second-to-last pedestal. He leaned in close, then lurched backward and jumped down, striding quickly across the chamber with a hand over his mouth. *Told you.*

"Know anything about this?" I asked, pointing to the keypad.

Tack nodded, his face still green-tinged. "I turned off the door locks so you could get in, but the motion sensors are still on."

My mouth went dry. "Did they reset after we came in?"

"I think so, why?" Then his eyes widened.

Noah grabbed Tack by the arm. "Are there cameras inside the silo?"

"All over the place." Tack shook him off with a scowl. "There's a monitor in the control room that cycles through the feeds, but I think we passed surveillance headquarters just now."

I shoved Tack toward the exit with both hands. "Go go go!"

We raced out of the lab, down the creepy white hallway, and through the empty living quarters. In the office section, Tack ran toward an open door. "Here!"

The room was narrow and dim, with four rolling chairs facing an array of monitors along the wall. The screens were divided into quarters, each showing a different view of the silo. Built-in desks below the monitors held hard drives and other equipment. On one sat a sleek black box with a flashing yellow button.

"What is that?" I asked in a shrill voice, thrown by one blinking light too many.

Tack squinted at the box, then groaned, his face going pale. "Shit! There's one of these in the control room. It monitors the miner's cage. Someone up top is calling for a ride." Tack's hand fired out and flipped a metal switch on the box. "Ha! I killed the power. The cage shouldn't go up now. But somebody's *inside* the silo, guys."

My heart skipped a beat. "But without the cage they can't get down here, right?"

Tack shook his head, jaw tight as he sucked in his lips. "There's a service ladder bolted alongside the track. I wouldn't want to climb down that way, but it's there."

"Let's see who it is," Noah said in a flat voice. Oddly, he seemed calmer than before. Stepping close to the monitors, he began inspecting the feeds.

He's more comfortable with action. Or is it the promise of violence?

"There." Noah pointed to the center screen. Movement in the bottom left quadrant. As I watched, skin tingling, a half dozen figures gathered within the frame.

One stepped into a halo of light. I'd know that sneer any-where.

Ethan Fletcher was standing on the highest catwalk, staring down into the abyss.

20

NOAH

"Not good."

Tack backed a step from the monitor, seemed on the point of bolting. But to where? They were already in the missile shaft above us. We were trapped.

"How?" I croaked, nervously squeezing my ear. "How'd they find this place?" I thought back to those footprints in the snow weeks ago, outside in the gravel lot. The ones I'd learned weren't from Min or Tack.

Tack shook his head in short, rapid jerks. "Doesn't matter how. They're here."

"Okay." Min's forehead scrunched, her fingers flexing as if she could squeeze an answer from her palms. "We have to get out of here. But we can't go up, and they *can* come down. So . . . we need another way out."

"You know one?" My eyes leapt to Tack, suddenly hopeful.

He'd been down here longer than us, reading the hidden binders. Maybe he'd discovered a bolt-hole.

But he just shrugged helplessly. "Don't look at me. And that's our plan? We run?"

"We don't have a choice." Min's hands curled into fists, her mouth a grim line as she watched Ethan and his team huddle on the catwalk. They'd given up on the cage, but Ethan was pointing at the ladder. "We're outnumbered two to one, and I'm sure they're armed. But there *has* to be a back door, right? Everyone builds a second exit. The people running Project Nemesis wouldn't have risked getting trapped from above."

Like we are now. I didn't say it. Her logic was sinking in.

"The supplies," I blurted, my pulse spiking as an idea took hold. "There are literally thousands of crates in the alcoves above our heads. All that material couldn't have been shipped through town. I don't care how good these Nemesis guys were, nobody could've moved that much freight through Fire Lake without people noticing."

Tack began nodding, one foot tapping the carpet like mad. "You're right. And don't forget about building this wonder bunker in the first place." He blinked, then his eyes widened. "Jesus, they must've bottled up the valley on purpose, with the only bridge on one side, and a secret route they controlled at the other end. It's the only answer that makes sense!"

A flicker onscreen caught my eye. I swallowed, pointed. Ethan and Toby had begun to climb down the ladder, followed a few seconds later by the Nolan twins and Derrick Morris. Sarah remained on the catwalk with her arms crossed.

"The gang's all here." Tack's hand shot to the desk, snagging a mouse. He fiddled with the commands and managed to zoom in. All five boys had rifles strapped to their backs.

I swallowed a string of curses. *My* rifle was stashed outside in the bushes, where Min had crawled from the ditch. All I had down here was my Beretta, and it was locked inside a drawer in the control room.

"Five descending, one topside." Min cleared her throat, nervously pawing her hair behind her ears. "They're all heavily armed, and we only have Noah's pistol. We've got twenty minutes, tops."

Tack shot to his feet. "I bet there are guns up there somewhere. There could be a freaking tank for all we know. We could race up in the lift, grab some firepower, and—"

"From where?" Min interrupted. "We don't know how the alcoves are organized. Ethan and his team might be closer to weapons than we are. And what if the ammunition is stored separately, or the guns are disassembled?"

Tack opened his mouth to argue, but Min rolled right over him. "Too many variables, plus we'd still be outnumbered. No. We have to escape, not start a firefight."

"She's right." I turned and jogged from the room, through the heavy wooden doors, not stopping until I passed through the bookcase and reached the control room. I unlocked the drawer and removed my pistol. Took a calming breath. Weapon in hand, I felt more in control. Then I hustled back to the security room.

They cut off whispering as I reentered. I could feel them both watching, and my cheeks burned. Did they really think so little of me?

Why wouldn't they?

Then Tack grabbed his forehead, blue eyes rounding in panic. "Oh fuck, Min, you're already down four lives." His voice rose to a squeak. "You *can't* take another reset."

My breath caught. In a blink, everything changed.

How had I forgotten? I'd been annoyed Ethan and those jerks were about to take control of the silo, but not devastated or anything. I'd knock out as many of them as I could, then gather my team and take it back. I was better at fighting than they were. I could have anything I wanted.

But Min.

She *couldn't* die again. She wouldn't come back.

The thought drove an icy spike into my chest. I shied from how it made me feel, like a dangerous animal loose in my brain. I thought I'd put all that stuff away. Min was an enemy, not a friend, and certainly not anything more. *I'd named her my nemesis*, for God's sake.

Min waved as if to swat away the concern, but I saw how her fingers trembled. "We just need to find a way out. And lock down this complex. And the Phase Two records room."

"I'll put everything back how it was," Tack said, already hustling out into the hallway. "But if I found it," he called back, "they will too. Eventually."

I glanced at the screen. Ethan and the others had stopped at the first level of alcoves and were poking around, jabbering excitedly to one another. My stomach curdled in knots. They'd control everything for the time being, and there was nothing I could do to stop it.

A dark thought formed in my head. Radical. But necessary?

"We should look for the back door," Min said, breaking my train of thought. She was watching me intently, eyes sparkling with hidden depths. What was it about a crisis that made her even more beautiful?

"Okay," I said with false enthusiasm. "If you were a secret bolt-hole, where would you be?"

Surprisingly, Min had an answer. "The computer chamber. It's the heart of this place."

"Our home," I said, then caught Min's flinch in the corner of my eye. But it was true. We were lines of code living inside the MegaCom, which was hidden beyond the control room by a curtain of solid steel. Everything else was an elaborate lie. *It's so hard to keep anything straight.*

Tack came racing back in. "I straightened the shelves and killed all the lights on the control level. The shaft lights won't shut off, though, which sucks. I'd have loved to make those bastards climb down in the dark. All that's left is to push the bookcase back into place and they won't have a clue what's back here. But we have to decide how to play this. Are we going out, or locking in?"

"Min thinks the way out is through the MegaCom room," I said. "Care to weigh in?"

Tack grimaced. "It's possible, I guess, but in case you didn't notice, there's an impenetrable metal wall standing in the way. How are we supposed to get inside?"

"What about the other doors back here?" I asked, moving out into the hall. A quick check of the office suite came up empty.

Tack and I ran back through the living quarters, but struck out there as well. "The doors in the lab wing were locked. See any keys in the control room?"

Tack shook his head. "I rifled all the workstations when I first got inside. There was nothing. Come on, we're running out of time." We sprinted back to join Min, who was tracking Ethan's progress.

"Any luck?" she asked. But the answer was plain on my face.

"They're coming straight down now, no more stops." Min looked at me, her expression unreadable. "We have to make decisions."

"I don't think we can hide," Tack said, anxiously cracking his knuckles. "Ethan has to suspect we're here—it's the only reason he'd bring a platoon. But you can't risk a fight."

I went cold all over, my insides quivering as I tried to think.

"It's okay," Min said, swallowing as she dry-washed her hands. "I'll surrender. They can lock me back up until you two break me out."

Tack shook his head adamantly, seemed horrified by the idea. "What if they just come in blasting? Ethan's never been a thoughtful type. Plus, if they find the records room—which they *will*—they'll learn the scoring system. And if they find the lab, they'll know your *exact* status!" His voice had risen to a shout. Tack was breathing hard, beads of sweat dotting above his lips. "Then Ethan will know he can put you out of the game for good, *and don't think he won't do it*. He could shoot you in a cell and we'd have no way to stop him. You couldn't even suicide your way free."

I glanced away. Tack was right. Min was in real trouble.

Min. Out of the Program.

Was that something I wanted? Was that something I could handle?

No.

I ejected the magazine from my pistol, checked the ammunition, then slapped it back into place with a reassuring click. Then I racked the slide and thumbed off the safety. I could deal with this. I was a match for anyone.

"I'll wait for them at the bottom of the shaft." My voice was as flat as the prairie. "They might suspect you guys are here, but they don't know about me. With a bit of luck, I might take out all five before they realize what's happening."

"Bad plan," Tack snapped. "They'll get you and me, then finish Min off out of anger."

I didn't miss that Tack had inserted himself into the fight. He was right that the odds were stacked against an ambush, but he also didn't understand. They had no idea what I could do these days. I could practically see in the dark.

"Let me try." I met Min's gaze dead-on. "I've got this. I can keep you safe."

Beside me, Tack tensed. Then his eyes widened slightly, a hand rising to cover his mouth. He nodded to himself. I couldn't tell what he was thinking, but he seemed to have come to some decision.

"Fine," Tack said. "We try to jump those guys in the shaft."

I nodded eagerly. I could do this. I was stronger than they could imagine. Tack could tag along if he wanted, but I didn't need him. But then he kept talking, and his plan made zero sense.

"But the gun stays with Min," Tack insisted, the line of his jaw firming as he spoke. "She *has* to have a way to defend herself. That's nonnegotiable. We'll just have to disarm a couple of them, or find weapons in the alcoves somewhere."

I blinked. Five on two was bad enough. But unarmed? We'd get slaughtered.

Min was about to protest, but Tack would not be swayed. "If we fail, maybe they'll think you're not down here. You could hide, then sneak past them later." He crossed his arms, setting his feet like two boulders. "*We* get popped and it's a bummer. *You* get hit and . . . I don't even want to think about it. This is how it has to be. It's the only way I'll agree."

I opened my mouth, then closed it. Looked at Min. Her chin trembled, gray eyes wide as she chewed her bottom lip. In that moment my heart melted. I realized I wanted her to have the gun, too.

I shoved my Beretta into her hands. "Careful—a round is chambered."

Min seemed on the verge of handing it back, but Tack reached out and stopped her. He took a deep, relieved breath, wrapping Min's fingers around the gun so it hung loosely in the air between them. "Remember how to use this?" he asked softly.

Min nodded, lines digging across her forehead. I could tell she was still conflicted.

Tack lifted the gun so that she held it with both hands. "Look for me at the meeting place when it's over."

Min's face crumpled. "Tack, I don't want you to get shot again. We can lock ourselves in here. They won't be able to reach us."

He gave a wan smile, sliding his hands around hers. "Too risky. This is the only way."

In a flash, I understood. But it was too late.

Tack squeezed Min's trigger finger. A thunderous bang echoed in the room.

Tack collapsed, eyes already glazing. Min screamed and dropped the gun. He hit the floor and didn't move. Then, mercifully, his body faded from sight.

"Clever son of a bitch," I whispered, pulling on my neck. Min's gaze slashed up to impale me, horrified. Shock had dulled her wits.

"You're safe now," I explained. "Tack gave a life to pull you from the brink."

Understanding dawned in her eyes, followed by anger. "He didn't have to—"

"He did," I said curtly, growing heated myself. "Wake up and take the gift. Tack just did a very brave thing. Now, no matter what, you'll live to fight another day. And he'll be out there waiting for us."

Min wiped tears from her face, eyes drilling me. "Us?"

I flinched. Looked away.

Was that what I wanted? Had everything changed so quickly?

Red lights flashed inside the room. Someone had reached the bottom level.

I scooped up the gun and shoved it back into her hands. Suddenly, I felt a thousand feet tall. If Tack could play hero, then so could I. I wouldn't hide. I'd go out and meet them. Beat them. "Lock the blast door, Min. We can't risk Ethan and Sarah finding what's back here, which means one of us should stay just in case. I'll take care of this."

I fired out of the room without looking back.

A shout at my back, followed by a string of curses. I ignored them, headed for the doors. Then a bullet whizzed by my ear and thunked into the wood, stopping me short. I glanced back over my shoulder. Min was standing in the hall, Beretta in hand, her face tied up in knots.

We locked eyes. Her gaze smoldered, cheeks still wet with tears. I was reasonably sure she'd missed me on purpose, but not 100 percent.

"I don't like being told what to do. Or getting left behind twice."

I smiled, then turned and pushed out of the suite.

Her footsteps followed as I stepped through the blast door. I grabbed the thick metal portal and swung it. For a moment Min was silhouetted in a nimbus of soft light, then the door slammed shut with a heavy clank. I pressed buttons at random until a red warning light appeared on the keypad. Then I heard the heavy locking wheel spin and knew Min had thrown the deadbolt on the other side. She was safely sealed away.

Quickly now.

I stepped out into the control room and shoved the bookcase back into place. Tack had killed the lights, but I could see by the faint glow of electronics. Satisfied the lab complex was secret once more, I trotted to the entrance and peered out. Light footfalls sounded in the darkened corridor—an attempt at stealth, but I heard. Then someone stumbled, hissing a muffled curse, and I had a target.

I pulled a hunting knife from beneath my sleeve. Almost chuckled at Tack's naiveté. Slipping into the black, I felt so alive,

I was bursting with it. I almost pitied whoever was in this darkness with me.

Ahead was a deeper shadow creeping closer along the wall.

My lips formed a snarl.

I lunged forward, arm and knife as one, and reveled in a scream of pain.

PART THREE

ANNIHILATION

21

MIN

The scalpel dug into loathsome gray paint, gouging a new vertical line.

Then I turned the blade horizontal and bisected the grouping. Fifty-five marks. One for each day I'd been trapped.

I placed the scalpel on my bedside desk and sat heavily. The room I called home was a small square, modestly appointed, with blue carpeting and a simple bathroom attached. It stank of dust and disuse, even after the two months I'd been living there. The only light was a halogen bolted to the ceiling, which cast a glare so harsh, I usually kept it off, relying on the illumination leaking in from the hallway.

I drummed my knees. Then, with a heavy sigh, I stood, straightening the charcoal-gray jumpsuit I was wearing. I frowned down at the black starburst symbol stitched above my heart. There were a dozen more uniforms like this one in the room's tiny closet. I'd been wearing them for weeks despite my revulsion for Project Nemesis. I might hate the manipulative bastards who'd repurposed this silo, but I really wasn't into doing laundry.

"No point skipping work," I muttered to my shoes.

Stepping out into the hallway, I strode past the kitchen, lounge, and game room, heading for the office suite. I'd already rehydrated and eaten a meal for this block of hours—day and night become hazy concepts when you never see the sun—and I was getting so good at pool it wasn't fun anymore. So I shouldered through the middle set of wooden doors.

The suite's main conference room contained a long wooden table surrounded by cushy leather chairs. A closed laptop at the far end was the only thing on its surface. I spent most of my time in this room, tooling around on the silo's closed network, researching Project Nemesis and monitoring the rest of the silo. Or just plain killing time. I was stuck in the lab complex with no way out, and no one for company.

Fifty-four days ago, Tack had tricked me into killing him. Then Noah stormed out to fight the world. I hadn't heard from either of them since.

I slumped into the chair before the laptop, filling a crease my body had shaped in the leather. Permanent Silo Resident Min Wilder, reporting for duty. I woke the computer and opened a program that displayed surveillance feeds. The lab complex I occupied had been built to serve as the silo's nerve center, even beyond the main control room. A dozen people could live and work back here in relative comfort. All major systems were fully automated, requiring no input from anyone.

I had food for literally *years*—stacks of MREs and dehydrated meals, some that weren't even terrible. With the blast door sealed and its physical locking pin engaged, this was probably the safest place in the entire valley. The perfect place to hide. And also die of boredom, but beggars, choosers, and all that.

So that's what I'd been doing. Because there was no way out except through the control room, and that route was blocked by assholes.

At first, they didn't even know I was there. How could they? They hadn't discovered the hidden file room behind the bookcase. I'd felt a flutter in my stomach every time someone approached it, but they'd always moved on.

There were cameras everywhere inside the main silo, but none in the lab complex. I could see them, but they couldn't see me. So I lay low, watching everything. After a week, I'd hoped they'd think I was long gone. That I'd been shot and killed in the firefight, or had taken my own life to escape.

A reasonable assumption. After all, I'd done it before.

I shivered. Hugged my arms. Rubbed them with my palms. My eyes strayed to a walnut cabinet against the far wall. I pictured the Beretta 9 mm resting inside it.

A reasonable assumption, unless you've done it before.

I shuddered more deeply this time, leaning back in the chair as I tried to control my breathing. My mind decided to play the torturer, looping memories of a cold muzzle pressed against my temple. Me pulling the trigger. Hot lead smashing into my skull.

I don't think anyone could do it twice. I knew *I* couldn't. I'd sit in this conference room for a goddamn year before taking that route again. Besides, another death would put me back on the razor's edge. That seemed like a waste of Tack's gift.

So I'd decided to settle in and wait. Bide my time. Eventually they'd slack, and I'd sneak past them and rejoin Tack and Noah. And perhaps I'd have done just that, if it hadn't been for Sarah.

Fucking Sarah.

From the moment she arrived, the girl spent every single day in the control room—which I'd learned was properly called the command center—reading Nemesis binders. Patiently. Implacably. Earbuds in as Ethan and others stormed this way and that, arguing about supplies. I watched it all.

The laptop in front of me connected to the silo mainframe, accessing cameras on every level. I'd observed—equal parts angry, bored, and annoyed—as Derrick and the Nolan twins went through the storage alcoves, recording what they found. I'd watched as Ethan came and went, never staying long, clearly uncomfortable being so far underground. I'd watched as Sarah worked her way through row after row of project files, learning the secrets Tack, Noah, and I had discovered on our first visit. I'd seen the exact moment she figured out I was still there.

I'd been watching idly, bored to tears. Sarah was sitting at a workstation, leafing through yet another black binder, persistence endless, stamina impressive. Then, abruptly, she'd stiffened, rereading a section as she traced it with a finger, a small smile stealing over her lips. When finished, she'd looked directly into a nearby camera and waved, mouthing hello and my name.

She must've found some reference to the lab complex, and then guessed I was still inside it. I'd felt a twinge of panic. Did the binders include another way back here? But the worry had proven unfounded—Sarah didn't find the hidden records room that day.

She would, eventually. Sarah was smart, and seemed determined to learn everything she could about the Program. Once she understood all the rules, she'd be a formidable enemy. I had to get out of there, but I couldn't come up with a way to do it.

I wouldn't risk my life unnecessarily. I had a buffer of one because of Tack's noble and stupid sacrifice, but that was still too close for comfort. What if people were still lurking outside the reset zones? Take me out just one more time after resetting, and that'd be it. Game over for Melinda J. Wilder. For keeps this time.

So I waited. Watched. Learned all I could. Sarah wasn't the only one who could make good use of her time.

Although, that was how she found me.

I'd been manipulating the surveillance program, keeping an eye out, when a chat box appeared in the bottom corner of my laptop screen. Sarah. She'd somehow spotted me inside the system. I shut down quickly and stayed offline for three excruciating days, but the damage was done.

Every day afterward, Sarah located me whenever I went online. At first I tried to ignore her, but a text box would pop up constantly, always with a friendly hello. And I found that I simply couldn't stay off the grid—that computer was my only link outside the complex walls. I needed it to stay sane. Eventually, I broke down and wrote her back, telling her to fuck off, but she just sent back a winky face.

In the days that followed, we chatted from time to time,

sometimes even through live video. Sarah's doing—she'd figured out how to make the cameras and microphones on our computers work. Resourceful as always.

"I had a hunch you were still here," she'd said the first time.

I'd swallowed. Debated closing my computer. But honestly, it had been so long since I'd seen another person—spoken to *anyone*—that even Sarah had been welcome company.

"Found a private spa," I'd replied, aiming for flippant. "The food is pedestrian, but the peace and quiet is to die for."

Sarah chuckled. "Ethan's sworn at least once a day that you took the coward's way out again, but I never believed him. Now he wants to dynamite a wall he's certain you're hiding behind. Can you believe him? *Explosives.* At the bottom of a hole in the ground, with thousands of tons of concrete hanging over our heads. I put an end to that idea."

I didn't respond. Was grateful someone was showing common sense, though I'd never thank her for it. The idea of blowing up anything near the MegaCom was insane.

"You can come out, you know." Sarah's steely blue eyes impaled me through the pixels. "I've explained to the others that it's pointless to shoot you. My old offer stands, whatever Ethan says. We could work together. You're a better ally than an enemy—you've proven that much."

I had to admit, I was tempted. Sarah was a lot of things, but typically not a liar. Then I remembered her threats in the sheriff's cell just before I pulled the trigger. All the nasty things she'd done to me in school. *We're all in this together.*

Sarah's heart was as black as ice. Plus, I doubted she could control Ethan in this. He had a grudge and wanted me eliminated. Given the chance, he wouldn't pass that up.

Fake smile. "Sorry, I'm having the time of my life in here. There's a margarita machine. Plus, so much to study," I finished significantly.

Sarah regarded me for a moment. "Your food will run out, Min. It's already happening up here. Ever since Noah torched the grocery store, well . . ." She shook her head, perfect lips curling with distaste. "Things have gotten worse."

"What do you mean?" As neutrally as possible. I hungered for news from outside. I could learn anything I wanted about the silo with the touch of a finger, but the rest of the valley was a black hole. I knew nothing about my friends.

Sarah's eyes glittered. She understood the power she had over me.

"Come out, Min." She glanced over her shoulder, then leaned in closer to the camera. "Or let me in with you. Unarmed. I'll tell you everything you want to know, and we can avoid this town of douchebags together."

My heart began to pound. What was she saying? Could I do that? Why would she want inside here? We were almost the same size—I doubted either of us could overpower the other enough to make physical threats a reality. Plus, I had a gun. I could hold her hostage.

Then a thought stopped me short. Was there something *she* needed?

The lab. The clones. Sarah didn't know what was back here.

She's probably as hungry for information as I am.

Sarah hadn't found the hidden records room yet. The location of this complex didn't appear in the online files. I knew—I'd searched the system repeatedly.

I studied Sarah's posture. Her casual manner. The nonchalance was feigned, I realized. This whole conversation had been carefully scripted. Sarah's fingers quivered slightly. She kept touching her nose. Now that I was paying attention, her whole frame reeked of caged eagerness.

Sarah didn't know where I was or what I was hiding, and it was *killing* her.

She's not the only one holding cards.

"No thank you," I said. "I value my privacy."

Her smile faded. The line of her jaw appeared. "Then I'll let you get back to it."

The link winked out. I tapped a security feed, watched her slam a fist on the desk. Then she smoothed her skirt, ran a hand through her strawberry-blond hair. A moment later Sarah resumed reading as if our exchange had never happened.

Cool. Composed. Clinical.

Sarah Harden to a T.

Three more days passed. Sarah didn't ping me, and I refused to consider contacting her first. I ate, slept, played pool, took showers. Watched the feeds. I avoided the lab area like always—I hadn't gone in there since the first week, and even then only to try locked doors. A key ring in the operations room had accessed a collection of smaller labs, examination kiosks, closets, and offices, but they didn't contain anything useful, the lab complex's final mysteries proving to be yawners.

Except for the last door on the left, the one closest to the glass doors into the clone room itself. *That* door had a keypad entry and refused to open, no matter what I tried. I wondered constantly what was behind it—I'd still never figured out how I opened the outer blast door in the first place—though part of me didn't want to know. I'd come across enough horrors already.

Eventually, I started thinking more and more about trying to escape. I knew Sarah would trip the bookcase eventually, and then things might get ugly. Armed with the info in those hidden files—the ones detailing the Program's rules—she'd be a nightmare to deal with. But there was simply no way out.

If I took the "dirt nap" route, this room would be permanently sealed. I was locked inside what amounted to a military-grade bank vault. No one could get in. The keypad on the blast door couldn't remove the six-inch steel pin I'd physically placed in the locking mechanism like a deadbolt, so it was essentially useless. That door wasn't coming open unless I opened it. I could deny the clone chamber to everyone simply by resetting.

But was that what I wanted? What if I needed back in here for some reason? I could doom the Program's whole mission, whatever it ended up being.

I was mulling over options for a diversion—set off the smoke alarms?—when I noticed movement on the feed. Sarah had bounced from her seat, the gleam of victory in her eyes. She arrowed straight for the shelving that hid the records room.

My heart sank into my shoes. She'd finally found the right page.

Sarah pushed on the bookcase and it hinged open. Her fingers came together to cover her mouth, like a schoolgirl pleased by a magic trick. Then she disappeared inside, where the cameras didn't follow. I debated racing down the corridor to the blast door, but there was no point. It wouldn't open, and I couldn't see through it.

Sarah didn't reemerge for eighteen hours. I counted.

I was jolted from a light doze in the security hub—the dark, narrow room where we'd first spotted Ethan's gang on the catwalk. The floor was vibrating slightly. Alarmed, I pulled up the security feeds, watched Sarah exit the hidden room and walk through the command center. She stopped on the lowest tier, gazing through the glass of the room's middle panel as the blast curtain rolled back, revealing the MegaCom chamber beyond.

Sarah's face was unreadable. What was she thinking, staring at the machine that housed our universe? Did it unnerve her? Make her feel small? Knowing Sarah, probably not. She simply watched, rubbing her chin, then turned and disappeared back behind the bookcase.

I strained to see into the computer room, but got no indication of whether my theory was correct—that another way out of the silo was hidden in there. I couldn't see much of anything through the security feeds, and the MegaCom chamber was the only other area without interior cameras. If Sarah had solved that particular riddle, she gave no sign.

Minutes later, her face popped up on a screen inside the hub. She was using a webcam in the records room. "Did you know the silo mainframe can manipulate the Program itself?" she said excitedly. "No wonder this was hidden."

I'd been examining silo schematics, looking for a way into the computer room from the lab complex. With the blast curtain deactivated, perhaps a new path had opened. *If there's a second exit at all.* Big, huge, monumental *if.* But I was growing certain there must be. A structure like this had to have a back door. Nothing else made sense.

I debated minimizing her, but Sarah's statement was too incredible to ignore.

"What are you talking about?"

She had a gleeful air, like a child who'd won a carnival prize. Sarah looked at me with genuine delight. It occurred to me that I might be the only person *she* could talk to as well.

"The Program," she bubbled, as if we were gossiping over brunch. "It has variables. I've been reading these software design books, and they say the whole system can be adjusted. We could change the environment in the valley!" Her face fell. "Not from *this* terminal, though. I need one with higher access."

Careful. She's fishing.

"Manipulated how?"

"All kinds of ways." Her enthusiasm was nearly infectious. I wondered if under different circumstances we might've been good friends. "Weather. Daylight. Even wild animals. Wouldn't you just *kill* to hear the birds sing again? It's possible! According to these manuals, anyway."

I couldn't believe it. Intellectually, I knew we were living inside a computer program, even though it was impossible to tell the difference. But to change our environment at will . . . The idea was amazing. Godlike. Terrifying. I mouthed a quick prayer that Sarah never figured out how to do it.

She seemed to guess my thoughts. "We could make this place *better*, you know."

I snorted. "Right. Better. Because that's been your goal so far."

Sarah nostrils flared. I'd clearly struck a nerve. "You can be so stupid, Min. For all your abilities, you're as blind as Ethan sometimes. Maybe worse. At least he knows what he wants."

Her words stung. "Don't talk to me about blindness," I shot back, heat rising to my cheeks. "You're enabling a dictator. *Own that shit*, Sarah. By propping him up, you're making it all happen."

Sarah's face flushed. She was furious, which surprised me. It went against her nature.

"You're such a child, Min," she said coldly, leaning back and resting her hands in her lap. "Do you have any idea what I've done for this valley? The circumstances I've prevented?"

I shook my head, frowning. "What do you mean?"

Sarah spread both hands palms up, glaring at me with disdain. "There are no rules here, precious little snowflake. Think about that. *No. Rules.* And we're surrounded by a group of high school boys hopped up on adrenaline. *Boys who can't die.* What do you think is keeping them in line?" She leaned forward, eyes narrowing. "Do you think this is as bad as it could get?"

I felt a creeping chill along my backbone. Found my tongue tied.

"I keep the monsters at bay," Sarah hissed, staring daggers at me. "I destroyed the liquor store the first week. I let Cash and Finn get drunk and smash everything. Then I gave all the boys stupid tasks to keep them busy. I convinced Ethan he needed perfect order to maintain control. I outlawed vandalism, because that can lead to worse crimes. Assault. Torture. *Rape.* What do you think is holding all that back?"

Eyes blazing, Sarah tapped the center of her chest. *"Me.* My influence. I was the only thing standing between society and chaos. I've known about this silo forever, but decided it was too big a deal for Ethan and Toby. I didn't tell anyone until Noah lost his mind and decided to blow up our food. I've spent weeks and weeks keeping a lid on things, preventing one disaster after another. But now I'm down here."

My breath caught. Footprints in the snow. Of course it had been Sarah. Her reset point was inside the fence. *How long has she known?* Before the Program? Had she been inside?

I was reeling, but Sarah didn't let up. She leaned close to the camera. "You know who the fucking *problems* have been? You and Tack, traipsing all over the valley and riling people up. Meanwhile, Noah's death squad has killed more people than everyone else combined."

"No." I shook my head weakly. "That's not—"

"You've *tried* to do right, Min. I'll give you that. And Ethan shouldn't have stabbed Tack in the church. That was stupid, and I don't blame you guys for losing it there for a while. But since then, you've screwed up every step of the way, and people are *dying* as a result."

I couldn't speak. Couldn't defend myself. God in heaven . . . was it true?

"Things have gotten bad topside." Sarah put a hand to her forehead, then ran it back through her hair a few times. Spoke in a calmer voice. "Since Noah torched the grocery store, food is short everywhere. Then a transformer blew, and power failed across the valley. Nobody has a clue how to fix it. That's a serious problem. Did you miss that winter arrived while you've been hiding? People outside are just trying to survive right now."

"So what are you saying?" I asked pointedly, trying to regain a foothold in the conversation. "Have you given up on empire and started running a democracy? If so, come right inside."

Sarah rolled her eyes. "Such a Girl Scout," she muttered. Then she took a heavy breath, refocusing. Something vulnerable slipped into her voice. "Let me in with you. Seriously, a truce. We can forget the others and stay safe together. Let these idiot boys destroy each other with their stupid wars. Fear of Ethan was the only thing keeping the valley from becoming a living hell, but . . . it won't last. Things are about to get worse."

I blinked. "You want to abandon everyone else and hide in here. With me."

Sarah nodded without embarrassment. "I accept your presence there as earned. Please accept mine." She licked her lips, eagerness sliding into her voice. "The terminal that can alter source code must be where you are. Think about it, Min. By tweaking the variables, we can accelerate this phase ourselves."

With a sharp shock, I understood what she was suggesting. My heart rate spiked, even as revulsion roiled my gut. "You want to turn the Program against our classmates. Literally kill them with it."

"It's going to happen anyway," Sarah countered, exasperation in her voice. "This phase doesn't stop until the Program is satisfied. But we don't have to be part of the chaos. We'll just turn up the pressure and let the lunatics sort themselves out, while staying out of the line of fire. It's *perfect.*"

We're all in this together.

I shook my head. Sat back and crossed my arms, unable to hide my disgust. "Fuck you, Sarah. I won't lock us in together so you can kill everyone else. You're insane."

Sarah's jaw clenched. I could almost hear her teeth grinding. Her whole body quivered for a moment, then she spoke in a clipped voice. "Fine. I'll take it from you, then."

I shrugged, suddenly feeling tired. "Bring it, bitch."

Her nostrils flared, but Sarah visibly calmed herself. Cocked her head slightly. "Do you know *why* you're always a failure, Min? Your whole pathetic life? It's because you lack commitment. I have it. So do the other betas, in their own ways. But not you."

Sarah sneered, no trace of empathy in her eyes. "I'll win because I won't accept anything less. Ethan will survive, too—he's so stubborn that it's actually impressive. And Noah?" Sarah snorted. "Noah's a zealot. He's completely given himself over to the cause." Then she flashed a shark's smile. "But not you. You'll lose, Min. Not because you're stupid, or incapable, or anything like that. You'll lose because you're too broken to adapt, and too weak to lead. People like you *always* lose. And then they're forgotten. Good-bye."

Her hand rose and the chat box winked out.

I gasped aloud, reeling. Tears stung my eyelids. She'd taken me apart as easily as breaking a vase, and the worst part was, she was right.

Every word of it.

I was about to lose it completely when an alarm began blaring from somewhere deep inside the complex. "What now?" I moaned, but I rose and hurried toward it, secretly grateful for a way to avoid what Sarah had said. I wanted to hide from the truth.

Leaving the office suite, I passed into the living quarters, nerves fraying with every step. The noise was coming from the lab section beyond. I really, really didn't want to go in there, but had no choice. I took a deep breath and pushed through the doors.

The last door on the left. The locked one. A yellow button was blinking on its keypad as an alarm sounded from a speaker above it.

I pressed the button without thinking, and the sound abruptly ceased.

A buzz startled me and I jumped back.

The door swung open on silent hinges.

22

NOAH

The toilet wouldn't flush.

I pressed my forehead against the cool bathroom wall. Resisted the urge to pound it with a fist. Then I reeled off a string of expletives that would've gotten me fifty laps back at basketball practice.

Great. Another thing that wasn't working. The power had been out for weeks, and we'd run out of fuel for the generator three days ago. Now plumbing? This "luxury" chalet was slowly falling apart.

I straightened slowly, then walked out, closing the bathroom door. I'd probably never open it again. Just pack up my stuff and move to a different room. Yeah, we'd reached that point.

The room stank from dirty clothes, old linens, and the unfortunate bathroom issue I was preparing to kiss good-bye forever. I needed some air. Scratching my scalp, I stepped out onto the patio. Was immediately socked in the chest by an icy blast.

The weather had turned bitingly cold. Pale morning sunlight

was spilling over the eastern mountains, sparkling the valley, but that didn't make it warm. I could see icebergs forming in the center of the lake. My ears and nose quickly lost feeling as I stood there, shivering, tempting fate like an idiot in a T-shirt and gym shorts.

Downtown far below was silent and peaceful. No lights, no sounds. Everything seemed frozen in place under a suffocating white blanket, one that coated dozens of charred, burned-out buildings. But even a casual observer could see that the valley was in shambles.

The summer camp? Gone. The trailer park? Gone. Both had burned to the ground in the fighting and been abandoned. Tack was still in a rage about his crappy mobile home.

I knew I didn't feel the cold quite like I should. I had the energy of two extra people now, at the very least. I'd fired the shot that eliminated Josh Atkins when he, Toby, and a handful of others attacked our base. On the rare nights I slept, I still dreamed about pulling the trigger, often waking up in a tangle of bedsheets, my body drenched in sweat.

That same day, Tack had X-ed out Cole Pritchard, a big brute of a kid who'd liked shooting squirrels growing up. Eliminations were coming fast and furious, as people got too close to the line. Everyone knew about the reset limit by now.

Josh. Cole. Gone and gone. I'd played sports with both of them growing up. Josh had started at center on the Fire Lake basketball team, used to set hard picks for me, roughing up any opponents who tried to play physical and throw me off my game. I tried not to think about things like that. If you thought of your enemies as people, they killed you first.

Excuses.

I grimaced, but didn't let the notion linger. Doubts had been hounding me 24/7 lately. I'd even had another panic attack. Alone, thank God. Try as I might, I couldn't isolate the weakness inside me and stamp it out for good. I had to accept that part of me would always be imperfect. I just couldn't let the others see. Certainly not with Tack around.

Tack.

Thinking about the kid made me queasy. Over the last two months, some people had waded into the deep end, in terms of violence—I was no role model there—but Tack had taken a flying cannonball that left even me shocked. Nothing meant anything to him anymore, except revenge. He was like a tornado of violence.

Some of my team had begun to idolize him. It was getting to be a problem.

As if on cue, the music started up again despite the early hour. Someone had found an old iPod loaded with nineties music, most of it terrible. Who had ever liked the Macarena? But then Kyle found Rage Against the Machine and suddenly, my squad had theme music.

"Killin' in the name of! . . . Killin' in the name of! . . ."

Heavy guitar riffs echoed into the valley. They could probably hear it in the liberty camp across the lake. With a sigh, I went inside, dressed quickly in jeans, hoodie, a jacket, and my game face. Then I stepped back out and hustled over to the ski village.

"And now you do what they told ya . . . And now you do what they told ya . . ."

The wooden buildings beside the chalet were a tight cluster

of shops, rental places, and cafés built for skiers taking a quick break from the slopes. The music was blaring from the main ski store, Moguls, an A-frame building in the center of the complex where Tack lived. He'd moved in a month ago, the day he first strolled up the mountainside, hands in his jeans, making no effort to disguise his approach. He'd been covered in frozen blood—said it wasn't his own—and only wanted to know if Min was here. She wasn't. No one had seen her in weeks.

Too long.

Tack and I had met eyes. We'd both feared the truth.

Min must've been eliminated.

The thought still made my breath catch, but the conclusion seemed inescapable. Min was impatient. I couldn't imagine her hiding down there with the clones for two whole months, doing nothing, cut off from everything. She'd had a gun and a life to spare. She'd done it before.

But Min hadn't made any attempt to contact us. Before joining me, rumor was that Tack had thrown himself against the silo over and over again, taking out Ethan's guards but mainly getting himself repeatedly shot to hell. He never even got through the first blast door. I could've told him it was impossible—I'd tried three times myself.

Then, abruptly, he gave up. Something convinced him she wasn't there anymore. So Tack had scoured the valley like an avenging god, calling her name, and taking on all comers who tried to mess with him about it. Finally he'd walked up to my base like he didn't care what happened next.

I shared his misery. No one could stay hidden that long, and why would Min want to? She was gone. They must've gotten her at the silo somehow, or she'd pulled the trigger a second time to escape.

Acid scorched my throat. My breathing became labored.

They'd probably gotten her again at one of the zones. Min would've reset with no margin for error. I felt a wave of sickly heat in my gut, but shook it off. I couldn't change it. I had to accept reality and move on.

So why did it still rip me open every time I thought about her? How come my mind tortured me with memories of how perfectly her body fit next to mine?

The nights we shared. The way her nose wriggled when she laughed.

Stop it. I couldn't do this every damn day. I had to deal with the threat right in front of me, masquerading as help.

Since Tack had joined us, his fury against Ethan had been relentless. He went out every morning despite the miserable cold. Sometimes he got one of them, sometimes they got him. But he stalked Ethan's gang with merciless determination, like an angel of death.

I did nothing to stop it. I knew I couldn't, and didn't want to look weak trying. Even *our* food was growing short, and with it my trump card over these people.

Sometimes it felt like failure drenched everything I tried. I'd already been worried my team could see through me, and was secretly questioning whether I should be the one giving orders. And then here comes Tack, with the single-minded obsession of killing everyone responsible for Min's absence. His rage was simple, distilled, and all-consuming. Appealing, in its way. Kyle had moved in with Tack immediately. Jamie and Richie joined them a few days later.

"*Killin' in the name of!... Killin' in the name of!...*"

I took a deep breath. Jammed all my misgivings into a box, then dropped that box through a hole in the lake ice. But they refused to sink all the way.

With Min gone, I just couldn't see things the same way I had before. It all seemed so pointless. Futile, just like she'd said. What did I care about "Phase Three," whatever it was, if I turned into a monster to make it there. Seeing Tack so completely given over to his anger was jarring. I'd been headed that way since the beginning. Did I still want to go?

I was stronger than him—Tack had more kills than me by far, but he'd taken only a single elimination that I knew of, and lost a life for practically every one he took. He didn't seem to care, making suicidal frontal assaults, blasting Ethan's people until they rallied and gunned him down, sending him back to the reset zones.

I had no idea how he managed to elude Ethan's capture teams, but he always did. Tack was a walking body count that had everyone in the valley quaking. And I was the one supposedly controlling him.

"*And now you do what they told ya... And now you do what they told ya...*"

I pushed into the ski shop. Sleeping bags and camp chairs were scattered across the hardwood floor, surrounding an outdoor space heater and a cooler filled with beer. Where they'd gotten it I had no idea—someone must've slipped some into the vans during the raid—but I chose not to make an issue of it. More than ever I had to pick my battles.

Tack was sitting in a canvas chair cleaning a Heckler & Koch MP5, a fully automatic submachine gun he'd taken off Chris Nolan after shooting him in the back. He glanced up when I entered, a caustic smile twisting his lips. Dark circles ringed his eyes, but his tongue was as sharp as ever. "Hey everybody, Fearless Leader is back."

Jamie and Richie were lying together on an inflatable mattress. They sat up as I entered, pushing plastic cups out of sight. As if I wouldn't notice. Kyle was asleep in a portable hammock, but was roused by a swift kick from Leah, who was huddled by the heater. He cursed loudly as he fell over backward.

The drinking didn't bother me much—so long as they weren't on watch—but I was more disturbed by the sweet-smelling smoke permeating the store. Still, I wasn't their guidance counselor, and all that stuff would run out soon anyway. I knew better than anyone how stress could be a killer.

So. Everyone was present but Leighton and Cash, who were on guard duty.

Everyone but me.

"And now you do what they told ya . . . now you're under control . . . And now you do what they told ya . . . now you're under control . . . And now you do what they told ya . . ."

"Turn that off," I said loudly.

Tack smirked for a moment, then snapped his fingers at Richie, who shut down the iPod. I didn't miss Richie looking to Tack instead of me. My teeth ground together. Things were worse than I'd thought.

"Do you have any idea how far that sound carries?" I said quietly.

Tack was buffing the stock of his weapon. "I'm pretty sure everyone knows where we are, Noah."

I struggled to hold my temper in check. "You're broadcasting when we're here and when we're not. You're giving Ethan information about us."

Tack's face reddened. He covered it by putting the gun aside and crossing his arms. "You afraid of Ethan's people or something? I've shot them dozens of times, and will happily do so again if they come visit. They're nothing."

I bit back a scathing reply. This conversation was public. "Tell that to Morgan."

Tack flinched, his eyes darkening. "She didn't keep a good count. It's not my fault she got eliminated."

I kept my voice level. Glacial. "You took her down the mountain and she didn't come back." I spread my hands in mock curiosity. "Whose fault is it, Thumbtack?" Before he could reply, I barked out an order. "Everyone give me a status update."

A short pause, then voices began sounding off.

"Even," said Leah.

"Neg-three," Jamie grumbled, and was immediately parroted by Richie. But when she slugged him in the arm, he rolled his eyes. "Or maybe neg-four. I took a lucky hit yesterday by the sanitation plant."

I frowned. Both were down lives, and Richie was on the brink.

"Pos-four, up one," Kyle said, with a smile that never touched his eyes. The "one" was for someone he'd eliminated. Kyle had

246

knocked out Charlie Bell a few days ago and seemed hungry for more.

I'd been watching him to see if he'd absorbed Melissa Hemby's elimination as well, all those days ago, after the explosion at the grocery store. But it didn't appear so. I'd asked him point-blank, and Kyle wasn't a good liar. It seemed that kills had to be direct for a transfer of power to occur.

Tack squinted at the ceiling, as if considering whether or not to answer. Then he met my eyes, and there was no friendliness there. "What's *your* number, Noah? I'm curious about the status of our mighty captain. Can't risk you, no sir."

Our glares locked, and in that instant all my insecurities melted away. If Tack wanted to do this right now, I was ready. I'd bury him. "Pos-five, up two. And you, Thomas?"

Tack broke first. He looked away, rolling his eyes as if bored. "Pos-eight, up one. Looks like you're still the elimination king."

I barely suppressed a shudder. God, what had I become? But something Richie said demanded attention. I glanced at him. "The sanitation plant?" I'd never listed it as a target. With a sick feeling, I knew what was coming.

Tack smiled smugly, shooting a finger-gun at his companion. "Richie and I took care of it last night. Good luck flushing those toilets, Fire Lake."

Heat crept up my chest, through my neck, and into my face. "*My* toilet didn't flush, Tack. Did you think about that?"

"The woods are right—"

I strode forward and grabbed him by the shirt, lifting him from his chair. Then I held him there, kicking and squawking like a caught chicken. "You don't get to decide things like that,"

I growled. "Not while you're living here. Do you understand that, Thomas?"

Tack stopped struggling, spat through gritted teeth. "Put me . . . the fuck . . . *down*."

I dropped him and stepped back, watching his hands. I'd needed to make a point, but you could never push Tack too far. When his temper broke loose, reason was left by the wayside. I didn't want to see what would happen if the room was forced to choose sides.

Tack straightened his shirt with an embarrassed jerk, red-faced, eyes blazing. Then he forced a nasty smile. "Whatever you say, boss. You're the expert strategist. Look how well you defended the silo."

Words like a slap. He was referring to Min, though he never said her name anymore. Tack blamed me for her loss, even though I'd given her my gun and had thought she was safely locked away.

Against my better judgment, I fired back. "I took out four of them with a hunting knife. By myself. In the dark."

"Not enough!" he shouted harshly. Tack spun, cleared his throat. A beat later he dropped back into his camp chair and resumed a casual posture. When enough time had passed for him to feel like he'd defied me, he shook his head, looking up and adopting a condescending tone. "You let Sarah Harden ace you with a *gun*. Not ideal, sporto."

I considered expelling him right then and there. He was too much of a wild card, and our feud ran deep. Tack would never forgive me for losing Min.

My eyes strayed to the rear wall. To a list of names inked in black marker.

The Dead List. Every eliminated person we knew about. Tack had scribbled Min's name up there himself, even though we didn't know for sure. It was the last time he'd spoken it out loud.

Tack followed my eyes. A vein in his neck started working, pumping in time to the grinding of his molars. When he looked back at me, his fury was directed elsewhere.

This was what bound us. Why he'd come here. Why I let him stay.

Tack wanted to destroy Ethan and Sarah, hurting them like they'd hurt him. My team was the best way to do that. And so, once again, our truce was cemented by mutual hatred. The enemy of my enemy is my friend.

"I won't go out again without telling you." The words cost him, but he said them.

"I'll make sure you have whatever you need when you do."

He glared at me a moment longer, then nodded. I nodded back. Felt a collective release of tension in the room. Then I turned and walked out before things could go south again.

Tack was a problem, but it would hold for now. I needed to get my head straight and decide what to do next. My team craved action. I had to provide it.

As I walked away, the speakers started blasting once more.

"Fuck you, I won't do what you tell me! . . . Fuck you, I won't do what you tell me! . . ."

23

MIN

I sat there staring at the open door.

In a cushy rolling chair, with my legs folded up beneath me, drinking Tang from a white sports bottle. I'd wheeled one all the way from the conference room down to the lab wing for sessions like this one. Staring sessions.

Because the open door was driving me insane.

Just as she intended.

I knew Sarah had unlocked it somehow. Zero doubt on that account. After her Dr. Evil pitch failed—*join me in the secret underground lair, and together we'll rule the world!*—she'd moved to the next plan. Sarah didn't waste time pouting.

She'd stopped talking to me, too, leaving me to stew over this new riddle. But I watched her on the laptop. Day by day, she was figuring out how things worked. I could barely track her movements through the computer system as she explored subfiles and processing routines, intent on learning everything she could. Frankly, I was in awe. Sarah Harden was the worst enemy I could have possibly selected. Hooray.

I pressed my palms against my cheeks, returning focus to the Pandora's box before me. Sarah obviously wanted me to go through this door. But why? Where did it lead? All I could see was a dimly lit corridor that took a hard right after a dozen yards. Back toward the command center. Back toward the computer room.

Possibly to *exactly* where I wanted to go.

Arrrrgh.

My basic theory hadn't changed. During construction, huge amounts of material had been hauled into the silo somehow. Surely it didn't all come down the shaft. Too much weight, but more importantly, way too public. Someone in Fire Lake would've noticed and raised hell. So that meant, logically, there had to be another way. And the only unexplored area left was the chamber housing the MegaCom. My gut told me this corridor led straight there. Given what I knew of the silo, it was the only possibility that made sense.

So. This hallway *had* to lead to the computer room. Right? RIGHT?

So why open the door? With the blast curtain retracted Sarah could see into the computer room, but not every corner. She couldn't say for certain what was inside, and her part of the silo didn't have a separate way to access it. Tack and I had checked.

So why open the door?

Did Sarah know if there was another way out? Did she suspect one, as I did? She'd read almost every binder in the building by now. The same idea must've occurred to her. Sarah didn't miss things.

So why open the door?

I didn't think she'd simply open up a way for me to escape. Not after our last chat. Which meant this had to be a trap. Was she hoping I'd get too curious? If so, it was working.

A quick dash? Sarah slept, and I could time it.

No. That's the trick. The minute I go, she's got me.

Or maybe there *was* a way out, and she just wanted me gone. She might have some clever trick to get inside the lab complex, but it wouldn't work if I was there to play defense. So she was encouraging me to leave.

Or maybe it never occurred to her that freedom might lie that way.

AAAAARRRRRGGGGH.

Not today.

I rose, trudged slowly down the gleaming white hallway. I needed caffeine. The only perk of living in this underground terrarium was a near limitless supply of space food. I entered the kitchen and poured instant coffee into a mug. I was reaching for the hot water dispenser when I heard it.

Thump.

Thump thump thump.

I froze, blood pressure spiking as I worried someone had gotten inside. A moment later the noise repeated. It was coming from the office suite.

Where I keep the gun.

Heart in my throat, I crept to the dividing doors and peeked through. The noise repeated.

No. Not the office. Someone was banging on the blast door.

"Oh, come *on*," I grumbled, shaking my head. I set my mug on a table and strode down the hall, pushing through the last set of doors to the sealed portal. There was an intercom button, and I pressed it. "That's six feet of solid steel, genius! You're not going to hammer it open."

Seconds later a muffled voice erupted from its speaker.

"Min, open up!"

Amused, I pushed again. "No."

"It's Derrick. We need to talk. Right now."

"Um. *No*." Did he think I'd lost my mind?

"I'm serious, Min! I'm not going to hurt you. I'm here to help."

I shook my head, eyes narrowing even though I couldn't see him. I hit the button again. "The last time we met, you tackled me, tied me up, and had me marched to a jail cell."

"Things are different now." A pause. "I'm *out*, Min. I'm done with these guys."

Interesting new strategy.

"Right. I'm sure Sarah isn't sitting right behind you." In truth, I hadn't checked the cameras in a while, but Sarah was *always* in there. Then I paused, momentarily thrown. Was she letting other people talk to me now? No one else had tried before.

No, it had to be a trick.

I pushed the button. "I spotted Mike and Chris rooting through the alcoves a half hour ago. Not buying it, Derrick."

"Look again."

Huh? I pressed to speak. "Excuse me?"

"Look. Again." Derrick's voice was dripping with impatience. "Eighth level, far left."

I bumped a fist against my chin. Derrick sounded . . . different somehow.

"Okay," I said to myself. "I'll play." With a sigh, I walked back to the security hub and checked the surveillance feeds. Silo shaft. Level eight.

Then I gasped in surprise. Two people were lying side by side in the last alcove on the left. I zoomed in until I could see their faces. Chris and Mike. Their chests gently rose and fell. But they didn't stir, appearing to be unconscious.

I straightened, began chewing a thumbnail. What were these guys playing at? The twins weren't dead, obviously. They were just lying there. This must be an elaborate scam.

They think I'm an idiot.

I stormed back to the blast door and jabbed the button. "I don't know how dumb you think I am, Derrick, but I'm not *that* dumb." I released the intercom and crossed my arms in a huff, unimpressed with my sentence structure but satisfied with the overall message.

"Min, it's not a trick! It's . . . *bad* out here now." Derrick's voice crackled through the tiny speaker. "Ethan and Toby, man. They've lost their minds! Sarah never comes out of the silo anymore, so there's no one checking 'em." There was a pause so long I reached for the button, but then his voice rattled once more. "They're straight-up *killing* people, Min. They have firing positions at the reset points and don't bother capturing prisoners.

They just mow people down until they stop popping back up again."

A hand flew to my mouth. Derrick's story was ghastly. Had it come to this?

This is what the Program wants.

"Min, please," Derrick pleaded. "Open up. They've even turned on their own. Toby and Mike keep taking people out on patrols, and sometimes they don't come back. We need you. Either that, or let me in!"

I wavered, heart pounding as I softly shook my head. I was starting to believe Derrick—that this wasn't a trap—but I couldn't see his face to be sure. Was he this good an actor, or had opportunity finally come knocking?

GO LOOK.

The notion made my eyes pop. Of course! I had a room full of clones behind me. Those machines had scores. Data. I could fact-check everything Derrick was claiming. And he didn't know it, either.

I pressed the com. "Hold on a second, Derrick. I have a way to verify what you're saying. If you're telling the truth, I'll be able to tell. And if you're lying."

"Whatever. Go. Just hurry. Sarah went into town, but she's never gone long."

That was true, at least. I turned and ran for the lab, pushing through three sets of wooden doors, ignoring my staring chair and the stupid open door that was tormenting me. At the entrance to the clone room I paused a moment, taking a deep breath, then slipped through the glass doors. Instantly, I pulled up short. I hadn't been inside there in weeks, and the change was stunning.

Darkened overhead lights. Everywhere. Perhaps a quarter of the room.

My hands flew to my mouth. All I could think were two names.

I raced among the pedestals, trying to remember the path Tack had taken. I finally located his tube near the back of the room and breathed a sigh of relief. Light on. Sensors green. Just to be sure, I climbed up and wiped condensation from the window.

He was there. His face looked peaceful. But then I saw his stats and nearly screamed.

Thomas Russo. Status: 8.

Oh my God.

Eight.

That number. What had Tack been doing?

In a mild daze, I went looking for Noah. Passing a darkened pedestal, I couldn't help myself. I climbed up on shaky legs and read the display.

Neb Farmer. Status: eliminated.

I remembered Neb standing in the rain at the summer camp. He'd never wanted to hurt anybody, but now he was gone. I stumbled back down to the floor, unable to make my feet work. Where was Noah's pedestal? I thought back to when Tack had called out to him. Walked down the row. There were two pedestals near the end—one gleaming, the other disconnected.

He's one of these.

Limbs trembling, I climbed the unlit pedestal. Rubbed the

glass. A girl lay inside, eyes open and unfocused, staring at the ceiling. Kayla Babbitt. I didn't know her well, but we'd had music class together. I felt a burst of relief, then a tidal wave of guilt on top of it.

I hurried to the next tube. Expelled a pent-up breath upon seeing Noah's face. Then I jumped down and headed for the door. I didn't check Noah's score. Didn't want to know.

I was firing past the conference room when I stopped short. I dithered a moment, then darted inside and retrieved Noah's Beretta from the cabinet. Better safe than sorry. Back at the blast door, I slammed the call button. "What the hell is going on out there?"

Derrick's voice crackled immediately. "It's insane, Min. The whole thing is falling apart. Please let me in and I'll explain everything. I'm unarmed."

Moment of truth. But I'd decided when I saw the darkened tubes.

Whatever was happening outside was madness. I couldn't sit on the sidelines while the world burned. I had to get out, find Tack and Noah, and somehow help put a stop to whatever was going on.

With a sigh, I grabbed the steel locking pin and hefted it out of place, dropping the rod with an audible thunk. Then I spun the heavy wheel, retracting the bolt. The door beeped, swung open on silent hinges.

I stepped back quickly and crouched, gun in hand. Ready for fight or flight.

Derrick stepped inside. He was breathing hard, eyes round. He clearly hadn't expected me to open the door. "Thank God.

I swear I'm not playing you, Min. Ethan and Toby started a slaughter. They'll shoot anyone they think is near the edge."

I swallowed the bile rising in my throat. "Then we have to stop them."

Derrick gave me a calculating look. "We *could* just stay in here. You've got food, right?"

"Not enough," I lied. Derrick's news had lit a fire in me. I had to get out of there. Had to see what was happening for myself. The thought of hiding no longer had any appeal.

Derrick grunted unhappily, threw a glance back over his shoulder. "Okay. Let's go then."

"There's something you need to see first."

He gave me a strange look—almost hesitant—but nodded. "What's back here, anyway?"

"You have to see it to believe it."

Derrick turned and closed the door. I waved him a few feet away, then reengaged the bolt, leaving the locking pin out for now in case we needed a quick escape. Then I led him down to the lab, gun in hand and keeping a safe distance between us. Derrick ogled the facilities along the way.

"Damn, Melinda. Nice. Living like a queen down here."

"Wait until you meet the neighbors," I grumbled. He shot me a confused look, but I held up a hand. Entering the lab area, I walked him to the glass doors. "Prepare yourself. This is a little . . . hard to see."

We stepped into the frigid chamber. "Pick a pedestal."

Derrick shrugged and took a few steps, then stopped, throwing a glance at me over his shoulder. "You coming?"

"Nope. I've seen it, thanks."

Eyes rolling heavenward, he took three long strides to a pedestal and climbed the steps. I watched him reach out and wipe the fogged glass. Bend close. Then he reared back with an unmanly yelp. "Holy shit! What's Hector doing in here?"

I almost chuckled. "I don't think that's him. At least, not the Hector inside the Program. Try another."

Derrick's mouth worked. His breathing had quickened to a pant. He leapt down, sped to the next tube, and peered inside. A hand rose to his forehead, then slid down his face. "I think I'm going to be sick."

I couldn't help myself. "Want to see yours?"

"No!" Derrick stumbled off the pedestal and careened into another before storming back to the door. "This . . . what . . . Min, let's get the hell out of here!"

"Don't you want to know what this is about?"

He shook his head violently. "Not now. Not here. Tell me when I can breathe fresh air."

What air? But I didn't press. Derrick was shaken, and I needed him functional to escape.

"Is the route clear all the way up?" I asked.

Derrick frowned unhappily. "I think Finn might be topside, waiting for Lars. If we're quick, though, we can—"

"Too risky. I have another idea. Let's go."

Questions seemed to tip Derrick's tongue as I swept past him, but he followed without comment. The magical open door loomed in front of me.

I spun to face Derrick, reaching up to grip his shoulders. "You're *sure* Sarah's not here?"

His palms shot up, his mouth twisting as if he'd bitten a

lemon. "She said she was going home to change. I haven't seen her since, and that was an hour ago."

I nodded. This was the opening I'd been waiting for. *Time to toss the dice.*

I stepped through the doorway, skin tingling, my pulse racing a mile a minute. I motioned for Derrick to follow, then snuck to the end and peeked around the corner. A second stretch of blank hallway led to another turn twenty yards on.

"Where does this lead?" Derrick asked, his dark temples damp with sweat.

"The room housing the MegaCom, I think." *I hope.* "There might be another way out from there. Let's go fast and quiet, check quickly, and if we don't find anything we can haul ass back the other way. Okay?"

Derrick nodded, worry lines crisscrossing his forehead. We scurried to the next turning. Beyond was another featureless corridor ending at another monstrous blast door. Reaching it, I grabbed the locking wheel and pulled. Was shocked when it opened without resistance.

Inside was a large hexagonal chamber. The air was warm, smelled of ozone and warm metal. Solid steel plates lined the walls. The room was empty but for the towering machine at its center, a sleek black monolith twinkling with red and green lights.

I stared at the MegaCom, eyes burning, surprised by the powerful emotions coursing through me. I was looking at a fake: a reflection of something that existed tangibly in the real world. But there, in *that* machine, whatever still constituted *me* resided as a line of digital code. A burst of electricity, traveling circuits at the speed of light, believing myself alive.

I shivered. Glanced up at Derrick, who must've been thinking the same. He rubbed his long arms and shuffled sideways, gazing at the tower with a repulsed frown.

Tick tock.

"Look for a passageway," I said, circling the machine, desperate for any sign of a hidden exit. But my hopes were already fading.

The floor was an unbroken expanse of polished stone. Steel walls, except for the massive panel that allowed a view from the command center. The wall plating stretched floor to ceiling, fit snugly together without visible gaps. I knew there had to be a power supply somewhere, but I didn't see any routes in or out, and we didn't have time to investigate.

Behind me, the door beeped.

I spun, watched in horror as it slowly swung shut.

"Oh shit!" Derrick ran and grabbed the handle. It refused to budge.

The keypad blinked red. I covered my eyes, felt a terrible churning in my stomach. It wasn't hard to put things together.

A voice sounded over the intercom. "Don't bother, it's locked."

Knowing what I'd find, I trudged over to the command center window. Sarah was standing on the lowest tier with some sort of radio in her hand. Her satisfied smile was one of total victory.

Sarah's eyes widened slightly as Derrick stepped into view. She regarded him coolly, then nodded to herself, lifting the radio. Her voice hissed from the door's intercom. "I should've seen it coming, Derrick. Good thing you're no smarter than Min."

The dig burned, but I couldn't dispute it. I'd thought she'd

261

given up on the door lure, or grown careless. *Stupid.* Sarah never gave up. Was *never* careless. She'd waited for me to take the bait, knowing I eventually would.

She spoke as if reading my mind. "I knew you'd be tempted. But there's nothing in there but a giant computer and two people destined to be very hungry." Her head tilted slightly, one finger extending toward the gun still gripped in my hand. "Or will you take the other way out?"

I tensed. Shuddered. Sarah didn't miss it.

Her expression grew pensive. "You can't, can you? No more lives to spare, Melinda?"

Derrick marched over and mashed the intercom button. "Well, *I* can." He glared through the thick glass, his other fist clenching and unclenching at his side. "I can come right back through the front door of this place, too."

Sarah shrugged. "If you like. But you won't find me. I have other plans." She swung her gaze back to me. "I assume the laboratory wing is *finally* open?"

No point lying. With the locking pin out, Sarah could get the blast door open.

"You won't like what you find," I replied, trying to keep my voice firm. Then I realized she couldn't hear me.

But Sarah understood. "You may be right." She began rubbing her chin, considering me. "Stick around, Min. I might have questions for you. If you work very hard to please me, I might let you out one day." She glanced back over her shoulder. The command center was empty but for her. "For now, however, I'm going to keep you two as my little secret. Maybe I'll even feed you. But only if you're good helpers."

She turned and strode to the closest workstation. Woke a computer and tapped a few keys. Then she looked up at us and waved coyly. "Bye, guys! I'll be sure to check on you in a day or two. That should give you enough time to think about what you've done."

The blast curtain began slowly rolling shut.

No. Not like this.

"Let us out!" Derrick roared.

I jerked up the Beretta and fired, but the bullet pinged from the glass without leaving a mark. Sarah laughed as the command center slowly began to disappear.

"Sarah, wait!" I shouted, a geyser of panic erupting inside me. "Don't do this!"

But the thick metal wall rolled forward, relentless, sealing the world from sight.

Her smirk was the last thing I saw before it closed with a boom.

24

NOAH

"Fall back!" I shouted.

Then I scrambled from behind a snow-covered log and bombed into the woods. Leighton ran beside me, chest heaving, blue eyes wide with animalistic fear. Bullets zipped past overhead, slamming into trunks and blasting out tiny explosions of bark and slivers.

The bastards were trying to flank us, just as I'd warned. But had Tack listened? Of course not! He'd barreled straight downslope with half my people seconds after the first shots were fired. Just like they'd wanted him to do. Now he was pinned down and useless.

I didn't know how many attackers were converging, but I suspected at least a dozen. They moved fast, too, ghosting through the snow-covered forest. Ethan's guys must've taken on eliminations. And now we might be totally screwed because Tack had ignored the simple military advantage of higher ground.

Leighton and I crossed another slope, reaching a wide tree fall covered in icicles and white powder. I had to grab his arm to get him to stop. Leighton's cheeks were flushed, his blond hair a frizzy, frozen mess, but he managed to get ahold of himself. We crouched behind the fallen pine trees, rifles trained on our back trail.

"Come on," I muttered. "Be as dumb as Tack."

An instant later five dark-hooded figures exploded from the bushes on the opposite side of the slope. They didn't even break stride, charging right out onto open ground. I almost smiled, then felt disgusted by the impulse. But they'd created this situation, not me.

"Wait until they're halfway across," I whispered to Leighton. "You take the left side, I'll take the right."

He nodded, jaw clenched, nostrils flaring. Ready to pay these bastards back for the fear they'd placed inside him.

Three. Two. One.

"Now."

I rose smoothly and pulled the trigger, dropping the lead attacker. The others skidded to a stop. They tried to swerve, take cover, get flat on the ground. But it did them no good. They were caught in no-man's-land, with nowhere to go. Leighton was screaming at the top of his lungs, unloading his magazine long after they'd all fallen. Finally, the chamber clicked empty.

Then we watched, holding our breath. Four disappeared, but one didn't. With a lump in my throat, I led Leighton out onto the run. We approached the crumpled form cautiously, but one look at the damage and it was clear the person had just been eliminated.

I was kneeling to see who it was when Leighton's whole frame spasmed, eyes glazing as he sucked in his bottom lip. He dropped his weapon, hands finding his knees as he quivered from head to foot. "Oh, man. I feel . . . I feel *amazing.*"

His kill, then. Whoever was lying at our feet, their power had flowed to Leighton.

Leighton choked and gasped until his breathing finally slowed. Then his head popped up, his gaze over-bright in the midday sun. "*Wow.* I get it now, Noah. Before, I thought you were just kind of a psychopath, but now I . . . I understand. That was the best feeling I've ever had. The Program really does reward you."

I looked at the broken body at our feet. *Some reward.*

I didn't chase the thought away. There was nothing dishonest about it.

Then a voice cut across the slope, turning my blood to ice.

"Freeze, assholes! Turn around!"

I locked eyes with Leighton, a hand creeping toward the pistol in my belt. My rifle was slung over my shoulder and out of reach.

"Move another inch and I'll blast you both. Don't test me."

I stopped. Rotated a slow three-sixty, raising my hands, silently cursing a blue streak for letting my guard down. Leighton mirrored my movements.

Someone in a blue jacket stepped from the bushes on the far side. He yanked down his scarf, revealing long red hair. Chris Nolan, one of Ethan's top guys. This was a disaster.

Chris smirked, his mouth opening to say something clever, but then his lips rounded in surprise. He tumbled forward like a sack of potatoes, a knife protruding from the back of his neck. Moments later he shimmered and was gone.

"What the . . ." Leighton dove for his gun and brought it up as another figure stepped from the tree line. My hand shot out to stop him from firing. I'd know that red jacket anywhere.

"Wait!" I pushed down the nose of Leighton's rifle. "That's Akio. He's with us."

Akio trotted across the slope, his face devoid of expression. I hadn't seen him in almost two months, and his absence had been eating at me. Min had seen Akio locked in one of Ethan's cells, but that didn't mean he was still with me.

"Good to see you again," I said guardedly.

Akio nodded. "Had some trouble in town." He glanced downslope at the main lodge, where the morning's skirmish had begun. "Guess you did, too."

Ethan and Toby had attacked the gate just after breakfast, luring Tack down and kicking off a fierce firefight. Sensing a trap, I'd stopped Leighton from following the others and taken him to scout our western flank. Sure enough, a second force had been sneaking through the woods. If they'd broken through Leighton and me, Tack and the others would've been surrounded, with a second force descending from above like an avalanche.

The chalet and ski village would've been lost. Our food. Supplies. Weapons. Everything. Gone in a snap of my fingers. I was furious at Tack for being so stupid, and at those idiots for getting swept up in it.

Something had to be done. Tack had almost cost me everything.

And then, suddenly, here comes Akio waltzing back up the hill.

The timing was a little too perfect. I watched him from the corner of my eye, but his face betrayed nothing. Then Leighton turned over the body at our feet and all other thoughts fled.

Leighton reared back, covering his mouth. "Oh, shit! It's Vonda Clark!"

I blinked. Turned away. Didn't need a new horror seared into my brain. Vonda was a big girl with deep brown skin and wide eyes. Her father had been deputy mayor, the guy who used to pardon a turkey every Thanksgiving. Vonda laughed a lot, had been addicted to Pokemon Go and pudding cups. Drove a sliver Ford F-150.

All in the past. She wasn't even a sequence now.

Suddenly, I felt like crying. Weakness stole in from every corner, tried to cut me down at the knees. But Akio's eyes were on me. So I squashed my feelings and hardened my face to granite.

Leighton was more transparent. He backpedaled away from Vonda, slipping and landing on his butt. Then he turned and threw up in the snow.

My sorrow turned to disgust. Leighton knew *this* was part of it, too. The power he'd absorbed required a corpse on the other end. How amazing was that feeling now?

Gunshots echoed up the slope. A male voice screamed.

I almost slapped myself. While I was sitting there twiddling my thumbs, a battle was hanging in the balance. "Leave her," I said without feeling, diving back into character. "There's still a fight on. We'll come back and bury Vonda later."

Leighton's face was a sickly green, but he nodded, hands

shaking as he wiped snow from his rifle. Akio said nothing, but made ready to follow as well. With a last glance at the body, I began stalking down the mountainside.

Ethan was responsible for this. He'd sent Vonda through the woods to attack an armed camp in broad daylight. That had killed her as much as Leighton.

Time to make him pay.

Two bodies, rolled in tarps, were lying side by side beneath the chairlift.

Everyone still breathing was gathered inside the ski shop. Me. Akio. Cash. Richie and Jamie. Leighton. Kyle and Tack had shown up last, having reset, Kyle red-faced and numb after trekking all the way across the valley—he'd caught a second death trying to evade one of Ethan's reset zone teams. Tack had slipped them without trouble. He always did somehow.

No music this time. The speakers were mercifully silent.

I thought of those no longer able to attend.

Zach. Morgan. And now Leah, my best soldier, wrapped up in plastic outside.

The tension in the room was palpable, probably because I refused to sit like everyone else. Eyes studied me when they thought I wasn't looking. Assessing. Judging. Worrying?

For once I didn't obsess over it. Barely noticed. My anger was a boiling river of lava flowing directly at one Thomas Russo, who was sitting in his camp chair, doing everything he could to avoid my eye.

"Leah Halpern had been with us from the beginning," I began, halting the whispered conversations midsentence. "She fought hard every day, and never complained. Always did her part. Leah was first-chair clarinet in the school orchestra."

I don't know why I added that last part. Something compelled me. A need to remember Leah as something human, a *person* rather than a pawn in a video game. But then Tack spoke and all other thoughts were scorched from my mind.

"We need to attack town," he said darkly, digging his nails into his jeans. "Those bastards killed Leah. We should repay the favor. We owe it to her."

I was striding forward before I knew it, reaching for him. Who knows what would've happened next. Except Tack had been expecting it. His left hand rose, pointing a gun directly at my chest. I halted, seething, barely able to control myself.

"You don't touch me again," Tack said, glowering. "Get that into your head."

My finger shot out, impaling him where he sat. "Leah is gone because you're an idiot. They fired a few rounds up a *near vertical snow-covered slope*, praying some moron would charge down into their trap, and you did exactly that. Tack Russo, the dumbest man in the valley!"

Tack's face flushed. The knuckles gripping his Glock turned white. "I made a mistake," he growled through gritted teeth. "But we beat them, so was it really?"

I laughed a little too loudly, emotions spiraling. "We? WE? *I* beat them, you jackass. Me and Leighton. If we hadn't thought to protect our flank, you'd have been stuck down there with your ass hanging out while Chris and his buddies took turns napping in your sleeping bag."

Tack went from red to scarlet. His gaze slid sideways, darting around the shop, and he obviously didn't like what he saw there. I had the room, mostly because I was 100 percent right, and everyone knew it, including Tack.

The gun barrel lowered. Tack scowled at the floor, every word ashes in his mouth. "Fine. I was wrong. It won't happen again." Then his chin rocketed back up. "But they *did* attack us, and we *did* win. We won the firefight down by the lodge, and you X-ed out a whole squad. Now they're vulnerable. We need to hit them hard as payback!"

"Yeah!" Kyle shouted. I saw tear-streaked nods from Richie and Jamie, Leah's best friends. Leighton wore a sour expression but held his tongue. Akio also said nothing.

The room balanced on a tightrope. I spoke quickly. "This raid could've been a feint. They tried to trick us and almost took the chalet, but the whole thing might be a ploy to get us to come at them. Assault *their* positions. It's easier to defend than attack, as we just proved, and there's a lot of high ground in town."

Tack looked at me like I was crazy. "You think Ethan and Toby are suddenly employing a multifaceted battle strategy designed to outwit us? Come on, Noah! Today's attack was classic Ethan Fletcher. Brute force. He probably thought using two teams was genius."

I squeezed the bridge of my nose. Spoke as calmly as possible, more to the rest of the group than Tack. "I don't worry about Ethan's plans. I worry about Sarah." Then I shook my head at him. "And if you don't, you're a fool." I couldn't help myself. "But you proved that this morning."

Tack shot to his feet. "You're one to talk! Such a *big* man on his daddy's mountain. But since I got here, all you've done is hide, anxious and uncertain, the Noah Livingston way." Tack slammed a fist into his palm. "We need to take the fight to them! *Decisive action*." Then he crossed his arm and met my gaze squarely. "Or maybe we just need better leadership."

I closed the distance between us, skin tingling with tiny flames, a fluttery, empty feeling expanding in my stomach. "Are you saying *you* should lead?"

Tack straightened, pupils dilated. He tried to meet my glare nose to nose, but I had six inches and fifty pounds on him. The optics weren't good, and he knew it. After holding his ground long enough to save face, Tack turned his back on me lazily and flopped back down into his chair. "I'm no leader, Noah. Never pretended to be." He flashed a crooked smile. "And this is your father's building, after all."

I brushed off the dig, riding a rush of adrenaline. I'd seen this showdown coming and had won it. No one had taken his side. I could breathe a little easier. For a few moments, anyway. But then Tack spoke again, putting me back on the defensive.

"I *do* have a plan."

My jaw clenched. I said nothing.

Tack leaned forward, speaking rapidly, pointedly not looking in my direction. "Like it or not, we have problems. Ammo is running short. So is food. Ethan's a cancer and controls the town. Sarah controls the silo, which is bad news—we don't know what's in those crates. There could be RPGs, machine guns, grenades, *anything*. We. Don't. Know."

People were shifting uncomfortably. I felt a trickle of unease myself.

Tack took a deep breath and continued. "We're protected up

here, but we're also kinda sitting ducks if they come at us with real firepower. Right now, they're scattered and licking their wounds. It's the perfect moment to hit town with everything we have."

"He's right," Kyle said immediately, almost as if he'd rehearsed it. "They won't suspect a counterattack so soon. We could cut right through 'em!"

I opened my mouth to speak, found I didn't have a good rebuttal. Tack seized the opportunity and kept going.

"It's not just this raid." He was animated now, talking with his hands. "Ethan's guys are still spread out all over the zones. Kyle and I ran from two different teams this afternoon. *That means Ethan doesn't have his fighters on Main Street.* His lines are stretched."

Tack looked at me then, and the animosity was shoved to the back burner. Tack really believed in what he was saying.

I rubbed a hand over my mouth. "What are you suggesting?"

"Ethan just moved his headquarters to Emerald Tower, right? Thick stone walls, eight stories, lobby with a bank. A good choice. So we go in heavy—one giant team stabbing straight for their heart. Ethan stores weapons in the vault, and everyone moved into the condos above it. If we destroyed that building, we'd cripple them! Then we take the jail cells, the stores, hell— we take everything. We could *break* them, Noah. Let's have dinner by the water tonight."

The energy in the room was rising. I could tell people liked the plan. But I was hesitant.

"We have seven people total," I said. "They have, what, maybe twenty?"

"At least half that number are out at the reset zones," Tack countered, and he was right. "And some of the rest aren't fighters. Jessica Cale? Please. Plus, we're better at this than they are. We've proven it again and again."

"We can do it, Noah." Jamie wiped tears from her cheeks. Leah's loss had hit her the hardest. She was the only girl left in my camp. "I want to see Toby's stupid face when his house burns down around him." Richie held her hand, nodding, wearing an ugly sneer.

I was plagued by a sudden indecisiveness. Felt heat rising under my collar. Eyes were boring into me from all sides. I needed a moment to think. Get my head straight. I couldn't let Tack bully me into a plan without testing it from every angle.

"I'll consider it," I said, firming my voice as best I could. "Everyone take five."

I knew I shouldn't leave them with him, but I was suddenly afraid my body might betray me. I had to be alone for a second, right that second.

I turned and headed for the door. Tack's voice arrowed across the room, striking between my shoulder blades.

"Don't take too long, Captain Livingston. Time is of the essence."

25

MIN

"Six, Min."

I squeezed my eyelids shut, then reopened them. Ignored him.

Derrick was sitting with his back to the door, staring at nothing. He'd called out every hour we'd been locked inside the computer chamber. After a few fruitless attempts to hail Sarah over the intercom, he seemed to have given up completely.

I was circling the MegaCom for the hundredth time, examining every screw in its jet-black casing. Finally, I heaved a sigh and turned to face him. "Look, I've spent a *lot* of time thinking about this. There has to be another way out. Some passage they used to get stuff into the silo in the first place."

His frown deepened. "Sarah said we're trapped. You think she doesn't know? She's read every scrap of paper in this tomb."

"She doesn't know everything," I snapped, though I could hear the hysteria creeping into my voice. Sarah was undoubtedly inside the lab complex as we spoke. "We just have to hope the way out is hidden. If she checks in and finds us gone, she'll think we took the . . . other way. She won't know the truth."

Derrick gave me a hard look. "Is the other way an option for you?"

I swallowed. Nodded. "I'm not done yet."

He looked away. "Then we should just go ahead and . . . and *do* it. This room isn't complicated. One door." He banged a fist back against the heavy steel portal behind him. "Locked. One supercomputer. Stationary. Nothing else. Staring at the Mega-Com isn't going to change things."

I waggled a hand at him. "Just let me think!"

He snorted, rolling his eyes. "By all means, Min. Find the magic exit."

We hadn't spoken much since the room was sealed. There wasn't a lot to say, though I could feel the sullen recrimination in his eyes. I'd led Derrick into this trap, underestimating Sarah even after promising myself I wouldn't.

She'd contacted us only once since closing the blast curtain, and then just to gloat. The intercom had abruptly hissed to life and her voice bounced off the metal walls. "Min, it is a *gold mine* back here. Why did you ever want to leave?"

I'd leapt to press the intercom. "Sarah, open the door. Please. We can work this out."

Laughter like nails on a chalkboard. "Oh, it's a *bit* late for that, Melinda. You had your chance. I can take it from here on my own." The speaker went dead a moment, then she was back, undisguised giddiness fluttering her voice. "You really can access the Program from here! The *source code*, Min. And you won't believe what the password is!"

My finger hovered over the button, but I had no idea what to say. The helpless panic of a caged animal ratcheted my pulse. What was she doing? How could I have been so stupid?

Sarah's voice returned, gleefully echoing across the room. "There are so many variables to the system. I think I'll make things more interesting. Did you guys miss wild animals much? Well, they're back!" Her tone became mock sympathetic. "Not that you'll see any in there."

"Piss off!" Derrick shouted, though he knew she couldn't hear him.

Her voice had crackled one last time. "This is amazing! I have complete control. I'm *never* coming out of here, Min. You really blew it. See you guys in Phase Three, though probably not!" The speaker had gone dead, and we hadn't heard from her since.

I rounded the MegaCom yet again, a square column six feet to a side and humming with energy and purpose. *I live in there. I'm part of that electricity.* Repressing a shiver, I turned from the supercomputer and began examining the chamber's metal walls.

"Why the plating?" I said aloud.

At first Derrick seemed determined not to answer, but then his hands flew up. "Magnetism. To keep the chamber clean. Because it looks scary. Who knows, man? What does it matter? It's not like we have power drills or a bomb."

"What if the plates were installed to plug an exit? A tunnel or something?"

Derrick pressed his forehead with his hands. "How. Does. That. Help. Us?"

I bit back a caustic reply, trying to get a feel for how the MegaCom was set up. "This thing has to have a power source. Some kind of battery, or engine, or generator. *Something* to keep it running."

"Yes, Min. Computers use electricity."

I spun to face him, irritation seeping into my voice. "Then where is it, Derrick?"

He opened his mouth, then closed it, his deep brown eyes growing squinty despite himself. "What do you mean?"

"What I *mean* is, where's the plug?" I did another quick circuit around the black pillar. "It has to have wiring connecting it to a power source. And they wouldn't build it in such a way that it couldn't be serviced." My hands spread from my sides. "So . . ."

Derrick nodded slowly, rubbing his cheek as he finished my sentence. "So there must be cables, and a way to access them. You can't just turn on this kind of hardware and never touch it again. The system must be crazy complex—it probably took years to debug."

Derrick rose for the first time in hours. Glanced up, then down. "I don't see a damn thing. The casing stops short of the ceiling and is built directly into the floor."

True. The bottom of the MegaCom was screwed to a steel platform. Which, in turn, was bolted to the floor, giving the whole apparatus an appearance of self-containment.

But that isn't possible.

"The wires must run through the floor," I decided, then shot

Derrick a level look. "Which means we have to do the same."

A quick exhale through his nose. "How the hell do we do that? That casing is airtight. Solid steel plates, screwed together like puzzle pieces. You gonna peel this thing open with your fingernails?" Derrick's shoulders slumped once more. "I'm not saying you're wrong, Min, but this is still a dead end."

A sour taste filled my mouth. *Dead end. Shit. It really might be.*

Derrick placed a hand against one seamless metal wall. "I bet there *was* another way into the silo. You're right, they had to get all that stuff in here somehow. But there's no reason to think they didn't block it once they were done. These might seal the back door."

Vitality seeped from my limbs. Derrick could be right. Why leave a way open once finished with it? They were trying to keep this place secret.

I glanced at the gun in my belt. My heart started thudding.

But if they sealed everything, the lab would have no emergency exit.

Derrick walked over and rapped the MegaCom with his knuckles. "Huh."

"Huh, what?"

He didn't answer, circling to the next side and knocking again. I followed him, questions forming on my lips but held at bay. Derrick tested all four sides of the monolith. His last set of knocks struck a different note. "Hello," he whispered, running a hand along the dark panel.

My fists found my hips. "Any time you're ready to share."

"This sounds hollow." Derrick's nostrils flared as he reared back to kick the panel, only just stopping himself. "But we can't get inside. Because we can't rip through solid steel with our bare hands."

"Not with our hands." I pulled the Beretta from my waistband.

Derrick's eyebrows nearly climbed off his forehead. "You're gonna shoot the MegaCom? Our lifeboat? The machine we literally *live* inside?"

I chambered a round. "This is a virtual re-creation of the MegaCom inside the Program, not the real thing. We'll be fine."

Eyes wide, Derrick tapped an index finger into his open palm. "You know that? You're *one hundred percent sure* of that? Because that's a helluva gamble."

"We either shoot this panel, or we shoot ourselves," I said flatly, crossing my arms with the gun in my hand. "Which do you prefer?"

Derrick bit his bottom lip, blinking rapidly. Finally, he gave a tight nod. "Screw it. Light the damn thing up."

"With pleasure." I took aim at the center of the panel, spreading my legs and bracing like Tack had shown me so many times.

"Not down the middle!" Derrick barked, waving his hands. "You'll hit something important, and what good is a bullet hole anyway?" He stomped over and adjusted my aim, easing me closer to the MegaCom while pointing with his finger. "Shoot the screws on the side, at an angle. There, there, and there."

"Right. Got it."

I rolled my neck. Measured my breathing. Lined up a shot and pulled.

The report was deafening, reverberating back at me from all sides. The acrid scent of gunpowder filled the air. But the Beretta had done its work. A corner of plating with a screw in it had been torn away.

Derrick rose from a crouch, grimacing with his hands over his ears. "Okay!" he shouted, holding up a pair of fingers. "Two more!"

The second shot was less clean. It took a third to blast the screw away. But Derrick was able to get his fingers into a crack and pull on the sheeting, bending it back a few inches. He stepped back, panting, a grin on his face. "Still can't see behind, but one more should do it."

I took aim. Blew a third screw to pieces, freeing up a six-foot section of casing. Derrick peeled back the dark metal like a tin can, revealing a tangle of wires inside.

Stacked blade servers ran up and down the MegaCom's guts, creating a central column that dropped through an open floor and descended into darkness. Bundles of wires surrounded it, connecting row upon row of other gleaming components I couldn't identify. The smell of ozone was strong, the array of blinking lights almost hypnotic. But I barely noticed this massive puzzle of hardware. My eyes were locked on a slender black ladder running down the left side of the interior.

"Boom!" Derrick clapped a hand on my shoulder, eyes alight. "It's like an iceberg. The biggest part is straight down."

I grinned back at him. "An iceberg thoughtfully equipped with a ladder."

"A way down."

"A way down might be a way out."

"After you, milady."

I shoved the gun into my jumpsuit pocket and stepped onto

a narrow rung. The way was snug, but wide enough for an average-sized person to squeeze. The chute smelled of hot wires and old dust, the only light coming from winking hardware. I passed through the floor into a cavernous chamber beneath it.

"Any lights?" Derrick called. "I can barely see these rungs."

"Hold on." Peering down, I could just make out a catwalk a few yards farther below my feet. I climbed down, stepped off the ladder with a clang, and spotted a metal box affixed to the railing. It had a switch. I flipped it, igniting a row of steel-caged lights along the catwalk and against the walls. This room was much larger than the one above. The catwalk hung in space roughly halfway to the floor, one end leading to a narrow tunnel cutting through the stone and disappearing from sight.

The MegaCom descended another twenty feet to the floor, its bottom third surrounded by a maze of pipes, transformers, tanks, and unfathomable machines, enough heavy equipment to fill a high school gymnasium. I spotted a sign posted at the column's base:

U.S. NAVY NUCLEAR POWER PLANT LEVEL
AUTHORIZED PERSONNEL ONLY

"Looks like we found the battery pack," Derrick said, then he glanced at me. "Should we keep going down, or try that creepy-as-hell tunnel over there?"

"Your guess is as good as mine." I took a deep breath, surprised at how glad I was to have him with me. We might've been mortal enemies only hours before, but I was extremely happy not to be down in that hole alone.

"I vote murder tunnel," Derrick said finally. "I don't know much about nuclear power plants except that I'm not trying to get near one. *Godzilla* scared me to death."

"Compelling. Lead the way."

I followed him down the catwalk and into the tunnel, praying the dim lights along its length wouldn't fail. We walked for what seemed like miles, twisting and turning, but always angling up. After the first dozen yards the passage became wide enough to drive a truck through. I was sure this was the route Project Nemesis had used to move things into the silo undetected. Which meant there should be a way outside.

After fifteen minutes we reached a place where the tunnel narrowed significantly, the walls creeping in on both sides until we had to walk single file. The concrete here looked newer than the passage behind us, and I got nervous, quick. Perhaps they'd sealed the way after all.

Then I spotted a tiny red light up ahead. The tunnel dead-ended into a blast door with a keypad like the ones above. It was locked.

"*No no no.*" I put my hands on my head, unable to accept that we were still trapped.

"Wait! What did Sarah say to you upstairs? About a password."

Tamping down my panic, I thought back. "She said I wouldn't believe what it was."

Derrick skewered me with a double-barrel stare. "That means you know it, Min. *Think.*"

I resisted the urge to punch him. He was right. I must know it, or Sarah's taunt made no sense. But what the hell could it be?

I chewed my thumb, mentally inventorying everything Sarah and I had in common.

Nothing. Sarah and I were as different as two people could be. We never hung out, never did anything together. The only thing we shared was a stupid quirk of . . .

Oh.

I tapped six digits into the keypad. It beeped once. Blinked green.

"Yes!" Derrick thrust both fists skyward, then winced as one struck the ceiling. Shaking out a bruised knuckle, he offered me five with his other hand. "Nice work, Wilder! What was it?"

"My birthday. *Our* birthday, I should say. Sarah and I share one."

All four betas did. I still didn't know what that meant.

Derrick shot me a quizzical glance. "But Sarah's birthday is—"

"It's a long story. I'll tell you on the walk, okay? Let's just get the hell out of here. I've been underground so long, I don't even remember fresh air."

"Gotcha." Derrick grabbed the handle and spun. The door creaked open, frigid winter winds enveloping us in an icy fist. I breathed deep. Felt a charge course through me.

I was out. I was alive.

I had work to do.

26

NOAH

I ran a hand across the waxy underside of the snowboard.

Pulled back my fingers with a sigh. The concrete floor squeaked as I turned down the next row of equipment, trying to calm my thoughts. This was a monumental decision. I had to think clearly, but my head felt like a block of wood.

I'd ducked inside a rental store a few doors down from the ski shop. I was alone, trying to sift through my feelings. Part of me wanted to give myself over to Tack's savagery and charge down the mountain, guns blazing. But a deeper, calmer voice was refusing to concede.

Tack assumed our enemies were stupid. Careless. But I knew better, maybe because I'd been friends with them in school and he hadn't. Sarah always thought of everything. She'd have considered all the angles even before Ethan's attack, and would've anticipated the current situation as a possibility. What seemed like an opening could easily be a trap.

Or was I just being spineless like Tack said?

I walked along another row, then another. I was in the gray cinder-block storage area in back, a utilitarian room packed with racks of skis, poles, and boards. I had fond memories of this place from when I was a kid, had even worked here one summer in junior high. Back in a life I could barely remember.

God, what was I going to do? Maybe I really wasn't cut out to lead.

I heard a bell jingle as the front door opened. I tensed, one hand automatically checking the gun in my jacket as I watched the swinging door. It creaked open and a head poked through. Akio. I didn't relax.

"Yes?" I said.

"Just checking in." Akio hesitated, then came through the doorway, short and slender, with spiky black hair and smooth features I could never get a read on. "You've been gone for a while. I saw you come in here and thought you might want to talk. Some of the others are getting impatient."

I caught his eye and held it. "And you?"

Akio seemed to understand what I was asking. He walked down the row to stand before me, then bowed his head. "They had me locked up for a while. Ethan and the others. I even saw Min when they brought her in months ago."

I knew that part. Min had told me. Her face popped into my thoughts, and I struggled to erase it. Another part of my old life, gone.

"She stole my idea, actually. Aced herself out to escape." Akio's eyes grew solemn. "I wasn't so lucky. They held me another three weeks, until Tucker got sloppy and left a fork on my dinner plate." A look of revulsion stole over his face. "We waited until nightfall, the ones who'd decided. Then we . . . ended each other, one at a time. The most horrifying jailbreak in history—a human murder chain. I went last. Ran myself into the wall."

No inflection. Akio seemed half dead as he spoke. I couldn't imagine the horror of what he was describing. He'd put the memory in a place without feeling, and I couldn't blame him.

"You did what you had to," was all I could say.

He nodded, took a deep, shuddering breath. "I stayed away from everyone after that. I . . . I was having a hard time. But Toby and those guys never stop. They burned me out of a house on High Street, then hounded me all the way to the quarry. The cousins took me in." He looked at me then. "Good people up there. I tried to convince them to link with you, but . . ." His gaze slid away, one hand rising to fiddle with a nearby ski. "Your reputation isn't the best these days," he finished.

I nodded, understanding completely. I had to be hard. That came with a cost.

"Why'd you come back?"

Akio ran a thumb along the ski. "I'd always planned to, it was just . . ." He dropped his arm. "I needed to work some stuff out. All this killing, I think . . . I feel like it's scarring me. Or maybe worse. Like it's changing who I am."

I licked my lips. Wanted to agree, but was afraid to. What if Akio was testing me?

I spoke softly. "No one could go through this and stay the same."

Akio's face twisted. "But it's more than that. I think we're losing our humanity. After each reset, I feel like I care a little bit less. It . . . it scares me. The voice inside that used to tell me to behave is fading."

The voice you ignore.

I put a hand on his shoulder, words of agreement tipping my tongue. But they never escaped. The swinging door hammered open and Tack walked in, hands on his hips, a scowl twisting his features. The time for softness evaporated.

Spotting us, he stomped over. "Noah, we need to go now. The whole point is surprise."

"I'll leave you," Akio said quietly, retreating for the door.

Tack watched him exit, eyes narrowed, then turned back to me. "Good. We're alone. Now you can stop posturing like a *Walking Dead* villain. We both know you're not cut out for this, so just give me 'permission' and I'll lead the attack. You can stay here and guard the hotel or something. Just stop standing in my way."

My pulse began pounding in my ears. The *nerve* of this smarmy little shit. "Go to hell, Tack. You're in *my* resort, with *my* team, as a guest. And you've already shown how bad you are under pressure. Leave the fighting to the big kids." A shot at his size, one I knew would land.

Tack didn't disappoint. His face purpled, chest heaving as he jabbed a finger at my face. "You stupid prick! The only reason *Min is dead* is because I left the fighting to you. You were a real hero that day—ditching her, alone, surrounded by enemies, so you could run and hide like the coward you are. You *abandoned* her, Noah. And now she's dead."

I don't remember making a decision.

My left fist flew, striking Tack across the face. Backed by my increased strength, the punch split his lip, sent Tack careening into the equipment rack behind him. Poles and skis tumbled everywhere.

He was up in a flash. Charged me like a bulldog. Tack's head slammed into my abdomen and the breath exploded from my body. We fell backward into the next row, flipping over it in a snarling mass and landing in a jumble of scattered gear.

Punching. Kicking. Clawing. The pent-up rage of weeks finally unleashed.

I planted a foot in Tack's midsection and launched him across the room. He hit the floor and skidded into the far wall, cracking a cinder block. I charged, tackling him as he tried to rise. Then I straddled his body and wrapped my hands around his throat.

Tack struggled like a fish, but I was bigger, had leverage, and had absorbed two eliminations to his one. I pinned him to the floor, squeezing. Watched his face turn bright red like a tomato.

I wanted to kill him. Erase him from this hill where I was king.

His struggles became more feeble. Tears streaked down his cheeks. An image flashed into my head: Tack putting a gun to his chest. Forcing Min to pull the trigger. Giving his life for hers.

I howled. Released him with a gasp. Was rewarded with a right hook to my chin.

I rose and staggered back. Tack tried to lurch after me, but

I shoved him to the floor. Backing away, I wiped my nose with a wrist that came away bloody. Tack scrambled into a crouch, blood dripping from his mouth, his chest pumping like a bellows.

We stared at each other, squinting, unsure what came next.

I felt something break inside me.

"Maybe you're right." I straightened, then my shoulders slumped. I put my hands in my pockets. All the pain in the world was swirling inside me. "You gave Min a chance. It never even occurred to me. I failed."

Tack's cheek twitched. He turned and spat blood onto the concrete. Then he rolled his eyes, expelling a high-pitched grunt. Tack rocked his head left and right before crossing his arms. "Oh, that's bullshit, too. There were six of them in the silo. No way you were getting them all, and you left her the gun. She was locked away."

An awkward silence grew. Stretched. Swallowed the room.

Tack's face twisted in a bloody half smile. "I enjoyed punching you."

I barked a laugh. "Likewise."

Then he stepped forward, eyes twinkling in the fluorescent light. "Let's do it, Noah. Let's take the fight to them. No more hiding, no more defending." His voice grew hard. "Let's make them pay for what they did to Min."

I squeezed my forehead, wavering. "What happens if it's a trap?"

Tack reached down and lifted a ski off the floor, then snapped it in half with his bare hands. "We handle that, too."

Something dark and ugly unfurled inside me. I found myself smiling.

Tack's face mirrored mine. He extended a fist.

I stared at it for a beat, then pounded it with my own.

27

MIN

Derrick fired four more times.

The bear roared, rearing up on its hind legs. Then it turned and thundered back into the forest, leaving a red smear on the understory.

"Why'd you do that?" I shouted in a cracked voice. "It was scared!"

My hands shook. The grizzly had appeared out of nowhere, bounding onto the woodland path and snarling at us, six hundred pounds of "you're screwed, kids."

Derrick gave me an incredulous look. "You know that bear isn't real, right?"

I hugged my arms to my chest. "Doesn't mean you had to shoot it."

His head flopped sideways. "You know that not-real bear could've ripped us to pieces, right? Then *eaten* us? With its teeth and claws?"

"You don't shoot at a grizzly," I clapped back peevishly. "That only pisses them off." I was being silly, and knew it, but I hated seeing animals get hurt. Even a giant fake one that might kill me.

So Sarah hadn't been bluffing. That bear was the first animal I'd seen inside the Program. How many were there now? Why would a bear be up and outside its den in the dead of winter? I got a bad feeling about this development. What else had Sarah unleashed?

Derrick was still shaking his head at me. "Is that how you wanna go out, Min? Mauled to death in the woods? I should shoot you, too. For being a jackass."

My hands found my hips. "Nice gun, by the way."

He had the decency to blush. "Okay, sorry. I lied. I do have a gun. But you know by now I'm not playing you, so can we please get past this teensy little dishonesty? I'm freezing to death out here."

We were south of the government land, in a remote corner of the valley. The sun was dipping in the western sky, but still held. Derrick and I didn't have a plan yet, but the path from the silo had gone this way, and it seemed as good a direction to head as any.

Beyond the silo's back door we'd found a narrow gravel track camouflaged by trees on both sides. After a mile it reached a tunnel that cut east into canyon country we'd been told our whole lives was impassible. A short debate had ensued.

I'd wanted to follow the road and see where it led, but Derrick wanted no part of that tunnel. Plus, he thought it was pointless. The simulation didn't extend beyond the valley, he'd argued, so the road couldn't lead anywhere. Odds were excellent it was somehow "blocked" like all the other paths—maybe inside the tunnel, deep in the dark, where we'd be blind and have to turn around.

I'd reluctantly agreed. So we'd plunged into the woods, angling south. Thirty minutes later, we'd met a bear.

"You've had a gun this whole time?" I grumbled, unwilling to just let it slide.

Derrick's shoulders rose and fell. "Call it an insurance policy. Let's move past it."

"Jerk."

The bastard winked at me. "At times. But I think we should focus on more important things, like not dying of hypothermia."

He was right. The temperature was down in the teens and, once again, I was in the woods without a jacket. My Nemesis jumpsuit was no match for Mother Nature—the swirling winds cut through the thin fabric like it wasn't even there.

Still, I was happy to be outside. Anywhere but trapped in that damn bunker. I inhaled deeply, soaking in the alpine scents. Pine sap. Wet leaves. Frozen earth. My eyes watered in the sunshine, and I blinked incessantly. Snowdrifts were swallowing my sneakers, tiny avalanches of ice sliding into my socks. But I was alive, on my own two feet, and free to move about as I pleased. That was something.

Then another icy gust bit through my jumpsuit, as if to remind me not to get cocky. I shivered uncontrollably, cold for the first time in weeks. The silo was always a sterile sixty-eight degrees. Adding days in my head, I realized it was now mid-December.

"Almost Christmas," I mumbled. "I completely forgot about it."

"No decorations in town yet," Derrick quipped. "I'm guessing Santa doesn't have virtual Fire Lake on his nice list." Then his voice grew serious. "I keep forgetting you haven't been out in two months. Things are different, and none of it's good. Downtown is torn up. Fires a week back burned all over the valley. You hear gunfire somewhere every single night. The place is falling apart. People don't act like people anymore."

I thought of the status number blinking on Tack's pedestal. Tried to ignore the queasiness it caused. "So what do you think we should do? I have to find a jacket right away, and your shoes are no better in the snow than mine." My stomach growled for the first time in weeks. "Food wouldn't hurt, either."

"That's the biggest problem," Derrick said, all six-plus feet of him shivering as he tried to stomp the cold from his sneakers. "Barely is any. Winter's here in full force, and the grocery store is gone, thanks to your psycho ex-boyfriend. And before you ask, I don't know where Thumbtack is. He might be running with Noah's crew, though. Two weeks ago I saw him shoot Chris in the back and take his machine gun."

The sick feeling in my gut grew stronger. "Where'd that happen?"

"Tack shot Chris at the library, then ran to the school. We lost him there."

I thought a moment. Tack liked sticking to himself. "He's probably in the trailer park."

Derrick's eyes slid away. He kicked a rock. "Yeah . . . I doubt it."

"What? What is it?"

Derrick blew out a breath. "The trailer park's gone, Min. After Tack popped Chris, Ethan and Toby went there with a bunch of kerosene and burned it down."

I swallowed, fighting back tears. "The whole thing?"

Mom's trailer. The only home I'd ever known. I hadn't visited it since the massacre at Town Hall—too obvious a place to look for me—but I'd often been comforted by knowing it was there. Her things had still been inside.

Derrick nodded unhappily. "They made sure. Tack wasn't there. At least, they never saw him."

Or they burned him alive, I wanted to scream. But I choked it back. Now wasn't the time. I sealed this new hurt in a safe and shoved it into a mental cabinet. I'd deal with it later, alone. "We need to resupply on this side of the lake, then," was all I said.

Derrick nodded, seemed relieved I wasn't going to break down. "From here, the liberty camp is closest."

I tapped a finger to my frozen lips. "Is anything there?"

Derrick shrugged. "To be honest, we've kinda ignored it. Those buildings are all cheap clapboard nonsense, and it's not close to anything. Place is probably abandoned. But I bet we can find some winter gear, at least."

I nodded in agreement. "If not, we can keep circling south of the lake, around toward the hillside neighborhoods. We'll find clothes there, maybe even food."

"Sounds like a plan. Let's get going. I wanna keep all my toes."

We started moving down the path again, eyes peeled for our grizzly visitor. The bear was nowhere to be seen, but the longer we walked, the more I felt a nameless anxiety stealing over me. I glanced at Derrick. His jaw was clenched, his lips moving silently as if arguing with himself. He must've felt it, too.

Then it hit me. Birds. I glanced up, spotted a hawk preening on a snow-covered perch high in a longleaf pine. It hopped back and forth a moment, then announced its presence to the forest. Focusing on the sounds around me, I heard other creatures chirping and squabbling.

I began scanning the canopy as I walked. Spotted a heavy brown squirrel skitter across a nearby branch. Sarah hadn't been kidding. She'd reintroduced animals with keystrokes. The implications were staggering. What else could she do behind that computer? Sarah was playing God, and there was nothing anyone could do about it.

But how? How can a player inside the Program manipulate it? Why didn't I figure it out?

I was stewing on that thought as we emerged from the woods in the southeastern-most corner of the valley. A mile later we reached the self-proclaimed liberty camp, a ramshackle collection of squatter buildings that had slowly built up over two decades and been grudgingly allowed to remain. Even before Nemesis, the camp had had a reputation for lawlessness and antigovernment hysteria, a den of unemployed drunks without many women or kids. It was a ghost town now.

Derrick and I halted near a beaten-earth circle surrounding a large communal fire pit.

"Jeez," he said.

"Not much to look at," I agreed.

Derrick rotated a slow three-sixty, surveying the camp as he blew into a fist for warmth. "You know, I've never actually been over here before. Toby used to come by to see his uncle, but I never went with him. It's even crappier than I thought." .

"Me neither." Though my body was almost completely numb from the cold, I wasn't eager to rush into any of the buildings. The camp had a distinctly creepy vibe, like some fake Old West town at a cheesy robotronic theme park. "My mom always wondered why Sheriff Watson never cleared this place out."

Derrick nodded, his face scrunched. "My parents, too. Everybody always worried about Fire Lake's rep as a tourist wonderland, but this freeloader camp was cool? How's that work?"

My teeth started chattering again. Creepy or not, I had to get inside somewhere. I began sizing up which shoddy tenement looked most likely to contain a jacket. "Don't forget, Watson worked for Project Nemesis, which meant the conspiracy probably made the call. I guess they preferred this area be undeveloped. And the people who lived here would never talk to any authority, even if they saw something weird. Makes sense when you think about it."

"Doesn't matter now." Derrick pointed in two directions at the same time. "Which disaster should we try first—the saggy barn with all the propane tanks, or that gem down there with a crate nailed to its side as a basketball goal?"

I shrugged. "Whichever's biggest, I guess."

Derrick clicked his tongue, removing his pistol from his pocket. "Saggy barn it is."

I frowned, then reluctantly did the same. Even took a moment to check the Beretta's magazine. Five rounds. Ammunition was going to be a problem soon, too.

Derrick waited until I was ready, then slunk toward the building's only door. I followed a step behind, listening carefully, one eye on the buildings surrounding us. Derrick reached out and tried the knob, then turned to me, eyes narrowing as he mouthed a word. *Locked.*

My pulse accelerated, but I took a calming breath. Could mean anything. Could mean nothing. I mimed a kicking motion. He nodded and took a few steps back. Derrick rolled his shoulders. Cracked his neck. Then he sprang forward, unleashing a long leg in an improvised karate kick. The heel of his shoe slammed into the knob and the door rocketed inward.

A shout from within, quickly stifled.

I dropped into a crouch. Teeth bared, Derrick pointed at me, put two fingers to his eyes, then aimed them at the camp behind us. I nodded, pivoting to watch our backs. Gripping his pistol tightly, Derrick sucked in a deep breath and rushed the doorway.

"Don't shoot!" a girl shouted.

"Hands!" Derrick thundered, his voice carrying from inside. I gritted my teeth, wanting to help him, but he'd been right. Someone had to make sure we weren't ambushed.

"Okay, okay! Just please don't shoot!" The girl said something muffled, then, "Put it down, Aiken. Don't be an idiot. Derrick, it's not even loaded!"

Aiken. Which meant the girl must be Anna Loring, his forever girlfriend. I hadn't seen either of them since everything started. Had they been hiding here the whole time?

"Drop it, Aiken." Derrick's voice was ice cold.

A moment hung in the balance, then I heard something heavy hit the floor.

"Keep watch out there!" Derrick shouted at me. Then, "You two alone?"

"Yes," Anna said. "I mean, no. We're alone in this building, but not the camp."

That got my attention. I took cover behind one of the tanks beside the door, began scanning the other buildings for signs of occupation.

"Don't tell him anything," a male voice snarled. Aiken Talbot for sure.

"Who else?" Derrick demanded in no-nonsense tone. "Don't mess around, guys. *I'm* not getting shot today, but you might if you play this wrong."

Not being able to see them was killing me. I slid closer to the open doorway, keeping my eyes on the rest of camp. Nothing moved anywhere. If there were others hiding, they'd chosen to stay that way.

"You're . . . you're not here to shoot us?" Anna said.

"Of course he is," Aiken spat, his words laced with venom. "Ethan's thugs are shooting everyone. Just do it already, you beanpole prick. We can take it."

Derrick spoke with as much patience as he could muster. "I'm not with Ethan anymore, and I have zero plans to shoot you. But that can change right quick if you don't answer the damn question. Who else is in this camp?"

"Not with Ethan?" Aiken scoffed. "Then who's outside?"

"Min Wilder."

"Bullshit."

"I'm here, Aiken!" I called. "And we're not here to shoot you."

"That's her." I heard the surprise in Anna's voice. "No way

300

she's working with Ethan, Aik. I think they're telling the truth."

"Glad you're finally on board," Derrick snarked, his irritation plain. "Now, pretty please, *tell me who the hell else is out there.*"

"It's just Hector," Anna said over Aiken's grunt of protest. "He's not even armed."

Hector Quino. I relaxed a bit. Hector was the nicest kid in our school, even ran the youth group. I couldn't imagine him hurting anyone.

Most of the tension had left Derrick's voice. "Okay. All right. Just you three?" There was a pause where someone must've nodded. "Then let's get him over here, please."

It took a minute to figure out how best to accomplish this. In the end, we all walked over to the basketball-goal house. Derrick kept his gun out, just in case. As we approached, I spotted a shadow by the window. A moment later the door swung open. Hector stepped outside with his hands up, breath misting, brown eyes wide.

I glanced at my companion. "Put it away, Derrick. Hector's not the type to play murder bait, and we're not here to cause trouble."

Derrick nodded, shoved the gun into his jeans. Everyone eased a bit. "You guys been out here the whole time?" I asked Anna.

A sour-faced girl with short red hair and beady doll's eyes, Anna never really seemed to smile. "Mostly," she said. "This hellhole is as far from everyone else as we could get." Her hand found her boyfriend's. "Those jerks already attacked Aiken once."

Anna and Aiken were Fire Lake's slacker power couple.

Short, slight, and sarcastic, forever in his cherished jean jacket, Aiken had greasy brown hair grown long during the months of isolation. He'd mouthed off to Toby early on—back in the church, before everything truly went to hell—and had taken a vicious beating for it. Add in Hector, who abhorred all forms of violence, and we'd found the trio least likely to ever side with Ethan and Sarah.

Aiken pointed an accusatory finger at Derrick. "You've been with them the whole time."

Derrick looked down at the ground. Shuffled his feet. "Well, not anymore. Not after . . ."

Hector surprised everyone by speaking. "After that?" He pointed west.

Derrick didn't look, a lump forming in his throat. "Maybe," he said quietly.

Silence fell. I glanced from face to face, then peered in the direction Hector had pointed. Didn't see anything. "What'd I miss?" I asked finally.

Anna tugged on Aiken's arm. "Let's just get insi—"

"You didn't hear about Starlight's Edge?" Aiken spoke loudly, clearly needling Derrick. "Your new pal didn't tell you what he and his buddies did at the summer camp?"

Derrick shouldered past Aiken. He opened the door to Hector's building and stepped inside without looking back.

I turned to Hector. His eyes were glassy.

"Murder," Aiken growled. "Toby and his jackboots stormed the place in the middle of the night, shot everyone living there, and then burned it to the ground. We could hear them screaming from here." Anna's shoulders began to quiver. Aiken wrapped an arm around her, glaring at the door Derrick had used. "Who knows, maybe Stretch in there led the charge? Those guys are monsters, Min. Nowhere is safe."

"Enough," Anna said, wiping her nose. "It's getting colder. We can talk in Hector's place." She pulled on Aiken again, and this time he relented. They headed toward the house.

I glanced at Hector. "You should stay with us," he said. "We don't have much, but it's safer than the alternatives. There's nothing out there but death now."

I opened my mouth. Closed it. Didn't know what to say.

Hector seemed to notice my jumpsuit for the first time. "What are you wearing, by the way? God, you must be freezing. Come on, let's get inside. We've got an incredible array of bad sweaters for you to choose from."

Hector held out a hand for me. I hesitated, then took it. We followed the others inside and shut the door firmly behind us.

28

NOAH

The shop was deathly quiet as Tack spoke.

Camping lanterns were lit, throwing orange pools of light. No one mentioned our battered faces. What had happened was obvious, but just as obviously, Tack and I had come back united in purpose. I'd called everyone together, then given him the floor.

Outside, night had fallen, and the temperature was dropping rapidly. The wind picked up, raking the mountaintop with swirling crystal clouds. Heavy clunks announced a hailstorm, fist-sized missiles thudding down like icy baseballs. The weather was eerie. Apocalyptic. It felt like a taunt. My anger at the Program smoldered just beneath the surface.

Yet Tack was oddly encouraged. What better conditions for launching a sneak attack?

I'd given him the okay. We would hit town with everything,

leaving no one behind. The Guardian had told me to win at all costs, so that's what I'd do. There'd be a reckoning with him, too. Someday. But Ethan and Sarah had to be dealt with first.

"The plan is simple." Tack was sitting cross-legged on the floor with everyone gathered around him. I stood at his side, providing implicit approval. "We take the fight to them, *tonight*, under the cover of this blizzard. We'll hit hard and fast, no stopping until we torch Emerald Tower and everything inside. Then we'll set a trap for anyone coming back to help them."

"And if they're waiting for us?" Leighton asked, knees pulled into his chest as he sat on a sleeping bag beside the space heater. "No offense, Tack, but I doubt they haven't planned for an attack. Our last one sure didn't work."

Tack nodded at Leighton's concern. "Last time, you had fewer people, and didn't use a distraction. We won't do that again." He avoided glancing at me, for which I was thankful. My previous attempt had been stupid and costly. I prayed we weren't repeating that mistake.

"What distraction are you planning?" Richie asked, yellow eyes gleaming in the lantern light. "That means some people won't be making the charge."

Tack hesitated, running his tongue across his teeth. His gaze bounced from face to face as he fidgeted with his fingers. I waited impatiently. We hadn't discussed this part. I could sense that whatever was coming next, I wasn't going to like it.

"Okay." Tack cringed a little, one hand scratching at his cheek. "This is going to sound crazy at first."

Bad start.

He took a deep, committing breath. "We need to pool our resources."

I looked down at him. "Pool them how? Everyone has access to the arsenal. We share everything already."

Tack squinted at the floor, then his head came up, a new resolve hardening in his eyes. "I mean our *human* resources."

For a moment, I just blinked at him. Then my eyes widened. "No."

His hand shot up, index finger extended. "Just hear me out!"

"Tack, you're out of your f—"

"There are people in this room staring at the death limit," Tack blurted quickly, over a rising chorus of murmurs. "We can't go on the offensive knowing some of you might not come back."

Cash and Richie shifted nervously. Jamie began chewing her hair. I moved around so I could see Tack's face, my implicit approval revoked.

"*Further,*" he forged ahead, "Ethan's best people are jacked up on eliminations by now. We'll have the element of surprise, but we need to match their speed and strength. And the only way to do that is by . . . sharing."

My mouth was hanging open. I glanced around, saw eyes widening as more of the others comprehended what Tack was suggesting.

Tack continued doggedly. "But there's another benefit. Ethan has two-or three-man teams at every reset zone, in the four corners of the valley. Any attack on downtown leaves those people at our backs. Bad idea. But my plan solves *that* problem, too."

I couldn't take it anymore. "You want us to kill each other. On purpose. That's what you're suggesting."

Tack winced, shifting his weight. "Well, I wouldn't describe it like that. But . . . yeah."

"Dude." Cash's hands rose to grip the sides of his head. "Dude."

Leighton was staring at Tack as if a stray dog had wandered into the room and thrown up on the carpet. Richie and Jamie were both shaking their heads. Akio kept his face guarded, but worry lines creased his brow. Only Kyle seemed to be giving Tack's insane idea any real consideration.

"We kill two birds this way." Tack made a face. "Okay, poor choice of words. But I'm serious! Our attack squad will get stronger while at the same time we're secretly sending people to ambush Ethan's reset teams. They'll never see it coming! It's perfect."

"Problem," I said immediately. "Weapons don't reset. We'd be sending unarmed people against armed groups that are specifically watching for them."

"Not true!" Tack countered, bounding to his feet. He took off his jacket and then, with a flourish, unzipped its waterproof liner and removed a long, thin knife. "Weapons integrated directly into clothing travel with you. I've tested it."

This stopped everyone short. If Tack was telling the truth . . .

"Guns?" I asked sharply.

"I'm not sure," he admitted, but then hurriedly added, "Knives *definitely* do, though. I haven't had the chance to test a gun, but that doesn't mean the same principle won't apply. And either way, our people won't be totally unarmed. Plus, it'll be pitch dark out, and they won't be expecting resets during a blizzard. Who'd be out fighting in this? They'll never see us coming!"

I opened my mouth to end this nonsense, but hesitated. There was a certain brutal logic to what Tack was saying. And if guns *did* slip through, that was a game changer. We could seize control of the valley in one swoop.

"Think about it," Tack pressed, clearly sensing an opening. "We hit downtown and torch their base of operations. While it's happening, they'll think help is coming, but instead *our* people attack from behind. We'll smash them! Ethan's crew will be totally uprooted, waking up at the reset points without weapons or supplies, in weather you can't survive overnight outdoors. If everything goes right, they might even surrender!"

Skeptical looks were fading, replaced by hungry expressions. Even I found myself daring to believe. If this worked, we'd *rout* those arrogant pricks. One bold, daring raid to finally break the stalemate.

"Let's do it."

The words were out before I could stop them. Tack beamed. Eyes shot to me. Suddenly it was *my* plan, and the others needed more.

Adrenaline surged through me as I barked out orders. "We pair off. One for the zones, the other for town." I felt invigorated. Inspired. We could do this. We *would* do this. I did the math in my head, sorting who needed a reset and who could spare one. "Strike team: Me. Tack. Jamie. Richie. Zone team: Akio. Kyle. Leighton. Cash. Wherever you guys reset, hit Ethan's people while they're zipped in their tents, then come join the assault on town."

Nods. Scattered cheers. Kyle circled the room, pounding people's shoulders, trying to jack everyone up. We were united in purpose. Then a pit opened in my stomach as I thought of the next step.

I'd just sentenced four people to death.

We assembled in the courtyard. The storm had risen in intensity, sheets of razor-fine snow blowing sideways and abrading exposed skin. Our jackets had been altered, handguns and tactical knives sewn directly into the lining. I prayed the ploy would work.

"Time to go!" I shouted over the wind, waving a hand. Everyone was bundled up like Arctic explorers, ski goggles in place so you couldn't see their eyes. It was better that way, given what we were about to do.

Four pairs reluctantly faced off in the snow. I removed a pistol from my jacket pocket and pulled the slide. Felt a deepening horror steal over me.

This isn't right. It's not how decent people act.

I shoved the thought away. It was too late for second-guessing.

Akio stood before me, trembling, and not likely from the cold. I was stronger than him and didn't need the kill, but Tack and I had to lead the town assault. Akio had the wiggle room to provide a life and would be invaluable attacking the zones. He'd go from one to the next, hunting Ethan's teams and keeping them off our backs. So I fiddled with my weapon, giving him a moment to compose himself.

Akio nodded. Stiffened.

I put the gun barrel to his forehead. Watched his chest heave in and out.

The revulsion inside me grew. My hand shook and I hesitated, but I was only making this worse for him.

A shot rang out to my left, followed quickly by two others.

Three bodies slumped to the ground, then vanished. But I stood there, frozen.

"Do it," Akio whispered. Head down, shaking all over. "Please, Noah, just do it now."

I bit down hard on my tongue. Felt tears freezing on my cheeks. Tack was striding over, chambering another round in his pistol. If I didn't shoot Akio, he would, and I'd look soft in front of everyone.

I'll give it back. I promise I'll give it back.

A cold wind swirled up from somewhere deep inside me.

With a silent scream, I pulled the trigger.

29

MIN

"I need to find Tack," I repeated stubbornly.

"You're nuts," Derrick said. "He's not the same dude, Min."

He was lying on a ratty three-seat couch, cocooned in a quilted blanket. The five of us had gathered around a wide brick hearth in Hector's house, the only feature in the building that looked well crafted. A crackling fire burned in its rugged iron grate.

I sat cross-legged in a rocking chair pulled close to the flames, soaking in the heat. It was pitch black outside. The temperature kept dropping, high winds tossing sheets of stinging sleet at the fogged windows.

Derrick sat halfway up, adjusting a borrowed Gonzaga Bulldogs toboggan on his head. "The valley is a nightmare factory right now." He pointed to several massive storage bins stacked in the corner of the single-room building. "That's the most food

I've seen in one place since the supermarket exploded. Enough for weeks. Thank God these liberty dudes were hoarders. Min and I would make five in this camp, which is enough to set decent watches."

"You're welcome to stay," Hector said, just as Aiken said, "Who invited you?"

Anna elbowed her boyfriend in the chest. They were wrapped in a blanket on the couch opposite Derrick. Hector sat on the floor between them, zipped into two fleeces, elbows on the wagon wheel coffee table.

"Stop being an idiot," Anna scolded Aiken. "Min and Derrick have guns *with actual bullets in them.* You were just saying how we need more people to protect ourselves. Well, they walked in the front door!"

"Kicked it in." Aiken sat forward abruptly and glared at Derrick. "Were you part of that summer camp raid, Derrick? Tell us now."

Derrick met his eye. Shook his head firmly. "I ran a snatch-and-bag crew at the southern reset point, Min knows that firsthand. But I've *never* gone out shooting. That's a promise." He looked at me then, and I could tell he was desperate for me to believe him. "Not once, on my life. Hell, that's why I'm stuck out here with you guys now."

"I believe you," I said. I did. I'd seen his face in the clone room.

Aiken was still scowling, but he nodded finally, slumping back into Anna's arm.

Derrick smiled brightly. "It's settled then. Are any of the other shacks livable, or am I bunking in with Hector?"

"It is *not* settled." My feet dropped to the floor and I rocked forward. "Hiding is a temporary solution at best. Right this minute Sarah is locked inside the silo, doing whatever she wants to the whole Program. Meanwhile, Ethan could decide to come burn this place down at any time. We need to *stop* the insanity."

"You could do it," Hector said. "You just have to show the others a way."

My eyebrows shot up. "Um, not likely."

"It's true." Hector's brown eyes glowed with reflected fire-light. "Everyone heard the Guardian mention you by name. Plus, you've opposed Ethan and Sarah from the beginning. If you stood up to them, I think people would rally around you. I know I would."

"Whoa, whoa." I rocked back in my chair and crossed my arms, shrinking into the fleece Hector had given me. "Most kids never gave me the time of day back in school—the ones who didn't actively pick on Tack and me, that is. I'm not trying to replace Ethan. I just want . . . We just have to . . ." I trailed off, unable to finish the sentence.

I didn't know what to do. Less than anyone, probably. I'd been hiding underground for the last two months, doing nothing. The idea that *I'd* lead a revolt against the most dangerous people in Fire Lake was laughable. Devin would've stood a better chance.

Devin's gone. Eliminated by Ethan for dropping a Hot Pocket. How many more will join him?

For a few heavy eyeblinks, I just wanted to go home. To curl up in my old bed and sleep for days. But my trailer was gone. Burned to the ground. I'd never have a home again.

"Someone has to lead," Hector pressed, unwilling to take the hint. "You're a fighter, Min. You don't give up. Everyone's seen it. Ethan's thrown you in jail twice, and you escaped both times. Who else can say that? If you don't step up against the other betas, who will?"

I barked an uneasy laugh, pulled my knees up to my chest. "Take it easy, Braveheart. I'm just trying to avoid being deleted."

I'd already told them everything. Reset limits. How the count worked. Eliminations. About Ethan's plan to jail everyone, and Sarah adding wild animals to the valley. Their eyes had grown wide as they'd listened to my misadventures around the lake with Tack, screwing up time and time again. Yet Hector suddenly wanted to knight me? Please.

Derrick had chipped in as well, describing the chaotic breakdown back in town. Toby and Ethan had grown secretive and unruly, no longer content to merely cage people. They'd unleashed a string of murders that had finally driven him away.

"The Nolan brothers burned down the whole marina on a dare." Derrick rubbed his face with both hands, eyes fixed on the wooden plank floor. "I screamed at them about it—Mike and I even scrapped a little bit. After that, they all stopped telling me things. That's why I didn't know about the raids. Toby and some others hit the summer camp, wiped it out, then tried to do the same at the quarry. The cousins are tough, though. Toby and the twins surprised them at first, and burned down that warehouse they had, but Carl and Sam pulled back into a mineshaft or something. They mowed attackers down for three straight days. Toby must've gotten killed seven, eight times at least. Just kept coming back at them until eventually even he gave up. Word is the cousins lost some folks and most of their supplies. They're starving now. That's when I left."

It was shocking. Appalling. These were just stupid boys. We'd had lockers in the same hall. Taken Spanish together. Chris Nolan and I once built a balsa wood tower for a project in seventh grade.

"What about Town Hall?" Aiken asked. "Did the Guardian ever come back out?"

Derrick sighed long and loud. "Nope. And the building is still pristine. Even fire won't touch it—Toby's tried everything you can imagine." His gaze slid to me. "Someone went in, though."

I sat up straight, eyes popping. "What?"

Derrick seemed to relish his little surprise. "The same day he blew up the grocery store, your boy Noah walked right up to the front door and stepped inside."

I stared, open-mouthed. Derrick giggled darkly. "Saw it myself. Noah was dragging one of his injured guys, and we cornered him on the steps. He retreated in past the columns. But when we charged, no Mr. Livingston."

I relaxed. "Then you hit him. They reset. Or maybe he slipped around you."

Derrick shook his head. "Nope. I saw the door. The keypad was blinking green for a hot second, then turned red again. I've been by there dozens of times and it's always just red, even when you fiddle with it. Someone went inside. But there was a gun battle going on behind me, so I had to book."

I was speechless. Began chewing on a fist, one foot dropping to the floor and tapping furiously. Why hadn't Noah told me? How'd he get inside? *What happened in there?*

Facts coalesced in my head. I'd somehow opened the blast door to the lab complex. Noah had gotten into Town Hall when no one else could. Were those things connected?

Then I nearly gasped. Sarah had accessed the Program by using our shared birthday.

Me. Noah. Sarah.

Beta. Beta. Beta.

Test patients chosen by the Guardian, in a program he designed.

If Noah got inside, maybe I can, too.

The Guardian. He was the only one who knew everything. If I could get to him, maybe I could stop all this. Shut the madness down all by myself.

"Yo, Min?" Derrick was waving a hand to catch my attention. "Where'd you go?"

I took a deep breath. Glanced from face to face. All eyes were on me.

"Actually, we need to talk about where I'm going."

"I'll never forgive you for this," Derrick grumbled, pulling his scarf tighter.

My teeth were chattering so badly, I could barely answer. "No one made you come."

He harrumphed, but said nothing. It was true he'd volunteered, and I was extremely grateful for it. I didn't want to be out in the dark alone.

We'd dressed in the warmest clothes Hector could scrounge. Jeans. Sweaters. Two ugly fleece-lined ski jackets—mine was a disturbingly bright shade of pink—and an unstylish assortment of mismatched gloves and hats. A flurry had kicked up, and the temperature was dropping off a cliff. Our path took us west along the lakefront, headed for the swanky docks below the southwestern neighborhoods. We walked past the charred remains of the summer camp, a stern reminder of what was at stake.

My plan was simple. Steal a boat, cross the lake, and sneak into Town Hall.

I didn't think beyond that point. Not yet. I had no idea what I'd say to the Guardian, or whether he'd listen to me. Or if he'd even be there. Or if I could really get inside. But I had to try. He was the only one who could reverse what the Program had become.

"It's gotta be ten below zero," Derrick moaned. "Coldest night of the year, by far. And hailing! How is that even possible?"

I stopped short, slapping my forehead. *Of course.* Derrick glanced back at me curiously, then sucked in a breath. We spoke in unison. "Sarah."

All the more reason I had to try this. Ethan and Toby had turned the valley into a war zone, but Sarah could make the environment itself a threat. We'd heard wolves howling as we set out, which quickened our steps in a way the weather never could. What else could she input to plague us?

We reached a long, sturdy pier capped by a tidy boathouse. Derrick and I scurried down its length as quickly as possible, a full moon lighting up the night sky and reflecting off the lake's icy surface. The boathouse had a large sliding door sealed with a padlock. We'd prepared for this—Derrick removed a set of bolt cutters from his jacket. He cracked the lock and we slipped inside, breathing twin sighs of relief.

Too soon.

Lights flicked on all along the ceiling.

Small boats were stacked four-high in racks to both sides of a central aisle. I glanced up, saw a rifle pointing down at me from a dinghy. Derrick grunted, eyes rounding. Another gun barrel was covering us from a canoe on the right.

"Don't fucking move!"

"Nobody's moving!" Derrick blurted, hands slowly rising. "Just chill."

Two heads appeared. Boys have said Casey Beam has the best smile in school, but it was nowhere in sight at the moment. She blew blond tendrils from her mouth, one eye squeezed shut as she aimed at my head. Lauren Decker glared down from Derrick's side, pug nose sneering, her brown hair pulled back in a loose ponytail. Soccer players both, they'd been inseparable since first grade, along with a third girl named Dakota Sargent. This wasn't a worst-case scenario, I didn't think, but their guns were screaming something different.

Lauren sat upright in the canoe, her gun trained on Derrick's chest. "Both of you drop everything you're carrying, strip down to your underwear, and then leave. One funny wiggle and you catch a bullet."

Derrick blinked at her, pressing fingertips to forehead. "Do you have any idea how cold it is outside? You might as well just shoot us."

"Suit yourself." Lauren flipped off the safety and worked the action on her rifle. "Tell Ethan to burn in hell."

"Wait!" I shouted, inching a very small step forward with my hands up. "He's not with Ethan anymore. He flipped."

"I need to put out a newsletter or something," Derrick mumbled, a ring of sweat dampening his brow.

Casey swung her legs over the dinghy's rail and dropped to the floor, as lithe as you'd expect from Fire Lake's all-state striker. "Why should we believe that?"

I snorted a mildly hysterical laugh. "Well, he's with *me*, for one. You think I'm palling around with Ethan these days?"

Lauren climbed down with considerably less grace to stand shoulder to shoulder with her friend. "Fine," she said, red-faced and puffing. "You can keep your clothes on, but everything else stays. Guns especially."

Derrick made a face like he'd smelled something rotten. "What, you guys are just robbing people?"

"It's a living," Casey said, and the megawatt smile emerged. "If it makes you feel better, we've done this a dozen times. You're the first to come to us, though."

Something clicked. "The fishermen," I muttered.

"Fisher*women*," Lauren corrected. "Did we mug you once already?"

I crossed my arms. "Tack and I avoided you. You looked like two ducks waiting to get plucked. We assumed no one could actually be that stupid, and went around."

"These ducks have claws," Lauren said with a smirk. "Others haven't been as smart."

I glanced deeper into the boathouse. "I assume Dakota is here somewhere?" Tack had never pinned those three down on his map. He'd be giddy for this new information. Then I remembered his masterpiece was likely burned to cinders along with the rest of the trailer park, and my mood went further south.

A shadow crossed Casey's face. Lauren's bottom lip began to tremble, one hand leaving her rifle to wipe her eyes.

"Dakota's gone," Casey said, in a voice as bitter as chalk. "Ethan has a lot to answer for."

I took another small step forward. "I agree. Let us help."

Lauren's gun barrel swung to face me. "Help how?" Casey asked coolly.

I told them everything. What we'd learned. Where I was going. What I hoped to do. By the time I finished, their rifles were sagging in their hands, forgotten.

"You really think you'll reach the Guardian?" Casey asked. "No bullshit, Min."

I shrugged. "I honestly don't know. But if I can, maybe I can do . . ." I spread my hands helplessly. " . . . *something*."

"Min might be the only person who can make a difference," Derrick said curtly, "so you've got to stand aside. We need our clothes, our guns, and"—he rapped his knuckles against a rowboat—"one of these bad boys."

"Not we."

I'd made a decision as Derrick spoke. This mission was incredibly dangerous, with no reasonable expectation of success. "You're staying with them." Derrick opened his mouth to protest, but I didn't give him an opening. "This is on me alone. I doubt you can get inside Town Hall anyway, so there's no point. You can't change that."

He stared down at me for a long moment. "Fine. But at least let me row you over."

"*So* . . ." Casey interrupted drily, "Lauren and I have decided to let you go. In case that's important to you."

I gave her a crooked smile. "Thanks."

Lauren snorted. "Frankly, you guys need our help pretty bad. I'd love to see this row-across-the-lake plan in action."

Derrick bristled at her rebuke. "What's that supposed to mean?"

The girls set their guns down, Casey slipping past us to re-secure the door. Lauren crossed her arms and smirked. "Look outside, genius. The temperature's been dropping all day."

It hit me in a flash. "Ice."

Lauren graced me with a condescending nod. "You don't need a boat, kids. Just some Yaktrax. Those boots were made for walking."

She jabbed a thumb over her shoulder toward the end of the pier.

"Town Hall is thataway."

The marble steps were covered in snow.

I climbed quickly, ruing the deep footprints I was leaving behind. Then I darted behind a column and expelled a relieved breath. Crossing the lake had been the worst hike of my life. I desperately hoped it hadn't been for nothing.

The blizzard had intensified the second I stepped onto the ice. After carefully testing my weight, I'd mouthed a quick prayer to the laws of thermodynamics and crossed at a near trot, heart pounding with every creak beneath my feet. But the sur-face held—I'd scrambled up a ladder at the downtown water-front and slunk into an alley. Up a block, around the corner, and I was there.

The building was dark and ghostly, yet undamaged, in sharp

contrast to the many other trashed and ruined structures along Main Street. A red light glowed beside the door. Since the moment Phase Two engaged, Town Hall had been impregnable. No matter what was tried, nothing marred the alabaster perfection of the Guardian's lair.

At least, I *thought* the Guardian was in there. No one knew for sure.

Noah does. He went inside and didn't tell me.

That stung my pride, even as it frightened me. I'd hoped something had shifted between us back at the silo. I'd been surprised to discover my anger leaking away, even as I fought to hold it. But I'd been wrong again. Noah still kept secrets. I didn't know him anymore. Maybe I never did.

I shivered, rubbing my gloved hands together as I crept between the marble pillars. I blamed Sarah for the vicious turn of weather, but that could be paranoia—December in Idaho meant heavy snowstorms were always possible.

But we're not in Idaho, and this isn't December.

Derrick was out in this mess, too, driving Casey's SUV back to the liberty camp. The soccer girls weren't actually living in the boathouse, they'd just been waiting out the storm there when we came stomping up the dock. The girls had taken over two small houses on a secluded driveway in the southwestern hills and grudgingly invited us to join them there, mainly because we had food and they were out.

Derrick's job was to convince Anna, Aiken, and Hector that seven was better than five, that real houses were superior to shacks, and then load up the liberty camp stores and get back undetected. He was in for a long night, same as me, though at least he'd spend it in a warm vehicle. I'd just walked across the Arctic Circle to get here, and still didn't know if I'd wasted my time.

A whirlwind of doubts spun through me as I approached the entrance. Perhaps Noah had found a key. Maybe the door only opened at certain times. My theory about betas having access could be me grasping at straws, forcing a pattern where none existed.

I'll know in seconds. Gritting my teeth, I reached for the handle. But before I laid a finger on it, the keypad flashed green, there was an audible click, and the door swung open.

I blinked. That was easy.

Warmth and light flowed through the opening, hooking me like a siren's song. I stepped inside and closed the door behind me.

30

NOAH

It was so cold I could barely breathe.

The snow attacked from all angles, swirling, dancing, dumping down on us, needling exposed skin like biting insects. By the time we reached the bottom of the slopes, my whole body was numb. No sane person would be out in this weather. The frigid gusts never slowed or faltered, pounding the valley with relentless icy fists. It felt unnatural, like a hurricane was parked over the mountains.

I'd tweaked Tack's plan for stealth. First, we'd waited two more hours to give our teammates a chance to reset. I didn't know how long that process would take, but everything needed to kick off at roughly the same time, so I made a best guess. The insane snowstorm should still ensure the element of surprise. I prayed they were moving into position now as well.

Second, charging straight down Main Street again seemed foolhardy, brought back memories of losing Zach. No, instead we'd swing around on High Street, above Main, bypassing the center of town. Emerald Tower was farther from us, beyond the sheriff's office and the sporting goods store, on the other side of town over by the marina. We'd get above it, then shoot down a side street and hit it from the north. We'd catch them looking in the wrong direction, if they were even looking at all.

Tack had thought a moment after hearing my strategy—I suspected he was testing the idea for any sign it might be me backing off—then agreed without a fuss. He just wanted to go. Hit them hard and hurt them. Pay them back for Min, one bullet at a time.

Now it was time. Soundless steps as we powered through the drifts. Visibility was no more than five feet. Everyone wore all-white gear lifted from the ski shop—it seemed impossible that anyone would see us coming.

Split into pairs, we entered town near the remains of the grocery store and scurried onto High Street, following it straight uphill two blocks before the road took a hard left and ran parallel to Main. I could barely see Tack shadowing me on the opposite sidewalk. We needed to go six blocks east, then turn back down toward the lake. A challenge in the terrible weather, but doable.

With my hood up and ski goggles in place, I was in my own little world. The muscle burn of working through deep snow had kept my mind blank, but as we scurried past the high school and town square, doubt began to plague me. I couldn't shake the feeling that I was forgetting something.

We passed Dr. Lowell's office and my mouth went dry. The reality of what we were doing crashed in on me, speeding my pulse and slicking my palms inside my gloves. I'd risked everything on this toss of the dice, something I'd sworn I wouldn't do again. But it was too late to second-guess. Not after what we'd done to our teammates.

Clipper Lane was a side street connecting the park neighborhood above town to the marina sector below. Reaching its intersection, I flattened myself against the wall of a bakery on the corner. Felt Jamie move in beside me. Tack and Richie fired across the narrow lane to take up positions on the opposite side.

Dropping to a knee, I peered down the alley as the wind ruffled my jacket. Even enhanced, I couldn't see much. The street was dark and gloomy, though diffused moonlight illuminating the clouds like snow globes gave everything a pale blue glow. God, it was freezing. The temperature had to be fifteen below zero. This was an all-time blizzard, something my mind rejected as illogical inside a simulation. Unless someone *wanted* it this bad. Was the Guardian finally losing his patience?

No movement. No sounds. Not that I could hear anything less than a bullhorn in these elements. I knew the tower was two blocks ahead, where this slick, snow-covered lane dead-ended into Main Street. We were directly above it, and would descend on that building like an avalanche. Blow the whole thing straight to hell.

I watched for a moment longer, then realized it was pointless. I couldn't see to the bottom of the alley. We just had to go.

Something emerged from the swirling snow and I reached for my gun, but it was only Tack. He knelt, cupped his hands to my ear. "No point waiting! Let's go now while the storm is intense!"

He shoved a grenade into my gloved hand. We had four left, one for each person on the assault team. We'd roll them into the lobby, then cut down anyone emerging from the wreckage. I said a quick prayer for the people inside who weren't fighters. There was nothing we could do beyond wishing them a speedy reset.

I gave Tack a thumbs-up, then lifted two fingers. He flashed an okay sign and disappeared back into the billowing snowfall. I turned, saw Jamie watching me with big eyes. I squeezed her shoulder and nodded. She swallowed, then nodded back. We bumped fists.

One hundred and twenty seconds later we started downhill, Tack and Richie moving in tandem across the narrow lane from Jamie and me. I kept it slow, not wanting to rush. We were still too far away to see the target.

The road grew slippery, black ice coating the pavement. Our pace slowed to a crawl. A false step here and I could slide down the street like a bowling ball, ruining our surprise. A voice inside my head was yelling something, but I was too busy balancing to listen.

We reached Library Avenue and the street leveled, but it still resembled a skating rink. We skittered across, then I frowned down at the next block. It was even steeper. Ice seemed to cover everything, and Jamie and I were forced to sidestep. Maybe creeping downhill in a blizzard had been a mistake.

I looked over at Tack and Richie, vague outlines in the darkness across the narrow alley. They'd stopped moving, seemed to be testing their footing.

I decided to risk a flashlight. The storm was blowing like

crazy and we were still half a block away. It'd take a warlock to spot anything in this weather. I powered mine and aiméd it at Tack. He started, nearly fell, then powered his own beam and centered it on me.

I lifted both hands to my shoulders, palms up. Tack looked left, then right, seemed to consider. Then he repeatedly pointed down toward Main Street. I took a deep breath and gave a reluctant thumbs-up. Killed the light. Then I motioned to Jamie and we began carefully working our way down again.

In less than ten steps, I knew we'd miscalculated. The ice had become a sheer, unbroken patch stretching across the lane and over both sidewalks. The voice in my head finally broke through. No way this was natural. The ice was too thick, too evenly distributed to be a result of the snowstorm. Which meant someone had put it there on purpose.

I spun to tell Jamie to stop, that we were turning back, but at that moment her feet shot out from under her and she barreled into me. We fell in a tangle of arms and legs, sliding down the sidewalk and into the street, picking up speed as we went. In seconds we reached the bottom and slammed into a thick, high barrier running between the corner buildings and blocking off the alley.

I rose to my knees, dazed. Heard a commotion up the alley. A second later Richie crashed into us headfirst, knocking me flat again. *Shit shit shit.* I scrambled to my feet, began testing the barrier in front of me with my hands, unable to comprehend what it was doing there. Two cars, parked bumper-to-bumper and piled high with hard-packed snow. The voice in my head was screaming for me to run.

We'd slid all the way down to Main Street. Beyond the suspicious car wall, Emerald Tower rose like a specter in the raging storm. I was somehow still holding my grenade, and had even managed not to pull the pin and blow myself to pieces. I shoved it into my pocket and helped Jamie stand up. Abandoning caution, Tack came sliding down on his butt to join us.

No alarm had sounded. Incredibly, we were nearly in position, although this six-foot-high barricade was a wrinkle we hadn't counted on. But we could still do this.

Something caught my attention back up the alley. Shadows moving within shadows.

No. Not shadows.

People.

"Tack, look out!"

He turned just in time to avoid a smoking red cylinder that came bounding down the ice-slicked pavement. I grabbed Jamie and dove to the side, pulling her out of its path, but Richie slipped and fell to his knees trying to dodge. The barrel hit him chest-high and broke open, covering him in flaming liquid.

Richie screamed, clawing at his engulfed clothing, but whatever it was burned too quickly. He collapsed in seconds, then shimmered and disappeared.

Tack was huddled against the barrier on the opposite side of the flaming wreckage. The stench of burning kerosene was overpowering, laced with a sweet roasting smell I didn't want to think about. Tack ripped off his goggles in surprise. "What the—"

"They're behind us!" I shouted, pointing up the block. "It's a tra—"

A second barrel came rumbling down. We dove to the sides as it exploded against the barrier, burning fuel shooting in all directions. A wave of heat enveloped me. I was smacking out flames on my jacket when the first bullets began tattooing the wall behind me.

"Climb over!" I yelled, grabbing the top of the snowpack and clawing my way over the left-hand vehicle, a dented Crown Victoria that looked like an undercover police car. A relatively simple move for a person with the power of three.

Tack followed easily on his side, but Jamie got hung up. I reached back and grabbed her hands, started pulling, nearly had her across when a loud bang rattled the wall, punching me backward like an invisible fist. *Richie's grenade!* A tongue of red enveloped Jamie. She made a sickly keening sound, a red stream leaking from her mouth as she slumped backward into the flames. Moments later, a second explosion roared, splitting the barricade in half.

Both grenades. Tack and I were picking ourselves up off the snow when spotlights sprang to life atop the corner buildings of the intersection.

Tack grabbed a fistful of my scorched jacket, eyes wild. "What the hell is happening?!"

I smacked his hand away, enraged by my own stupidity. "It's a trap, you idiot! They were waiting for us!"

Tack stared at me, shaking his head. "Impossible! How could they know?"

We were crouching next to the mangled roadblock as fire consumed it. I wanted to rip Tack apart with my hands. "The whole thing—their attack, our counter, even the target we chose—it's exactly what they wanted. We walked right into it!"

Tack grimaced in horror, his cheeks reddening in the biting cold. I took no joy in it. Jamie and Richie were gone and we were pinned down with enemies all around us. To make matters worse, the snowfall was tapering off, robbing us of our primary cover.

A whistle blew. Two dark forms blurred from the tower lobby directly across the street. My lips pulled back into a snarl. Only an enhanced player could move like that. Then a rifle opened up. Tack and I flattened on the snow-covered ground, covering our heads as bullets pinged off the pavement, curb, and smoldering vehicles behind us. When I glanced up again, Toby and Ethan were standing a dozen yards away.

"Nice to see you boys!" Ethan called, his face a dark silhouette in the harsh spotlights.

Toby pulled down his balaclava, flashed a lopsided grin. "Hey, Noah. You screwed up."

Tack rose slowly, staring daggers at the pair. "Just do it. I'll be back."

"Maybe," Ethan said, and I could feel the satisfaction in his voice. "But you'll have to find a new place to sleep tonight." He stepped into the light wearing a smug smile. His arm shot out, pointing east.

My heart stopped beating. Ignoring the danger, I staggered to my feet and into the street. Pulling off my goggles, I squinted in the direction my enemy was pointing. Far up the mountain, a spectral orange glow danced in heavy winds. My stomach constricted like a black hole.

The chalet was burning. Probably the lodge, too, and the ski village. All of it. Our home.

The fight drained out of me. I covered my eyes with a gloved hand. Wondered vaguely what had happened to our reset zone teams. I was probably about to find out.

"No cells for you guys," Toby said, grinning like a kid on Christmas morning. "Enjoy your trip through the hard drive." He raised his rifle and worked the charging handle. I didn't even flinch.

A chorus of howls erupted in the darkness.

I lurched a step sideways, the hairs on my arms standing. Something deep within my primal brain began jabbering.

Ethan half turned, was peering down Main Street. "What the hell?"

Five sinewy apparitions appeared at the edge of the spotlights' range. There they paused, seemed to regard us. Toby spun to face them, unsure.

A low growl carried on the wind. The shapes moved closer. Resolved into hazy forms.

Wolves. Big ones.

Toby was staring at the animals in shock. "Where'd these bastards come from?"

I shook my head to clear the shock, survival instincts kicking in. Something major had changed, but I needed out of this jam before I could deal with it. Ethan and Toby were staring at the pack, thunderstruck, guns trained on this impossible new threat. It was then I realized I still had a grenade in my pocket.

I withdrew it slowly, catching Tack's eye. Then I pulled the pin and tossed it underhand near Ethan and Toby's feet, where it disappeared in the snow. Tack fidgeted in the corner of my eye, and then a second green orb landed a few feet to the right of the first.

I spun and dove, covering my head with my hands. Toby's head turned as Tack began racing in the other direction. "Not so fa—"

The ground bucked as twin booms rattled my teeth. Canine voices howled. When I lifted my head, Toby and Ethan were lying on their backs in the street. The wolves were gone.

Toby's left leg was missing, severed at the knee. He sat up, glaring at the bleeding stump with a scowl. Then he laughed wildly and collapsed backward onto the snow. "Ah, crap." Toby put his gun in his mouth and calmly pulled the trigger. He disappeared an instant later.

Ethan began moaning on the ground. I staggered to my feet and ran after Tack, was pounding up the block when a hand snaked out from a storefront alcove and grabbed my jacket. I fought whoever had me, swinging wildly, until Tack's voice sounded in the darkness. "Stop, you idiot! It's me. There's someone else down the street."

"Of course there is," I shot back, but I melted into the shadows beside him. "They were ready for us no matter which way we came. They *baited* us, Tack. And we ran straight into their arms."

Tack backed against a locked door, eyes pained. "I . . . I thought . . ."

A cruel streak burgeoned inside me. A need to blame this fiasco on anyone but myself. "All you thought about was *killing*. More lives in your column. And look where it got us!"

Tack's face spasmed. Then he thrust his nose an inch from mine, spittle flying from his lips. "You own this too, Noah. I proposed the plan, but *you* agreed. You don't get to be leader at meetings but pass the buck when things go bad. This mess belongs to both of us!"

I shoved him away from me, the fire in my chest turning to ice. "You know what, Tack? You're right. It was my fault for listening to you. But that was the last time. We're done working together."

Tack spat on the ground. "Couldn't have said it better."

Movement out in the street. We'd been arguing loudly. Foolishly.

A halogen flicked on. I glimpsed a face—Mike Nolan, staring down the barrel of a pump-action shotgun. Then glass shattered all around me as shots boomed. Ropes of agony punched through my chest. My neck. I tumbled to the ground and everything went black.

31

MIN

I was standing in a large atrium.

The Fire Lake town seal embedded in the floor with tiny red stones. A crystal chandelier hung from the dome high overhead. Before me, a grand staircase led up to the main council chamber, flanked by heavy wooden doors set at intervals in the atrium walls. One stood open, soft orange lamplight spilling from its cozy depths. The lintel above it was engraved.

MAYOR'S OFFICE

My skin began to crawl. I felt hot all over, a nameless pressure building inside me. My limbs felt wrong, *compressed* somehow, as if my bones were stuffed into a body too small to hold them. I wiped my palms on borrowed jeans. Then I slipped off my jacket and removed Noah's Beretta from its pocket.

Deep breath. I squared my shoulders and marched through the door.

He was there.

The Guardian was sitting behind a wide mahogany desk topped by a brass lamp, a laptop, and a single manila file folder. He was tapping away at the keys, dressed in the same black suit he'd worn every time he'd murdered me as a child.

His jacket was off—a new wrinkle. I spotted it hanging from a coat stand in the corner. The ubiquitous silver sunglasses were missing as well. For the first time in my life, I could see my tormentor's eyes.

Gray green, with flecks of gold. Hard eyes. Tired eyes. They remained glued to the laptop's screen as I slowly crossed the room.

The mayor's office was long and spacious, with a vaulted ceiling and wainscoted walls. Two chairs faced the desk, sandwiching a small table. A cut-stone fireplace hosted a sultry blaze, the scent of burning cedar mixing with old cigar smoke.

Without looking up, he gestured for me to sit. "Welcome. Grab a chair."

I nearly shot him then and there. Limbs trembling. Teeth clamped as bile rose in my throat. Of all the ways I'd imagined this might go, this wasn't one of them. My constant executioner had greeted me like a secretary called in to take a memo.

The hell I'd do as told. I stood behind a chair, keeping the Beretta out of sight. My other hand gripped its leather backing with white knuckles.

"That won't do you any good," the Guardian said, closing his laptop. He looked at me then, steepling his fingers before his face. "Guns don't work inside this building. Programmer's privilege." He sat back in his chair and regarded me, an index finger tapping his chin. "I'm glad you're finally here, though. I've been a little disappointed by how long it took."

The gun rose and I pulled the trigger in one fluid motion.

Click.

Nothing. My jaw tightened. I pulled again. Then again, and again.

Click. Click. Click.

The Guardian sighed. "I told you it wouldn't work."

I tried to control the rage coursing through me. I hadn't come here to shoot this man—I wanted answers, a way to stop the violence—but a lifetime of hatred, fear, and pain was bubbling to the surface.

Click. Click.

With a howl of frustration, I threw the gun at him. Flinched as it bounced off an invisible barrier and landed on the burgundy carpet. The Guardian's seascape gaze never wavered. He didn't seem to blink much.

"You can't do that, either. This place is my . . . refuge. We won't be disturbed."

My fingers curled into fists, impotent fury shaking my limbs. I had to calm down. I had to think clearly. Throwing a tantrum wouldn't get me what I wanted.

"You're a monster."

"Maybe. Maybe not. Will you sit while we discuss it?"

I stared at the Guardian for a long moment. Then I circled the chair and sat. He opened his mouth, but I spoke first. "I want you to stop the Program."

One coal-black eyebrow rose. "You want me to end life on Earth?"

I winced, then bit back a scathing reply. If this was to be verbal sparring, so be it.

"I want you to stop forcing people to kill each other," I amended. "End the eliminations. Make the valley peaceful again. If this is our . . . *existence* now, then fine. But there's no reason it has to be a murder-happy circle of hell. You control the variables, so you control what happens. I want you to stop being a prick."

He surprised me by shrugging. "Actually, I don't control the variables. Not anymore."

My eyes narrowed. "What do you mean?"

"I've been locked out of the system." He smiled, unblinking, sending shivers down my spine. "Remarkable, isn't it? A classmate of yours has actually taken control of the MegaCom's OS. I'm powerless to do anything about it. Happily, I have no intention of trying."

An icy spear pierced my rib cage. I swallowed. Didn't want to ask, because I already knew the answer.

"Who?"

"Sarah Harden. The master terminal in the silo lab complex is a control portal for the Program. She's been studying and guessed the password. Harden controls the system now, not me."

My face burned. "She guessed the password because you made it her birthday."

"Your birthday too, Min."

"*Why?*" I slammed a fist on an armrest. "Why would you do that?"

"You haven't guessed?" He leaned forward, placing his elbows on the desktop. "Maybe you haven't been asking the right questions."

I gaped, at a loss. He was hinting at something he thought I should know, but I hadn't the faintest idea.

The Guardian cocked his head slightly. "Why were you able to enter this building? Why was Noah? Why were you able to access the lab complex? Because I *designed* it that way, Min. The beta codes have permissions others do not. They can even access the Program directly and adjust parameters, should they be clever enough to figure out how. It was the very least I could do after everything we put you through."

"No," I whispered, my feet pressing down against the floor. "No. No. No. No."

The Guardian tilted his head again, this time in what appeared to be genuine confusion.

"Don't you *dare*." I bent closer to him, chest heaving, my anger burning hot and acrid like a lightning strike. "You don't get to casually *aside* all the times you murdered me. The worst moments of my life—of *anyone's* life."

My hand rose, quivered as I ticked off fingers. "When I was eight, you pushed me off a cliff. When I was ten, you forced me into a creek to drown." My voice inched up an octave, the words speeding in time with the blood pumping through my veins. "On my twelfth birthday you ran me over with a car. At fourteen, you *smashed my head in with a rock*. All leading up to my wonderful sweet sixteen: the day you shot me in my bedroom, the last safe space I had."

Tears burned in my eyes as he watched me, stone-faced.

"I never understood what was happening, and no one believed me. I thought I was crazy for years. I had almost no friends. *Zero* boyfriends. Just a regular date with a pitiless murderer on my even-year birthdays. *That's* what you put me through, you psychopath. Noah, too. You don't get credit for anything with me."

I was shaking. Could barely breathe. But I'd be damned if he was going to see me cry.

The Guardian regarded me solemnly. Then his gaze dropped. He flattened his palms on the desktop, as if he didn't know what to do with his hands. "You're right, Min," he said softly. "I'm sorry. I did what was required, but what you and Noah experienced . . . it beggars the imagination."

He pressed a fist to his mouth and cleared his throat. Had that been a catch? Then the imperious green-gray eyes rose. They were misty. Regret seemed to fill them. For an instant he looked like a broken man.

Realization smacked me in the face. "It's you," I whispered.

"Excuse me?" He tried to pull the mask back into place, but I saw through it.

"It's you," I repeated. "Not an avatar. You're the black-suited man. The *real* one. You're alive inside the Program like us."

He flinched, then smiled faintly, knowing I'd caught him out. "I thought it'd be less difficult if you all thought me a robot. Emotions can run high. But yes, I uploaded myself just before Nemesis came. In the end, I didn't trust anyone else to complete the task."

I half rose, then fell back into my seat. My head was spinning. I couldn't think of a single intelligent thing to say. "I hate you," was all I managed.

He chuckled without humor, fiddling with his tie. "Tough but fair. Your instincts have always been good, Melinda Juilliard Wilder. That's why it's been so disappointing to watch you mis-

340

trust them." The Guardian—Black Suit—leaned forward, eyes suddenly intent. "I made you the centerpiece for a reason. You were tested hardest because you were strongest. The most capable. You can win this thing, Min. The others are sheep, but you . . . you're indomitable. If only you'd stop resisting your abilities. Take command. Take *control*."

My lips pulled back in a rictus of disgust. "I'll never do the things you want me to do. I *reject* you. I reject this whole world. And I'll fight it, no matter what the consequences are."

The Guardian stared at me. I held his unblinking gaze, though inside I was screaming. Then he slumped back with a loud sigh. The Guardian glanced away, a finger tracing idle circles on the armrest of his chair. "Stubborn to the end."

My turn to shrug. "I guess you bet wrong on me."

His eyes snapped back, impaling me with a baleful glare. "To think that I expected more of my only daughter."

Time stood still.

The Earth stopped spinning.

My heart froze, every synapse in my brain firing at once.

The album of lonely memories composing my car crash of a life all strobed at once, even as I tried to blank them from my mind. I gripped my head, denying what he'd spoken.

I couldn't, though. It fit. Goddamn everything everywhere, but it fit.

Mom. She must've known.

Turns out I was going to cry after all.

"You have to understand, Min." His voice cut like a razor blade. I stared at the floor, blubbering a watery curtain. After learning of my mother's involvement in Project Nemesis, I'd thought nothing else could surprise me. No new secret could hurt.

I'd been wrong.

The Guardian kept on, each word an injury. "Even before you were conceived, I knew the world was doomed. Nemesis had been detected as far back as the 1960s. The news was so terrible that a decision was made to never share the information with anyone." Leather squeaked as he shifted in his chair. "Project Nemesis investigated every method of survival conceivable, but nothing would work. We couldn't colonize a new planet outside the grip of the dark star, and nothing human could survive on Earth once it came. When they finally hit upon the idea of digital uploads, I was brought on board."

My head rose. Wiping away tears, I studied his face, picking out details that matched my own. This was my absentee dad. The ghost in my life. Two people I hated with every fiber of my being had suddenly combined into one.

Yet I hungered for details.

"What happened with my mother?" I choked out.

A small smile creased his lips. "I never intended to have kids, not with what I knew was coming. But the silo was about to begin construction, and I was in Fire Lake on a recon op. She was something, Virginia. I didn't find out about you until months later, when the town was officially selected and I returned. To say I was surprised is an understatement."

I snorted, voice thick. "So you put me in your experiment. How wonderfully insane."

He ran a hand over his mouth, as if trying to wipe away a

bad taste. "We needed test subjects to determine whether the concept could actually work. I knew the beta phase would be horrific—there was no getting around it—but if it was successful, *these would be the people who survived.*"

He looked at me with a fondness that made me shudder. "You'd just turned six, the apple of your mother's eye. She loved you more than you can possibly imagine. I'd just been promoted to head of programming, and my first task was to select a target group."

The Guardian drummed the desktop with his fingers. I listened, enraptured, all else forgotten. Secrets about my life that I'd accepted as lost forever were being laid bare by this nightmare of a man.

He chuckled darkly. "I decided to commit a tiny fraud. I had DNA testing done at your elementary school, all kinds of blood work and analysis. No one knew I had a daughter there. Then, armed with this data, I told my bosses an incredible lie. I claimed, *convincingly*, that the process under consideration would work only on a severe subset of individuals, all born within a twelve-month range. *Your* class of kindergartners. Further, I invented a specific date for an ideal electromagnetic brainwave signature in relation to Earth's gravity and the orbit of the sun. It was perfect bullshit, but meticulously papered with reams of pseudoscience. They accepted my report without question."

The Guardian leaned forward. "Can you guess which date I gave them?"

I swallowed, mouth gone dry. Then I nodded.

"September 17, 2001." He laughed hysterically, his shoulders

343

shaking in an explosion of hyena chuckles. "I spent four billion dollars of taxpayer money to get your birthday included in Project Nemesis."

My finger shot out at him. "And then you started killing me."

His laughter died. The green-gray eyes tightened. "It was unspeakable," he said quietly. "I'll never be clean of it. But making sure you were a beta patient was the only way. At the beginning, we didn't know how many we could upload." He glanced at the fire, orange light flicking in his irises. "In a way, Noah's deaths were harder. He wasn't my child. Just a scared little boy." He paused, eyes gleaming brighter. "I insisted it be me who did the . . . the fieldwork. I couldn't let anyone else bear that weight. I . . . I really am the monster you describe."

My voice nearly broke. "Try it from my end sometime."

His gaze snapped back to me, cold lines re-forming in his features. When he spoke again, his voice was clipped and emotionless—a soldier giving a report. "The murders were necessary to see if the encoding and regenerative cloning would work. There was no other way to do it. Processing the betas tested both project goals."

"What goals?" I blurted. "What did killing me accomplish?"

The Guardian held up a finger. "Mission goal number one: develop the ability to digitally preserve a human being as an insertable line of code. We got that done rather quickly, actually. We're all just numbers and electricity when you get down to basics." He added a second finger. "Goal number two: perfect the capacity to fully regenerate a human being from these pure lines of data."

He curled his fingers into a fist. Brought it crashing down on the desktop. "What I did was inhuman and miserable. I've paid for it. I never had a life, either. But I was *saving* you—one of four dozen souls who would survive the apocalypse while *billions* died. It nearly broke me, but I'd do it again. You're here, and still in play."

I launched to my feet, arms flying up. "In play for *what?* You keep saying you 'saved me,' but did you really? What about my soul? Do I even have one anymore? And if I do, why are you making me destroy it with all this . . . *chaos?*"

He waved a dismissive hand. "You don't understand."

"Why the eliminations?" I demanded, putting my knuckles on the desk and leaning forward. "What happened to those kids? Are there backups? Fail-safes? Can you bring them back?"

He didn't answer. With a growl of aggravation, I learned forward and slapped the shield separating us. "Why the killings, *Dad?* Why make your precious test subjects fight like starving animals if you only wanted to save us?"

The Guardian propped his chin in the crook of one hand, two fingers pressing against his temple. True anger flashed in his eyes for the first time. "What do you want me to tell you, Min?"

I straightened. Crossed my arms. "Tell me the true purpose of the Program."

"Fine."

My heart skipped a beat.

The Guardian interlocked his fingers before him and spoke in a dispassionate voice. "The Program is a Darwinian evolutionary model designed to grind the preliminary subject group down to a more stable core. Its purpose is to refine the source code."

I swallowed, still standing at the foot of his desk. "Yes. But that's not all."

He sniffed. "No, it's not. And I suppose telling you now won't make any difference. You've seen the clones."

I thought of the pedestals deep in the silo. "I know that's how you brought the betas back to life in the real world. By cloning us after each murder. But I don't know why you abandoned that idea, or why you had clones created for the others but never used them."

The Guardian shook his head. "We didn't abandon anything, Melinda. We executed betas in the test phase to determine if our cloning process was viable. We had to know if we could bring raw data back to life."

I frowned, confused. "But how is that not abandoned? You can't bring people back to life anymore. The planet is destroyed."

"For now." Before I could react, he swung his arms wide, indicating the room. "Did you really think *this* was my endgame? An interminable existence inside a few microchips, forever roaming the hard drive as squibs of electricity?"

A well opened in my stomach. The pieces were there, but I couldn't slot them.

The Guardian continued, relentless. "What you saw in the lab were bodies *waiting* to be animated, Min. In the future. The surviving codes will be inserted into living bodies. The human species will return to planet Earth."

I swayed, fell back into my chair. All the blood in my body rushed to my head. The office pulsed in and out of focus as my vision narrowed to a point. Suddenly, everything made sense.

All things but one.

"So why make us kill each other?" I whispered, terrified that I knew the answer.

He stared at me, remorseless, a judge pronouncing sentence. "There's a carrying capacity. The MegaCom can only safely regenerate a specific number of subjects. You must survive the cull if you want to return to life." His shoulders rose in the slightest of shrugs. "May the best codes win."

I covered my face with my hands. "How many?"

The Guardian shook his head. "I won't tell you that. You might see it differently, but knowing would be a terrible burden. It's better that you don't."

My mind began shutting down. I couldn't think. It was all too much. I wanted to escape the crushing weight of what he'd told me. But another question snaked from my lips before I could stop it.

"My middle name is Juilliard. Mom said it was from you, but she never explained."

The Guardian took a deep breath. "Virginia and I met in the Skyline Café. We were both a little tipsy that night. She asked me my name, and I told her it was Juilliard."

I snorted, disappointed. "So, another lie then."

He smiled. "No, actually. For a fraction of a second my guard slipped, and I told her my real name. A disastrous mistake. By protocol, I was supposed to erase her. Project Nemesis was the blackest op in human history, and didn't tolerate loose ends. Instead, I told her everything. Every detail of the threat facing humanity, and my work to thwart it. An unsconscionable breach of security. They'd have shot me on the spot, and rightly so."

My eyes rounded. "She never told, did she? Not anyone. Not even me."

His chin began to tremble, ever so faintly. "Never. She was my priestess, your mother. The only person I ever betrayed the project to. I left the next morning with a clear conscience and her promise." My father looked at me then, and for the first time there was . . . something. A faint connection between us. "You were a miracle that sprang from that single night. And when she named you Melinda Juilliard, it was to remind me. I was to keep you safe."

I stared, unable to form words. Felt a stirring of sympathy I'd thought impossible. But then reality crashed back in.

"I won't lead a slaughter of my classmates," I said. "There has to be a better way."

The Guardian shook his head sadly. "When humanity returns, the Earth will be a very different place. Only the most determined—the most ruthless—will survive. There is no better way. This is the *only* way."

My lips parted to challenge him, to *make* him see, but the words never escaped. A loud tone echoed across the office.

The Guardian's eyes widened, then his mouth hardened into a white line. The tone sounded a second time. I realized it wasn't confined to the room, or even the building. It was everywhere and nowhere at once. Then Sarah's voice boomed in my eardrums.

"Hi, you guys! It's Sarah. Big news! I've managed to gain access to the MegaCom—can you believe it? To celebrate, I went ahead and initiated a new command. To all the sideline-sitters out there, be warned: *the meek shall not inherit this Earth.* At exactly midnight tomorrow, all codes with negative kill ratios will be automatically eliminated from the Program. I figure this will speed the phase along nicely. Good luck, everyone! Bye!"

The announcement ended. My eyes shot to the Guardian, who merely shrugged.

"You'd better go," he said. "I can't stop it. In the end, this is probably a blessing."

"How can you say that? *I'm a negative ratio,* Dad!"

I saw the slightest wince, yet his eyes became ice chips. "Then you know what you have to do. Find the will. This isn't without purpose, Min. Reanimated codes may have to battle on a daily basis to survive. You might as well get used to it now."

Something snapped. A switch flipped inside me, and my mind went on autopilot. Like a robot I put on my jacket, picked up my gun, then turned and stumbled into the atrium. Through the front door and outside into the frozen night.

I couldn't focus. Couldn't breathe. Couldn't make my last words disappear.

I was a negative ratio.

If I wanted to be reborn one day, I'd have to kill to stay alive.

32

NOAH

I came to in the northern woods.

Min's old clearing, above town. A lucky break—this was the closest reset point to the ski chalet. Maybe I could salvage something. Then my eyes popped as I remembered to check the weapons in my jacket.

The gun was there! Tack's trick had worked. I removed it with a prayer of thanks, then chose the least likely way to exit the glade and took off into the woods.

The storm was over, but the temperature remained shockingly cold. After a few hundred feet of skulking I passed through the invisible barrier. A second later something sharp bit into my legs. I cursed in surprise, pulling out my flashlight. Flicking it on, I discovered a double line of barbed wire blocking my path.

I retreated a step, puzzled, and bumped into the invisible barrier. I'd crossed out of the reset zone and couldn't go back.

Cold horror crept through me as I put the pieces together.

The snare was ingenious. I was trapped inside a narrow corridor between the barrier and the wire. If they'd done this at all the reset points, everyone exiting was a sitting duck.

And I was holding a lit flashlight, announcing my presence. I clicked it off. Too late.

Crack. Crack.

The first shot took me in the shin. The second struck my side. I dropped, howling in pain for the second time that evening. Heard footsteps. I felt the instinctual fear of a hunted animal. They could keep doing this to me until I ran out of lives.

The gun!

It was in my hand. But I was wounded in the frozen woods, with no place to hide and no chance of getting medical attention. Hands shaking, I stuffed the gun back into my jacket liner and zipped it up, just as a deeper shadow appeared outside the wire.

I rose. Snarled. Charged.

Crack. Crack.

The lights went out again.

I was in the cave. *My* old reset point.

Later that same night, though I didn't know how much.

I sat on the stone floor in the darkness, hugging my legs to my chest, completely drained. I needed to regroup. Recover. A quiet moment where I wouldn't be shot the instant I raised my head.

I stayed like that for a long time, huddled in a ball, but eventually the cold crept in and forced me to move. Removing the pistol from my jacket liner again, I crept outside. The little pond was frozen solid, covered in a white blanket. The snow had stopped completely.

There were only two ways down from this location, and both would be guarded.

But I had a surprise for them.

Just get away. Get away and you can hide.

I walked straight down the main path, boots clomping in the snow. I knew exactly where the barrier was and felt the electric charge of passing through it. A few yards beyond I found the wire. Two silent forms emerged from the woods. One ignited a lantern. The other held a gun loosely in his hand. When the light bloomed, both had big smiles on their faces.

Tucker Brincefield. Chris Nolan. They looked smug to see me.

Chris nodded to the wire. "Noah! My man! I bet you didn't expe—"

I shot him twice, pivoted and blasted Tucker before he knew what was happening. Then I took the time to make sure of them both. As their bodies disappeared, I stripped off my jacket and carefully crossed the wire. If there was another team lurking out there, they didn't appear. I was almost disappointed.

I walked downhill in a daze. Everything I'd planned, every hope I'd carried, had been reduced to ashes. I'd let myself be outsmarted and outplayed. Now I had no base, no team, not even a place to sleep.

My feet slowed, then stopped. My shoulders sagged. The sobs came, and they didn't stop for a while. When I finally got ahold of myself again, I recognized I was in trouble. Freezing.

Starving. Mentally destroyed. I had to get in from the cold, in more ways than one.

I needed a familiar place to get my head together.

Only one came to mind.

With the gait of a condemned man, I turned my feet toward home.

PART FOUR

EVOLUTION

33

MIN

I stumbled into the boathouse, shivering hard enough to crack my teeth.

Derrick wedged the door shut behind me. I was surprised to find him there. It was close to one in the morning, and he'd spent a long night ferrying people and supplies.

"How'd it go?" he asked. "I heard explosions from in town and got worried. Plus, you catch Sarah acting like the voice of God?"

I nodded sharply, but didn't want to talk about it yet. My mind was still numb from the Guardian's revelations and Sarah's bombshell. I wanted to get warm, get something to eat, and go over everything in my head before I shared.

"I'll tell you everything once we get to Lauren and Casey's place."

"Change of plans," he said, rubbing his gloved hands together.

"I picked up the liberty campers and all the food, but the spot those girls are using is no good."

"What do you mean?" I asked.

He shook his head with a frown. "With all the snow that came down, we're more likely to get trapped in that cul-de-sac than anything. Plus, on the way driving back I picked up two strays—Corbin and Liesel. They're all that's left of the summer camp crew. The blizzard made them desperate enough to flag me down."

I chewed my thumb, working the problem in my head. "Okay. So. We need somewhere we won't get snowed in."

"High ground," Derrick said. "A big place, too, if possible. There's been gunfire all night and people are scared. I don't know what's going on, but it's big. When we got to the girls' cul-de-sac, three more folks showed up out of nowhere. Darren, Benny, and Rachel Stein. Sarah freaked them out so bad that they followed my headlights." He paused and eyed me significantly. "Is she for real, Min? Are people on the downside of the count about to fade out?"

I swallowed. Nodded again. "Sarah has control of the system. We need to get somewhere safe, then I'll explain."

He gave me a hard look, curiosity burning in his eyes, then huffed a frustrated breath. "Fine. Later. But you *will* spill the beans. In the meantime, where the hell should we go?"

"Where's everyone now?"

"This ranch house in Lakeshore Estates, but it's not gonna work. Big windows, no upper floor. It's on a corner lot with two cross streets, and the yard is some kind of garden maze. You could probably sneak a tank all the way up to the back door and we'd never notice. But I can't think of any place better. These homes obviously weren't built with defense in mind."

"I know a place," I said suddenly. Almost smiled at the irony of it.

"Where?"

"Top of the hill, Derrick. Where else?"

He squinted down at me, lips parting to complain about my caginess, but then he stopped, eyes widening. "You mean *Noah's* house." Derrick puckered his mouth, nodding as he thought it over. "Yeah, that might work. It's way up there, and there's only one way in. The snow won't bury us, at least."

Noah's father owned an enormous mansion in Winding Oaks, a ritzy gated community one neighborhood over from here. The last property on the highest cul-de-sac, up near the canyon rim, it had few neighbors and plenty of space. Even better, the house's physical security was state-of-the-art. I'd spent the night there once, in what seemed a lifetime ago—*ha ha, actually it was a few*—before everything fell apart. Going back there now felt incredibly weird, but it really was the most defensible spot on this side of the valley.

"You still have a car?" I asked.

He nodded. "Casey's SUV, but the storm jacked up all the roads. I *think* we can make the drive in two shifts, but no promises."

"Then let's go. We need to relocate ASAP."

Ten shaky minutes of plowing through drifts got us to the ranch house. The southwestern neighborhoods rose steeply, streets and houses built into the canyon wall so everyone had a lake view. Property values increased the higher you climbed, but the narrow lanes were buried in snow, and a few times I was sure we were about to slide right off. When Derrick finally parked, I let out a sigh of relief.

"Don't get comfortable," he grumbled, pointing up the mountain. "Noah's house is all the way up there."

Inside we found Casey and Lauren standing in a corner of the living room, eyeing their new companions with distrust. Corbin and Liesel were sitting quietly on the floor with their backs to a wall, Corbin a bulky, red-haired farm boy with pale skin while Liesel was tall, plump, and plain-faced. Both gave me a small wave.

Hector was perched on a red couch with Aiken and Anna, who were holding hands and whispering to each other. Directly across from them, in chairs pulled in from the dining room, were Benny Erickson and Darren Phelps. They also had their fingers entwined.

Rachel Stein was standing behind them, slender and coldly beautiful, her luscious black hair framing dark, angry eyes. I hadn't seen any of those three since the Town Hall massacre. Derrick told me they'd been hiding in Lakeshore Estates the entire time.

Everyone stood as we stamped our feet on the doormat, knocking slush from our shoes. Eyes bored into me—some hopeful, others steeped in distrust.

"It's good to see you all," I said.

"Did you talk to the Guardian?" Aiken blurted.

"I did."

"How'd Sarah make that announcement?" Lauren cut in. "Is she serious?"

"Yes, I think she is." Then I held up a hand as questions bombarded me. "I'll tell you everything once we get to a safe place to spend the night. Derrick and I have been discussing it, and we think the Livingston house is our best bet. It's defensible and shouldn't get snowed under. Thoughts?"

"Why should we go anywhere with you?" Rachel said, crossing her arms and cocking her chin imperiously. "Ethan hates you, and targets you specifically. I've been on my own for weeks, and in all that time no one has tried to shoot me, attack me, or burn down my house. But that seems like an average morning for *you*, Min."

I met her disdain as calmly as I could. "The game's changed, Rachel. Our enemies are on a rampage for eliminations and have declared war on everyone. Hiding won't save you anymore, but there is safety in numbers."

"Or a bigger target," she fired back. "No one even knew I was alive until tonight. If this stupid blizzard hadn't buried my house, I'd—"

"Sarah's controlling the weather. We have to figure out how to stop that."

Voices erupted, demanding explanations. How did I know so much? Where was Sarah? How could she make a *valley-wide* proclamation? I let it go on for a few seconds, then whistled shrilly, silencing everyone. "I told you, I'll answer every single one of your questions as best I can, but *after* we secure a place to stay."

"Benny and I have been fine on our own until now," Darren said defiantly, coal-black hair swirling atop his round head. He glanced at Benny, who put a supporting hand on his shoulder.

"I get that things have changed—I heard Sarah's PA—but why should we throw in with you?"

A fair question. One I honestly couldn't answer well. But I was certain we needed to stick together right now. "Come up to Noah's with us," I said. "For at least one night. We can drive, and there's plenty of room there for everyone to crash. Give me a chance to explain what's happening. If what I say doesn't work for you, fair enough, you two can ghost and maybe ride this thing out alone. I won't hold it against you."

"We'll come," Benny said abruptly, tucking shoulder-length black hair behind his ears. Darren shot him a sour look. Benny shrugged, squeezing Darren's knee and speaking to him in a low voice. "One night. I want to know what's going on."

Darren sighed. Then his eyes narrowed, a vein working in his neck as he glared around the room. "Benny and I will be staying together. If anyone has a problem with that, you'd better say something now."

Impossibly, I barked a laugh, smiling quickly to draw the sting from it. "Not an issue. We've got bigger things to worry about than who sleeps where." Darren's thick black eyebrows knit together, but he nodded curtly.

Corbin and Liesel both agreed, and Casey and Lauren were already pulling on their coats. Anna was speaking softly to Aiken, who nodded as he and Hector began attaching Yaktrax to the bottom of their boots. But Rachel was still standing like a statue, her nose scrunched back like she smelled something foul.

I met her glower and flared an eyebrow. Her dark eyes flashed, then rolled skyward. "Fine. Whatever. One stupid night. Congratulations, Min. You've manipulated me with news I want to hear."

"Thanks, Rachel."

She flipped a dismissive hand. "I'll drive, too. My Range Rover is down the block."

Twenty minutes later our caravan pulled onto the highest street in the valley, then up the large circular driveway at its terminus. Noah's front door was locked, but I knew where a key was hidden. Inside, the house smelled of dust and disuse. It was clear no one had been there for months.

The vaulted foyer opened into an expansive great room with floor-to-ceiling windows overlooking the lake. The kitchen was to the right and we immediately swarmed it, but there was nothing salvageable. Grumbling, Derrick walked back outside to haul in the food stores from the liberty camp. Others wandered off to explore, or collapsed onto the great room's comfy chairs and long sectional couch. A few slipped upstairs to claim bedrooms.

I was organizing a group meal with Liesel and Hector when Darren emerged from a corridor that accessed the garage. "Guys, this house has a backup generator. Look for fuel!"

That sent everyone scrambling, checking closets and pantries until Corbin came flying in through the door to the deck, smiling ear to ear. "We're in business! Benny jimmied open a storage shed out back. There's a half dozen canisters." He and Darren disappeared outside in a rush. Five minutes later the lights came on. I actually squealed in delight.

We ran around turning off everything we didn't need while

Derrick cranked the heat up to eighty. Blessed warmth began spilling from the vents. Hector discovered that the gas range worked and started opening boxes of pasta. "I call first shower!" Rachel shouted, bounding up the stairs.

An hour later—fed, scrubbed, and almost content—we gathered in the great room, where Lauren and Casey were watching *Battleship* on Blu-ray. I was about to call for everyone's attention when the front door abruptly swung open.

Noah stormed inside, pistol in hand, his face an angry mask. "You think you can—"

He saw me and stopped dead, eyes popping. The gun slipped from his fingers.

I gaped back at him from across the room. Hair wet. Wearing pajamas I'd borrowed from his dresser. *How?* How was he standing here right now?

Noah was staring at me as if nothing else in the world existed. As if I was oxygen he needed to breathe.

"You're alive." His whole body trembled. Then he sprang forward, shoving past the others to wrap me in a bear hug. I froze, uncertain what I was feeling. Whether I wanted him to touch me. Then his shoulders began to quiver, and I realized he was crying.

Noah. The boy who'd kissed me. Held me. Shot me in the back.

My emotions writhed like snakes, battling for supremacy. Part of me was repulsed by his embrace, while another part wanted to grip him by the neck and smash my lips against his. I didn't know what to do. What to say. A room full of people were staring at us, open-mouthed, as time stood still.

Noah slid down to his knees, still clutching me around the waist. He buried his face against my leg. "I'm so sorry, Min. For everything. I got it all wrong."

My hands found his soft brown hair. But I still didn't know what to say. Then I finally noticed the two others who'd trudged inside with him and were standing awkwardly in the foyer. Leighton Huddle. Akio Nakamura. They were staring at Noah, eyes wide.

Noah didn't seem to care about any of it. He stood abruptly and released me, but his green eyes stayed locked on mine, brimming with such pain and self-recrimination that I felt my walls crumbling. Noah looked like a man who'd found a lifeboat but knew he was still adrift far out at sea. A man sending up his last signal flare.

"I know I don't have any right to ask this of you," Noah said. The room had gone deathly quiet, everyone hanging on his words. It felt like a bad reality show, but one look at Noah's face left no doubt he was sincere. "But please forgive me."

I took a step back. Turned away. I wasn't ready for this. People were watching, and I . . . I didn't know how I felt. We'd been down this road before.

I'd trusted Noah completely, and he'd betrayed me just as completely.

I looked back at him, a deflection forming on my lips. But when our eyes met, I saw a need so great, a torment so complete . . . it took my breath away. My mind flashed back to the night we spent together in the trailer park. Me, sobbing, inconsolable over Tack's death. Noah holding me, gently brushing the tears from my cheeks.

Noah had been broken by Project Nemesis. His father had abandoned him. His doctor used him. His friends never understood him. I'd struggled with the horrors of being a beta patient, but at least I'd had Mom and Tack to round out my life. Noah had fought his war alone.

I reached out and took his hand. "I'll try, Noah. That's the best I can do right now."

His shoulders sagged in relief. "Thank you, Min. I won't let you down again. I promise." He wiped at his cheeks, seemed to realize we weren't alone for the first time. Noah cleared his throat awkwardly, then addressed the others. "Everyone is welcome." He looked around the room, nodding at people he hadn't noticed. "Some of you I haven't seen for a long time. I'm glad you're okay. I'm glad you're here."

Rachel huffed loudly. "We didn't come here because of you, Noah. Everyone in this room knows what you've been doing in your sick little kingdom. You're no better than Ethan, maybe worse."

"You *burned me alive*," Derrick grated, fists clenched at his sides. "Don't think I forgot just because you let me sleep over."

Noah flinched. He stepped back and leaned against the fireplace, stuck his hands in his jeans pockets. Deep lines crisscrossed his forehead as he stared down at the carpet. More than a few glares followed his movements. *I* might've extended Noah an olive branch, but it was clear not everyone felt the same way. I opened my mouth, thinking to divert the spotlight, but needn't have bothered.

Rachel fired a heated glance at me. "We're *here* because Min lured us into a blizzard with the promise of important news."

Rachel spread her hands with practiced contempt. "Well? Out with it. What did you learn?"

"Find a seat." I waved at the chairs and giant sectional. "This is going to take a while."

I stood before the hearth as they settled onto the couch, the carpet, anywhere a person could fit. Noah slid past me to stand by the giant windows on my right, away from the others. He kept watching me when he didn't think I was looking. Despite the chilly reception, each time I caught him, he couldn't stop a grin from quirking his face.

When everyone was settled, eleven sets of eyes regarded me with varying levels of suspicion. *Deep breath. Take it brick by brick.* But there was no sense in starting off slow.

"Earlier this evening, I spoke to the Guardian."

Sharp intakes, but no one interrupted. I glanced at Noah and saw him wince. I held up a hand before he could confess to his own visit. Mouthed, *I know.* Noah's jaw tightened, scarlet blooms exploding on his cheeks, but he held his tongue. I continued swiftly before anything else could distract me.

"The Guardian revealed a lot of things, so I'm going to summarize the major points first." I tried to keep my voice level and firm. "I'll give a full blow-by-blow later, and I swear I'll tell you everything I can remember."

Nods. Words of assent. A few frowns. Rachel stiffened and crossed her arms, eyes smoldering. But she kept quiet.

I took a deep breath. Where to start?

"I was able to get inside Town Hall," I said, choosing my words with care, "because beta patients have more access inside the Program. The Guardian designed it that way. You all know there are four of us. Ethan. Sarah. Noah. And me. We can get into places that are off-limits to others. Open certain restricted files. Sarah has taken full advantage of this, and found a way to manipulate the system. She even locked the Guardian out."

Incredulous faces, but they'd all heard her insane announcement.

"Where is she?" Leighton asked, pawing blond curls away from his face. He'd stripped off his jacket and sat side by side with Akio at the foot of the coffee table. "We should find Sarah and . . . I don't know. Stop her somehow."

I shook my head. "She's deep inside a secret base. Untouchable. Believe me, I know." I told them about the silo and its hidden lab complex. My two months underground, and what I'd learned about Project Nemesis. For most of them, this was the first they'd heard of a massive military facility lurking beneath the eastern woods. Hands began squeezing foreheads, rubbing faces, and raking through hair. With each new detail, the tension grew. It was getting harder to breathe.

The only thing I held back was the clone room. I wasn't sure how much of that I should share. Only I knew the Program's ultimate purpose, a secret as dangerous as any weapon in the valley. How would the others react to the prospect of rebirth?

With my biggest mistake laid bare, Rachel didn't miss the chance to seize on it. "So you had control of this . . . complex, and just *gave* it to her?" Her voice was acid. We hadn't gotten along back in school, and that didn't appear set to change.

To my surprise, Derrick spoke up in my defense. He leaned forward on the couch so he could see her. "Shut up, Rachel. Min was alone in there for almost sixty days, holding out, with Sarah harassing her day and night. Things changed because of *me*. I got her to open the door, and in the process we fucked up. But that's life. Stop trying to blame someone for this."

Darren interrupted as if he hadn't heard the other comments. "Let me get this straight. Sarah is locked inside some impenetrable bunker and can mess with the whole damn game. Meanwhile, you're chatting up the Guardian in Town Hall. Ethan's been shooting anything that moves for a week, and Noah"—his gaze swung to find him, eyes hard—"no offense dude, but you've been the valley's leading psychopath since this phase began." Then he surprised everyone by laughing darkly. "Be straight with me, Min. Why should we trust any of you?"

I opened my mouth to answer, but Noah spoke first.

"That's a fair question." Everyone shifted to regard the tall boy in the corner of the room. He spoke calmly, seemed at peace for the first time since entering the house. "I thought doing what the Program wanted was all that mattered. So, I did. I thought resets were a way of life. So, I didn't worry." He shook his head. "I couldn't have been more wrong. About everything. Inside a computer or not, we're still *us*, and we need to act like human beings, even if that's not what we are anymore."

Noah suddenly pointed at me. "Min never forgot that, not for a second. Even when the rest of us did." His voice caught. "Even after some of us gave her reason to hate everything. She could have hidden in the silo forever, but she came out to fight. So I'll listen to her now, and you should, too."

Dead silence as all eyes zeroed on me. I swallowed, mouth gone dry.

For the first sixteen years of my life these people had never

369

looked to me for anything. Most disliked me. The idea that Min Wilder from the trailer park would matter to the rich kids of Fire Lake was a joke.

Except no one was laughing.

They were watching. Waiting.

"I'm with Min, too," Derrick said. "She's gotten out of more scrapes than y'all know. She's also the only one Sarah is afraid of." He shook his head, frowning down at his hands. "I ditched Ethan and his crew because I thought there had to be a better way. We need to start trying to find it."

My skin prickled. I felt a noose tighten around my neck.

"Let's stop dancing around this," Hector said, surprising everyone by speaking forcefully. "We need to elect a leader, and Min is the best choice. I vote for her to represent us."

And just like that, the question was out there, and couldn't be taken back. The room fell silent. I held my breath, powerless to stop what was happening, or help it, and equally unsure which I wanted.

"Okay, sure." Darren fired a sarcastic thumbs-up at me. "Team Min." He looked to Benny, who nodded through his long black hair. Votes of agreement sounded from Corbin and Liesel. Casey and Lauren locked eyes for a moment, then nodded slowly, as did Akio. Leighton wore a frown—perhaps thinking *he* might've been chosen—but our former class president shrugged and added his assent as well.

I felt the weight of their hopes. Their fears. This wasn't what I'd wanted, but I couldn't run from it any longer. I was a beta patient for Project Nemesis. My *father* was the Guardian. We were living in a world of his design.

I owed my classmates for what was happening. Had a debt to repay.

"If you want me to lead, I'll do the best I can."

Seconds of excruciating silence, then applause broke out. The mood broke, if only for a moment, voices shouting out loud to release the tension. Stupid cheers sounded, swelled, echoing to the rafters like we'd won a state title. Everyone needed this, even me. We were alive. We were present. We would not go quietly into the night.

Only Rachel seemed unmoved. "This has been *adorable*, really," she shouted, killing the vibe. "But I'm interested in what you're going to *do*, Min. You have a plan, right?"

The acclaim died. Everyone watched me intently, hoping I had all the answers.

"We have to be smarter," I began, searching for the right words. "We need to rally *everyone* who isn't with Ethan. No more tribes. No more guarding our own little corners. We have to stand united against what's happening in town."

Corbin spoke up, red hair flopping over his pale cheeks. "But how? The summer camp got torched, and only Liesel and I escaped. I heard the quarry got hit, too. Nobody knows what happened to them. With Toby and the twins running all over, blocking reset points and shooting everyone they see, we don't even know how many people are left."

I nodded unhappily, taking a seat on the hearth. "It's a problem. In the last week some of the bigger camps were destroyed. People are scattered and afraid."

Noah surprised me by sitting at my side. "The ski chalet is gone," he said grimly. "Ethan burned it tonight. There were eight of us living there, but I led my whole team into a trap and we got slaughtered." Noah nodded to Akio and Leighton. "We found each other by dumb luck while stumbling through the storm. But with the resort gone, I have no idea where the rest will go." He ground his teeth. I could tell the guilt was killing him.

Then he grimaced. Stole a glance at me, something uncomfortable flickering in his eyes.

In a flash, I knew what it was.

I grabbed his arm. "Was Tack with you?"

Noah nodded, but the tension in his muscles told me there was more. Something I wasn't going to like. I was about to badger him for details when Casey's voice broke in.

"There's a big problem at the reset points," she said. "Those townie bastards ran barbed wire around the force fields, trapping anyone resetting in between." Casey shivered, worrying her blond ponytail. "People caught up in that mess might not make it out."

I focused on Casey, unwilling to be distracted. I'd ask Noah about Tack later, when I had him alone. I had to tell him about the clones, too. Him and Derrick. I wanted their thoughts in private before I told everyone else.

First act of leadership—hiding the truth. Bravo.

"So if everyone's scattered," Benny asked, "how do we unite them?"

"I think we should light a beacon," I answered, the notion forming as I spoke. "This house is one of the highest points in the valley. You could see a bonfire up here from almost anywhere. I say we announce ourselves."

"To whom?" Rachel scoffed. "Ethan and Toby? You're nuts. We're trying to *avoid* an attack, not encourage one."

I hesitated, but the more I thought about it, the more I liked the idea. "It's definitely a risk, but our presence won't stay secret for long. We have lights on, for one. Plus Ethan and Toby scout, and there are too many of us to stay hidden. We need to increase our numbers before they can take us down."

"We're not helpless up here, either," Noah said in a cold tone that gave me pause. "We can defend this block while gathering people willing to join us. In fact, this might be our only window. We should take it."

Others spoke, some for the idea and some against, but in the end they looked to me.

"Your call," Derrick said with a wry smile, as if he knew how much I hated responsibility.

I exhaled deeply. Made a decision. "Let's show Ethan we aren't afraid. Let's put up a big-ass sign that says we're right here. And that this valley doesn't belong to him."

Nods. Mutters of agreement. Even some pumped fists, the prospect of our defiance straightening a few spines. Excited conversations broke out. Corbin and Darren began plotting out how best to build the bonfire. Rachel turned her venom toward criticizing Ethan rather than me. I hadn't told them everything—and we still hadn't discussed Sarah's message—but it felt like we'd turned a small corner. We were working together. Had a plan. Despite our differences, progress was being made.

Then Noah's TV winked on by itself, and the world crashed down around me.

Sarah's face appeared. She was sitting in the security hub, smiling into a webcam. Noah gaped at the image for a moment, then ran to his kitchen. Sarah's face filled the TV in there as well. Noah ripped open the deck door and stepped outside, then came back shivering. "My neighbor's pool house is showing it, too."

"Can she see *us*?" Liesel whispered, eyes rounding in terror. But Sarah didn't react, bouncing her head back and forth as if she was waiting on something.

"I don't think so," I said. "But I don't know—"

"Hey, guys! Me again." Sarah spoke causally, as if making a dull entry into a video log or something. "I've been searching for a way to eliminate people directly, but apparently that's impossible." She mugged an exaggerated frown. "*Bummer.* That would've made things so much easier. But I did figure out how to do *this*." She swirled her fingers next to her face, then clasped her hands together and shook them on both sides of her head. "I'm a TV star! Whoo-hoo!"

All eyes were glued. No one could breathe. Liesel was crying, head buried in Corbin's chest. I stared, rooted to the spot, unable to even twitch.

Sarah held all the cards. We could only wait and see what she played.

"*Anyway*, I thought I'd still stir things up a bit." She straightened her posture like a beauty queen and continued in a mock-serious voice. "*Thus the following decree*: in addition to tomorrow evening's status deadline, all reset zones . . . are now . . ." She spun a finger in front of her face, letting it rise dramatically, inch by inch, before arrowing it back down onto a keyboard. "Canceled! From this point forward you'll just reset in place. Immediately." She winked. "Try not to get stuck in a bad spot. Take care, you guys!"

She tapped another key and disappeared, leaving a dozen freaked-out teens staring at a blank screen. Eyes swung to me, hungry for answers.

I opened my mouth with no idea what to say, but was spared that indignity.

The doorbell rang.

34

NOAH

The bonfire burned in my yard all night.

To my surprise, people trickled in immediately despite the storm—Kyle and Richie right as Sarah's insane telecast ended, startling everyone half to death. A lucky break. They'd seen the house lights and needed to get in out of the cold. I hugged them both, thrilled to have more of my people back safe. Both seemed stunned by my show of camaraderie. They edged away from me, but I didn't care.

Then came Floyd Hornberry, country strong in his signature denim overalls, his Afro grown into short, frizzy dreadlocks over the months. At the quarry since the beginning, he said the place was now a burned-out wreck—no food, no shelter, nobody left. Toby's attack had eliminated Trent Goodwin, and he hadn't seen any others since. He was happy to join us.

Another pair arrived just before dawn. Floyd nearly broke Maggie Knudson's back with a hug, her curly red locks bouncing as he lifted her off the ground. She freed herself and hurried back outside, calling an all clear. Moments later Cenisa Davis appeared, short and prim, swimming in an oversized blue parka. The quarry kids went upstairs to catch up, or maybe to grieve, commandeering a bedroom and locking themselves inside.

As the darkness receded, I stepped out onto my back deck in sweats, a mug of instant coffee warming my hands. The sun slowly crested the mountains, sparkling the frozen lake. A crisp, clear morning after a savage storm. Puffing in the fierce cold, I walked to the far end. Snow was piled everywhere, a sea of unblemished white running to the bottom of my cul-de-sac. No one was sneaking up that way unannounced.

I nodded to Akio, who was standing in the driveway with Leighton. We'd set up watches all night. I'd taken a graveyard shift—hadn't slept before or after, bouncing around, trying to get everyone settled in relative comfort. I had fifteen house-guests, the most people I'd been in the same place with since the massacre at Town Hall.

Since you shot Min in the back and gave your loyalty to a machine.

I winced, knuckles tightening on the mug. Then I let the scolding fade. Those days were over now. I'd apologized, and, miracle of miracles, Min was trying to accept it. It was time for a new leaf.

Seeing Min had cracked all my defenses. I hadn't dared hope she was still alive after all that time, yet there she was, standing in my own living room. Weighing me in those bottomless gray eyes.

I'd made a vow on the spot. I would never be on the opposite side from her again. I'd put her judgment above mine, as I should've done from the beginning. Min was a candle in the darkness. For better or worse, I'd follow her lead from now on. The Program would just have to get over it.

Movement at the foot of the street. My senses slammed into high gear. I stared, shielding my eyes against sunlight reflecting off the newly fallen snow. A group of figures was laboring up the hill.

I whistled to Akio. Pointed two fingers at my eyes, then aimed them down the street. He nodded, signaling for Leighton to follow, and began creeping down the block. I hurried inside and through the house, ripping my jacket from a hook by the front door as Floyd came down the stairs. "Visitors hiking up the street," I told him. "Unknowns."

The big guy didn't hesitate, grabbing a coat off the rack and following me outside.

"You armed?" I asked, eyeing the trail Akio and Leighton had left in the snow.

Floyd shook his head. "Mine's upstairs. Should I go get it?"

I pulled a Sig Sauer P226 from my jacket, a replacement for the Beretta Min had agreed to keep carrying. "Just hang right here. If I'm not back in two minutes, wake up everybody and be ready."

But before I took a step, a familiar whistle sounded the all clear.

"That's Akio," I told Floyd, relaxing. "We're good. Could you go get Min, though?"

Floyd slapped me on the back and disappeared inside. A minute later Akio and Leighton trudged into view with several others following. My heart sank when I recognized the leader.

Then someone in a bathrobe flew past me, bounding into the snow with no shoes on.

"Tack!" Min shouted.

I ran after her. "Min, get back here or you'll freeze to death!"

She ignored me. Tack had perked at his name, then seemed to finally recognize who was screaming it. With a bellow of delight he shot forward, meeting her in a hug at the center of the cul-de-sac. For a moment they both jabbered at once, then Tack noticed Min wasn't properly dressed. "Get inside, you head case. Can't have you dying of pneumonia the second I find you alive." But his smile was irrepressible. It occurred to me that I hadn't seen a genuine Tack smile for weeks. Maybe ever, now that I thought about it.

They hurried for the door, Min shivering head to foot. Tack shot me a hooded glance. For Min's sake, I nodded, letting him enter without a word. But it was going to be a short stay for Thomas Russo. We'd said everything that was needed back in town.

Three others approached with Akio and Leighton, and these people were much more welcome. The cousins walked side by side—Carl scowling, Sam grinning—while Hamza Zakaria brought up the rear. I nodded to my guys as they joined me and waited for the newcomers.

Carl and Sam stopped halfway up the driveway and waited. Hamza, one of the smallest kids in our class, was struggling through the heavy snow. I hadn't seen any of them since the beginning.

Sam pointed to the bonfire smoke still rising over my house. "We took that to be an invitation. Were we wrong?"

I shook my head. "You're more than welcome. Quarry go bad?"

Sam hawked, spit to the side. "Toby and Ethan burned down our warehouse. We retreated to the mine and made them bleed for a while, but then they found some way to collapse the opening. We were stuck inside for days. Had to take the only way out we could."

Carl put a finger to his head and mimed a shot.

"We lost innocent people," Sam growled. "Kharisma Rutherford. Emily Strang. I owe those ruthless bastards." He nodded toward the house. "We found Tack at a reset zone. Last night Sam and I hit three of them, taking out Ethan's teams and cutting the wire. But the fourth zone flared up like a laser show before we came close, then it disappeared. We checked, man. It's just . . . gone."

"Sarah turned off the zones. I'll explain inside."

Sam scratched his cheek, eyeing me. "Ethan, Toby, and Sarah. You against them?"

I nodded. "To the bitter end."

"Then we're with you." They both took a step forward, but I held up a hand. The cousins frowned. Hamza looked nervously from face to face, unsure where this was going.

"Just one thing," I said. "We've chosen a leader. You have to agree to follow the orders of the person in charge. No exceptions."

Sam snorted. "Your house, your rules, Livingston. But we don't follow *anyone* blindly."

"I'm not talking about me."

Carl's eyes narrowed. "Then who?"

I smiled tightly. "Your word, please. Now, or else it's back down the mountain for you guys. After breakfast, of course. I'm not heartless."

The cousins shared a silent conversation. Finally, Sam shrugged. "Okay, Noah. While we're here, we'll follow your mysterious leader. Care to fill us in now?"

I stepped aside, waving them toward the front door. "Min is running the show. Welcome to the resistance."

Carl chuckled darkly. "Min, huh? After you shot her in the back? Well, could be worse. She's definitely got guts." He placed a hand on my shoulder and looked me in the eye. "I'm already impressed she's tamed the Grim Reaper of the slopes."

He released me with another snicker. I gritted my teeth as the trio trudged past. What hurt most was that Carl was right. I had a lot of ground to make up in the eyes of my classmates. But an even bigger problem was sitting in my living room right now. Tack needed to be dealt with. But how was Min going to react?

I nodded to Akio and Leighton as they resumed their watch and headed back inside.

A half hour later everyone reassembled in the great room. We were twenty-four strong now, with good fighters in the mix. A force to make the monsters in town take pause, except all anyone could think about was Sarah's deadline.

Min spent the first five minutes outlining the Program's tally system and cutoff line. Then I spoke, explaining how power transferred between players. Many had worked out the basics on their own, but for a few, this was a total revelation.

Some in the room had been hiding since the first day. Others had been on losing sides in last week's running battle. Negative ratio numbers abounded, and Sarah had said those players would be eliminated tonight. Nerves were frayed to the breaking point, a dangerously tense mixture of clenched jaws and tapping feet.

"Let's start with who's safe," I suggested. "Who has a positive count?" Hands went up around the room, mostly guys who'd been in the thick of the fighting. Me. Tack. Carl. Sam. Floyd. Kyle. Corbin. Akio. Casey and Lauren. And Darren, surprisingly. Eleven people altogether.

Min rubbed her mouth, not speaking up, so I continued. "Who's even? The way I heard Sarah's proclamation, those people should also be safe. She specified a *negative* status."

This group was a mixed bag—those who'd been hiding the whole time and managed to avoid the violence, kids who'd fought but had also taken their fair share of hits, and people from the bigger groups who'd managed to mostly stay away from battle. Derrick. Leighton. Hamza. Aiken. Anna. Rachel. Six players sitting right at zero.

The last group had the fidgeting hands and chewed fingernails. They were underwater. If Sarah was telling the truth, they'd automatically be cashed at midnight unless something was done. Maggie. Cenisa. Liesel. Richie. Benny. Hector.

And Min. She was in the most trouble of all.

I tried not to let panic take hold, but my gaze strayed to the elimination list Kyle and Tack had reconstructed on the wall. There were new names there that cut like knives. Sam had told me Jamie and Cash were gone, along with his friends Jacob Allred and Greg Kozowitz. All four were found at reset points, hung up in the wire. I felt a surge of fury at Sarah and Ethan for arranging something so sinister.

Our best guess was that something close to forty people were left in the valley, but we couldn't say for sure. Nobody felt safe, not even those gathered in this house. How many more had to go? What number was the Program grinding toward?

I can't lose Min again. I won't.

Min cleared her throat and the room quieted. Her eyes were mournful. "You've chosen me to lead, and that means a lot to me," she said softly. "But I'm not sure I can. I might not be here tomorrow, and it won't help the group if I drop out at a crucial moment." She swallowed, then found some core of inner strength and continued in a stronger voice. "Sarah Harden did this. I know where she is. So I've decided to go to the silo and try reasoning with her. It's probably guarded, so I'm going alone. We can't have any more people risking unnecessary hits with the deadline coming. You'll need to pick a new leader while I'm gone."

"She'll never listen to you." Derrick sat forward on the couch, his knees almost up to his shoulders. "Sarah wants to speed things up. You'd just be gift-wrapping yourself for elimination the old-fashioned way."

Min shrugged. I saw the helplessness lurking in her eyes. She knew her plan was doomed but would do it anyway. "I can't just sit here, Derrick. This is our best option."

"There's another way."

All heads turned.

Tack was sitting alone on the floor against the back wall. He was staring at his hands. It burned me that I hadn't thrown him out of my house yet, but I hadn't spoken to Min. She didn't know what he was like now. How warped and twisted his logic had become.

And suddenly, I knew exactly what he was going to say.

Tack looked up, and for once the sarcastic smile was absent. "No one's going to like this, but I think we care about each other enough to do what needs to be done." Our eyes met, and the pleading I found there stifled the scathing rejection I'd been preparing.

He's right. God help us, but he's right this time.

Min's eyes widened. "Tack, no," she whispered.

"*Yes*, Min." He eased to his feet and strode over to the hearth. Tack glanced at me for support. "No games this time, Noah. It's about saving people."

I felt strangled, but one look at Min made the decision for me. "You're right."

Tack nodded, and it was like something had loosened inside of him. He turned to address the group, suddenly teeming with energy. Min was gaping at me, but I didn't meet her eye. I needed Tack to win this argument. *I won't lose her again.*

"Do one of y'all want to explain what the actual fuck?" Derrick said peevishly.

"Min said there's only one way," Tack answered, addressing the room. "But Sarah won't back down from this. You guys know that. Not when she's locked up safe and we're stuck out here. Sarah hasn't fired a shot in this whole war, so her conscience will be clean. It's time to accept reality: *we* got ourselves into this position. But we can fix the problem without her, too."

Sudden intakes of breath. Covered mouths. People were

picking up Tack's drift, the idea striking minds like a series of guided missiles.

"I'm pos-seven," Tack said, his voice trembling slightly. He stood before the hearth, commanding every eye in the room. "I did some . . . some bad things to get there. But I'm willing to give back to help everyone else."

And there it was.

"You want us to *kill* each other?" Rachel scoffed, never one for subtlety. "That's insane!"

"What's more insane, Rachel?" I heard myself counter, stepping over to stand beside Tack. "Trading a few resets, or letting people in this room drop dead at midnight even though we could've prevented it? Are the old rules worth more to you than Hector's life?"

Rachel winced, jerked her head away. Startled glances darted like pinballs. I'd put a face on the problem and made it real.

"But it won't work," Leighton said brusquely, holding up a hand when Tack looked set to bite his head off. "Logistically, I mean. How many times are we supposed to sprint across the valley, getting back here? Even if we started this instant, it'd take all day, and we'd probably lose more people sending them through the zones."

"But Sarah shut *off* the zones," Sam blurted, his dark eyes rounding. "Carl and I saw one power down ourselves—the barrier really did disappear. She said that we'll reset *in place* now. Intentional or not, she gave us the means to make Tack's plan work."

That quieted everyone. Skeptical looks were turning speculative.

"You're talking about a group commitment to wholesale murder," Hector said quietly. "Everyone involved would be scarred by it. I couldn't ask that of another person."

"Would you take it as a gift?" I caught and held his eye, like I had at the shattered bridge all those weeks ago. "I don't want you to die, Hector. I'll gladly take a bullet to stop it from happening."

He smiled sadly. "I couldn't do that to you. But the offer means a lot, Noah."

Min held up a hand, was slowly shaking her head. "What you're suggesting . . . the scale . . . it'll be horrible."

Tack planted himself in front of her. We bumped shoulders as I did the same.

"Neither of us is letting you die while we can prevent it," Tack said. He punched my arm and I nodded firmly, in total agreement. "I'll clamp a pin around your finger and run away with the grenade if I have to."

"No one has to be eliminated," I said. "And you can't help anyone if you're not here."

Min covered her eyes. "So many deaths," she mumbled, but weakly. The cold logic of Tack's plan was percolating through the room. I saw resolve cementing on several faces.

Darren lumbered to his feet, looked down at Benny with watery eyes. "I've got two extra, and you're down one. You better shoot me *right now* or I swear I kick the crap out of you."

The room laughed, quickly stifled. Benny looked away, then nodded.

Darren glanced at me, determination radiating from his posture. "A test run?"

386

I looked to Min. Head down, she seemed to be arguing with herself. Then her eyes rose, glittering in the lamplight. "Tack is right. We're a community now, which means we take care of each other."

Min nodded to Darren. He extended a hand to Benny, who took it, allowing himself to be pulled up from the couch. Darren put an arm around Benny's waist, whispering softly in his ear as they walked toward the front hallway. We watched them go, some shocked, some crying, some horrified.

Everyone understood what was happening. Benny was going to kill Darren in my garage. The meeting dissolved into whispered conversations as they disappeared from view.

Min swallowed. "I'll do it. I'll take a second chance if offered."

"Done," I said immediately, before Tack could get a word out.

Min wobbled slightly, wiping her eyes. Her bottom lip trembled as she nodded.

A weight flew from my shoulders. This was my chance at salvation. A way to offset some of my previous betrayal.

Tack spun me by the shoulder, his mouth opening to protest. I grabbed his arm and made him meet my eye. "I owe a debt, Thomas. I took a life from Min. This is my chance to give it back. *Please.* You can help whoever else needs saving."

Tack flinched. He glanced at Min, who was staring at the floor. Then he jerked free and walked away without a word.

I tried to care about Tack's feelings, found I couldn't. Something was fusing inside me. A bubbling joy, completely wrong for the context. For the first time in months, I *knew* I was doing the right thing. My body sang with the possibility of a second chance.

Min was trembling from head to foot. I reached out and took her hand.

"This is going to be *terrible*," she whispered. "What if I can't get the memory out of my head?"

"We'll make new ones. But you have to be here for that to happen."

I felt Min lean into my side. Carefully, slowly, I wrapped an arm around her shoulders, worried I might spook her. Or repulse her, the stain of my sins still an impenetrable wall between us. But Min burrowed in, resting her head on my chest. I blinked, hoping this wasn't a dream.

I heard Tack's voice from across the room. He'd taken a knee before Hector, extending a hand. "I got you covered, boss," Tack said. "I'd like you to stick around."

Emotions warred in Hector's soft brown eyes. He hesitated, unsure. Around the room, people were pairing up, grim-faced but determined as they worked out the math. I turned back to Min. She was crying silently.

Kyle approached us and spoke in a low voice. "You know this makes us weaker," he said with a frown. "We're lowering the individual strength of our best fighters. Meanwhile, Ethan and Toby are practically gods now. We'll be at a huge disadvantage."

I shot him a dark look. "Doing this makes us stronger, not weaker. We take care of our own. You think the negative-status people in town are getting the same deal? How many folks will *Ethan* lose tonight?"

"Why would Sarah do that?" Hamza asked, joining us. "She's hurting her own cause."

Min grimaced, seemed to snap back into focus. She squeezed

my arm and stepped away. "Sarah doesn't care about them any more than us. She's a team of one right now. She just wants the eliminations to continue."

Derrick was nodding with every word. "She might as well be the new Guardian."

Kyle walked over to Richie and shrugged, then the two shook hands. Carl and Sam were talking quietly with Cenisa and Maggie. Corbin was in a heated argument with Liesel, who was crying and shaking her head. Tack plopped down on the couch next to Hector, and the two laughed about something.

I decided to check on Benny and Darren, feeling sick to my stomach thinking about the logistics of assembly-line homicide. The brutality of what was about to happen made me shiver. But I had to be strong. I couldn't let Min down.

I found them standing inside my empty three-car garage. There was a snowmobile on a lift in the far corner, plus my father's prized fly-fishing gear spread out on a battered aluminum workbench. Relics of a different world, one where you didn't save a friend's life by letting him kill you.

"I don't want to do this," Benny was saying, shoulders heaving as tears coursed down his cheeks. It was cold in the garage and his breath misted in little white clouds. "You're asking me to *shoot* you, Darren."

Darren's voice was rough. "I'm asking you not to leave me, Benny. I'll be fine. I'll be *right back*. We're out of other options."

Benny brushed long black hair from his snotty face. "What if Sarah was lying?"

Darren barked a laugh. "Then I'll be right back after a short walk."

I could barely look at either of them. "Do you guys need . . ."

Darren shook his head sharply, removing a weathered Colt 45 from his jeans. "This was my dad's. I don't know what he'd think of me right now, but . . . it'll get the job done." He cocked the hammer and shoved it into Benny's reluctant hands.

My stomach lurched. "Okay. I'll wait on the other side of the door. You guys take all the time you need."

Darren sniffed. "Thanks. Hey, Noah?"

I paused, one hand on the knob. "Yeah?"

"You're all right, man."

"Thanks, D. See you *both* in a minute."

I waited in the hallway. Endless moments passed, then a loud bang echoed from beyond the door. My heart began beating out of my chest. Seconds later the door flew open and Benny stormed past me, both hands pressed to his face. A few more beats, then Darren emerged, legs shaking in an unsteady walk. His shirt was missing, but he gave me a thumbs-up.

"You pop right back in place," Darren said in a strained voice. "But the blood . . ."

"Understood. I'll take care of it. Go get warm."

Darren put a hand on my shoulder, then stumbled away down the hall. When he was gone, I peeked behind him. The stain on the concrete nearly cost me my lunch. We had six more people to go, and they couldn't walk into this.

There was a hose in the garage. I'd do my best.

Sam and Carl paired off with Cenisa and Maggie. Floyd and Hamza joined them for moral support. Ten minutes later the quarry group came back from the garage together. Shaken, but safe. Then Kyle bumped fists with Richie, the pair cackling darkly as they went to even up their strength.

But not everyone agreed to the plan. Try as he might, Corbin couldn't convince Liesel.

"I won't do it," she vowed, setting her jaw in a hard line. "I won't shoot my boyfriend over Sarah's bluff."

Min knelt beside her chair. "It's not a bluff, Liesel. Sarah can access the source code. The Guardian told me so himself. That's how she makes those announcements. You have to take this threat seriously."

Liesel shook her head, red-rimmed eyes glued to her shoes. "I won't shoot someone just to stay in this nightmare. No. That's the end of it."

Hector was equally intransigent, no matter how much Tack and I pressed him.

"My religion forbids it," he said, standing in the kitchen with us as we tried to persuade him. "Even worse, Tack would have that memory forever. I'm sorry. I know you both mean well, and I don't judge anyone else's choice. But I can't do it."

I lashed out, angry at him for being so stubborn. "I already have the memory of you jumping off a bridge. *That* haunts me. Tack is offering this freely, eyes wide open. Just take it." But Hector refused to be moved.

As the afternoon wore on and people got used to the idea, some of the stronger players began convincing people stuck at zero to take a life, moving them off the bubble. A vote was held, establishing a baseline goal of everyone at no worse than positive-one. It took a little arm-twisting of those who'd already had to shoot someone, but in the end we hit the mark.

Akio helped Leighton. Floyd gave to Hamza. Casey and Lauren had spares for Aiken and Anna. Tack spotted Derrick and Rachel, the latter taking a sick delight in shooting him.

The process was simple. Two people strode to the garage and laid out a fresh drop cloth. One shot the other, being careful to make it instantaneous. The donor would collapse and blink out, then come back in the exact same spot seconds later. The hose was necessary after every reset, the water salted to avoid freezing. It made my garage a grim place. When this was over, I was never going in there again.

As nightfall approached, I began hounding Min. She'd put it off all day, professing a need to help organize things, but I knew she was simply avoiding what had to be done. Now there were no more excuses. It was our turn.

"I'll go with you," Tack offered.

We shook our heads in tandem. "Just be here when I'm done," Min said. Tack frowned, but stepped aside and watched us disappear into the garage. I closed the door, set out a fresh sheet, and then pressed the Beretta firmly into her hand.

She stared down at it, not moving.

"Don't think about it," I whispered. "It's not real, and I'll be right back."

Min's shoulders began to quiver. "Noah . . . I don't . . . I can't . . ."

My heart broke for Min, but I wasn't having it. This was to keep her alive. I had to make this happen whether she wanted to shoot me or not.

I took her by the hand. Lifted it gently, pointing the gun barrel at my chest. "I can do it for you. Just close your eyes and—"

"No." Min pushed away, wiping her eyes with her wrist. I was about to argue furiously, but I misunderstood. She took a series of slow, deep breaths, trying to get her body under control. "I agreed to this, so I have to take responsibility. I'm supposed to be a leader. I can't pretend it's not happening, or pawn the pain off on you."

"I'm ready." Then I snorted a nervous laugh. "Do . . . do you want me to kneel? I want you to get a clean shot."

Her eyes grew tortured and I regretted the words. "Just turn around."

I nodded, spinning to face the opposite wall. Steeling my own nerves. Then I felt the cold weight of a gun barrel pressed against the back of my skull. Seconds ticked past, or maybe it was hours. The wait was worse than anything I'd ever experienced, but I didn't complain. She *had* to do this. Whatever she needed, I would endure.

A stifled sob. "I'm so sorry, Noah. I'll make her pay for this, I swear it."

"I know," I said in an odd, tight voice. "I forgive you. Do it."

A last breath, in and out.

Bang.

The next thing I remembered, I was lying on the ground in a puddle of warm, slick blood. My own. Min was covering her face and sobbing uncontrollably. The gun rested on the ground beside her.

I rose unsteadily to my feet, scooped up the Beretta, and jammed it back into her hand. I turned away a second time. "Don't stop," I said blearily. "It's better if we go quick."

"Noah, I—"

"Do it!" I shouted. "Don't think, just shoot!"

"I can't!" she shouted.

I spun, grabbed the gun by the deadly end and forced its barrel up to my forehead. "You *will* finish the job, Min! Don't make what just happened mean nothing."

She flinched, then bit her lip. Spun me back around. Another lifetime passed, then . . .

Bang.

I was down again. The drop cloth was soaked through with dark red liquid. I opened my eyes, saw Min shaking silently as she hugged her chest with both arms. I staggered to my knees, tried to reassure her with an outstretched hand, but I was blinded by the lights. "I think . . . just maybe I'll stay right here, okay?"

Min let out an inarticulate cry, like an animal in pain. I closed my eyes as she thrust the gun barrel against my forehead.

Bang.

The room was teetering. My arm flailed as Min tried to pull me up. "I'm so sorry, Noah! I . . . this . . . I can't get the image . . ."

"One more," I wheezed, holding up a shaky red-tinged finger. Her eyes bulged and she tried to pull back, but I caught her by the arm. Blood coated her sleeve as it dripped from my saturated hands. "We agreed. No one stays at zero."

Min screamed, shoving me down and tearing at her hair. Then she ran and picked up the gun from where she must've tossed it, whirling to aim at me from across the room.

I laughed, untethered from reality, my head swimming in a vortex. "Don't miss, oka—"

Bang. Bang. Bang.

I don't remember rising. Akio was there, helping me walk.

Derrick had his hands on his knees, staring and breathing hard. Min was gone.

Someone said she'd run upstairs and locked herself in a bedroom. I wanted to follow, but Casey insisted I change clothes first. Looking down at my sodden sweatshirt and jeans, I had to agree. She ran to get me something while I stood there, shivering, blood running down my legs.

Then Tack appeared, gently handing me a towel. "You okay?" he asked.

I tried to nod. Think I did. I ran the towel over my head. It came back scarlet.

Tack lifted my chin, forcing me to meet his eye. "Did you get it done? All the way?"

I nodded for certain this time. "Shot me f-f-four times. She's safe."

Tack's whole body relaxed. He squeezed my shoulder, then surprised me by wrapping me in a quick bro hug. "You came through, man. Hero stuff. Whatever problems I had with you before, I'm over it. And I'm . . . I'm sorry for the things I did."

I blinked. Blinked again. Was surprised to find I shared the sentiment. Maybe I was more out of it than I suspected. "Same. It's b-buried. But you gotta excuse me a s-second, because I'm definitely going to th-throw up now."

Tack chuckled and ushered me outside. My prediction proved accurate.

Hours ticked past. Min eventually emerged from the guest room, pale but otherwise composed. I gave her a hug to show how fine I was. She only flinched a little.

We ate dinner in shifts, stood guard, watched a Godzilla movie. And waited. The bonfire still burned outside, but no one else came. As time streamed forward, everyone began stealing glances at Hector and Liesel. More tearful appeals were made, but the pair refused them all—one polite and sad, the other scared and defensive.

Finally, we all gathered as the clock neared midnight. No one had gone to sleep.

"Hector, *please*." I sat next to him on the couch, poured out everything I had. "There's still time. I can cover you. One pull of the trigger and you're safe."

He shook his head, eyes glistening. "Not safe, Noah. Damned. But thank you."

I rose, mouth opening to scream, ready to shake him in frustration—prepared to *make* him kill me—but at that moment the grandfather clock began to chime.

Panic engulfed me. I strode to the window and looked out at the lake, refusing to watch. Corbin was holding Liesel's hand, his face slack. Some, like Rachel, watched avidly, entranced by the horror of the situation. Others fled the room.

The clock chimed on.

Ten. Eleven. Twelve.

I squeezed my eyes shut. Hoped for a miracle.

But Corbin's anguished cry was the answer I'd feared.

35

MIN

We laid their bodies in the shed.

The ground outside was frozen, much too hard to attempt a burial. It would stay that way until spring, if one ever came to this godforsaken digital valley.

Corbin took off in the night. One minute he was with us, staring at Liesel's lifeless body. The next he was barreling wildly through the trees and down the street. Sam and Floyd wanted to go after him, but it was pointless. Corbin had to find his own peace, same as everyone.

Noah was taking Hector's loss hard. Not everyone would notice, but I knew the signs. Flat tone. Robotic motions. A blank countenance to hide the anguish. Noah had tried everything he could think of to convince Hector to accept a life, but Hector wouldn't be swayed. I tried not to think about it.

There were lots of things I couldn't think about.

My mind flashed back to the garage. Noah with his back to me, shoulders hunched as he urged me to pull the trigger.

Four times, each more difficult than the one before. Tears had streamed down my face. I'd never forget the awful sounds, or the stench of gunpowder mixed with blood and singed hair. I never wanted to touch a gun again.

But I would. Had to. Inside the Program, I'd never be without one.

The scene replayed over and over in my head. Shot. Fall. Vanish. Then Noah would reappear, struggling to rise each time, his body and clothes repaired but the blood and gore on the ground, the walls, and the front of my shirt telling a different story.

Shot. Fall. Up.

Shot. Fall. Up.

Shot. Fall.

Each time he'd begged me to do it again, even as he lost control of his body. They were the worst minutes of my life, and that's saying something. I'd run away when it was over. Left him there alone, choosing to hide and weep rather than face what I'd done. It had taken me hours to compose myself, and even then it was mostly for show. Later, after Hector and Liesel were lost, I'd surrendered to sleep too long deferred.

This morning I felt stronger. Yesterday had been a nightmare beyond description, but we'd gotten through it. Almost everyone had survived. We'd evaded Sarah's scythe by working together, a fact we could be proud of.

People were looking to me for what came next. I didn't have an answer yet. The bonfire was still smoldering—by now Ethan and Toby had to know where we were. They could be staring across the lake right now, watching Noah's house as I sipped tea by the kitchen window and looked back at them.

There was a noise behind me. I turned as Noah came into the kitchen.

"Hey," he said.

"Hey."

He joined me by the window. For a moment we stood quietly at each other's side, gazing down at the frozen valley. The temperature was still polar—a thermometer on Noah's deck read exactly zero. I imagined Sarah snickering as she fine-tuned the crappy weather. I had no idea what to do about her. She was untouchable. Left unchecked, she'd grind us into dust.

"I don't think we can stay here," Noah said.

I eyed him with a frown. "Why do you say that?"

He stepped back and leaned against the island, crossing his arms. "Fuel, first off. The generator needs four canisters every twenty-four hours, and my dad and I only stockpiled twenty. That gets us through a few more days, but then . . . back to the Stone Age."

My spirits deflated. "I can't think of a better place to go. Carl says the quarry is wrecked. The trailer park burned, and was never great anyway. Same with Starlight's Edge. The liberty camp is just a bunch of shacks that can't be defended, and you said the ski resort was out of commission, too. That leaves the downtown area, which Ethan controls, and these neighborhoods across the lake. Your house is the highest point over here, with a single access road. I think we're stuck here by default."

Noah clicked his tongue. "Another storm like the last one,

and we could get cut off. My backyard ends in a twenty-foot vertical cliff down to the next street. The cul-de-sac really is the only way in or out. Plus, we don't have enough food for this many people. If Sarah keeps on adding these insane obstacles, we're going to *have* to make a play for the village."

My mouth worked, but nothing came out. I didn't know what to do. Suddenly all my doubts and fears piled on top of me and I couldn't breathe. "I . . . I don't know . . ."

Noah eased forward and wrapped an arm around my shoulders. Drew me close. I leaned into his embrace, trying to siphon off some of his strength. I put my head against his chest as he pulled me in. I felt a sudden urge to connect, my body responding without conscious thought. To lose myself for a few moments would be such bliss.

A throat cleared. I looked up, then jerked back from Noah, heat rising to my face. Tack was standing across the room, eyes burning.

A hand rose to smooth my hair. "Tack, hey! I . . . we . . ."

Tack spun and walked out. I closed my eyes, then covered them with a hand.

I felt Noah beside me. "Is there something I should know?"

My eyelids snapped open. "What?"

Noah's shoulders thrummed with tension. "You guys were living together for months. If there's something you want to tell me—"

White-hot rage exploded inside me. I'd been lost in a moment, but these two idiots had shattered it completely. God, what was I thinking? "Why would I have anything to tell *you* about, Noah? I was alone with Tack all that time because you betrayed me."

400

Noah winced, a hand rising as if to ward off a blow. "No! I mean, I know. I didn't—"

He was interrupted by a loud tone. Our eyes met, then we rushed into the great room. Sarah's face was filling the TV once again.

"Greetings, neighbors!" she said cheerily.

Feet pounded as people rushed in from all over the house. In moments, everyone not on guard duty was present, watching nervously as Sarah twirled her hair.

"*Sooo* . . . my last adjustment didn't go as well as planned." Sarah had an elbow on the desk and her head in one palm, piercing blue eyes zeroed on the webcam. "I thought it would clear the field *much* more than it did." Her expression became mock-stern. "Some of you have gotten tricksy. Well played."

I looked at Noah, who was worrying his chin as he stared at the screen. My eyes slid to Tack, who was watching me. His gaze darted away.

Derrick was standing behind the couch, muscles taut as he leaned forward and gripped its back. "Listen to her. She's laughing. Sarah's lost her damn mind."

"Psychopath." Casey was sitting in front of him and gnawing her blond ponytail, one leg bouncing up and down on the carpet. She glanced at her best friend beside her. "I can't believe we used to eat lunch with that bitch." Lauren just glared at the screen with her arms crossed.

"Here's the deal," Sarah continued, oblivious. "I'm *bored*. I hate it in here. The food is all disgusting baggies of vegetable paste, or dehydrated crap made for living on Mars. But the *good* news is that variables keep unlocking in the MegaCom OS.

This thing is like an Advent calendar. We're *so* close to ending the phase, you guys. I just know it."

"What the hell does *that* mean?" Leighton shouted. He was immediately shushed.

Sarah rose and stepped out of sight, spinning her laptop to face a large whiteboard. Two columns were drawn in black marker. "I took the liberty of tallying up all the eliminations, and this is where we stand."

I stopped breathing.

Sarah had recorded everyone, in and out.

Kyle ran to our list and began scribbling furiously. I watched, unable to blink, as Sarah calmly went over names.

"Last night's deadline eliminated *five* people," she said, her lips puckering as if she'd eaten something bitter. "You guys are either a lot more bloodthirsty than I remember, or way more generous than I anticipated. Regardless, that leaves thirty-five of you precious snowflakes out there, plus me." Her shoulders rolled in a lazy shrug. "Whatever final number the Program wants, it's less than that. So we're going to have to work a little harder."

"She really is a monster," I whispered, rubbing a hand over my mouth. "Those names mean nothing to her." Then Maggie gasped, half rising as she pointed at the screen.

"Oh my God. Look! Corbin's name is on the eliminated list!"

The air left the room. Heads dropped. Tack cursed and punched the wall, leaving a hole in the plaster. Corbin had run away last night, distraught at Liesel's elimination, headed only he knew where. Somehow he'd gotten himself scrubbed. It was a gut punch.

Sarah kept right on talking. "Now here's the *crazy* part. Right this moment, nearly every player left in the Program is in one of two places. Except for me, of course." She made a pouty face, then used air quotes. "There must be 'serious meetings' going on at Emerald Tower and—you're not going to *believe* this—Noah Livingston's house! I can't see inside either one, though. Not allowed. And that *bugs* me, if I'm being honest. I want to know what you guys are talking about. It might even be *me*."

I'd never wanted to strangle someone more in my life. This truly was a game to Sarah. Twenty-eight classmates had been deleted to nothingness, yet she was annoyed it wasn't happening *fast* enough. It made me sick.

"Damn," Leighton grumbled. "She just gave away our position."

Darren glanced up from his spot on the carpet next to Benny. Gave Leighton a flat look. "Dude, we lit a freaking signal fire two nights ago. Decent chance they already knew." Then he looked at me, his thick black brows forming a V. "If this silo is so important, why is she there alone?"

I'd been wondering that as well. Had Sarah cleared the place somehow? Kicked everyone else out? Then the answer hit me like a slap across the face. "They're planning something! Ethan and Toby."

Tack walked over to Kyle's updated list. "There are twenty-one of us here. That means only *fourteen* are left in town. We have way more people!"

"Ethan can't afford to be spread out anymore," Noah said, chewing his knuckles as he watched Sarah onscreen. She'd sat again and was typing while absently fiddling with her hair.

Sarah was playing God with our lives, but had the demeanor of someone checking email in an Internet café.

Sam spoke then, sitting with his back to the far wall beside his cousin. "Consolidating their position makes sense. The reset zones are gone, and Sarah can manipulate the environment until we're forced to abandon this hilltop. If I were Ethan, I'd stay put in the tower and wait us out."

"He won't, though." Derrick straightened to his full height, a frown drooping the corners of his mouth. "They might have fewer people, but all those dudes have taken eliminations. Most have two. Ethan has *fighters*, and they get bored quickly." He began counting on his fingers. "Ethan. Toby. Mike and Chris. Lars. Finn. Tucker. Spence and Ferris. They're not gonna sit around counting canned goods, not without Sarah to keep them in line. You haven't seen them lately. Toby's a rabid dog, and the others aren't much better. I can't believe the girls over there keep sticking around."

Before I could respond, Sarah's body stiffened, her posture radiating eagerness. "Oh, *interesting*." Ice-blue eyes sparkled as she read something we couldn't see. Then she looked directly at the camera and winked. "I'm going to try something new. See everyone later!" Her image blipped from the screen.

"I do *not* like her," Cenisa muttered, drawing some gallows chuckles.

I turned to Derrick, who was now pacing behind the couch. "Where *are* the girls in this?" I glanced at Kyle's list of active players. "I get that Jessica, Zoë, and Colleen stayed—they're Sarah's best friends—but what about Susan Daughtridge and Alice Cho?"

Left unsaid were names in the eliminated column. Girls I hadn't seen since the beginning. Never involved in fighting, they must've been wiped out by the status change. The life-sharing we'd accomplished clearly hadn't taken place in town—Sarah's deadline had taken as many people from Ethan's camp as mine.

Derrick shuddered, eyes troubled. "Jun Son Li and Kristen Fornelli were workers. Never touched a gun, never took a bullet. They must've been sitting at zero. If those two are out . . . they got pushed over the edge."

My stomach lurched as bitter recriminations flew around the room. One reset might not seem like much, after all we'd been through, but if Ethan and Toby had taken lives from those girls right before the deadline, it was murder. There was no way around it.

"Susan and Lars are together," Leighton said, eyeing the list, "so it doesn't surprise me she stuck. She and Colleen even worked on a reset team. Same with Zoë. But Alice Cho? I can't remember seeing her in all the weeks I was living downtown. And Jessica is useless."

Noah walked over to the hearth, squeezing my arm as he slipped past me. He turned to address the group, jaw set, eyes hard as diamonds. "They have twelve fighters, and they're good, but we have more. There are *fourteen* guys in this room."

"Since when did sex matter?" Casey shouted, with Lauren scowling at her side. "I learned to shoot when I was ten years old. If you want to go head-to-head for the deed to this place, say the word. I've sent Toby packing twice. Don't count up penises and assume you know the score."

"She's right." Hamza barked a laugh, wiping sweaty palms

on his pants. He sat at the far end of the couch, his tiny frame almost comical beside his giant friend Floyd Hornberry. "For the record, I don't have a *clue* what to do with a gun. I'm great with laundry, though."

Everyone chuckled, releasing some of the tension. Sarah's whiteboard, while ghastly, had shown us we were the larger group. Any way you sliced it, that was a relief.

"We still need a plan," Benny said quietly. It was the first thing I'd heard from him since he'd shot Darren to stay in the game. "Sarah won't let up until all of us are gone."

Heads turned to me, and I felt my blood pressure rise.

Me. The leader. Right.

I paused to marshal my thoughts. Sarah had given us the lay of the land, but had anything really changed? "Let's inventory what we have," I said. "Food. Fuel. Vehicles. Weapons and ammo. Then tonight we'll reconvene and make a decision."

"Decision about what?" Tack hadn't left his corner since Sarah appeared, staying as far from Noah and me as possible. There was going to be trouble with him, I could feel it. But I didn't know what to do. Mainly because I didn't know what I wanted.

If Noah sensed my concern about Tack, he ignored it. "We need to decide whether to stay put or try talking." He swallowed. "Or if we should attack."

"Talk?" Sam nearly spat on the carpet, then glanced at Noah in apology, his eyebrows merging on his forehead. "Seriously?"

I spread my hands, trying to regain control of the conversation. "Everything will be on the table. That's all I'm saying."

Sam glowered, but nodded stiffly. Grudges ran deep. I personally doubted negotiation could work, but we had to at least consider the possibility. Maybe the swing in numbers would soften Ethan's stance. Or maybe we could drive a wedge between him and Sarah.

Noah clapped his hands together, gathering eyes. I watched him, wondering what kind of man he truly was. Whether my feelings were betraying me. Whether I cared if they did. I didn't look at Tack.

"You heard the boss," Noah said. "Let's get to work."

36

NOAH

The visitor arrived at sunset three days later.

We were just finishing dinner, wondering how much time the generator had left, when shouts erupted outside. Then Floyd barreled in, ice coating his overalls to the waist. The weather had turned nasty again, vicious winds whipping down from the peaks with the promise of more snow. I ran to meet him in the foyer.

"Company, Noah!" Floyd's hands were on his knees as he tried to catch his breath. "Me and Hamza were on watch. He came with his hands up."

"Who?" I demanded, already moving past him. The wind caught the front door and nearly slammed it into my teeth, but I got a hand up in time. "Someone looking to join us?"

Floyd's head swung back and forth, his dark cheeks still bellowing. "It's Ferris Pohlman. Says he has a message from Ethan."

My heart rate spiked. What did Ethan want? "Get Min. I'll bring him in."

Floyd nodded and hurried upstairs. I threw on the closest jacket, removed my pistol and checked the magazine, then stepped out into the bitter cold. I spotted Hamza, Lauren, and Casey at the bottom of the street. Guns drawn, they were wading up the cul-de-sac surrounding a skinny figure in a red parka. I waited for them where I stood.

"You search him?" I called as they got closer.

Lauren nodded, held up a small pistol. "He had this."

"I *handed* you that," Ferris whined, sunflower-blond hair curling atop a narrow, pointy head. "Noah, can we please go inside? I'm freezing my ass off out here."

I didn't move. "Tell me why you're here."

Ferris rolled his eyes. "I already told these guys. Ethan sent me. He has an offer."

I stiffened. Crossed my arms. "Well?"

Ferris gave me an appraising look. "So you're in charge of everyone now?"

I frowned. Was getting ahead of myself. Min should be the one to question him, not me. "You're right, let's go inside. Don't think about doing anything stupid."

"Your house has lights on, Noah. I want in there. No stupids, I promise."

We found the others hastily assembling. Ferris moaned with pleasure at the warmth, unwrapping his slush-caked garments and piling them on the floor. "Man, this is *nice*. I walked straight across the lake, which was a mistake. Colder than Santa's balls with that wind."

He was making small talk, but I read the tightness in his shoulders. The hard line of his jaw. Ferris was sweating even after shedding his extra layers. Nervous. Maybe even scared. I glanced at Min, who was standing by the hearth. She flared an eyebrow. I shrugged. *Hear him out, I guess.*

"Ferris," she called, silencing murmurs. "Come over here where everyone can see you."

"You?" Ferris seemed taken aback. He glanced around quickly. "Seriously?"

Derrick gave Ferris a hard look. "You gotta problem with that?" He stepped over Anna and Aiken to get in the smaller boy's face, squinting down at him like a prosecutor. "What are you doing here, Ferris? Ethan never gave you any big jobs before. But now you're his ambassador or something?"

Ferris edged away, his face reddening. "No one else would go, all right? Not with Noah's reputation. Ethan needed a messenger, and I . . . I took the deal he offered."

"What deal?" Min said sharply.

Ferris lifted his chin. "That's between me and Ethan. Now do you want to hear this or what?"

Min regarded him for a moment longer, then nodded, indicating with a hand that he should address the whole group.

I turned to the four kids on guard duty who'd followed me inside and were standing at the edge of the foyer. "Lauren and Casey, you two go back down the street. Be vigilant. Hamza, you and Floyd circle the house, then one of you watch the cul-de-sac while the other mans the back deck. Make sure nothing funny's up. If anything seems the *slightest* bit off, sound the alarm."

Though I knew it pained them, they agreed, heading back out into the gathering darkness. I wanted eyes everywhere, whatever our guest claimed. Derrick's suspicion had struck a nerve with me—Ferris Pohlman was prickly and annoying by nature, an odd choice for diplomat.

I stepped back into the great room and stood behind the sofa, listening intently. I spotted Tack in his corner, beside the hole he'd punched in my wall. Our eyes met briefly, then he looked away. He hadn't spoke to Min or me since finding us together in the kitchen.

Ferris was clearing his throat. "First, Ethan wants everyone here to know that *Sarah* is the one jacking the weather around, and that he's pissed off about it, too." Ferris snickered. "And he *is* mad, believe me. I don't think she's welcome back in town anytime soon. There were some wolves, a bear, and all kinds of craziness. Anyway, that's not us."

Min spoke up. "You're saying Ethan isn't in control. That Sarah's running the Program."

Ferris made a pinched face. "Wasn't she always? Anyway, I was supposed to say that part about the weather and I did. Moving on." He swallowed, as if summoning the courage to speak his next lines. Whatever was coming, I sensed it was going to start a fight.

"Ethan demands that everyone report to the sheriff's office by tomorrow night." Ferris nervously licked his lips. "He calls for your unconditional surrender. There might be more of you here, but our people are pretty juiced from eliminations and aren't close to the deadline. How many of you can say that?"

"Not a chance," I said immediately, although a sliver of worry

411

began worming through my gut. Most in this house were just above the cutoff. We'd worked hard to rehabilitate the group—everyone had at least one spare reset, for comfort's sake—but in a war of attrition we were doomed.

"Surrender my ass." Derrick stepped forward and got chest to chest with Ferris again. It had the feeling of history between these two. "How'd those guys get so charged up, Ferris? You want to talk about *that*?"

Ferris clamped his mouth shut, a sickly flush infusing his cheeks. He looked away.

"Yeah, you don't wanna talk about mowing folks down at the zones, do you, champ?" Derrick's voice smoldered with condemnation. "You manned one of those posts, probably shot some people in this room. But now we're supposed to walk down Main Street with our hands up, knowing more people still have to go?"

"They *made* me do that stuff, okay?" Ferris's eyes darted the room, looking for a safe landing spot and not finding one. "You found a way to bail at the silo, sure, but I never had the chance! Town is like a prisoner camp now. Nobody's allowed anywhere without one of the Sith Lord assholes watching you. You think Toby and Mike were nuts before? They don't care about *any-thing* now. They just want to end the phase."

Now Min got into Ferris's personal space. "Then why in the world would we surrender?"

"Honestly? I don't know." Ferris backed up, then barked a harsh laugh. "I think Ethan sent me to screw with your heads. But facts are facts—if you try to fight, they'll crush you. This was probably just to rub your noses in it." He took a breath, then spoke in a rehearsed manner. "Ethan orders you to appear at the jail, unarmed, by sunset tomorrow, or else . . ." He shrugged, then pointed to Kyle's list on the wall. "You'll join the others."

Ferris nodded, rubbing his beanpole arms with his hands. "There. Message delivered. I'm done. You guys got any cigarettes?"

"That's ridiculous." Tack stormed forward, unable to hide his temper. "Ethan's offering nothing? That's his negotiating stance?"

Ferris shrugged. Voices erupted in anger. The room seethed, people rising, shouting and pointing fingers. Ferris stood in the center of it, cringing inside a ring of resentment, a helpless pout on his face.

Something didn't feel right. Ethan could be petty and cruel— and he'd never be accused of being a genius—but he was also a man of action. Sending Ferris to taunt us like this didn't fit his style. Plus, it would only put us on guard.

Unless . . .

I walked to the door, put on my coat, and stepped out into the night. The cold hit me like a stomach punch, though the wind had died. I had floodlights on all around the house, pools of illumination in the otherwise seamless black. I walked over to the driveway, then down into the cul-de-sac. It was too dark to see our post at the bottom of the street, so I whistled. A second later I heard the proper return. Lauren and Casey were on the job.

Shrugging, I headed back up the drive. Then stopped. I turned slowly around, taking in the night sounds. I stood there a moment as something nagged at me. The answer came.

Hamza. Floyd. I'd told one of them to stand watch here after they circled.

I jogged back up toward the house and called out. "Floyd? Ham?" No response. My pulse increased to double time. I hurried past the garage and started around back. A twig snapped and I froze, listening intently, casting my senses out like a net.

Nothing. So I called out again, and got no answer.

I cut across my yard to a set of stone steps running down its middle. They descended to a crushed-stone path that disappeared into the woods, a wild stretch of forest ending with a sheer drop to the houses a street below. That cliff was unclimbable, especially in this weather, so there'd been no reason to set a guard there. Yet as I knelt, I saw footprints in the snow. Coming *up*.

I spun. Someone was supposed to be watching the deck.

I took a running step, but tripped and went sprawling. I rolled, then nearly screamed. Hamza's face was half buried in the snow.

At the same moment, I heard someone cough.

I flattened myself beside Hamza's lifeless body. Tried to control my breathing. Then, slowly, I craned my neck to look back up at the house. As my eyes adjusted, I spotted movement under the deck. Something flickered in the darkness beside the HVAC units.

I carefully withdrew my Sig Sauer and put my finger on the trigger. Slid over poor Hamza, mouthing a word of prayer. Then I slithered toward the house, inches at a time. I didn't know where Floyd was. Had no time to yell for help. Enemies were prowling the property, and I had to stop them.

Footfalls in the snow. I whirled, spotted Floyd jogging toward me, gun in hand.

"Noah?" he called. "You okay? Seen Hamza?"

"Floyd, get down!"

Bullets peppered the snow around him and he dove for cover. I rose to a knee, fired into the gloom beneath the porch. Someone screamed, then a barrage of lead whizzed past my head. I dropped flat as three shapes emerged and raced down through the yard, vanishing into the woods.

I fired after them as Floyd scrambled to my side. "You hit?" he hissed, the whites of his eyes reflecting moonlight.

"No. But they got Hamza." My voice hitched. "Twice, I guess. He's gone."

"Bastards!" Floyd was reloading, his chapped lips forming a snarl. He lurched to his feet, preparing to give chase, but I grabbed the sleeve of his beefy forearm. "They were messing around under the deck, Floyd. Then they just ran. Why?"

Floyd was breathing hard, nostrils flaring in rage, but he kept his head. "We'd better check, I guess. I'll cover you."

I pounded his shoulder in thanks, then scurried for the deck. The wooden structure rose on long stilts and was bolted to the back of the house. The space beneath was roughly eight feet high and ten deep, sheltering the HVACs and essential utility hookups. I crept in slowly, wary of traps, but it quickly became obvious I was alone.

I snapped on my flashlight. Swung it in a slow arc. Noticed a small gray block molded to the gas line below the meter. Something was jammed into it. A cell phone. Cheap, by the look. As I watched, the display blinked on. 2:00. Then 1:59. 1:58.

My eyes popped. I turned and ran, barely missed cracking my skull on a crossbeam. "Bomb!" I yelled at Floyd, not pausing as I sprinted up the steps to the deck itself. "Get away from the house, Floyd! Get Lauren and Casey!"

I didn't hear his reply as I slammed into the back door. Mercifully, it was unlocked. Bursting into the kitchen, I found everyone else still huddled in the great room, interrogating Ferris. All eyes whipped to me.

"Bomb!" I shouted, waving my arms. "Under the house! Everyone get out now!"

No one moved. They all blinked at me in surprise, even Ferris. Min's face went white.

"What's going on, Noah?" she said.

I could barely speak, the clock in my head paralyzing my tongue. "In one minute this room is going to explode! His visit is a trick! Go, now! *There's a bomb under the deck!*"

People leapt to their feet. Faces turned to each other, eyes wide. But no one was running for the door. Derrick grabbed Ferris by the shirt and dragged him close. The weasel-faced boy began screaming that he didn't know anything.

They weren't moving fast enough. It wasn't real to them yet. In a panic, I aimed my gun at the ceiling and fired over and over, yelling, "Bomb!" between each pull of the trigger.

The stasis broke. Everyone bolted for the front door, but they were putting on jackets and scarves, taking way too much time. I screamed at them, dragging Min by the hand and shoving people before me. "Get out! Get out! Forget the jackets! Go! Go! Go!"

People finally got the message, abandoning their gear and

416

charging into the bitter cold. I stood by the door, propelling them out one by one. Min hesitated, waiting for me. I thrust her at Tack, and he tugged her outside.

The front stoop became clogged with bodies. Someone fell.

A dragon's roar erupted behind me. Orange light rocketed up through the floor, swallowing the great room in a molten fist. Then something vast and unseen lashed out and struck me in the chest, and I remembered nothing more.

Stars. Colors. Spinning vortices. Endless void.

I awoke in ash and debris. My consciousness floated on an ice-tinged breeze.

A tinny ringing, but the world was silent.

Burning fire. Fierce cold. I stared at a hole in the side of my house.

My hearing came back all at once, like a tuned channel.

The growl of flames eating wood. Snapping gunfire. *Ping. Ping. Ping.*

Screams. Grunts. Howls. Dark streaks in the snow.

Something moved beside me. Then it rose with a startled gasp. A moment later the shadow fell again, making a terrible gagging sound. It rolled to face me, features slack, eyes fixed and unblinking like a doll.

Bye, I thought kindly, adjusting the ski hat on the doll's sticky red hair.

I blinked. No. Not a doll. Maggie. She wasn't moving. Didn't disappear. That meant something, something bad. But I couldn't remember what.

"I think I hit my head, Maggie," I gurgled, throat raspy and wet. I staggered to my feet, found that the left one didn't work. It didn't appear to be there.

I was in my front yard. My house was breathing a black mist. Shattered windows. Frames broken to pieces. I suspected I'd flown through one of them when the dragon coughed.

People were running all around me. Ducking behind trees. Moving in pairs.

Others were across the street. These were bad people. They wore black masks and waved shiny metal objects.

I could tell something was wrong with me. This event was important, but I couldn't get my thoughts to process. Suddenly dizzy, I sat down in the snow. Maybe someone would help me.

Clouds of white smoke swirled in the sky above. Rising and falling. Dancing like leaves. Sometimes gray pieces fell in waves. Shards of soft glass. I opened my mouth and stuck out my tongue.

Phantoms flew from place to place, screeching, clawing, pointing their hands at shadows. Sometimes they'd collapse and lie still. Heaps of ragged cloth. Bags of potatoes. A discarded toy, dropped and forgotten.

Then, a miracle. They would shimmer. Disappear. Then snap back. Jump up and shake like a wet dog. I laughed. Clapped.

One girl stood in the golden halo, barking words that flew like arrows. The others swung on the fiery lines she cast, dancing for her, forming walls. Shields. Knife points.

Min. Min, bathed in light. The others revolved around her as she spun webs.

It was beautiful. She was beautiful.

The demons were disappearing more often now. They turned

and melted back into the trees. Shapes followed, shouting, hounds on the scent. I tried to go with them, but I fell forward on my face.

I rolled. Could see my house again. Except it had been transformed. A sinuous red pyramid, wreathed in black, stretched into the night sky. I gasped, tears streaming from my eyes as orange hands tried to embrace me. Then I was floating, flying, my house racing the other way.

No. *I* was moving. Someone was dragging my shoulders.

I looked up. Scorched face. A terrible scowl. I felt sad for this person. Wanted to make him feel better. But I could only say one thing. "I hit my head."

The face pulled close. Yelled. I knew that voice. "Tack," I whispered, suddenly able to speak. "But that's not your real name."

"Lie still, Noah." He wouldn't look at me. "You're . . . It's not good."

"Bad," I agreed. But truthfully, I felt okay. I didn't feel anything at all.

More thunderous cracks. Tack spun, then swore, diving to the side. I managed to roll onto my stomach. Saw a line of telephone poles. No, trees. The demons were back, poking from the branches.

My vision doubled. I tried to blink. Found I couldn't.

"I think I hit my head, Tack." But he was pointing down the driveway. A demon fell. I cheered weakly. Good job, Tack.

I tried to clap, but my hands wouldn't move. The world slipped into a soft dream.

Min. Bathed in white. *So beautiful.*

I awoke gasping. Scrambled to my knees. I'd been lying in the snow in front of my house, which was burning like a monstrous version of the signal bonfire. Gunfire sang on all sides. I spotted Tack crouching behind a woodpile to my left and scuttled over to join him.

"Good to see you back," he croaked, assault rifle in hand, his eyes glued to the tree line across the cul-de-sac. "You were—"

"Let's not dwell on it," I interrupted, shivering at the memory. The blast had tossed me from the house and broken my body. It was a mercy I'd finally bled out and reset. Now I was back—*remade*—and in the game. And intensely, overwhelmingly angry.

Then I felt a stab of panic. "Where's Min?"

"Shed out back." Tack was watching the darkness for movement, hunting another target. "She improvised a command post there."

"Then why are you here?!" I demanded, searching my jacket for a weapon. I found the pistol I kept inside the lining and checked the mag. Good to go.

"She *ordered* me to guard the driveway." Tack dropped behind the logs to reload. "You should see her—barking out commands like General freaking Patton. I did as I was told." But I could tell it was grating on him. Tack yanked back the charging handle like he was strangling a rattlesnake. He was worried about Min, too.

"You're right," I said. "Sorry. What's the situation?"

"They hit us from both sides after the bomb went off. The

whole house went up." He looked at me then. "If you hadn't warned us . . ."

"Got lucky. Now let's pay them back."

Tack grunted. "It's quiet up here. I think they bounced. Let's check in with the others."

I nodded. We rose and scurried across the driveway. Nearly tripped over two still forms lying beside the garage. Heart in my throat, I knelt to check. Finn Whitaker. And poor Ferris, the world's worst emissary. Neither were on our side, but I felt empty just the same.

Tack pulled me by the arm. We sped around back, nearly got lit up by Sam and Carl, who were hunkered behind an over-turned picnic table and covering the approach.

"Don't shoot," I hissed. "It's Noah and Tack!"

"Hurry," Sam growled. "They're everywhere. Tell Min we can't stay here."

We passed their position and ran down to the shed. Min was there with Akio and Derrick. Behind them, Anna and Rachel were huddled in each other's arms, cheeks stained by ashes and tears. Min glanced up, and I could see the relief in her eyes.

"Casey and Lauren were cut off and fell back into the neigh-borhood," Derrick was saying. He nodded as we joined the grim conference. "I don't know where they are now."

"Those girls can look after themselves," Min said. "I know where they'll go. As for everyone else—we've got the cous-ins guarding the driveway, Darren, Benny, and Leighton are watching the path behind us, and Richie and Kyle are down in the woods. Any word on Floyd or Aiken?"

Akio shook his head. "They got hit right out the front door, but they both got up and ran into the neighbor's yard. They could be fine."

"What about Cenisa?" Min asked. The way her lips trembled, I knew she feared the answer.

"Gone." Derrick ground his teeth, eyeing the floor. "Dropped twice. Didn't get up."

Pain flared in Min's eyes. "I haven't seen Maggie, either."

"She's gone," I said softly. There was a moment of silence, then Derrick punched the wall. "I'm gonna *kill* Ferris," he seethed, shaking out his hand.

"Too late," Tack said flippantly. "Someone beat you to it. Finn, too."

Derrick blinked, then sniffed hard. "This is crazy, man. I used to play soldiers with those guys as kids. What the hell are we doing, y'all?"

"Trying to stay alive," Tack fired back. "They came to kill *us*, remember?"

"We can't stay here," Akio said, deftly changing the subject. "The house is gutted and it's too cold outside. We need a new base." As if to emphasize his point, the wind rattled the shed's wooden doors, stoking the fireball only steps away.

"They're still out there." Derrick's eyes were tight. "I saw Toby, Mike, and Lars working together. Benny said he spotted Chris and Spence in the woods." He glanced over at me. "They came up that cliff-side in the backyard. I thought it was unclimbable too, but we forgot how jacked up they are now."

I grabbed my hair with both hands and pulled, tasted ashes in my mouth. *I didn't set a guard there.*

"I popped Tucker by the garage," Akio added, scratching his cheek. "He got up, though. That makes eight in their attack at least, counting the dead."

"Has anyone seen Ethan?" Min asked, and for a moment there was murder in her eyes.

Everyone shook their heads.

Her shoulders pushed back. "Akio's right, we need to move. And if they attacked us *here*, that means they can't be *there*." She spoke briskly. "Get everyone together. We're making a run for town. There are buildings we can occupy and defend."

"The library!" I blurted, feeling a surge of inspiration. "It's too big to blow up in a sneak attack, but there aren't many ground-floor windows. We should have enough people to secure it."

Min nodded. "Good idea. Go! We'll move as soon as we're all together."

It took ten more minutes to get organized and gather our remaining supplies—mostly weapons and ammunition we'd been smart enough to leave in one of the SUVs. I spent the time creeping through the snow, anxiously whispering at where I thought our people were stationed. Thankfully, we didn't see an enemy the whole time. Perhaps they were retreating. If so, we had to move fast.

Min's plan was smart, but required speed. We needed to beat them back to town, or at least slip by them before they guessed our intentions. I was hoping they'd assume we'd just move a few blocks over and lick our wounds. Instead, we'd get behind Ethan's lines and give him a nasty surprise.

Our number had dwindled to fourteen. Min put me in charge of the caravan, but our vehicles had been disabled in the firefight. So many flat tires. We had no choice but to walk. I sent a team of four to scout the street—the cousins, Darren, Benny—while the main group traveled behind them. Min, Rachel, Anna, Derrick, and Leighton were guarded by me, Tack, and Kyle. Richie and Akio brought up the rear. Everyone moved at a fast walk.

Good news arrived first. Floyd and Aiken burst from the woods halfway down the block, Aiken and Anna colliding in a hug that could've broken bones. Spirits buoyed, we continued to the valley floor. Min wanted to check the boathouse for the soccer girls, then circle the lake and sneak onto Library Avenue. A decent strategy, until it all went wrong.

We'd reached Shore Point Road, were a hundred yards from the docks when they hit us from both sides. The deadly crossfire began with no warning. Sam, Akio, and Kyle were instantly cut to pieces.

"Everyone down!" I shouted.

It was so dark I could barely see, but shadows were moving on the road. I was lying side by side with Benny and Floyd. We fired into the black, pausing only to reload. Bullets whizzed overhead. I heard a grunt behind me, glanced over to see Darren's face go slack. But he phased back in seconds later and rejoined our line. Then Carl flopped down in the snow beside him.

"Hold them here," I shouted, then shimmied back and scurried in the other direction, passing where Anna, Rachel, and Aiken were cowering with their hands over their heads. Another line had formed on our opposite flank. Sam and Tack were shoulder to shoulder with Min, Akio, and Leighton, everyone firing into the gloom.

"They've got us pinned," Sam said. "And they're using automatic weapons." A ripping sound like a buzz saw echoed in the night. We made ourselves small as the deadly hail scythed through the air above us.

Sam was right. They had us trapped out in the open. Sitting ducks. I was planning a blind charge into their teeth when a quick succession of pops sounded ahead. The automatic firing stopped. Moments later Casey and Rachel ghosted from the darkness.

"They're all down on this side," Casey shouted, "but they won't be for long. Let's go!"

I didn't argue. Rising to a knee, I yelled back the way I'd come. "Everyone, fall back this way! Now!"

The other side was still taking heavy fire. They ripped off a long barrage, then sprang up and retreated toward me, gathering the group in the middle. We all followed Casey and Lauren as they dashed off the road and onto the frozen lake.

Min stopped at the edge, waving everyone forward. "This way! Hurry! They won't have any cover on the ice, and can't surround us." When the last person ran past, I grabbed her hand and we rushed toward the boathouse end of the dock. Though slick, the lake ice was puckered and covered in snow, giving decent traction. The others had gathered by the last pylon and were counting off. One was missing.

"Anyone seen Leighton?" I called out.

"Here!" a voice shrilled. Leighton was somehow behind

everyone, just now running out onto the ice. "They're right on me!" he shouted.

A machine gun screamed again, and we cowered under the dock's pilings.

"Get the others away," Sam growled as Leighton finally slipped and slid his way to join us. "Carl and I will hold them here, then we'll meet you at the library. Go!"

Min seemed about to protest, but there wasn't time. "Don't wait too long," she said, then gripped Sam by the shoulder. I began herding everyone else out onto the open lake ice, into the howling wind and suffocating darkness.

Moments later gunfire echoed, a rapid firefight fit to wake the gods. It ended abruptly. The sound repeated as we worked farther out onto the lake, then did so again.

The cousins were holding the door closed. I said a prayer for them. As silently as ghosts, we slipped into the infinite black and disappeared.

The crossing was slow and painful, a slipping, sliding mess of falls and curses. Whatever time we might've saved by taking a direct route was being squandered by the snail's pace we were forced to endure.

But finally, the ruined marina's dark outline hove into view. I was trudging beside Min, who seemed lost in thought. I put an arm around her and her head jerked up, lips smiling faintly before the frown returned. I knew she was worrying about how to take care of everyone. What we were going to eat tonight. Where we'd sleep. How to protect us from the stalking murderers our classmates had become.

I wanted to say something comforting, but no words sprang to mind. I didn't have the answers. Then the first grumblings shook the ice, and all other thoughts vanished in an onslaught of dread.

Min's eyes went as wide as dinner plates. "Oh, no."

I remembered Sarah's expression on the webcam. Like she'd found something new.

A low rumble reverberated from the surrounding mountains. The ice beneath our feet began to vibrate, then hiss and snap. I felt the deep, primordial panic of a land creature suddenly aware of a bottomless depth of water beneath its feet.

"Run!" Min shouted.

We took off like a flight of panicked birds, racing as fast as the ice would let us. The roaring increased. I saw hairline cracks spiderweb beneath my boots, then whole sheets began to crack apart.

Around the valley, invisible peaks groaned. Out on the ice, the once solid surface broke into pieces, large sections popping up and calving sideways like icebergs.

The marina was close—less than fifty yards away. We could make it.

With a shriek like a screaming baby, a massive sheet of ice reared up beside me. Tipped sideways. I watched in horror as Floyd and Lauren slid soundlessly into the black water, twin Os on their faces. Then the berg overturned completely, covering them both.

Casey stopped, screamed, but I grabbed her by the arm and pulled her toward shore. More huge chunks were shaking apart. We had seconds to reach solid ground. After a few yards

Casey shook me off and raced ahead, crying as she ran for safety.

The kids with the best footwear reached the wharf first and began scrambling up ladders. The ice began to shred all around us. I took another step, felt my sneaker go through. In a panic, I spun, losing my footing and sliding toward a yawning patch of open water.

My legs went in and the cold was impossible. It seeped into my bones, stunning me, turning my muscles to jelly. I began to slide down into the inky depths, mind blank, limbs slack and useless.

Something snagged the back of my jacket. Pulled me back from the edge. My brain jolted into action, began to function again. I gasped, whipped my arms out, flipping over to look behind me. Min was on her butt with my jacket hood gripped in both hands, dragging me across the ice. Yelling at me the whole time. Then Derrick and Tack appeared, and together they hauled me upright.

"Em fiiine," I said through chattering teeth. "Guhhhoo."

I staggered the last few yards, grabbing the bottom ladder rung just as the ice dissolved beneath my feet. I was pulled, towed, and cajoled up to the dock, then managed to stumble down to the stone wharf under my own power.

Blinking like an invalid, I peered around. Though it was dark, I could see buildings up and down the block. There was a fire burning in the southwestern hills—my house, spreading to consume the woods surrounding it. With the wind howling, nothing would stop the conflagration from burning down that whole section of the valley.

Min and Tack were arguing, gesticulating wildly. Something about a library. Min pointed at Town Hall and shouted something, while Tack vehemently shook his head.

It all became too much.

I crumpled to the snow-covered flagstones and passed into a dreamless sleep.

37

MIN

"Busy night, you guys! Find a TV!"

Sarah's voice echoed off the library's thick granite walls. My eyes snapped open, scratchy and tired. I ran a hand through my tangled hair, stumbling to my feet in the study room I'd commandeered for a few hours' rest. I stepped out into the stacks and hurried to the atrium. There were screens there. Sarah's stupid face was leering from every one of them.

People appeared quickly, some armed, some wiping sleep from their eyes like me. Dawn was fast approaching. I couldn't find Noah. Maybe he was still out.

We'd taken over the building hours earlier. Most everything else in town was destroyed, except for Town Hall, of course. The Guardian's lair stood like a gleaming white scar, unblemished despite the rubble surrounding it on all sides.

The sheriff's office had collapsed. Sam told us—last to arrive, frozen to the bone but unable to contain his grief. He'd lost Carl out on the ice, his only consolation that his cousin had taken Tucker down with him. Two more classmates, gone. I was getting numb to the losses, and that scared me more than anything.

I didn't know where Ethan and his thugs were. For the moment, I couldn't bring myself to care. I wanted to grab Sarah through the screen and throttle her with my bare hands. Instead I watched, heart in throat, waiting for whatever new horror she was about to inflict upon us.

She was sitting in the conference room as I had so many times, wearing a gray Nemesis jumpsuit. This was the first time we'd seen her in one—I guess washing her other outfit each day had finally lost its appeal.

Her whiteboard had been updated. The results took my breath away.

"Nine players were eliminated last night," Sarah said in a matter-of-fact tone, "making it the bloodiest day in Fire Lake history. When this is over, we should have a holiday commemorating our community's loss." She took a deep breath, rolling her delicate shoulders. "*But* . . . this silly MegaCom is stubbornly insisting it wasn't enough. I wish I could tell you how many more of you have to go, but I can't. Sorry, kids."

Nobody said a word. Raging against our circumstances was pointless. We just waited. Drained. Fifteen wrung-out teenagers quickly nearing the limits of our endurance. No one could take this for much longer.

Sarah leaned forward. "Yes, that earthquake last night was me. And I'm sorry if it was nasty, but I simply *cannot* stay down here any longer. I . . . I just can't. It's creepy. I don't know how Min lasted as long as she did."

I noticed signs of wear in her demeanor. Her voice was sharper than usual. Her eyes were a little redder. Sarah's blond hair hung lank and lifeless, as if she hadn't bothered to bathe before broadcasting. I knew how isolating the lab complex could feel. What it was like to have zero variation hour after endless hour. Apparently it was affecting Sarah even worse than it had me.

She sat forward, pressed the tabletop with her index fingers. "So here's the deal: I'm ordering everyone to town square at dawn this morning. Let's bring this thing home. You guys can form up and . . . and . . . finish whatever needs to be done." She sat back and crossed her arms. "If you *don't* show, I'm going to key in another earthquake, only this time I'll turn it all the way up. That'll level every remaining building in the valley. Hell, every remaining everything."

Sarah huffed a sigh. "Right now I'm giving you a sunny, pleasant, crisp winter morning to work with. No more snow. No wind. I'll even take wildlife back offline. But I'll drop the temp to a frosty negative forty and have freaking polar bears prowling the streets if you don't do what I say. Does everyone get it? I hope so. Bye now!"

Her face winked out.

I gaped at the screen, mind racing, but every path it took hit a dead end. Sarah held all the cards. She could make this world our enemy.

I turned, found everyone watching. Noah had appeared and was standing next to Tack. The others stood in a ragged semi-circle. Derrick. Casey and Leighton. Sam. Kyle. Richie. Akio. Aiken and Anna. Benny. Darren. Rachel. Fifteen refugees.

Some looked to me hopefully, others with doubt in their eyes. I understood. I doubted, too. But I had to be strong for them.

"We have to do it," I said. Mutters broke out, but no one contradicted me. "I'm not suggesting we give a single inch to Ethan, but I don't see how we can avoid this meeting." I waved a hand at the cracked roof above our heads. "This building can't take another earthquake. We need a break to recover, but we won't get that chance if Sarah shakes our house down."

Tack was frowning at the floor. "We don't all need to go."

I shook my head. Wanted to reach out to him, but he was still a closed door. "You heard her, Tack. Sarah knows exactly how many of us are left. She probably knows where we all are. She said everyone, so that means everyone. When have you known her to make an empty threat?"

"Min's right." Noah stepped forward, caught a withering glare from Tack he didn't see. "We should show up and listen, and maybe buy some time. But this isn't surrender. We'll go armed and ready for anything."

"I *want* to see them." Sam's scowl was carved in stone. He hadn't spoken to anyone since reporting his cousin's elimination. "I want to look into their eyes."

"There are still more of us," Derrick said. He leaned back against one of the long library tables, trying to warm to the idea. "We scout ahead, set up on one side on the common. Everyone carries. If Ethan and those boys want trouble, they can get it."

"You don't decide for me!" Rachel was standing between two stacks, arms crossed so tightly, I thought she might squeeze the oxygen from her lungs. "If I don't want to go, I won't. Sarah can kiss my ass."

I took a calming breath, then spoke to the whole group. "I can't compel anyone, but I take Sarah's threat at face value. I don't want to see what she can unleash. I'm going, and I hope you all come with me."

Rachel snorted, but then balked as eyes bored into her. "Fine! But if this is another trap, don't forget who walked us right into it. Sarah and Ethan have *always* worked together."

That was my fear as well, but I didn't see another solution. Dawn would break in less than an hour. We just had to be ready for anything.

My group spread out along the northern edge of the square. We'd come cautiously, scouting the route, wary of any ambush. But no one had bothered us as we covered the three blocks to the center of town.

Sarah was true to her word.

It was a beautiful morning, bright sunlight revealing the valley's destruction in horrifying detail. The lake was a shattered picture frame of broken chunks and loose icebergs. My heart broke, thinking of the classmates we'd lost in its depths.

Across the water, the southwestern corner of the valley smoldered, whole neighborhoods consumed and rendered to ashes. Just like the trailer park, the summer camp, the ski resort, and so much else. Main Street was in ruins, with only one building in ten still standing.

Except Town Hall. Its gleaming facade leered pristine white, like a giant middle finger.

Fire Lake had been an idyllic alpine village. Now it was a disaster area, a burned-out wreck of a place, barely recognizable.

We had done it all. To each other. With almost no prompting. There was a lesson there, but I was too tired to care.

"Look alive," Noah called out. He pointed across the snow-covered common to where another group was approaching. I hadn't seen them assembled in months. The sight made my skin crawl.

With the weather improved, hats and gloves were off. No goggles or scarves. I could see faces. Eyes. I clutched my weapon tighter.

It was jarring, that a simple meeting could feel so tense. So fraught with violence and danger. God, what had we become?

Ethan led, backed by Toby, the Nolan twins, Spencer and Lars. A quartet of girls walked behind them: Jessica, Colleen, Zoë, and Susan. Ten in all. Five less than my side, but those boys almost rippled with caged violence. They moved like hunting cats, eliminations making them strong. Some of my people were barely hanging on. If a fight broke out, they'd finish us.

That's what Sarah wants. I can't let it happen.

Movement to my right. Alice Cho stepped from the ruins of Sacred Heart and approached the square alone. She made no move to join either group, seemed ready to bolt at the slightest provocation.

"Hiding this whole time?" Tack whistled. "Jeez, Alice. You get the gold medal."

"Three coming over," Noah said. "They made a show of putting down their guns."

Ethan was striding toward the center of the square, followed by Toby and Mike. I took a calming breath. "Let's go meet them."

"Unarmed?" Tack said sharply.

"If they did, so will we." I passed my gun to Casey, then addressed the group. "I'd like Tack and Noah to come with me. I don't think many more should go. Derrick?"

He scratched his cheek, then shook his head. "Pass. I ditched them and that might be a distraction. I'll stay here and keep a watch out for tricks."

I nodded, signaled for Tack and Noah to follow. They handed off their guns and we started across the field. Sam shoved his rifle into Akio's hands and joined us. I didn't stop him. The only survivor of those who'd lived at the quarry, he'd earned the right to say his piece.

The summer camp group had been wiped out completely. Noah's team was cut to the bone. People who avoided the larger camps had come out best in the end, though if we hadn't united, we'd all have been ground to dust.

Still might be.

We met by the fountain, broken again like it had been on the last day of our lives. I remembered waking up right here, all those weeks ago. Our first moments inside the Program. Would my last be in the same spot?

Ethan wore a sweater and jeans. His face was leaner, harder than before. His hands never seemed to stop moving. No smug smile this time. No condescending laugh. His gaze was almost vacant. He stared at me without speaking for a long moment. Behind him, Toby had his hands in his pockets, a wry smile on his face. Mike's glower was soaked in bitterness.

I decided to speak first. "Ethan, we can't go on like this.

We're tearing each other apart. The Program wants us to fight, but we don't have to. We can still decide how to live."

"You're right," he said roughly, surprising me. "It *can't* go on like this. This phase has to end. We have to reach the next level."

"Ethan, I spoke to the Guardian. Just days ago. I know the final purpose of the Program."

"You think I don't?" he shot back, his voice trembling, rising with a manic tinge. "Sarah told us everything. We can be re-born. *Alive*, Min. Think about that. What wouldn't you do to be real again?"

"Kill people who never caused me harm," Sam spat in an-swer, his dark eyes boring into Ethan. "But you sold your soul because a computer told you to?"

Ethan flushed a deep red, but Toby bumped his friend's shoulder reassuringly. "You're one to talk, Sammie," he said with a lopsided grin. "Take a look at the company you keep. How many people has Noah reset? And Tack? Boy howdy! He's been a regular Angel of Death. Not sure you fellas can get up on that high horse with Melinda."

"Enough!" Ethan shouted, startling everyone. "I didn't come here to argue about things with no meaning. I came to offer a truce."

Everyone looked at him in shock, Toby most of all.

"What kind of truce?" I asked cautiously.

Something dark moved behind Ethan's eyes. "I want Sarah *out* of that silo. She's locked the whole thing off somehow." His finger shot toward me. "But you know a back door. Get me inside, and I'll leave you alone. *I'll* make Sarah pay for what she's done. For the lies! For her *disloyalty*."

Spittle flew from his lips. His glare wandered in and out of focus, as if he was imagining the harms he'd inflict upon his former partner. It scared me.

I didn't know how to respond. Noah looked equally baffled. Sam turned and spat on the ground. I glanced at Tack, who was watching Ethan like a lit fuse.

Toby glanced at Mike, then reached out and tugged Ethan's arm. "Dude, we need to—"

Ethan shrugged Toby off, nearly knocking him to the ground. "Sarah goes next! I want that bitch to suffer for what she's done to us. Afterward, we can decide who moves forward. I'm willing to trade—"

Bang.

Ethan's eyes bulged, then he looked down at a ragged hole in his chest. He staggered sideways, turning as he fell to the ground.

Toby was behind him, pistol in hand, an annoyed look on his round face. "Ain't gonna be no truce, Ethan. Hell, there's probably not even a Phase Three. You've gone soft, son. No good."

Ethan slumped in the snow, his breath coming in rasps.

Toby continued like he was scolding a puppy. "*This* is the world we live in. We're home, *right now*, and you've been slipping for weeks. Time for you to go." He looked up, then turned the gun on me. "You too, Min. No Girl Scouts in Toby Town."

Everything happened at once. A blur hit Toby from the side. Noah, moving faster than thought. Gunfire erupted from both sides of the square, and the field exploded into chaos.

Mike and Tack were wrestling on the ground, faces screwed up in exertion. Sam stepped in front of me and took three shots to the chest. He spun, pushed me back toward our line. "Go!" Then he collapsed.

I sprinted away, taking cover behind a park bench. The rest of my team was doing the same. I spotted Alice Cho as she bolted back inside the remains of the church, a rabbit going to ground.

I was about to signal a retreat when Kyle started yelling, "There are more of us! Attack! Don't let them get away!" He charged the other side of the square, drawing most of our fighters with him.

The sky abruptly darkened, heavy clouds rolling in. I felt a rush of freezing wind. Sleet began to fall in seconds as thunder rumbled the heavens. A bolt of lightning struck the field and sent Chris Nolan flying. He landed and didn't move, shimmered in and out before popping back to his feet, only to be mowed down again by Kyle. Then Kyle stood over his body, unloading on Chris every time he tried to get up. I turned away in horror.

Noah and Toby were still fighting in the center of the common. Toby lifted Noah over his head and threw him across the snow-covered grass. He was impossibly strong, and moved like a snake. "You're all sheep!" he screamed, shooting indiscriminately at everyone around him. "Why would anyone ever want to leave this place?" Then he laughed as Derrick tackled him to the ground. "We're *gods* here, don't you see that?!"

Something whistled by my head. Then a wall of heat slammed me and I was flying, end over end, to land in the street. I hit the ground hard, heard the bones in my shoulder crack. Looking back, I saw a smoldering crater close to where I'd been standing. Grenade? Lightning? I didn't know. The pain was excruciating. My vision swam in and out.

The world was a catastrophe of light and dark, explosions and gunshots. There were fights all over the square, nightmare scenes playing out on a carpet of white. Kyle had fallen into a blast hole created by something Lars threw. Spence and Mike cornered him, periodically firing until they nodded to each other and raced away.

They made it ten feet, then a line of bullets dropped them. Casey and Akio leapt over a bench and kept up a steady barrage, knocking the boys down each time they reappeared. Spence finally managed to scramble to safety, but Mike lay unmoving on the grass. Then my friends were blown off their feet as something exploded between them. There was a burst of light behind me and I turned, saw the battered church erupt into flames and collapse in on itself.

I'm in hell. This is hell.

Toby shook off Derrick and shot him, then grabbed Leighton by the shirt. Dropping his gun, he unsheathed a KA-BAR knife from his belt and stabbed Leighton in the chest. Toby lifted him into the air on its point, waiting, screaming an insane war cry.

Others stopped fighting around him, aghast. Toby was covered in blood, his face fixed in a horrifying smile. Leighton shimmered. Reappeared. Toby stabbed him again.

Tack raced over and grabbed Toby's arm. Toby kicked him away, then dropped Leighton and pulled a pistol from his waistband. Before he could fire, Ethan tried to tackle him, but Toby sidestepped in a blink and tripped him, then shot

Ethan five times in the back. Leighton was just returning on the ground. Toby put a boot to his chest, then unloaded the rest of his magazine.

Everyone in the square had stopped moving, staring at Toby. He was watching Leighton, waiting, only this time Leighton didn't shimmer. He lay still, sleet piling up on his chest.

Toby sighed, his eyes glazing as they rolled back in his head. Then he looked around, as if noticing everyone else watching him for the first time. Enemies stood shoulder to shoulder in a loose circle, staring at Toby like he was a wild animal.

Ethan rose to his feet, face slack. Noah put a hand on his shoulder and eased him back.

"Put the gun down, Toby," Noah said.

Toby smiled darkly. "You think I need it?"

He charged, faster than thought, and hit Noah with both fists to the chest. There was a sickly crunch. Noah flew backward and landed in a heap. Tack charged Toby's back, but Toby unleashed a blurring backhand that caught him across the neck. Tack's head flopped at an unnatural angle, and he fell to the snow.

"Do you see now?!" Toby shouted. Leighton's blood still ran down his chin. He stood in the center of us, cackling, impervious to the sleet coating him in ice.

Noah was slowly getting to his feet. Tack shimmered, then flipped to his back, staring up at Toby with haunted eyes. He tried to roll away, but Toby stomped a boot down on his back, pinning him to the frozen ground.

I stepped forward, my broken shoulder screaming in agony. "Toby, that's enough! It's over. Look around you."

The fighting had ceased. A few bodies littered the ground, their faces covered by the deepening slush. Some had fled, but most stood in a ragged circle around Toby. No one moved as he pivoted slowly, meeting every eye and finding no support.

Toby stopped rotating. Wiped his face and forced a plastic grin. "Ethan, man. Come on. We're good. I was just playing. I knew you had plenty of resets left."

Ethan let out a shuddering breath. Shook his head slowly. "No. I've been listening to you for too long. This . . . this has to stop."

Toby's eyes slid, searching for allies. Neither of the Nolans was present, which meant they were done. "Lars. Spence. We got plans, remember?"

Both boys looked away.

"This isn't a fantasy kingdom, Toby." I waved a hand despite the pain in my shoulder. "The valley is destroyed. *We burned everything down.* We've got no food, no power, no places to stay. People are all that's left. Lives are the only thing left to preserve."

Toby began muttering, patting his pockets. He removed a spare magazine from his jacket and ejected the empty one in his pistol.

Angry rumbles traveled the circle. Casey and Derrick raised their weapons. So did Ethan. I threw up a hand as Toby popped the mag home and racked the slide. "Toby, don't do this. It's not too late for anyone. We'll go see Sarah and stop her. I can talk to the Guardian. When he sees that we refuse to fight anymore, he'll *have* to adjust the rules. We just need to work together. No more dying."

Toby stopped moving. The gun hung loosely by his side.

He glanced down, seemed to abruptly realize he still had Tack pinned to the ground. Toby lifted his boot and my friend scrambled clear, joining the circle between Darren and Richie.

Toby stared at the crimson slush coating his boots. Breathed a deep, full-bodied sigh. "You don't understand, Min." His voice was almost a plea. "We're already dead."

His hand shot up. A frozen moment as the sights zeroed me, then a loud crack.

Darkness.

Void.

One and zeroes.

My body bucked to a sitting position, both hands clutching my forehead.

Gunfire echoed around me. I covered my head and curled into a ball, eyes squeezed shut. My last reset was gone. One more bullet would end me for good.

But no slugs pierced my skin. I peered through slitted eyes, saw that I was outside the circle, which had tightened around Toby.

Noah. Ethan. Derrick. Akio. Lars. Spence. Tack. Casey. Sam. Richie.

They stood united on the field.

They were putting Toby down.

"No! Wait!" I scrambled to my feet, but then Tack was there, wrapping an arm around my waist and holding me back. "It has to be this way!" he hissed. "He's lost his mind, Min!"

I struggled, but I was still dizzy. "This isn't better!" I shouted. "We can't become him!"

Toby fell again. Lay still. Shimmered. Bounded back to his

443

feet. He regarded the circle around him with disdain. "You're all sheep! I'm a god now, can't you see that? You *can't* kill me!"

Another round of shots. Down he went.

It went on and on, until finally, Toby failed to rise. People dropped their weapons, staring vacantly. There were no more sides, no goals, just a dozen horrified teens slumping down on the blood-soaked snow.

"Bury him," I heard Noah say in a strangled voice. "We have to bury them all."

He began dragging Toby toward a fissure in the earth. Surprisingly, Ethan walked over and joined him. As they carried the body away, the sleet abruptly halted. The sky lightened, thunderclouds rolling away to the east. Bright sunshine poured down, warming my skin. The temperature climbed in seconds.

I felt a rush of hope. Was it over? Had Phase Two finally been completed?

Others emerged from hiding. Jessica, Colleen, and Susan crept around the corner with their hands up. Anna and Aiken appeared with Darren and Benny, Rachel reluctantly following on their heels. I watched the smoking ruin of the church, hoping against hope, but Alice Cho never came out.

Twenty teens assembled on the green.

All that remained of the Fire Lake High School sophomore class.

Except Sarah, the bitch.

I stared at Town Hall, praying the door would open and reveal the Guardian. That he'd tell us we didn't have to do this anymore. That we could grieve, and heal. Instead, Sarah's voice boomed across the common. My heart shriveled on the vine.

"Hello, everyone. Bad news, I'm afraid."

We all stopped moving. Heads dropped. Hands covered faces. Many stood still with their eyes closed, like barnyard animals silently awaiting the fatal blow.

Sarah's voice surrounded us, everywhere and nowhere. Rougher than before. The playful tone was gone, as if her self-satisfaction had abruptly evaporated. Had she watched the nightmare that just played out? Was there a level of suffering that affected even the unflappable Sarah Harden?

"The system has revealed the final number we need, and you're not going to believe this." There was a pause. "It's twenty. Two-zero. That's one less than our current head count. I leave it to you to solve the problem."

The echoes died. Frightened gazes began circling.

My lower jaw trembled. I just wanted it to be over, and now this.

Rachel began backpedaling slowly, preparing to bolt. A few hands strayed toward pockets.

"Everyone wait!" I shouted, freezing people in place. "Please. Nobody run or do anything stupid. Don't panic. No matter what, we're not going to . . . to . . . to do what Sarah's suggesting. Let's talk this over and form a plan."

Shoulders relaxed. I waved everyone in to form one group. Surprisingly, they came.

"We have a truce, and we're not going to break it." Nineteen teens were gathered around me, listening. Praying I had an answer. I tried my best to give them one. "Sarah can't eliminate anyone directly, she's already admitted it. So there's no reason to panic right now."

My finger shot toward Town Hall. "The Guardian is inside there. Betas can access the building. I'm going to go talk to him."

"Why would he change anything?" Ethan said. "He's just a function of the system."

I shook my head. "He's real. As real as you and I are, at least. He told me so himself." My throat worked, but I refused to lie anymore. No more holding back. "He's an uploaded sequence like us. More than that, he's my father."

Gasps. Quickly transforming to shouts demanding to know why I'd never said anything. Suspicious glances impaled me. Noah was staring, wide-eyed, rocked. Tack was hunched at his elbow, both hands gripping his hair.

"I only just found out," I said. "Two nights ago. My whole life I never knew who my father was. I never worked with him, or knew anything about Project Nemesis. But he chose *our* class to preserve because . . . because I was a part of it. He wanted to protect me from Earth's destruction. But now he has to stop this. I won't give him a choice."

Noah had a faraway look, like he was seeing things clearly for the first time. Tack was grumbling, his face a mask of frustration.

"How can you force him?" Derrick asked. "He might be your dad, but this is his life's work. What makes you think he'll change things when we're so close to ending the phase?"

I swallowed. "Because if he doesn't, I'll eliminate myself."

Silence like death. Noah's gaze snapped to me, filled with horror. Horror and something else, a conviction firming behind those soft green irises. He strode forward and put both hands on my shoulders. "No," he said softly.

My eyes burned, but I fought back the tears. "It's the only way he'll listen."

Noah smiled, a finger stroking the underside of my cheek. "This isn't on you. Whatever comes next, we need you to be in charge. You're our leader. You have to take us forward."

He kissed me then, in front of the others. His touch was electric, and soft, and sad. My breath was stolen as he released me and stepped back. "They don't need me, though."

Noah removed his pistol from his pocket. Everyone took an involuntary step back, except for Tack, who was staring at Noah with undisguised hate. The kiss he'd given me had been a physical blow.

I shot forward, reaching for him, my fear and anger exploding at once. "Noah, no! That's not an option."

He caught my hand. The sun shone down on his wavy brown hair, setting fire to his eyes. I caught a whiff of pine sap, heard the slow trickle of water through the fountain as a soft winter breeze caressed my skin. Time seemed to stop, as if the Program had been paused.

Who knows? Maybe it had.

Noah wiped his eyes, then met mine. "The first thing I did in the Program was betray you. I've never truly atoned for it." He smiled then, with genuine relief. "Now I can. It's not up to you, Min. It's up to me."

I was frozen in place. This was *wrong*, but I realized I couldn't stop it. My eyes darted frantically, searching for support. No one else spoke out. Noah was offering a sacrifice to the group, and they were willing to take it.

Noah smiled at me with the warmth of a thousand suns, eyes intent, as if memorizing my features. "Do well," he whispered. Then he handed his gun to Tack, who nearly dropped it in surprise.

"I've got two lives left," Noah said curtly. "I know it's asking a lot, but I can't pull the trigger twice."

Tack blanched, tried to hand the pistol back. Noah refused to take it.

"What, you think the local psychopath will happily shoot you?" Tack shouted in a ragged voice. "No way, Noah. I'm done. I . . . I made mistakes too, when I thought Min was gone. I'm not making another."

Noah fixed him with a cold stare. "It's me or her, Tack. Remember that. We both know she isn't bluffing."

Tack's face screwed up in a ball. He dropped the gun, shoulders heaving. "Fuck you, Noah! You want to play Jesus, do it your goddamn self."

"Stop it right now, both of you!" My paralysis snapping, I stepped over and got in Noah's face. "This isn't necessary. *You don't need to be a hero.* Nobody does!" My voice broke. "Don't leave me, okay? I forgive you. I . . . I love you."

I kissed him then, hard on the mouth. Poured all my emotions into it, doubts and hopes swirling and colliding like ships in a storm. For an instant we connected on the deepest level, two digital sequences merging in perfect mathematical harmony.

Noah broke away, breathing hard. "Thank you for that. Thank you so much, Min. I love you, too." Then, wiping his eyes, he looked past me and nodded.

Hands found my shoulders, pulling me back. Derrick and Ethan. I struggled as I realized what they were doing. "No! No!"

"He made his choice," Derrick said through gritted teeth, eyes red. "Let him be a man." He looked up at Noah. "We won't forget this, brother. Not ever."

Noah nodded, his mouth forming a hard line. "Take care of her. Let her take care of you."

"Noah, don't!" My eyes shot to Tack, who was watching me as if every dream he'd possessed was in ruins at his feet. Then his mouth formed a snarl. He scooped up the pistol and aimed it at Noah's head.

Noah's throat worked. He nodded at Tack. "Do it. It's my decision. This isn't on you, Thomas. I'm giving myself up. And if you don't get your head straight and watch out for her, I'll haunt your ass."

"The hell you will," Tack said roughly, hands shaking. Then he turned to face me. Tears leaked from the corners of his eyes. "And you're wrong, Min. Sometimes you do need to be a hero. You always knew I loved you, right?"

Before I could respond, Tack put the gun to his head and pulled the trigger.

38

NOAH

BANG.

I jerked back in shock as Tack fell. Landed with a thud. Never moved.

Min's scream tore across the square. I stood, blinking, unable to process as she threw herself on his body, crying hysterically.

No shimmer. No movement. The crazy bastard must've known he was on the line. He'd stolen my gift right from my fingers and given his own.

Hands reached for Min, but she swatted them away, blubbering, beyond consolation. I stood over her, frozen like a statue.

This wasn't how it was supposed to go. I was about to redeem myself. I was going to make good on my mistakes. Part of me was furious with Tack—always the hero, always the grand gestures—while another part of me sagged with relief.

"Min," I started, but got no further. I didn't know what to say. There were no words. Tack was really gone this time. He wasn't coming back.

As if in response to my thought, Tack's body vanished. Min was left gripping air. She shot to her feet in surprise, an impossible hope blooming on her face. "Did he . . . did he reset?"

Derrick ran to the crater where we'd laid the others to rest. "Toby's gone, too. They're all gone!" He spun, eyes narrowing. "What the hell's happening now?"

Suddenly, the sky blinked. A flash of white, then everything went black. A moment later the sun returned, beaming down on a completely different valley.

Every building in town was back, standing in perfect condition. The statue by the fountain was restored. Clean air, with no trace of smoke. I looked down at the lake and its lapping blue waters. Realized I was hot, suffocating in my winter jacket. I shed the garment to the verdant grass beneath my feet—no snow, no blood-drenched slush—and let a gentle mountain breeze ruffle my scruffy hair.

Jessica Cale pointed across the lake. "Look! The fire's gone!"

It was true. Near the edge of sight, my neighborhood rose in tiers from the opposite shore, familiar bay windows gleaming at its highest point. I had to squint, realized my senses had dulled to normal.

Fire Lake was restored, everything back to the way it had been when we'd first awakened in this very square, months ago. It seemed like this time, the *Program* had reset.

"Phase Two," Derrick breathed. "It's over."

Min was on her feet, eyes wet, the only one not gaping in wonder at the restored valley. I understood. Tack was truly gone, left behind in the nightmare. Twenty of us remained, but he wasn't one of them.

"He gave me everything," Min whispered. "Over and over." She looked at me, all the hurt in the world filling her eyes. "I killed him, Noah. It's my fault. If it weren't for me, he'd be here."

I crushed her in a hug. "Don't even *try* to think that. Tack made a choice. He saved us."

Min buried her head in my shirt, shuddering as her fingers clawed my chest. I wanted to say something perfect, to fix the pain inside her, but I knew that was impossible. Min had lost her best friend and felt responsible for it. There's no pushing that kind of guilt aside.

"Holy crap, look!" Ethan had stripped down to a T-shirt, was pointing at Main Street.

The door to Town Hall stood open.

The Guardian was striding onto the square.

Min pushed away from me, glaring hatred at her father. I was afraid she'd charge him—gnash her teeth and beat him with her fists—but then the energy seemed to drain out of her all at once. She simply watched Black Suit approach the fountain and turn to face us.

I felt an instinctive panic, gazing upon my longtime tormenter, yet I gathered around him with the others and waited. Maybe we really were the sheep Toby named us.

"Phase Two is complete." The Guardian clasped his hands before him as if concluding a sacred ritual. "Congratulations. You've survived the refinement process and been selected for regeneration. You'll live again."

Even after the slaughter of the last few days, people couldn't suppress their smiles. Something budded inside me that I hadn't felt in months: hope. Suddenly, there was a light in the darkness.

This terrible, brutal, despicable man was offering it to me. I wanted it more badly than I could possibly describe.

"My best friend is dead," Min said bitterly, staring at her father. "Thomas Russo. Went by Tack. You never knew him because you abandoned me for my entire life, but he was a good person. He shot himself in the head to finish your game. I hate you forever, Dad."

Black Suit removed his sunglasses, revealing crestfallen gray-green eyes. I took an involuntary step back. Seeing something human in this man—the beast that had stalked and killed me as a child—made my stomach churn.

"Last night I created a subroutine," the Guardian said. "The eliminated codes have been placed in a loop. They will continue to exist inside the MegaCom for as long as it runs, in virtual Fire Lake, under the conditions you see now. The day will repeat itself endlessly. So you see, they won't even know they've failed. It's the best I could do for them. I did this for you."

Min stared at her father, a fierce intensity sharpening her gaze. But whatever she wanted to say at that moment, she kept it bottled inside.

"Can you stop Sarah?" Ethan demanded. "I want her to pay for what she's done."

The Guardian turned his cold regard on him. "Recriminations serve no further purpose. Sarah Harden has no control in Phase Three. None of you can harm each other from this point forward. Note that your weapons are gone."

My hands darted to my pockets. He was right—the snub-nosed .22 I always carried was missing. Empty searches by others confirmed that the Guardian was telling the truth.

"Sarah played the game better than the rest of you," the Guardian said, "and without the malice many of you held. There's no point in grudges now. You all did what you thought was best. The Program made demands, and you responded. From this moment forward, you are one team. You are the future of life on Earth. Put away your petty grievances. They won't serve you where you're going."

"Where is that?" I blurted, unable to keep the words from escaping.

The wisp of a smile curled his lips. "You're going home, Noah. Out of my grasp forever, and well wished. It's time for you to return to life."

"Now?" I didn't understand. I glanced at Min, but she was somewhere else entirely. What the Guardian was saying made no sense. "You showed us the real Earth once before. It was all lava flows and choked skies. Nothing could survive there. How long will we have to wait?"

This time the Guardian smiled with genuine contentment. "Your minds adapted so well to the programming. This really has been a triumph for me, if I may toot my own horn. Surely you understand that time here is a variable like everything else."

My mouth opened. Closed. I had no idea what he was talking about.

"How long?" Akio asked, his smooth cheeks scrunched in thought. "It's been close to three months by my count, but what's the real number?"

The Guardian spoke matter-of-factly. "This Program has been running for one million, three hundred and thirty-four thousand, seven hundred and forty-six years. And eight days."

People cried out in shock. Ethan blinked rapidly, like a confused toddler. Rachel was shaking her head, one hand covering her mouth. I stumbled sideways, unmoored, unable to process the enormity of what he'd just said.

"Earth has healed, as it always does in the wake of Nemesis." The smug bastard seemed to be enjoying himself. "It became inhabitable several thousand years ago, but Phase Two had to run its course."

I felt light-headed. Staggered. We'd been squabbling for control over this tiny patch of existence for . . . *eons*. The thought made me seasick. Others were just as floored. Jessica Cale had wilted into Colleen Plummer's arms. Sam sat down on the grass, hands on his head.

Min weaved between the others to stand before the Guardian. She met his eyes and stared into them. A tense moment passed, then her hand snaked out to slap him across the face. Except it stopped short, arrested by some invisible force mere inches from his cheek. Black Suit never flinched.

Min lowered her hand. Her head dropped to her chest. "What happens now?"

He spoke formally. "Project Nemesis is nearly complete." A ripple flitted across the Guardian's face, quickly covered. "The goals have been achieved. Are you ready to be reborn, daughter?"

Min nodded without looking up.

"Then lead your classmates to the silo. It's time to reenter the world."

The walk was surreal. We moved east down Main, headed for the government land. At the edge of town we reached the grocery store, restored to its former glory. Even stocked—Ethan actually had to unlock the door before we poured inside and started gorging ourselves. Weirdly, it felt like a celebration. Laughter sounded among the shell-shocked survivors.

The Guardian said nothing, smiling faintly. His indulgence killed my appetite. I dropped the Klondike bar I was eating and walked past him, found Min waiting outside.

I put my arms around her and we stood together silently, drinking in each other's presence. She was as stiff as a toy robot, but when I asked what was wrong—what *else* was wrong, I guess—she only kissed my cheek and stepped away. Eventually the others came out and we continued down the road.

The silo's outer door was unlocked, as was the blast door at the end of the corridor. We reached the missile shaft and circled the catwalk. "Noah, Ethan, and Min will come down in the first cage with me," the Guardian ordered. "The rest of you can descend afterward in groups of four. Derrick, come down in the second group and gather everyone in the command center, then lead them to the lab complex. We'll be waiting."

Derrick nodded stiffly. Ethan stepped into the cage first, strangely quiet. I led Min to the opposite side. The Guardian stood between us and we started down. No one said a word at first, but as we passed the alcoves, Ethan finally spoke out.

"Survival supplies," he muttered, waving a hand at the stacks of dusty crates. "This stuff wasn't meant for us *here*—it's for back in the real world."

The Guardian nodded. "Everything you'll need to rebuild society, assuming you don't waste your energies fighting amongst yourselves, or take foolish risks."

Awestruck, I scanned the cavern with fresh eyes. "How long did you plan this operation? Not the project, but *you*, personally. How many years did you work down here?"

The Guardian glanced at Min, who didn't seem to notice. For a moment I thought he wouldn't answer. Then, "All my life, Noah."

We slid into the chute, dropping to the command level beneath the shaft's concrete floor. The cage jerked to a halt and I opened the gate. Elevator doors parted, and the Guardian led us to the command center. There he paused a moment to regard the MegaCom, visible through the center panel, its blast curtain rolled back once more. The Guardian breathed deeply, then turned away, crossing to the bookcase and triggering the hidden release. The blast door at the far end stood open and we entered the lab complex.

Sarah was waiting in the conference room. She stood at the opposite side of the long table, arms crossed tightly over her chest. Her eyes seemed red, but her posture was steady. Ethan sneered at her, a look of pure loathing contorting his features. Sarah met his glare squarely, then shrugged, turning her attention to Min.

"I did what I had to, Wilder. No hard feelings."

Min shook her head softly. "Does it even matter now?"

Sarah pursed her lips, nodded. "No. But you should know this was never personal for me. I wanted to survive."

"Oh, yes!" Ethan spat, his shoulders quivering. "You certainly did what you had to do."

Sarah's gaze flicked to mine, a flush coloring her cheeks. Then she regarded Ethan coolly. "I kept you alive, and now you're here. Be grateful."

Ethan's finger shot out, angry words ready to explode, but the Guardian cut him off.

"Fighting now is pointless," he scolded. "You each demonstrated your ability to survive and adapt, or you wouldn't be here. Be content with your success."

Ethan spun, stalked from the room. Sarah relaxed slightly, sitting down in a chair and licking her lips, her blue eyes narrowing as she appraised the Guardian. "I assume my access has been revoked?"

He nodded, taking a seat as well. "That's over."

I pulled out a chair for Min, and she slumped into it, but it was like she wasn't really there. I began to worry. Min had been totally disconnected since we left town square. I knew Tack's loss was eating at her, but for some reason I didn't think that was all. Min didn't look devastated, she looked . . . edgy. Distracted.

It took twenty minutes for Derrick to arrive with the others. The Guardian rose immediately and led everyone down the corridor to the clone chamber. It was cloaked in semidarkness, harsh lights shining over less than a third of the pedestals. Those who'd never seen the room before huddled together, apprehensive, staring at the grid of metal tubes. Everyone knew the rumor of what lay inside.

The Guardian clasped his hands behind his back. "Phase Two is complete. In a moment, I will accelerate the Program to the third and final phase: regeneration. System prep will take a few hours, but I wanted you to see this room. These tubes are empty now, but back on Earth, new bodies will be generated inside them to match your exact genetic blueprints. Then your unique electromagnetic signatures—the digital sequences you are now—will be inserted. You'll live again."

His gaze drifted to where Noah and I stood. "The cloning process has been tested. It works. You won't notice a thing. This morning I ran diagnostics on the MegaCom, waking these functions for the first time in more than a million years. Everything responded perfectly." The Guardian's voice rose. "This is the most important scientific event in the history of mankind. An incredible achievement of ingenuity, mechanics, and durability that will culminate in a new genesis for the human race. Be proud you're a part of it. Now, go and relax. The blast door leading out has been sealed for your protection, but the lab complex has diversions. The hour of your rebirth is almost at hand."

We were dismissed.

We went.

I followed Min to the living quarters, trying to think of something to say. She'd remained silent during the Guardian's speech. Tack would know just the right joke to snap her out of this funk, but I was hopeless in these situations. I began to worry that something was very wrong, or that she'd given up completely.

"You lived alone down here for two months?" I ventured.

Min's head whipped to me, her gaze darting over my shoulder. The Guardian walked past us, heading toward the office suite. He hesitated a tick, breaking stride as if to stop and speak with us, but at the last second he continued on. When the doors closed behind him, Min grabbed me by the arm and pulled me into one of the sleeping pods.

"Looking for some alone time?" I joked lamely.

Min shut the door and spun, eyes gleaming. "Did you hear him?"

I pulled a face. "He said a lot of things, Min."

"About the other codes," she said impatiently, as if I should've been thinking about it, too. "They're not erased! He put them in some kind of *Groundhog Day* feedback loop."

My heart sank. I reached for her. "It's better than nothing, Min. At least—"

She slapped my hands away, speaking excitedly. "If the eliminated codes aren't erased, that means they're still inside the MegaCom somewhere. In this system, with us. They're not gone, Noah! Tack isn't dead."

I blinked. Hadn't thought about it that way. "Well, I guess—"

Min was too amped to let me speak. She slammed a fist into her open palm. "If Tack can be inserted into a loop, he can be inserted into a clone. We just have to hack the system. Make the Program bring *everyone* back."

I was shaking my head without meaning to. Improvisation had never been my strong suit. "But the Guardian said the carrying capacity is twenty. That's what all the murder madness was about."

"I don't believe him!" Min's fingers dug into her sides. "Do you really think a computer of this magnitude can't manage a few redundancies? The MegaCom has been running for *a million years*, Noah. I'm sure it can handle more than 'best practices.' That prick just doesn't want to risk it!"

I rubbed my temple, flustered by what she was suggesting.

Unsure *I* wanted to risk it, either, but I'd made a promise. "So what do we do?"

"Find out how to hijack the system." Her hands shot forward and grabbed the sides of my head. "We don't get into those tubes until *everyone* is with us. I won't leave Tack behind. I *won't*, Noah."

"Okay, okay!" Trying to wriggle from her grip. Min planted a rabbit kiss on my lips and let me go. "We'll find a way. Somehow." Then my shoulders fell. "You know what that means though, right?"

Min nodded. We spoke at the same time.

"Sarah."

39

MIN

We found her in the conference room.

The rest of the survivors were scattered across the living quarters. Some sat quietly in the lounge, alone or in pairs, while others packed the game room and were boisterously blowing off steam. I heard whoops of laughter. High-pitched voices talking over one another. I saw Derrick and Spence shooting pool together against Casey and Susan. In that space at least, the sides had made peace. The war was over. Maybe we all really could forgive, or at least forget.

Anna and Aiken had disappeared into one of the sleeping pods. Jessica and Lars were pretzeled in a lounge chair, dozing. Benny and Darren sat together, whispering quietly as Benny sketched on a notepad. The stress of the game was fading. People were starting to accept that it was over.

A few heads were down. Ethan sat in the far corner of the

lounge, not talking to anybody. Akio was by himself in the kitchen, staring at his hands, as if trying to reconcile the idea of being downloaded back into a living body. Rachel paced the corridor and chewed her bottom lip. Nervous to leave, or fearful of what lay ahead?

Noah and I pushed into the office suite. The Guardian was nowhere to be seen, but the door to the security hub was closed. I assumed he was inside using the master terminal, inputting the commands that would send us back to life.

Sarah was in the same chair I'd favored, the one at the far end of the table. She looked up from a laptop as we entered, eyes wary. "If you're looking for a fight, I'm not interested."

Noah quietly shut the door. He eyed Sarah with something close to revulsion, but didn't speak. This was my show.

"Are you locked out of the system?" I moved briskly, snagging a chair and pulling it side by side with hers. Noah followed to stand behind me, arms crossed.

Sarah raised an eyebrow, but made no other move. "Yes, sadly. There was a function suite I could use before, but it's gone. I can still *see* everything, but I'm just an observer."

"Show me," I said, tucking my hair behind my ears. I'd work with the devil himself to bring my best friend back. To bring them all back.

Sarah regarded me curiously, her eyes briefly glancing to Noah. "Tell me why."

"I want to see the loop he mentioned. Where the other codes are intact. Or was that just a pretty lie?"

Sarah leaned back and crossed her arms. "And if they're intact?"

She was sharp. Sarah never missed the long game. There was no point lying, either.

I looked her dead in the eye. "If they still exist, I want to include them in the regeneration process."

Sarah was quiet a moment. Something moved behind her eyes. Then, "The Guardian said the capacity is twenty people. He designed and built the system, so he must know its tolerances. Even if what you suggest is possible—and assuming we could somehow figure out how to do it—you might overload the Program. You could kill *everyone*."

I kept my voice level. "All or none. That's a risk I'm willing to take."

"And *you* get to decide?" Sarah leaned into my personal space. "We're talking about the future of the human species, Min. Maybe the only sentient beings in the universe. In *creation*. You'd really gamble the future of . . . of *consciousness itself* for a lost friend?" Her voice was sharp, but there was something else, too. It was almost like she was really asking.

I met her stare for stare. "If mankind requires what we were forced to endure in order to survive, then maybe it deserves oblivion. The Earth can just replace us with something better. But what's right—what's *human*, Sarah—is to try to rescue our classmates. Now, *will you help me*, or does Noah need to remove you from this room?"

To my complete surprise, Sarah nodded. "It can't hurt to look."

She pulled the laptop closer and began typing, searching files and subfolders, checking routines, demonstrating a faculty within the system I couldn't hope to match. I realized quickly that we couldn't do this without her.

"Oh." Sarah paused, drumming her bottom lip. "Interesting."

"What is it?" I felt Noah lean over my chair to see.

"This application here." She tapped the screen with a finger. "It's new, and behind a hefty firewall. But the password was never activated. It's a closed system set to run on its own."

My pulse quickened. "Open it."

Sarah clicked a pull-down menu. Selected *View*. A box opened, almost like a media player. We all sucked in a breath.

We were watching Fire Lake from above. Onscreen, dozens of people were picking themselves up off the ground by the fountain in town square. Though groggy at first, soon they were scrambling around in panic, shouting to each other in voices we couldn't hear.

"The start of the Program," Noah breathed, his nose even with my ear. "Day one."

"That jerk could've given them a better day," Sarah huffed, wiping her nose on her sleeve. "They'll spend eternity running around in circles. Still, it's better than nothing. They still exist." But she was staring intently at the screen, as if searching for something.

I wasn't listening. I watched one specific figure—a short, slight kid with unruly hair—as he dashed from person to person. Then he cupped his hands to his mouth and began bellowing.

I didn't need sound. Tack was calling my name. My heart broke into a dozen pieces.

"I will *not* leave him like this," I said roughly, eyes burning with tears I refused to shed. "How do we get him—*them*—out of there?"

Sarah gave me a level look, then pointed to a figure onscreen. "Even that one?"

Toby was glancing this way and that in confusion, one hand scratching his bald head.

I didn't hesitate. "All of them."

Sarah sat back and sighed. "Like I said, my hands are tied. I can access the system but can't change anything. And I certainly can't copy things in or out. Not without the Guardian's fingerprint log-in and master password. You don't happen to have those, do you?"

I rose abruptly, driving Noah back a step. "Say that I did. Could you do it? Could you restore them?"

Sarah was silent for several heartbeats, as if she'd gone somewhere in her own mind. Then she reached for the keyboard and began typing. A minute passed, then two. I began to think she was simply ignoring me, but finally Sarah waved at the screen. "There."

A simple box was streaming endless ones and zeroes. I examined the folder and application.

`Regeneration. Participants: Phase Three.`

"That's us." Sarah's voice tightened as she watched the numbers fly by. "I'm not certain, but if a sequence is listed here, I think the MegaCom will schedule it for regeneration. But I can't add or delete anything." She closed the laptop with a snap, startling me. "Noble idea, though. I'll admit it—you touched me."

"Stay here," I commanded, already headed for the door. "Both of you."

I beelined to the security hub. Crashed through the door, found my father sitting at the master terminal with folders spread out around him like he was launching a Mars mission. Who knows, maybe this was more complicated.

He glanced up, then back at the screen without moving. "What you're trying won't work. The system is locked."

"I saw the loop," I spat, anger heating my skin like a furnace. "It's *horrible*. Tack will spend every day never finding me."

The Guardian squeezed the bridge of his nose. "I never planned to preserve failed codes. I did that for you, as a favor, but there's no way to write a new environment. I had to reuse the original model. It's either that or deletion. Say the word and I'll erase the whole thing."

"Why not regenerate *everyone*?" I insisted, ignoring that we'd had this argument before. "The more people reborn, the better off we'll be."

"Study after study refuted that claim." He rubbed his face. For the first time I noticed how tired he was. "Do you have any idea how long we investigated this problem? How many simulations we ran? I spent over a trillion dollars perfecting this software, Min. *The optimal number was determined to be twenty.*"

I opened my mouth to protest, but he cut me off. "Research determined that the selection process needed to be an exceedingly difficult survival challenge, emotionally and physically. Everything you experienced was measured, tested, and quality-assured a million different ways, by the most advanced mathematics and psychoanalytics devised by man. Not to mention the very basic fact that the MegaCom could overload if we go outside its design parameters. It turns out that cloning human beings from pure lines of digital code is really goddamn complicated!"

He was shouting by the end, but I didn't care. "Nowhere in there did I hear that it can't be done. You're just afraid to try."

He rose and stepped close, glaring down like . . . like . . . well, like an angry father. He put both hands on his hips. "Do you know what day today is, Min?"

I shook my head slowly, thrown.

"It's your birthday. Impossible, I know, but I checked and it's true." He gripped me by the shoulders, our first-ever contact that didn't involve my death. Intensity bled from his eyes. "This is more than just science, Min. It's *fate*. Hate me if you must—I understand—but I *have* to see this through. I'm sorry."

The room tilted. I sagged in his hands, but he didn't let me fall. Then I reared back, shaking loose from him as a wild desperation took hold. He wasn't going to help. Tack would be stuck forever. Then a question struck me I'd not considered yet, one so simple it stopped me in my tracks.

"What about you?" I asked. "What's your place in this new world order?"

He went still, the mask I'd seen many times re-forming. This was the face he'd used to kill me, his own daughter, over and over. All so that one day I might outlast the apocalypse.

"I've had enough of life and death," he said, his voice cold iron. "The moment after I engage Phase Three, I'm deleting myself forever."

40

NOAH

I gaped at the Guardian.

I had one hand on the knob, the door merely cracked. I hadn't been able to wait any longer. The thought of Black Suit alone with Min was still poisonous to me, even now.

Min was staring at her father. Words seemed to bubble on her lips but didn't spill out.

He cleared his throat. "Trust me, it's better this way. For all of us." He rose and stepped past Min, then paused. Reaching back, he put a hand on her shoulder. Min didn't pull away, but every muscle in her body tensed. "We're minutes away, kid. I'm connecting the MegaCom. It's almost over."

Black Suit nodded to me and exited, disappearing deeper into the complex.

Min's chin dropped to her chest. I pulled her into my arms. She didn't resist, but was still coiled like a spring. "Tack gave himself up to save the group," I began, but she flinched and pushed away.

Twin fires burned in her eyes. "We owe him the same. Come on."

Min fired into the hallway, forcing me to scramble to keep up. I followed on her heels as she stormed through the living quarters, ignoring the others, her mouth set in a grim line.

"Where are we going?" I hissed.

"I'm taking a player off the board."

Min slowed at the paired doors to the lab wing, carefully pushing one open and peeking inside. She held still for a second, then slipped into the white corridor beyond. It was empty, with no sign of the Guardian.

The last door before the clone chamber was slightly ajar. Min hurried straight for it.

"He went in here," she whispered. "To the MegaCom chamber. There's a blast door on the other end of this hallway just like the others." She pointed to a keypad. "It can be sealed—that's how Sarah trapped me before."

Min spun to face me. "I'm going to lock the Guardian inside."

"What good is that going to do?"

"I don't know, but it'll buy time. Run tell Sarah to engage these locks in sixty seconds. She'll also need to change the pass-codes somehow, but she can do it. *Make* her do it."

A thousand questions dogpiled in my head, but Min shoved me with both hands. "Go! Count from now!"

I turned and ran, counting Mississippis. A few people hailed me as I raced back through the living area, but I ignored them, sprinting for the conference room. I reached the doorway in twenty seconds. Sarah looked up from the laptop, surprised, wiping the corners of her eyes. Had she been crying?

"Back for more?" she said, flashing a bitter smile. "Where's your girlfriend, Livingston? Regretting past choices?"

"Door locks!" I gasped. "The ones you used to trap Min. Engage them right now!"

"Why would—"

"No time! I'll explain everything after, just trip the locks and change their passcodes. Do it *now*, Sarah. Please! I swear it's important."

Sarah eyed me skeptically. Then she turned and began typing. A mental alarm went off—sixty seconds had elapsed. I was about to urge her to hurry when she emphatically tapped a final key and sat back, crossing her arms. "Okay, done. Now what was that about?"

I exhaled. "The doors are locked?"

"You want me to repeat myself? I can still manipulate a few silo systems from here, if not the Program itself."

Just then Min came charging in. "It worked! He's trapped inside."

"Who's trapped?" Sarah demanded. "Inside where?"

Min rushed to Sarah and pulled a chair close again. "We just locked the Guardian in with the MegaCom. Can you see if he's already connected the hardware?"

Sarah held up both hands. "Slow down, sudden best friend. Why are we imprisoning the guy who's gonna release us from dystopia?"

"Because we're not murderers, Sarah. Even you. Now, can you please tell me whether the system is connected or not?"

Sarah sat back and pressed her palms to her eye sockets. She took a long, deep breath, then raked both hands through her hair. Head tilting skyward, Sarah stared at the ceiling. "Pushed to where I want to go," she muttered. "By the girl *I* said lacks commitment. What are the odds?"

I blinked at Sarah, saw an equal befuddlement take shape on Min's face. But neither of us had a chance to speak. With an odd groan, Sarah lurched forward and began typing. Min opened her mouth to say something, but Sarah put a hand to her face and shushed her. More keystrokes, then, "The cloning system is online. This whole command interface is pretty idiot-proof. All the Guardian has to do to start the process is set the timer and engage, although we're supposed to physically get into the tubes for some reason. Then, boom. Wake up on the other side."

"And you can do it from here?" Min asked.

Sarah slumped back in her chair again, eyes filled with exasperation. "*No*, Min. I told you, I can't do anything to the Program without the Guardian's password and fingerprint signature. So this little sideshow is pointless. All we can do is sit down here and die of boredom until we let him out and he starts the cloning process."

Min rose, began pacing. "Can we get eyes on him right now? I never found a way to see into that room."

"There *are* cameras. Not accessible from this laptop, though. That was your mistake. Only a high-level security interface—there's one in the command center, and the master terminal in the security hub."

"Let's go." Min shot for the door, seemed relieved a next step had been placed in front of her. In the hub she didn't sit, but rather began pacing the narrow room instead. "Show him to me."

Sarah sat at the master terminal. "I know these cameras well. I spent days watching them, waiting for you to slip up and go into the computer room. *And you did*," she finished, singsong smugly.

Min ignored the jab as the MegaCom appeared on a wall screen. It looked the same as before—tall, black, and imposing. The section I'd shot open to escape with Derrick was magically repaired, but a smaller panel stood ajar.

The Guardian was standing before the blast door, shoulders heaving as he pounded it with a fist. Sarah tapped a key and his voice filled the room. "—useless and stupid! You can't do anything without me. So open this door and let me finish the job!"

Min glanced at Sarah and raised her palms. Sarah reached over to a small black box and flipped a switch, then tapped a button beside it. Min nodded, pressed. "In case I wasn't clear before, I'm *not* going back without everyone," she said into the mike. "So either give me the password or prepare to spend the night in there."

The Guardian grabbed his head with both hands. Grunted in frustration. "I can reset out of here any time I need to, Min."

Sarah spoke before Min could. "Correct me if I'm wrong, but won't you just reappear in place? I disengaged the reset points. And I thought you said we couldn't harm each other in this phase. Can you even reset at all? Plus, how would you do it? Are you going to run into the wall until it kills you?"

The Guardian stiffened. Was silent for a second. "I can use the escape route. It's a long walk, but—"

"I locked and scrambled that blast door, too." Sarah giggled wickedly. "Fool me once . . ."

"Then I'll disengage the cloning system! You won't be able to—"

"That doesn't change *your* position," Min said. "I'm not letting you out until you agree to regenerate everyone."

A spasm crossed the Guardian's face. "Exceeding parameters might crash the system. I'm not going to jeopardize everything I ever worked for—including my daughter's life—and the *future of humanity*, on some sentimental high school bullshit."

Sarah sat bolt upright. "Daughter? What's he—"

"Then we'll do it without you!" Min shouted. "Sit in there with your computer and rot!"

Min snapped off the feed.

Sarah was staring at her in shock. "So many secrets today," she said finally, her cool returning. "Well, listen up, *daughter*. I know that probably felt good, but he's right. Nothing's changed. We'll have to let him out eventually."

Min sagged. I saw the fight leak out of her. I started pawing at my chin, desperate for a way to help.

"The cloning program," I said abruptly. "Show it to me. Where does the password go?"

Sarah shook her head, but pulled it up. "We're gonna play the guessing game? I tried for two solid hours once and got nowhere. It's not our birth date, FYI. And it doesn't matter if we get it right anyway. We can't *guess* the Guardian's fingerprint, and we need that, too."

Min sat down next to Sarah. "Try 'Nemesis.'"

Sarah rolled her eyes, but complied. Password denied.

"Try 'Virginia Wilder.'"

Denied.

"'Fire Lake.'"

Denied.

It went on like that. Sarah bitched and moaned—demanding details about Min's secret family relationship—but she entered everything Min suggested. Nothing worked, and we were back where we started. The Guardian could've chosen any phrase to protect the system. We didn't know him as a person. Guessing was hopeless.

Then something occurred to me. We did know one thing about the man.

We knew he was Min's father.

"This whole thing," I began, eyes on the carpet. "He did it for you, Min."

The girls stopped carping and looked at me. I tried to expand the thought, talking it out in hopes an answer would present itself. "The Guardian rigged Project Nemesis to include you. It was always about saving *your* life, first and foremost."

Sarah's gaze switched from skeptical to intrigued. Min was squinting at nothing, her attention turned inward.

I went still, fingers entwined and pressed to my lips. I was close. I could feel it. "Did Black Suit ever give you anything, Min? A token. Or trinket. Maybe something your mom wore? Any tiny thing that might tie the two of you together?"

Min's eyes rounded. Then, slowly, she nodded.

She turned to Sarah, spoke no louder than a whisper. "Juilliard."

Sarah's brow furrowed. "Juilliard?"

Min nodded again, her whole body trembling. "It's hard to spell. J-U-I—"

"I know how to spell Juilliard," Sarah snapped, inputting the word. "I'm surprised you do, but if you think—"

A female voice purred from the speakers. "Welcome, Dr. Bolton. Please depress the touch plate for identity confirmation." Yellow lights began snaking around a small plastic square on the desktop.

Sarah cocked her head, blue eyes shining with reflected light. "Okay, wow. Nice job. But we're still stuck."

Min had a hand over her mouth. It took me a moment to realize she was crying. I stepped over and wrapped my arms around her from behind. Hugged as hard as I could. Sarah turned awkwardly.

Min sobbed for a few moments. Then she gently peeled away. Wiping the tears from her eyes, she reached out and reengaged the microphone.

"Dad?" she said in a tremulous voice. "Can you hear me?"

"I can, Min. You know that guessing my password won't do you any good."

Sarah reached for the keyboard, no doubt to put the feed onscreen, but Min stopped her with a hand. The monitor remained dark as Min spoke again.

"The password was your gift." Her voice was thick, as if each word cost a heavy price. "You said you did all this for me. I want you to prove it. Let me into the system."

"I can't do that, kiddo." There was sorrow in his disembodied voice. "For your own good. And you can't break in, either. The system uses my DNA, not just a fingerprint. Nothing you can do will fake that. Now please, let me out of here so I can finish my work."

Min waited a long time before replying. "If you ever truly cared about me, you'll let me do this. You'll let me try."

"Min, the MegaCom—"

"May be stronger than you know. It's lasted for ages. I believe it can sustain us all."

A long pause. "You'd risk everything—the whole world, Min!—on a hope?"

Min laughed softly. Nodded though he couldn't see. "What's more human than that?"

Goose bumps erupted on my arms. I loved her in that moment, wholly and completely. "I would, too," I said roughly, adding my voice to hers. "We all go or nobody. I . . . I think the betas should get to decide."

"Min. Noah." The Guardian's tone was inching toward desperate. "Think about what you're asking. Literally thousands of people poured their lives into this project, with the single goal of guaranteeing humanity's survival as a species. I can't gamble that on . . . emotion."

Sarah's fist hit the desk. "Oh, screw that," she said harshly. "And your freaking God complex. We can decide this for ourselves. If we don't survive, no one will be around to regret it anyway."

I glanced at her in shock. She shrugged, looked away. I did not understand Sarah Harden.

"You convinced *her*, too?" He sounded genuinely surprised.

"Dad. Please."

There was a long, audible sigh. Then nothing. I was tempted to ask Sarah to call up the camera, but something about the darkness felt right.

The lights around the touch plate flashed, then died. The terminal in front of Min woke, a command box blinking onscreen as the computerized voice returned. "Identification verified, Dr. Bolton. How may I assist you?"

Sarah gasped. Her hands shot to the keyboard. The camera feed reappeared onscreen. The Guardian was stepping back from the MegaCom. He put his hands in his pockets.

"He did it," Sarah whispered. "He gave us access."

Then, as we watched, Black Suit put his back against a metal wall and slid heavily to the ground. "Okay, Min. You decide."

"Thank you," Min breathed, barely able to form words. "Thank you for . . . everything."

Min disengaged the mike. Wiping her eyes, she faced Sarah. "You can make this work?"

Sarah reopened the application containing the eliminated codes. *Copy. Cut.* Then she switched to the regeneration program, calling up the list of sequences. *Paste.*

A red warning flashed. The voice returned. "You have exceeded the maximum number of allowable regenerations. Please delet—"

Sarah called up another box and clicked *Enter.*

"Override confirmed. System ready for Phase Three regeneration."

I was barely able to contain myself. "Is that really it? Are we good?"

Sarah was trembling. "I think . . . yes. If we engage the system, it'll try to complete its instructions." She grabbed Min's forearm and forced eye contact. "There will only be one shot. By attempting this, we may kill everyone instead."

"You're not afraid to gamble, are you, Sarah?"

Sarah full-on laughed. "I *hate* gambling." Then her gaze grew inscrutable. "But you're not the only one who . . ." She trailed off, then shook herself, her blue eyes hardening as they flicked to the camera feed. "What about him?"

Eyes closed, the Guardian was resting with his head back against the steel wall.

Min ran slender fingers over her lips. "When we're ready to engage, set the timer for two minutes. Then release the security doors. He won't have time to stop anything."

"No offer to join us? A bit harsh, isn't it? He did let us into the system."

Min was staring at her father's image. "He's finally doing the right thing. I don't want to give him the chance to sabotage himself."

There was nothing else to say. We divided responsibilities. Sarah and Min set to work on the program, scanning the procedure files the Guardian had left scattered around the command console. I walked to the living quarters and yelled from the hallway. "Everyone, listen up! The system's about to engage."

People spilled into the corridor. Seventeen anxious faces regarded me.

"Inside the clone room is a pedestal with your name on it. Atop each one is a metal tube. That's your regeneration unit."

"You mean coffin," Darren joked, and some laughed.

"Think of them as escape pods," I countered with a wry smile. "Ready to take us home. Everyone needs to climb inside and lie still. The process is supposed to be painless and timeless. We're almost there, guys."

"Where's the Guardian?" Ethan asked, edging forward from the back of the crowd. "Why are *you* telling us what to do, Noah?"

I took a deep breath. Sarah wanted to lie, but Min had been adamant. The others had a right to know. I agreed. "Sarah, Min, and I have taken over control of the system. We locked the Guardian in the computer chamber and hacked the MegaCom."

Eyes bulged. I kept going, *fast*, before a revolt could break out. "We've found a way to bring *everyone* back. Even our eliminated classmates. I won't lie—it's a risk to override the Program's restrictions, but I believe it's one worth taking. No one should be left behind." I quickly explained what we were proposing, and how we could execute it.

Voices erupted, some shouting angrily. Fear spread like a disease. My stomach clenched as one person after another thundered in protest. Then someone screamed above the rest, and the room went silent.

Ethan strode straight for me and I tensed, my heart sinking deeper than the silo. How would we control a riot down here? This only worked if everyone cooperated.

He grabbed me by the shoulder, then spun, facing the group. "Noah's right." His gaze seared into the others. "Don't you see? He's giving us a chance to get our dignity back. We . . . we did awful things out there. People are gone who shouldn't be. Why should we go forward if they can't?"

Murmurs. Nervous eyes and shifting feet. Ethan had surprised everyone, perhaps even shamed a few. But they were still uncertain, worried about their own survival.

"They can really do it?" Derrick asked, chewing his knuckles. "Sarah and Min know how to make it work?"

I nodded. "The Guardian even gave us permission. We just have to trust the computer."

Derrick ran his hands over his scalp, then shrugged. "Hell, why not? We've been living inside this beast for ages, or whatever. Might as well let it take us all home." He scowled at the group. "Come on, y'all. You know we can't just leave people behind. Not if we can help it. Who wants to live with that on their soul?"

Slow nods. Arms around shoulders. It was now or never to get a vote. "Show me hands. Who's willing to give the others a chance?"

One by one, they all went up. Even Rachel's at the last.

I felt a surge of love for these people. "Whatever happens next, that vote is something we can be proud of. Now get to your escape pods."

The matter decided, we walked to the clone room. Beyond the doors was a surprise—every pedestal gleamed under brilliant overhead light. As people began searching for their tubes, voices erupted in shock.

"Noah, look at this!" Derrick called. I hustled over and climbed a pedestal to join him. Inside the tube, a still form appeared to be sleeping. I recognized the face immediately.

"It's Hector!" I blinked, then the answer came. "When Sarah added the eliminated codes, they must've come online." Elated, I gripped Derrick by the arm. "We're ready!"

Derrick nodded. "Unless we flame out in an explosion of overloaded circuits."

"Real nice, dude."

"Just saying."

Derrick reached over and hugged me, slapping hard on my back. "You did good, Livingston. See you on the other side." He jumped down before I could recover.

It took a little time, but everyone found their places. People slipped inside the tubes. I circled, checking each one, making sure everything was airtight and secure. Then I noted the locations of the girls' pedestals and hurried back to the security hub.

They looked up as one.

"Good to go," I said, flashing a thumbs-up.

"Did you tell them?" Sarah asked. Min was chewing her bottom lip.

"They voted. Unanimous."

"Seriously?" Sarah pressed her fists to her cheeks and shook her head. "You must've given one hell of a speech. How'd you persuade Ethan to risk his neck?"

"*Ethan* gave the speech. These people aren't who you think they are, Sarah."

She blinked. "Well well well."

Min shook off her astonishment. "Are they loaded?"

I nodded. "Not just them. The eliminated players are in their pods, too."

"Tack!" Min was already rising, but Sarah pulled her back down.

"Sit! If this works, hugs all around later, but for now stay focused."

Min frowned sourly but nodded, dropping into her seat. She

started calling out commands for Sarah to input, the two working together like NASA engineers.

I paced behind them. Would this work? Were we idiots? The head programmer of Project Nemesis had specifically said this was a mistake. That we'd fry the MegaCom and erase ourselves. But we were doing it anyway.

A spike of anxiety tore through my gut. I realized I very much didn't want to die.

Earth. I wanted to see it again. Breathe real air. Have a heart that beat.

"Okay." Sarah turned to Min. "We're ready. Any last words for your father?"

Min glanced at the screen. Swallowed. A trembling hand switched on the microphone.

"Dad?"

"Yes, Min?"

"Do you want to come with us?"

His head rose, as if considering the idea. Then he slowly shook it. "The future belongs to you guys, Melinda J. I'm the past. Good luck."

A tremor passed through Min. Her voice cracked. "I forgive you," she whispered.

The Guardian's whole body relaxed. "Thank you, Min. Thank you."

Min wiped her nose. Then her hand shot out and killed the mike again. "Open the doors."

Sarah looked at her sideways. "But I thought you—"

"He's not going to stop us." Min cleared her throat. "I don't want to keep anyone caged anymore. Let's leave that in the past, too."

Sarah pinched her nose, then shrugged. Tapped a few keys. Onscreen, I saw the keypad beside the door flash green. The Guardian glanced up, but made no move to stand.

"Okay friends, moment of truth." Sarah pointed to the master terminal. The counter was set for two minutes.

Engage?

"Once I start the program, we just hustle down and get into our pods. The computer will do the rest. Understood?"

"Yes," Min said. They both looked at me, and I nodded.

We all stared at the command for an endless moment. I glanced up at the security feed, noticed that the MegaCom chamber was empty.

My lips parted, unsure, but Min spoke first.

"Do it."

41

MIN

I grabbed Noah's hand and held it.

Together we jogged down the corridor, trailing Sarah to the clone room. Noah seemed nervous, and I couldn't blame him. Who knew what future we headed toward? Once inside I was nearly blinded by all the lights, which warmed my heart. *Sink or swim, together.*

"See you on the other side," Sarah said drily, striding toward her pedestal. Then she stopped short. Turned. "You surprised me, Min. I never saw you coming. I'm impressed." Her ice-blue gaze flicked to Noah. "If I don't ever see you two again, well, I won't hold a grudge in the afterlife. Cheers."

Then she mounted her pedestal, opened its tube, and curled inside. The lid shut, sealing with a pneumatic hiss.

"Was that supposed to be friendly?" Noah said.

I shook my head. "Best she could do, I guess."

Then Noah's lips found mine and I wrapped my arms around

him, squeezing, losing myself in his warmth. My body smoldered, heat arcing from my mouth, to my limbs, my heart, every corner of my being. I wanted to live in that moment forever, but he pulled back, breathing hard.

"Clock," he gasped. Noah glanced back at the entrance, opening his mouth as if to speak, but then a tone sounded from the speakers.

"Right," I sputtered. I grabbed him again and mashed his face with another kiss. "See you soon, Livingston. I love you."

"Love you, too." He gave me a crooked smile, his eyes drinking me in. "I can't wait to greet you with my real body."

I laughed. Punched his shoulder. Then I released Noah reluctantly, watched him hustle across the room. The hole inside me was gone, the last of my anger evaporating.

The computerized voice sounded inside the chamber. "Thirty seconds to regeneration."

Around the room, monitors sprang to life. Pipes rattled. Machines woke from an endless slumber. It was time.

I opened my tube. Climbed inside. Watched the door lower and seal shut.

Here we go.

"Ten seconds to regeneration."

Please please please don't let me have killed everyone.

The timer ticked down to zero. Something hissed in my tube.

Everything went fuzzy, then white.

I felt a jolt of pure electricity, like I'd stuck a fork in an outlet.

Then my mind bent like a balloon animal and I shot screaming into the void.

I croaked a strangled cry.

My skin was on fire, tingling head to foot.

Eyes burning. Watering.

An incessant clanging echoed close to my head.

I licked my lips, tasted wet metal.

The smell of ozone was everywhere, mixed with hot plastic and rubbing alcohol.

I gasped, kick-starting my lungs. Nearly threw up. There was something in my mouth. I ripped it out, noticed suction cups running up and down my arms. I began slapping them away, trying not to hyperventilate.

The tube. I'm still inside it.

I was wearing a jumpsuit of some kind, made of paper. The glass window was dark and I couldn't see through it. The only light within my coffin was a pair of angry yellow sensors glowing by my head.

Had it worked? Was I still inside the Program or out? What about the others?

I started banging on the lid, making the same clanging sound I'd heard earlier.

Others. Trapped like me.

I kicked harder, my panic level rising. Then I noticed a button near the latch. I smashed my finger against it and the seal released, the lid hissing open with a push.

I sat upright, ran both hands over my head, pulling off a light cotton cap. I was in the same clone room as before, but all the overhead lights were doused. Everything was covered in inches of fine gray dust, like the surface of the moon. I sneezed, swirling dirt into the air.

Not the same room. The real *one.*

I nearly fell getting out as the banging started up again. I staggered over to the next pedestal. Pressed a button on the outside of the tube. The lid rose and Aiken Talbot leapt out like a startled cat, nearly landing on top of me as he tumbled to the ground.

"What happened?" he rasped, lying on the floor, the left side of his paper jumpsuit now coated in grime. "We alive?"

"I don't know." I jumped down and helped him to his feet, then gave him a quick hug. We'd never been close, but I was enormously happy to see another living person. He squeezed me back just as hard.

"Did everyone make it?" Aiken asked.

I released him. "Help me open the other tubes!"

Aiken's eyes widened. "Anna!" He ran to the next row. I went the opposite direction, jabbing another button. This tube held Carl Apria. He wasn't moving. My hands rose to cover my mouth. Carl had been eliminated on the last day, out on the lake. Had the process not worked for him?

Then his eyelids fluttered open. He stared up at me in shock.

I nearly screamed in relief. "Hold on, Carl!"

I removed the tube from his mouth and started pulling sensors from his arms. He sat up slowly, shaking his head, his face drenched in sweat. "So weird. I was back on the first day, but Sam was gone . . . and then . . . now . . . how did . . ."

"We restored you. Carl, we *all* made it. Help me with the others."

But lids were rising all over the room. Groggy teens cried out in the darkness. I ran to the door and flipped a switch, activating LED overheads that hadn't burned in millennia. Most refused to illuminate, but enough did.

I started counting heads. Five. Ten. Twenty. *Thirty.* Then something slammed me from the side and I toppled over, punching and kicking like a demon.

"Oof! Ow! Uncle!" Tack rolled onto his side and spat. "Okay, bad idea by me."

I blinked, unable to breathe. Afraid to trust my eyes. Tack was beside me, alive. Back from the dead yet again. My chest heaved as tension spilled from my body. I wrapped him in my arms, tears trickling down my cheeks.

"It's okay, Min," Tack said in a shaky voice. "You did it. You brought us back."

A throat cleared. I glanced up, saw Noah, relief and anxiety battling on his face. He nodded at Tack and forced a smile. "Good to see you again, Russo."

Tack grimaced. "Please don't tell me it was *you* that saved everyone."

Noah snorted. "Nope. Min did it all."

Noah offered a hand. Tack regarded it a moment, then let Noah pull him upright. I bounced up beside them and grabbed Tack by the ears, kissing him on the forehead. "You are my best friend, and I love you. Never, ever leave me again."

Tack blushed. Turned away. "Deal." Then he heaved an enormous sigh, a shadow of his old grin returning. "How many girls are in our class again?"

I hugged him a second time, then threw my arms around

Noah. Held on for dear life. By the time I let go Tack had slipped away, helping others exit their tubes. Voices rose around us, nervous questions already flying as the eliminated players were brought up to speed.

Derrick was circling the room, gripping shoulders as he counted. "Sixty-two, sixty-three, sixty-*four*." He smiled as wide as the ocean. "Perfect attendance again."

Sarah found me and extended a hand. "You were right," was all she said. Then her gaze strayed over my shoulder. Something melted in her expression and Sarah slipped around me, striding across the room to wrap her arms around a dazed Alice Cho.

I stared at them in shock.

"I told you to *hide*," Sarah scolded, cupping Alice's face in her hands.

"I did. The roof fell on my head."

I looked at Noah, who was gawking at the pair. But there wasn't time to dialogue.

Commotion in the corner. Several boys were surrounding Toby, who was sweating as he backed away, eyes darting from side to side. Noah pushed into the group, shielding Toby behind him. "Stop it! That shit's over with now. We made it through. What happened inside the Program stays there forever. Understood?"

Noah turned and extended a hand to Toby. Toby stared at it, wide-eyed, then whirled, banging into a pedestal as he stumbled away. The other boys muttered darkly, eyes following his retreat. Not everyone was ready to forget.

Then Ethan barged to the front. Heads turned as he put

fingers to his mouth and whistled shrilly. Shoulders tensed. A few people began eyeing the door.

"Listen up!" he shouted. Then Ethan pointed at me without looking. "I vote that Min Wilder is temporarily in charge. We do what *she* says until we figure out the best way to govern ourselves. Does everyone agree?"

There was a loud cheer of assent, mixed with a few stunned looks from people who'd been eliminated. "Opposed?" After a few seconds of tense silence, Ethan nodded sharply, then turned. "Well, how about it, Min? What the hell do we do next?"

My eyes traveled the room. Anxious stares reflected back at me.

Releasing Noah's hand, I stepped forward to stand beside Ethan.

Deep breath.

"I think we should go outside."

In the end, eight of us went.

The lab complex felt like a crypt, or a modern version of an ancient Egyptian burial chamber. But most of the lights worked, and the blast door disengaged at Sarah's commands. We all changed into the sturdier gray Project Nemesis jumpsuits, then rode up the rattling miner's cage in two shifts, reconvening at the top.

Me. Noah. Ethan. Sarah. That the betas should go was unanimous. The class viewed us as a unit now that we'd finally stopped fighting.

The second group had been a subject of mild debate, but

in the end Derrick, Sam, Corbin, and Casey joined us, loosely representing the other alliances from inside the Program. We'd have to work on that. Old fault lines would be hard to totally erase.

Toby had lurked in the back of the meeting, hands fidgeting as he watched everyone else. From the looks he was catching, he had reason to feel nervous. I worried about leaving him down there alone, but I honestly hadn't wanted him along. He was a problem without an easy solution.

The ride up was silent, everyone appreciating the moment—and worrying that the rusted track would fail. We passed level after level of alcoves, stuffed with filthy crates. Our provisions for this brave new world, cached literally eons ago.

This was a real place, with no more resets. No bonus lives. No forgiveness.

We hit our first setback on the upper catwalk. When Derrick and the others arrived, we circled to the exit, but the tunnel was blocked by rubble. Mild panic set in until I told the others about the back door through the MegaCom chamber. Grumbling in annoyance, we were about to ride all the way back down when Tack pointed at the ceiling.

"The emergency ladder," he said, rapping his knuckles against iron rungs bolted directly to the stone wall. "It keeps going up."

I followed with my eyes, squinting at the giant slab of concrete overhead. Spotted a small hatch where the ladder met the roof.

I pointed. "Anyone up for trying that?"

Noah swallowed, began to sweat. He hated heights.

"I'll do it," Tack said.

"Me too," Ethan echoed.

Tack glared at him for a moment, then nodded stiffly. He tested the lower rungs with his hands. Satisfied, Tack began to climb. Ethan waited for him to clear a few rungs, then followed after him. Up they went, both making a concerted effort not to look down. My stomach lurched just watching their progress.

At the top, Tack banged a fist against the hatch, earning a shower of ultrafine rust and a squawk from Ethan. Hooking the topmost rung with an elbow, Tack tried to turn the wheel, but it refused to budge. A futile minute later he said something to Ethan, who climbed up to join him. Together they pulled, swinging precariously out into space.

Metal groaned. The wheel slowly turned. Three revolutions and the hatch swung down.

"More ladder!" Tack yelled. Then he and Ethan disappeared up the chute. I waited impatiently, tapping a foot on the catwalk as I stared into the chimney-like hole they'd vanished through. Minutes passed. Noah put his arm around my waist.

A *real* arm. Somehow I could tell the difference. He felt more solid. More there.

Maybe I was crazy, but the dust tasted more bitter than it had in months. Echoes rang truer. I smelled soot and earth with clarity. Details were finer. Sharper. My heart beat more powerfully.

I was probably imagining it all, but it *felt* true. Looking around, I sensed that others were experiencing the same thing. We were *alive* again. Back. Made flesh. No longer safe from death, but real and free.

Ethan's feet reappeared, then his face, flushed with excitement. "There's a way out! You guys aren't going to *believe* this. Come on!"

"Come where?" Sarah shouted, face paling. "Up there?"

I grinned, patting her on the shoulder. "It's a day for adventures, right?"

She grimaced, but no one could really stay behind. Not now. One by one we climbed, disappearing through the hatch. I went second to last, with Noah following. He insisted on watching my back even here. Plus, heights.

I focused on each rung, never looking down. My heart fluttered as I transferred from one ladder to the next inside the chute, but I made it and continued up. Another twenty yards brought a second hatch into view.

Beyond was a circle of blue. I climbed quicker now, eager to exit the confined space.

The circle grew, a cobalt orb beckoning me higher.

Finally, I reached the top rung.

A blast of heat hit me, slicking my skin. Someone gasped.

I pulled myself out of the hole.

Sink or swim, together.

Eyes tearing, I stepped forward into a nimbus of shimmering golden light.

ACKNOWLEDGMENTS

I think I dread writing acknowledgments more than I worry about writing books. This is because I spend the whole time drafting these pages *absolutely terrified* that I will leave out key, obvious people who were fundamentally important to both the making of this story and just keeping me sane in general. This fear, this FOLO, haunts me, always, even now, as I watch you read this section in the already-printed book, lurking behind you behind the curtains. Nonetheless, I will once again endeavor to give proper credit where so much is due. As always, to anyone not listed here who rightfully should be, know that it's not because I'm ungrateful for all you've done to help me on this writer's journey, but rather because, like always, I'm an idiot.

Genesis is a dark, twisty, crazy novel that I put a lot into, and it took a lot out of me. It would not have been possible without the borderline superhuman efforts of my wonder-editor,

Ari Lewin. Thank you for all the time you've poured into Project Nemesis, and for enduring those mid-afternoon phone calls with me, when I haven't spoken to anyone else yet all day and have THOUGHTS. Thanks as always to the incredible teams at G. P. Putnam's Sons and Penguin Young Readers, including (but by no means limited to) Bridget Hartzler, Jennifer Dee, Elyse Marshall, Amalia Frick, Dana Li, Jennifer Besser, Christina Colangelo, Erin Berger, Emily Romero, Kara Brammer, Caitlin Whalen, Lindsay Boggs, Felicity Vallence, Katherine Perkins, and countless, countless others. Man, I love being a Penguin. March me where you will.

Cheers also to Venetia Gosling, Kat McKenna, Jo Hardacre, and the whole team at Pan Macmillan. This has been a wonderful partnership, and I hope it continues long into the future. I will soon travel to England and hug you all. Fiercely. You have been warned.

Endless, bottomless thanks to my agent, life coach, and partner-in-cackles Jodi Reamer. Everything that is happening now happened because of you. I cannot praise you enough. More effusive thanks to Jennifer Rudolph Walsh, Margaret Riley King, Anna DeRoy, Janine Kamouh, Simon Trewin, and the team at William Morris Endeavor. You've been there every step of the way, and I'm eternally grateful. And thanks, Mom. Again.

Heartfelt, joyous thanks to my Vermont College of Fine Arts advisors who help shape *Genesis* from, well, its . . . genesis. Tim Wynne-Jones provided acerbic and witty critique on the very first baby draft, helping me find my story. An Na then gave it heart and depth, shepherding me to a completed manuscript. Further refinements and tweaks were added by Kekla Magoon, Shelley Tanaka, and David Gill, and the book is so much better for it. And no mention of my MFA experience could possibly fail to mention my beloved Tropebusters, who listened to and provided encouragement and feedback on my very first drafts, and also shot bizarre ghost videos with me in a schoolhouse subbasement. You guys are the best. I ain't afraid of no Trope. (To Elizabeth, Sarah Hunter, and Allison: Go Lake Monsters.)

And here I must separately thank the beating hearts of my VCFA experience, my Airbnb roommates Ally Condie, Robin Galbraith, and Salima Alikhan. I can't express how much fun I had living in the unit below yours for two years of Vermont's blazing summers and freezing winters, all while I was working on this book. I miss our late-night chats already, and look forward to many future retreats. The author's lounge is always open.

Special thanks to author Cynthia Leitich Smith and Professor Scott Pinkham of the University of Washington for helping me with a hyperspecific question regarding Native American tribes of the Pacific Northwest. Your taking time out of busy schedules to help me get something correct is much appreciated.

My career doesn't even happen without the unflinching support of my YALL-family. I'm raising a glass right now to Margaret Stohl, Melissa de la Cruz, Kami Garcia, Veronica Roth, Alex London, Rafi Simon, and Jonathan Sanchez, as well as West Coasters Marie Lu, Tahereh Mafi, Ransom

Riggs, Leigh Bardugo, Holly Goldberg Sloan, and Richelle Mead. Further thanks to Tori Hill and Shane Pangburn for actually doing everything, and managing to smile (mostly) all the way through it. YALLFEST and YALLWEST are my favorite weekends of my year, and that's because of you. YALL MEANS ALL.

Particular thanks to my do-everything, keep-me-in-line assistant, Emily Williams. If you got an email response from me this year, it's because Emily reminded me. She's basically in charge now, and that's a very good thing.

Thank you to my fellow authors who have supported the Project Nemesis series with their precious time, open arms, and thoughtful praise: Ransom Riggs, Carrie Ryan, Renée Ahdieh, Ally Condie, Jay Kristoff, Victoria Aveyard, Alex Bracken, Margaret Stohl, Melissa de la Cruz, Kami Garcia, James Dashner, Marie Lu, Stephanie Perkins, Danielle Paige, Ryan Graudin, Rose Brock, Lauren Billings, Melissa Thomson, Lauren Oliver, Sabaa Tahir, Alex London, and Veronica Roth. You've endured my venting and/or whining more times than any human should have to. The world is beautiful place, and I know this because you are in it. I am blessed to work in a field of such generous colleagues. Know that you've got a friend in me.

I need to specifically thank two authors who have become my support system. To Ally Condie and Soman Chainani: I have no idea what I'd do without you. Don't ever change or leave me behind. Thanks for always being in my corner.

Most important, thank you to my beautiful wife, Emily, and my wonderful children, Henry and Alice, to whom this book is dedicated. I love you all very much, and thank you for sharing me with the road. Also, thanks to Wrigley and Fenway for being hilarious, evil cats, and Soldier and Turk for being good dogs. We have a full home.

Finally, to my readers, please know that you make everything worth it. As I said before, I will repeat here again: your support has given me a career that I love and a happy, exciting, fulfilling life. Thanks upon thanks until the end of time.

TURN THE PAGE FOR A FIRST LOOK AT

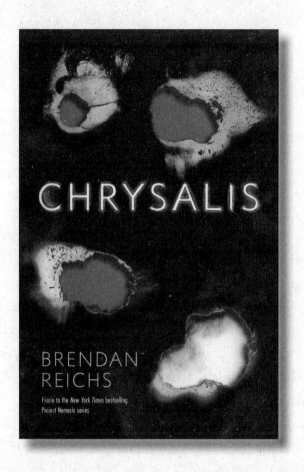

BOOK THREE IN
THE PROJECT NEMESIS SERIES

NOAH

I ran as fast as I could.

Legs pounding. Sweat oozing. As the sun peeked over the eastern heights, illuminating the valley in a soggy haze.

I could barely keep my impatience in check. The paths were too waterlogged for an ATV, so I'd set out on foot. The trek from Ridgeline usually took four hours, but I was determined to make it in three.

I had to. Everything had gone to hell while I was gone.

I took the most direct route possible, straight through the woods on the north side of the lake rather than my usual hike across the southern flatland. Thorns ripped at my flesh as I barreled through the undergrowth, ignoring my burning lungs. I scolded myself for leaving the village while a thunderstorm was gathering, but honestly, when wasn't one?

Sam's crew had a busted filtration system—without a spare

valve from the silo stockpile, they'd have been drinking from a stream like cave people. The trip had to be made.

I'd witnessed the lightning display from their camp in the western peaks, chewing on my fist beside Floyd and Hamza as bolts rained down. Then something exploded in Home Town. I'd wanted to sprint back immediately—cabins were *burning*—but the Ridgeliners persuaded me it was suicide to travel in that weather.

The thought of Min battling chaos without me gnawed my insides. I'd nearly bolted into the night a dozen times. But it was the worst storm any of us had ever seen, and that's saying something. When its leading edge reached our position we'd retreated into a cavern to hide like mice.

Now I was minutes away from home, growing more and more anxious about what I'd find. The trees thinned and my speed picked up, though new streams ran everywhere and soon I was drenched from the waist down. My boots made awful squishing sounds with every footfall.

The first thing to hit me was the smell. Smoke. Charred wood. A noxious, oily stench that could only mean something mechanical had burned. That or fuel. Pushing through the last line of trees, I was prepared to encounter pandemonium.

Instead, I found . . . no one.

Not a living soul.

I ran down to the square, discovered the wreckage of supply buildings 3 through 7. Taking mental notes on what had likely been destroyed, I looked around, baffled. The village common was always busy at sunup—there weren't a lot of other places to

3

be. Admittedly, Home Town was less crowded now than when the whole class had been living there, before the incident three months ago, but still. There should've been a dozen people puttering around on a slow day, and this wasn't that.

What the hell?

I heard a noise behind me and whirled. Nothing. But then it came again—a sniffling, sobbing cough from somewhere down by the stream. I jogged closer, trying to ignore the stitch in my side, and found Hector and Vonda huddled over four long bundles wrapped in blue tarps.

My heart stopped.

Hector looked up. "Noah."

"Who?" I blurted, hands trembling, as I stared at the tarps.

Head down, Vonda's shoulders shook silently. Hector's red-rimmed eyes lost focus.

"Jamie. Lars. Morgan. And . . . Finn."

Vonda exploded in a heart-wrenching wail. Her hands dug into her thick black hair as she rocked back and forth. Hector reached out and squeezed her shoulder. Vonda and Finn had been together since inside the Program.

My breath caught. I felt tears on my cheeks. It was so much worse than I'd thought.

"Vonda, I . . . I'm so sorry." I knelt and put an arm around her, and she collapsed against my chest. We sat like that for a long moment, but the questions couldn't wait. "Hector, where is everyone? Did they *all* go for a resupply?"

Hector seemed to startle back to the present. "No. They're at the silo. There was a cave-in last night, and people are trapped inside. You should go, Noah. Vonda and I will stay to prepare the . . . our friends."

He didn't say dead. Couldn't yet. I understood.

Death—something we'd treated as a minor inconvenience for so long—was real again. The bodies in those tarps wouldn't reset. They'd never stand up and stretch, ready to laugh darkly about how they'd bought it that time before going about their day.

Then Hector's words fully penetrated and I shot to my feet. "Who's trapped? How many?"

He shook his head. "I don't know. Min's up there organizing a rescue. I'm sure they could use your help."

I nodded. Looked at Vonda, wanting to say something comforting. But the words wouldn't come, and I'd be bad at delivering them even if they did. So I turned and raced up the path. My muscles screamed in protest as I made the ascent. I'd been running for several hours and didn't have much left in the tank. The trail was now a muddy slog riddled with puddles. Last night it must've been a river.

Five more minutes of hard going and I reached the silo's front entrance. I heard the commotion before I saw it—at least twenty of my classmates were dragging rubble away from where the tunnel had been. But the whole mountainside had collapsed on top of the opening. It took me all of ten seconds to realize the effort was futile.

Min and Derrick were standing to one side, conferring quietly. I ran to join them, swallowing Min in a quick hug. She gripped me back tightly.

"Noah, it's awful." She ground a fist into her leg as she spoke. "The door is buried under thirty feet of debris. We can't move these giant boulders, and we can't drop in through the top hatch because there's no way up there now. There's *nothing* up there now."

I gripped the back of my neck. "But there's no reason to assume anyone inside is hurt, right?"

"We don't know, because nobody's answering the radio." Derrick frowned at his walkie-talkie. "This entire side of the hill broke apart, and I swear some of it's not out here. If anything fell down through the shaft, it might've jacked up the catwalks, the alcoves, and who knows what else. This is a disaster."

I ran a hand through my sodden hair. Tried to think deliberately. "Who's there?"

Derrick glared at the wreckage as if to clear it by sheer will. "The collapse happened before anyone from the village reached the door. A blessing if the silo's roof really did cave in, though we were all stuck out here in the rain like jackasses. But Sarah and the other princesses are down there, and those boulders literally weigh tons. How are we supposed to move them?"

Min was shaking her head slightly. Her bottom lip quivered. I knew she was thinking about those four tarps down by the stream. "We just keep digging," she said abruptly. "Until we force a way through. I'm not giving up."

"We'd need a forklift to lift some of those stones." I chewed the inside of my cheek, testing the problem in my head. "Or the whole team of four-wheelers, pulling at the same time. But the village depot exploded, and the rest of our fuel is down there in the storage alcoves."

Min's gray eyes found mine. "We have to get them out, Noah. And this isn't the only way inside."

"You mean the back door?" I answered, surprised. "It's a dead end."

Derrick glanced at Min. "Nobody's used that since we came out of the MegaCom. I went down once, just to take a look. The power plant level is dark and nasty, plus I heard weird noises." He crossed his arms. "The back tunnel runs directly toward the cliffs. In case you missed it, that side drops straight to the ocean. What good does that do us?"

"But it's there." Min grabbed my forearm. "Derrick and I can—"

"—stay where you're needed most," I broke in smoothly. "You two run this whole island. You have to be here and make sure no one freaks out. I'll take Akio and Kyle, and we'll check it."

Min seemed ready to argue the point, but I cut her off again. "I'm the official inter-camp liaison person guy, right?" I flashed a grin. "So let me 'liaise' with Sarah and her cheerleader coven while you handle the big stuff." I stepped close, spoke in a softer tone. "You and Derrick need to keep everyone together. There's a ton of work to do in the village, including some unpleasant stuff. This is our worst day since—"

I winced, tried to pull the words back. The last thing I wanted Min thinking about was the accident with Carl. But one look and I knew it was too late. Min blamed herself for what had happened, and always would.

"Okay." Her voice was strangely flat. "Take a radio and call up the minute you reach them. We haven't heard a word, and I'm starting to . . ." She flexed her fingers in a gesture of help-lessness. "Just go fast. Please."

I wrapped her in another quick hug, then jogged to where several teams were hauling rubble away in buckets. The effort looked hopeless—house-size boulders had fallen directly onto the entrance, crushing the tunnel and blocking any path to the blast door. Still, our classmates were trying.

I spotted Akio and waved. Then, scanning quickly, I yelled for Kyle. The two hurried over, chests heaving, and faces covered in orange dust. Both had lived with me inside the Program at my father's ski chalet. I trusted Akio with my life and usually picked him for the harder jobs. Kyle I was less comfortable with—he'd pulled a fast one on me once, during a raid, and had seemed too comfortable with the slaughter in general—but he was fearless to the point of recklessness. I knew he wouldn't punk out if this got tough.

Kyle wiped his mouth with a dirty backhand. "What up, Noah? This is a real mess."

"Any chance we get through?" I asked.

Akio shook his head. "We might be able to dig around the boulders, but I doubt the door survived."

"Then we try a different way. Up for a climbing expedition?"

Kyle grinned like he'd won a prize. Akio nodded, but worry lines dug across his forehead. "The back tunnel?"

"That's the idea."

Akio frowned. "Even if the door's intact, how will we reach it? That side faces the water."

I pushed aside a tidal wave of doubt. "Let's see what we find and go from there. Nine girls are stuck at the bottom of this tomb. We have to get them out."

"Don't forget Devin." Kyle snorted derisively. "He moved

down two weeks ago. Their majesties let him stay because they need someone to cook and clean for them. I kid you not."

I gave him a sharp look. "Four people died last night, Kyle. Do I need to ask someone else?"

"Oh, crap. No. My bad, man." Kyle's face fell so quickly, I almost felt bad for snapping at him. Almost.

"Forget it. Let's just hope we can get inside. Come on."

• • •

Back in the village we grabbed several lengths of nylon rope and three sets of climbing gear. Then we tramped around the mountain, scrambling up bluffs and powering through scrub as we circled the massive cylinder. Once buried deep underground, the silo now stood at the outermost edge of the island, its eastern side fully exposed to the elements and dropping hundreds of feet to the ocean below.

I shivered every time I saw it from this angle. The silo looked like a bird on an unsteady perch. A few hundred more feet of erosion and our supposedly indestructible lifeboat would've crashed into the sea along with the rest of Idaho. It was a freaking miracle we'd survived.

Scanning the seaward-facing concrete, I tried to visualize where the back exit should be. So much had changed while we were inside the Program. I squinted into the sun, probing the pockmarked surface with my eyes, but came up empty. I was about to suggest we go back for binoculars when Akio's finger darted out. "There."

He'd spotted an indentation maybe forty yards to our right

and a dozen down. But I couldn't see if there was a door. "Could be," I agreed. "But how do we check?"

I glanced at the top of the silo, unreachable now with the mountainside gone.

Can't get up, can't go down. What a mess.

But Akio had seen more than just the possible entry point. "There's a ridge below us that runs around the silo. I think we can get above the opening and rappel down to it."

I blinked at him. "Rappel. Down the cliff. Over the ocean."

Akio shrugged, the ghost of a smile appearing on his lips. "You have a better idea?"

"I do not." My throat worked, but there was no other way. "So let's do it."

Akio took the lead. We worked along a sharp defile to reach the ridge. It was a full three feet wide—plenty big enough to feel comfortable if there hadn't been a hundred-yard death drop on the left side. As it was, I could barely breathe.

I heard Kyle gasping behind me and took solace knowing I wasn't the only one about to crap his pants. For his part, Akio moved confidently, circling to a wider cleft above the indentation. Once inside there, I put my back against solid stone and tried to slow my stampeding heart.

"We're lucky." Akio patted a triangular spike of rock jutting up in the center of the cleft. "We can tie off on this. I was worried two of us would have to anchor the line with body weight."

I shivered, thinking about *that* insane prospect, as Akio began securing ropes. He produced two sets of carabiners and snapped them in place, then handed me an ascender. "For the climb back up. Wouldn't want to forget."

I shoved mine deep into a pocket. There was nothing left to do but go.

"Okay," I said. "All right. Okay."

"One of us should stay here," Akio said. "To watch the lines."

Kyle's hand flew up. I shot him a dirty look, but nodded. I was in charge. I had to go over the side.

Akio offered to go first, but I shook my head roughly. If I didn't do it now, I never would. I clipped in and took a deep breath. Every kid in Fire Lake had gone rappelling at one time or another at Starlight's Edge summer camp. This wasn't novel. But a quick zip down a scouted pitch on lines laid by professionals was a little different from stepping off a vertical cliff above a death drop and hoping Kyle didn't accidentally let you die. We had no idea if this was even the right place. I'd have to climb back up either way.

Just don't look down. That's always good advice, but especially now. Don't. Look. Down.

Three deep inhales.

I stepped backward off the cliff.

The line played out easily. I worked cautiously down the face, being careful with my speed. After three bounds, I reached the indentation and was forced to look between my feet. I blanked out the crashing waves far below, focusing on the opening. It was a small cave of roughly the same dimensions as a school bus. I lowered myself to a lip where I could stand and scrambled to safer footing.

A weathered blast door was tucked into the back of the recess before me.

I let out a huge sob of relief.

I called up to Akio, detached from the line, and approached the door. There was a wheel-locking mechanism. As Akio landed softly behind me, I grabbed it with both hands and yanked. The wheel didn't budge.

My heart oozed through my shoes and off the cliff. This door hadn't been opened in millennia, and was exposed to the sea. *Of course* it didn't just spin, and we'd brought nothing to cut the oxidation. This ball of rust might never open. Why hadn't I thought of this before?

Akio unclipped and joined me in the back of the cave. We tried the wheel together, but it might as well have been part of the mountainside. I collapsed with an exasperated grunt. Akio sat down beside me and squeezed his forehead.

"We probably should have thought this through a little more," he said.

"You think?"

"I bet the door is rusted shut."

"You are clearly a master of door science."

"It would've been better if we'd brought something to grease the wheel."

I chuckled sourly. "Let's have this conversation up there next time."

"Deal. Of course, the door could also be locked."

I pressed my fists into my eyes sockets, then petulantly kicked the door. With a weary sigh, I fumbled for the radio in my pocket. Kyle could run back to the village and get what we needed. If the door was locked . . . well, that would be that.

I was fiddling with the frequency when the wheel next to

12

my head abruptly started rotating. My eyes bugged. I grabbed Akio's knee. We scrambled to our feet as it spun several times, then stopped. Hinges groaned as the portal swung inward.

Sarah Harden poked her head out. "Took you long enough."

I blinked. Opened my mouth. Closed it.

Sarah's blue eyes rolled skyward. "A thousand tons of rock just rained down on us. Did you think we'd just sit around waiting for you bozos? Please tell me you fixed a rope."

She stepped from the tunnel, followed by a sniffling Jessica Cale. One by one, three more people emerged. Alice Cho. Susan Daughtridge. Colleen Plummer. All were dirt-smeared. Most were crying. I peered past them into the tunnel, expecting the rest of the silo squad, but no one else appeared.

I aimed a confused glance at Sarah. She shook her head.

My whole body went cold. "Where are the others? Tiffani and Kristen? Devin? Are they trapped somewhere?"

I glanced at Alice, who was staring at nothing. Colleen and Susan were hugging each other and wouldn't meet my eye. "They're *dead*," Jessica wailed. "The roof caved in and they all died!" She slumped to her knees, sobbing, and covered her face.

Sarah watched Jessica with distaste. No tears marred her eyes. Then she looked at me and I nearly shivered. "Tiffani, Melissa, Emily, Kristen, and Devin were having dinner in the command center. The rest of us were in the living quarters. The blast door between the two sections was shut, which probably saved our lives. When we tried to open it . . ." Sarah grimaced, the first human thing she'd done since emerging. "It's gone. They're gone."

Akio turned to stare at the ocean. I shook my head, unwilling to accept what I was hearing. "It might just be blocked. The rest of the shaft could—"

"I connected to a working camera in one of the storage alcoves," Sarah said curtly. "The silo's entire ceiling collapsed down the shaft, crushing everything outside the lab complex. The command center is pulverized, Noah. So is everyone who was in there." She crossed her arms to reveal cracked, bleeding nails. "It's not like we didn't try."

I gaped at Sarah, horrified. Five more classmates, dead. *What am I going to tell Min?*

"I assume you have a way up from here?" Sarah said. "We've been waiting by this door for hours. It's the only way in or out now, and I was getting worried no one could reach it from above. The lab complex isn't damaged, and we sealed it, but I want to get topside and see what happened." She glanced at her companions. "The others didn't want to stay underground alone."

"Up. Yes." I shook my head to clear it. "We have ropes. Kyle is—"

A concussion thumped from somewhere deep inside the tunnel, followed quickly by two more. The stone shook beneath our feet. My eyes met Sarah's as a crunching sound echoed along the passageway, growing louder by the second.

Sarah flew to the open door, dropping a shoulder against the heavy steel. Akio and I leapt to flank her and together we forced the portal closed. Sarah turned the wheel, then jerked back as something heavy clanged against the door from the inside. The mountain groaned one last time, then went still.

I slid down on my butt and wiped grime from my eyes. "Will things stop breaking around here, please?"

"No way," Sarah whispered, dropping down beside me. The others were all panting like we'd run a marathon.

I rested my head back against the door. "No way what? The tunnel imploded. Thank God we got here in time."

Sarah grabbed my shirt, yanking me close. "Two major collapses in one day? Inside a military-grade disaster bunker that stood for over a *million* years? Get your head out of your ass, Livingston."

I gently extricated myself from her grip, then ran both palms over my face as the last twelve hours fell in on me like an avalanche. "What are you saying, Sarah? I'm too tired for games."

She shook her head with disgust. "I'm *saying*, Noah, that a storm didn't cause this damage. It's too much."

That got my attention. "If not the storm, then what?"

She leaned back next to me, staring off into the distance. "Not what, you idiot. *Who*."